SEASON OF THE
BRUJA

PRESS

AN ONI PRESS PUBLIC

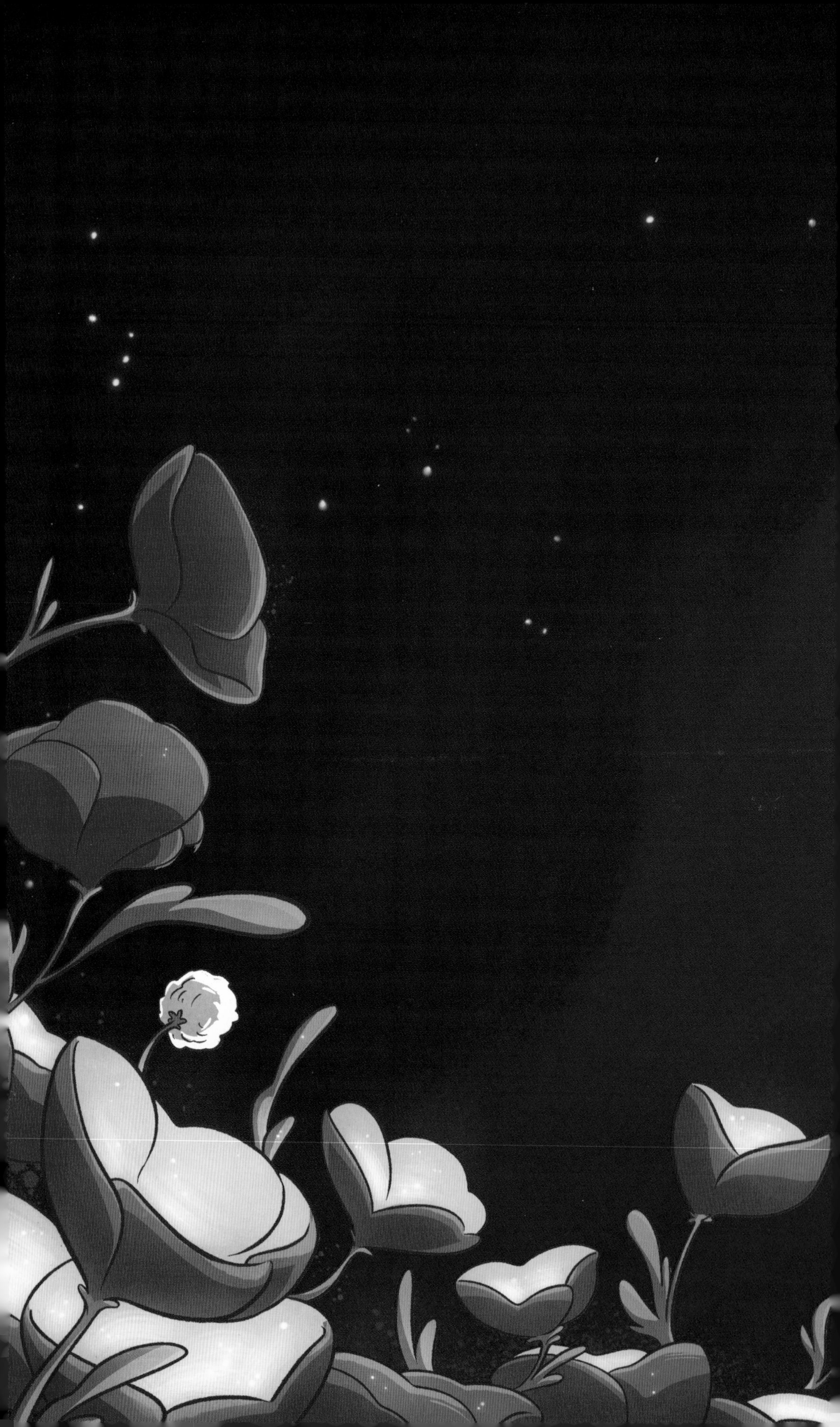

For Jenn, who worked tirelessly
and supported me so that
I could chase my dream.
—AARON DURÁN

For my colorful Diana, always.
To my favorite ornithologists Soph and Guille,
and also my support team: Raúl, Arkaitz & Fran.
You rock!
—SARA SOLER

SEASON OF THE
BRUJA

WRITTEN BY **Aaron Durán**

ILLUSTRATED AND COLORED BY **Sara Soler**

LETTERED BY **Jaime Martinez for AndWorld Designs**

EDITED BY **Shawna Gore, Desiree Rodriguez**, AND **Gabriel Granillo**

SPANISH LANGUAGE CONSULTANT AND SENSITIVITY READER: **Adriana Nodal-Tarafa**

BOOK DESIGN BY **Sarah Rockwell**

LOGO DESIGN BY **Leigh Luna**

PUBLISHED BY ONI-LION FORGE PUBLISHING GROUP, LLC.

James Lucas Jones, president & publisher • Charlie Chu, e.v.p. of creative & business development • Steve Ellis, s.v.p. of games & operations • Alex Segura, s.v.p of marketing & sales • Michelle Nguyen, associate publisher • Brad Rooks, director of operations • Katie Sainz, director of marketing • Tara Lehmann, publicity director • Henry Barajas, sales manager • Holly Aitchison, consumer marketing manager • Lydia Nguyen, marketing intern • Troy Look, director of design & production • Angie Knowles, production manager • Carey Hall, graphic designer • Sarah Rockwell, graphic designer • Hilary Thompson, graphic designer • Vincent Kukua, digital prepress technician • Chris Cerasi, managing editor • Jasmine Amiri, senior editor • Amanda Meadows, senior editor • Bess Pallares, editor • Desiree Rodriguez, editor • Grace Scheipeter, editor • Zack Soto, editor • Gabriel Granillo, editorial assistant • Ben Eisner, game developer Sara Harding, entertainment executive assistant • Jung Lee, logistics coordinator • Kuian Kellum, warehouse assistant

Joe Nozemack, publisher emeritus

onipress.com
@onipress

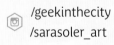

/geekinthecity
/sarasoler_art

First Edition: October 2022
ISBN 978-1-5493-0816-1
eISBN 978-1-63715-080-1

Printing numbers:
1 2 3 4 5 6 7 8 9 10

Library of Congress Control Number 2021949910

CHAPTER 1

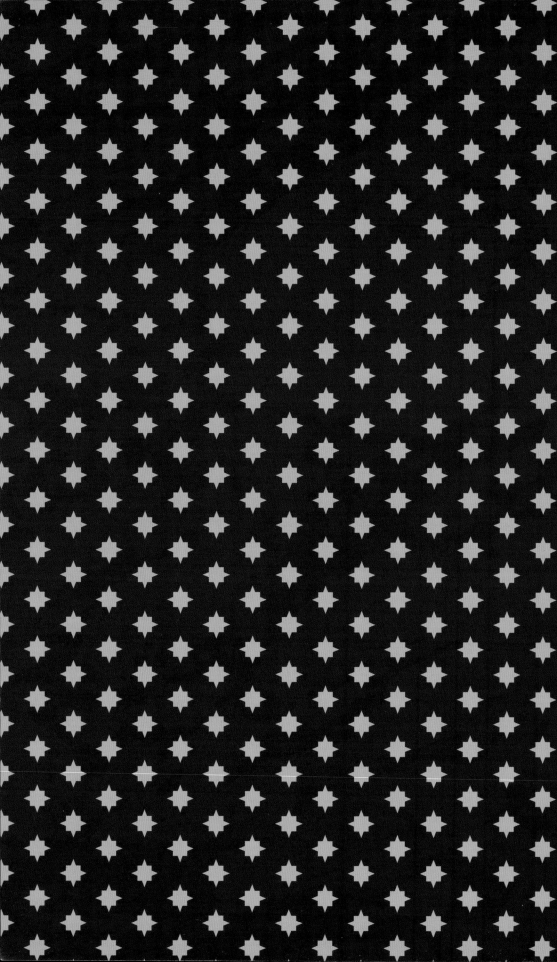

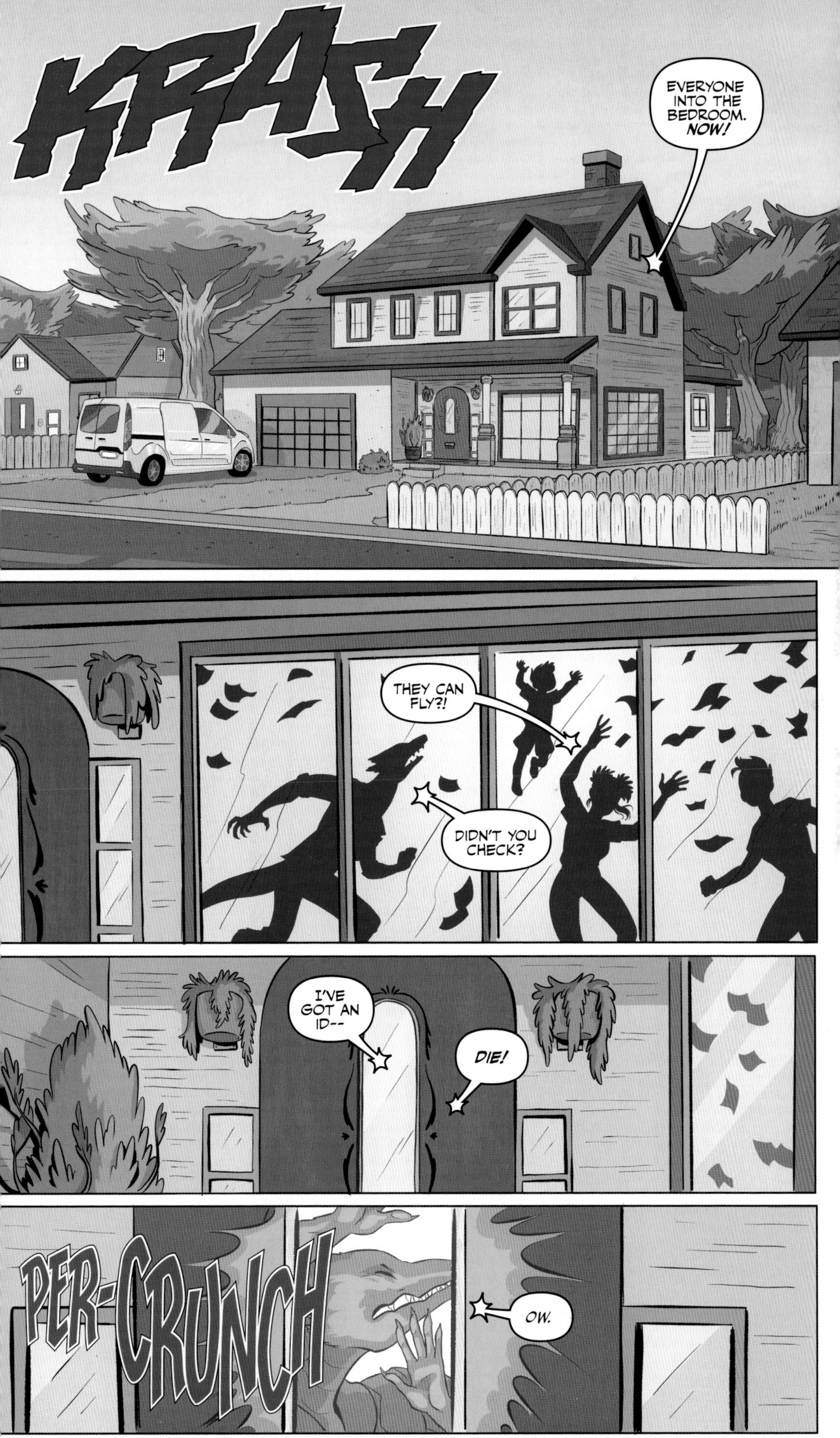
KRASH
EVERYONE INTO THE BEDROOM. NOW!
THEY CAN FLY?!
DIDN'T YOU CHECK?
I'VE GOT AN ID--
DIE!
PER-CRUNCH
OW.

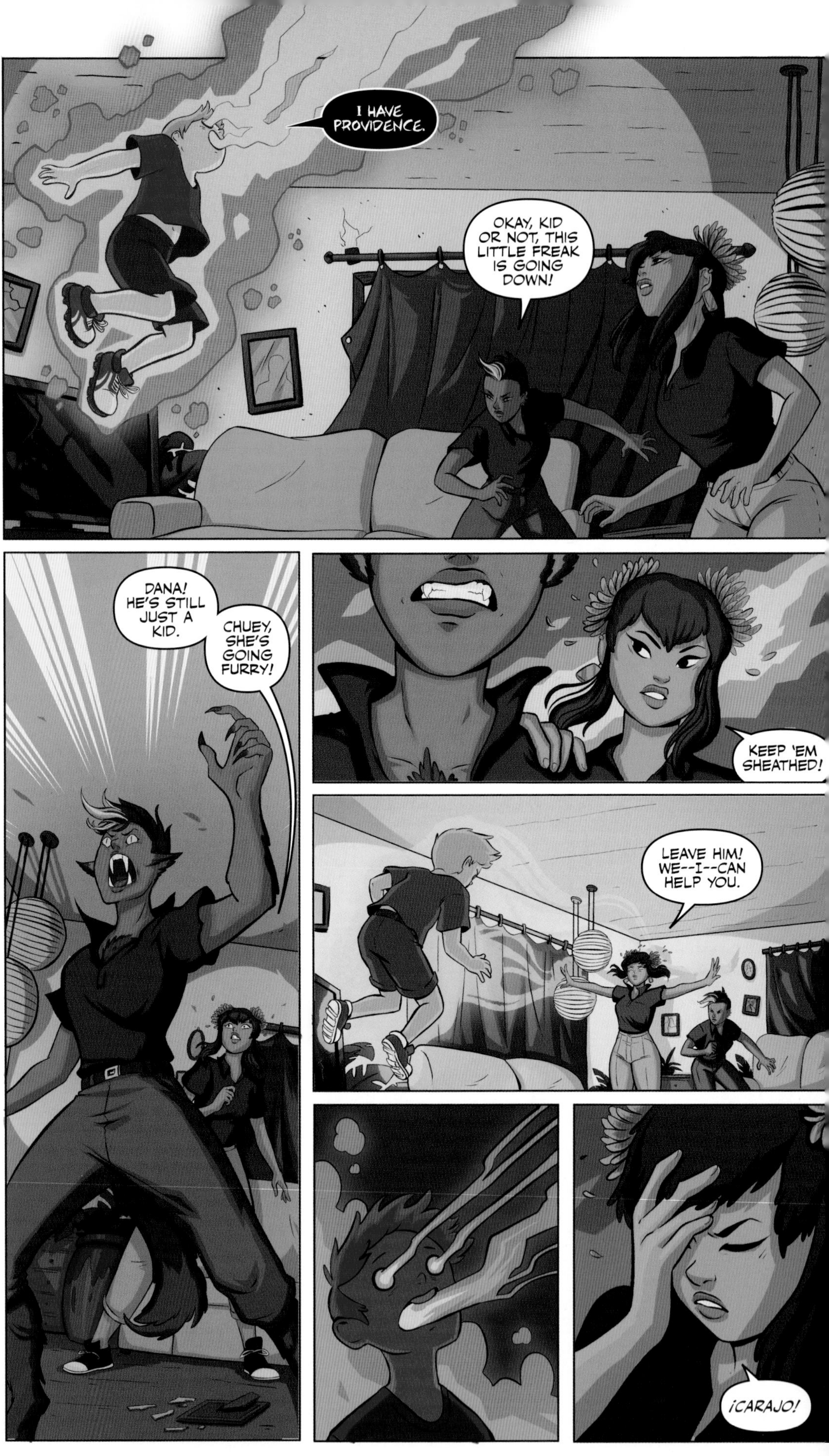

I HAVE PROVIDENCE.
OKAY, KID OR NOT, THIS LITTLE FREAK IS GOING DOWN!
DANA! HE'S STILL JUST A KID.
CHUEY, SHE'S GOING FURRY!
KEEP 'EM SHEATHED!
LEAVE HIM! WE--I--CAN HELP YOU.
¡CARAJO!

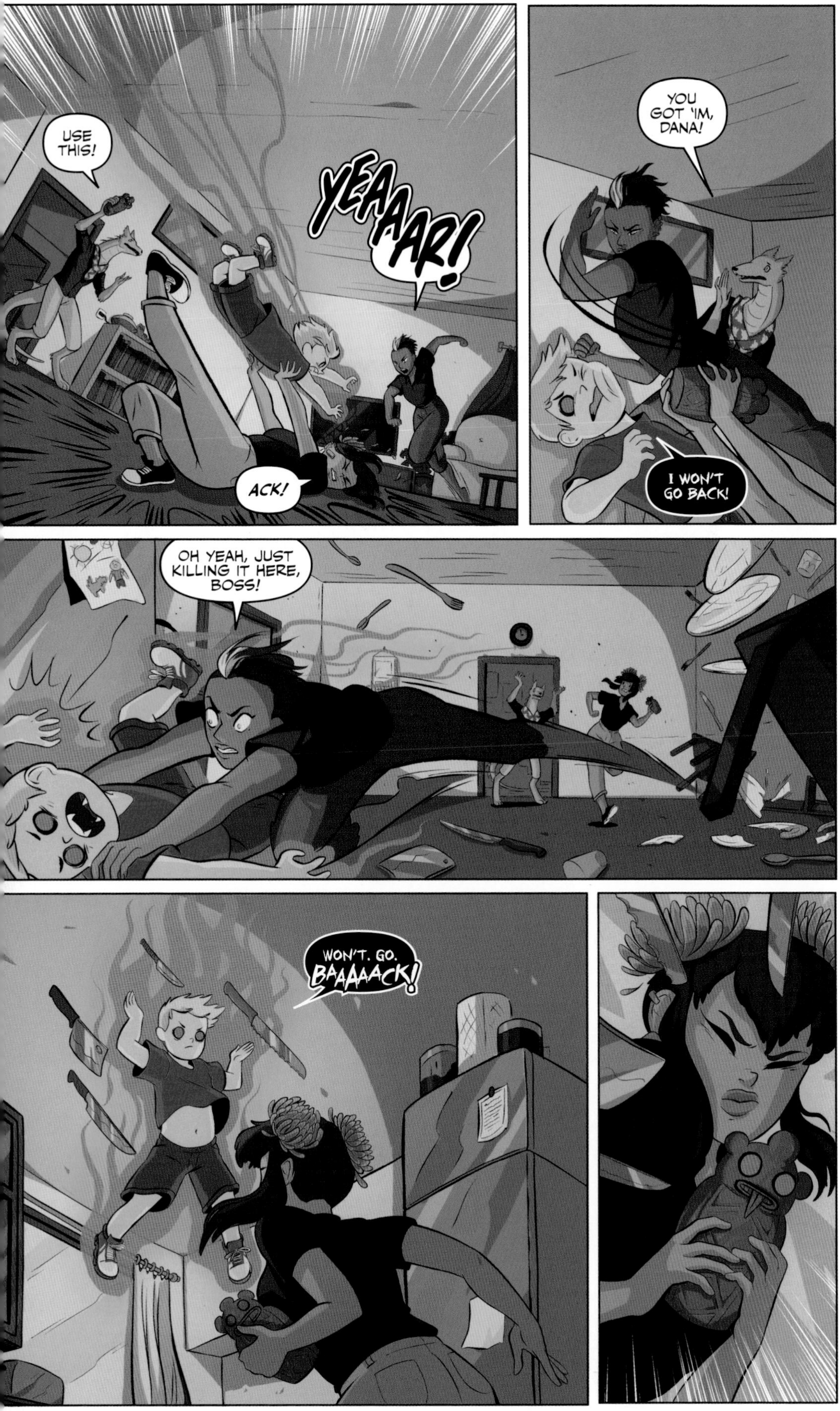
USE THIS!
YEAAAAR!
ACK!
YOU GOT 'IM, DANA!
I WON'T GO BACK!
OH YEAH, JUST KILLING IT HERE, BOSS!
WON'T. GO. BAAAAACK!

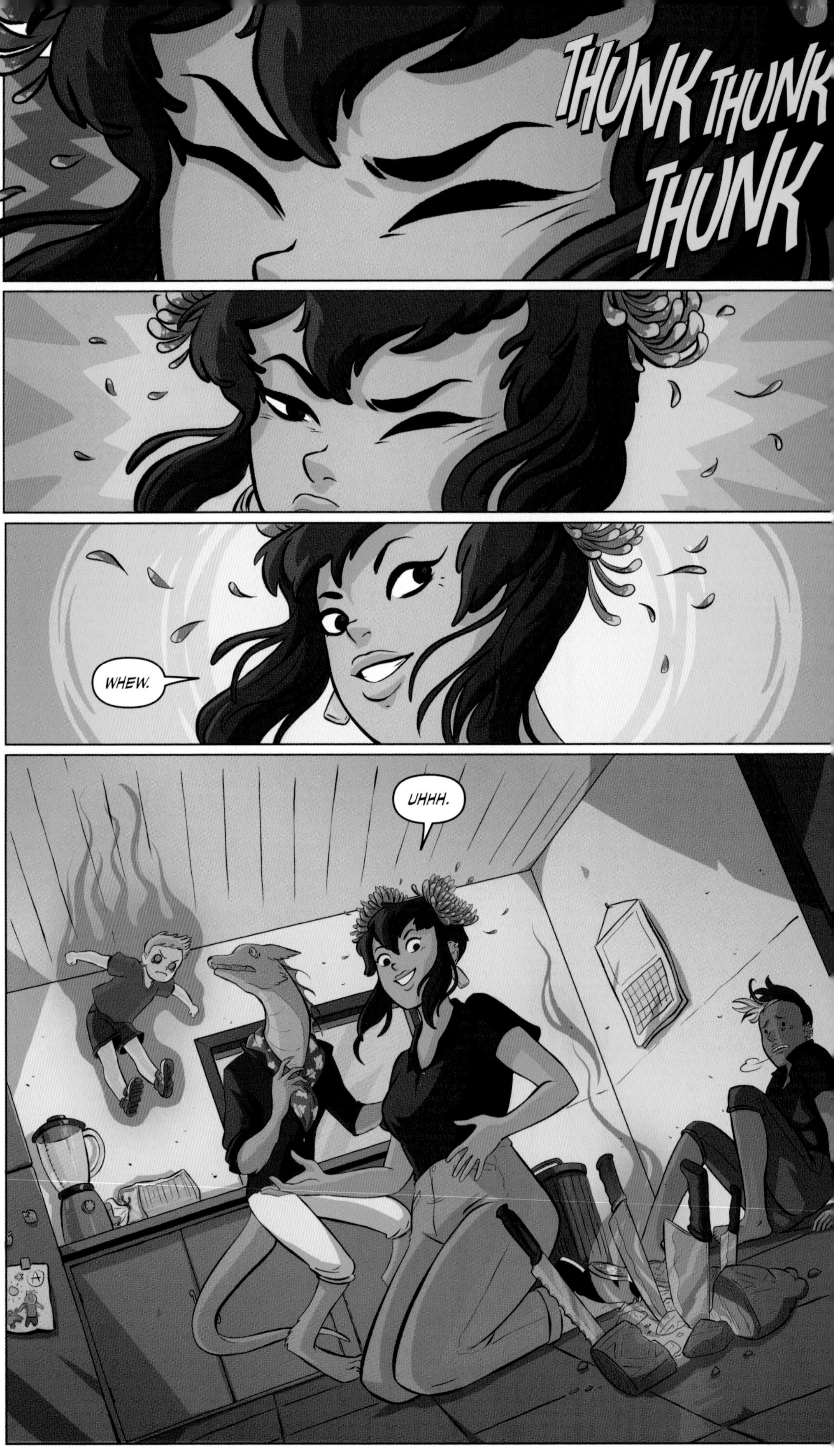
THUNK THUNK
THUNK
WHEW.
UHHH.

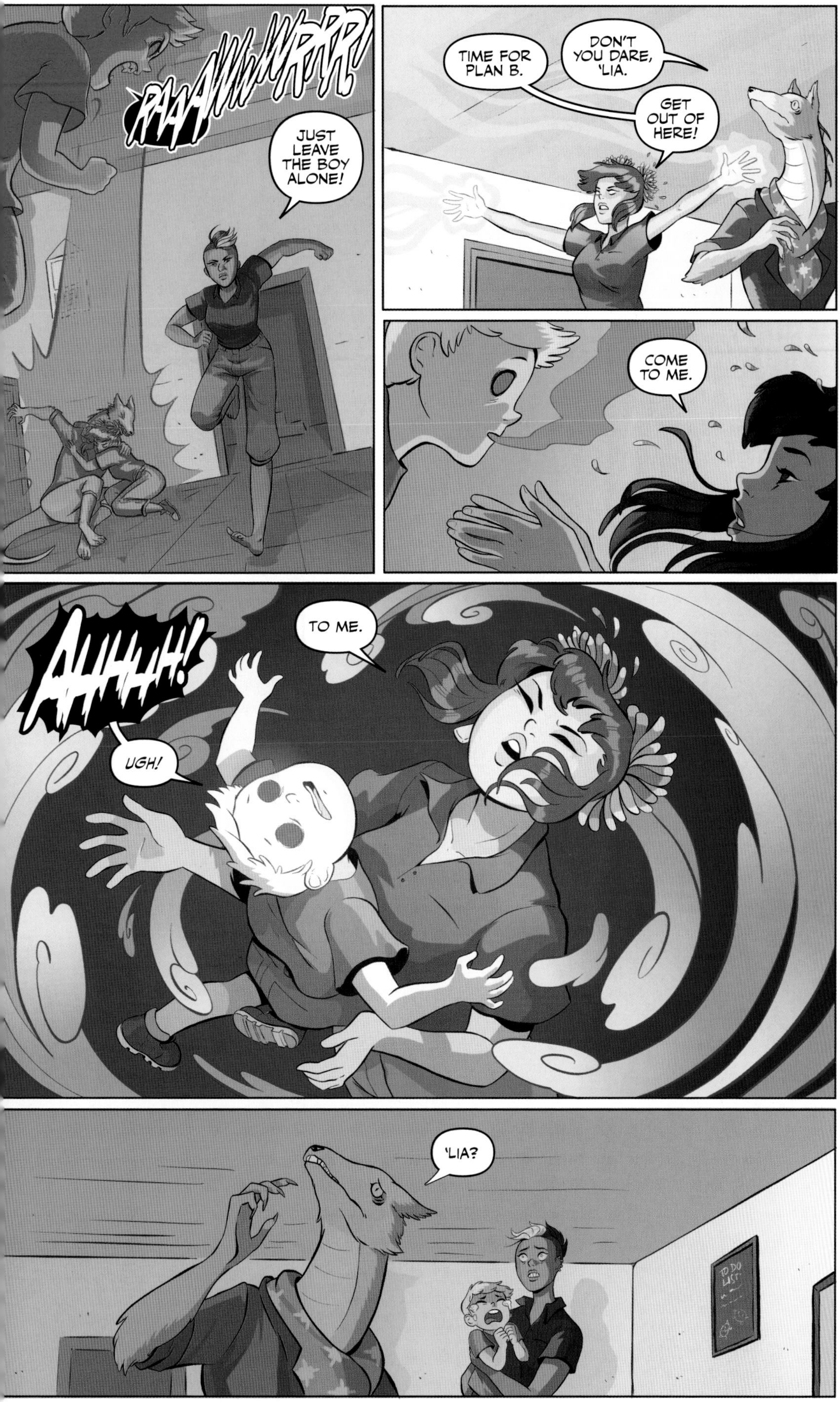
RAAAHHHHHRRRR!
JUST LEAVE THE BOY ALONE!
TIME FOR PLAN B.
DON'T YOU DARE, 'LIA.
GET OUT OF HERE!
COME TO ME.
TO ME.
AHHHH!
UGH!
'LIA?
TO DO LIST

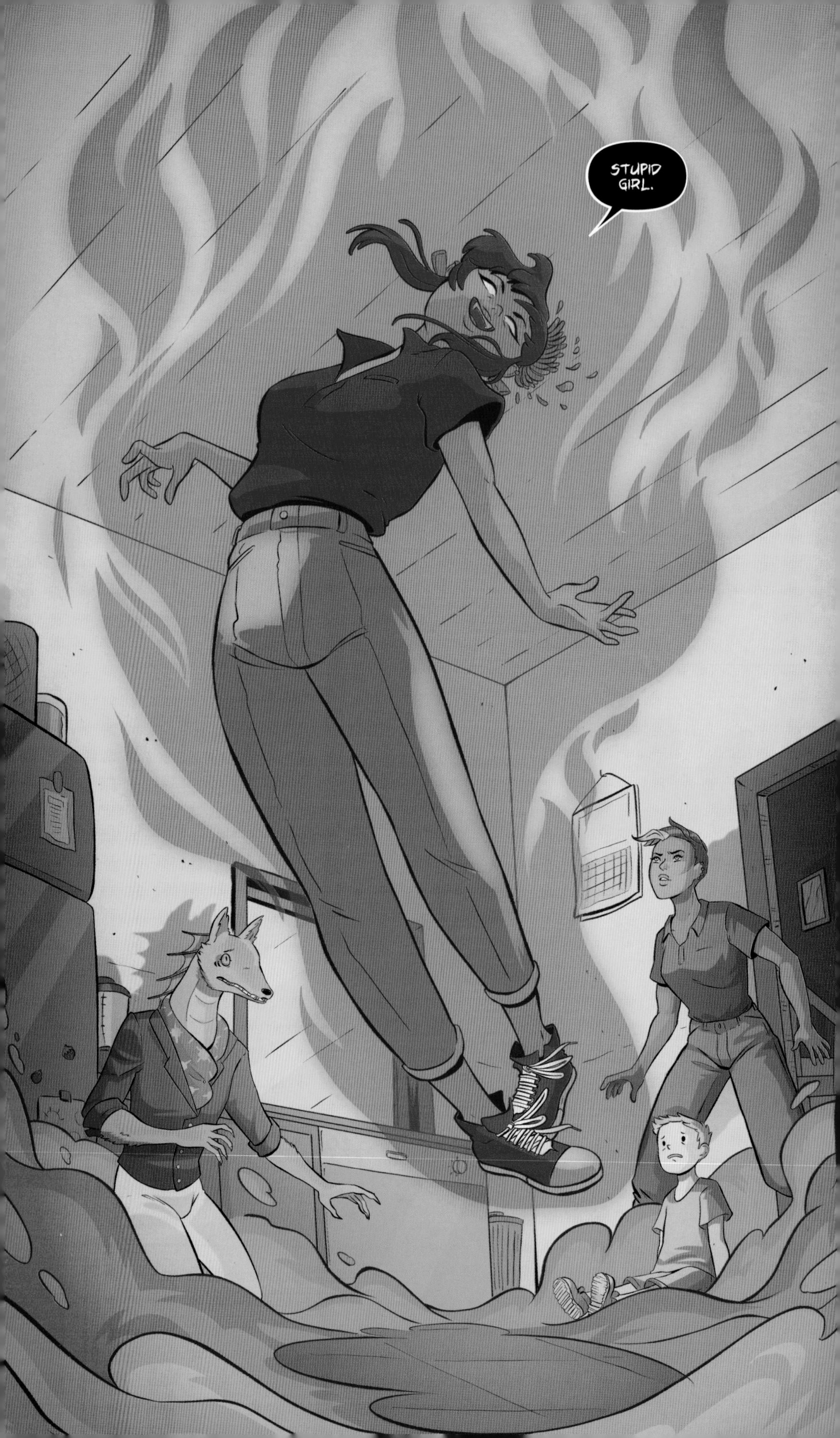
STUPID GIRL.

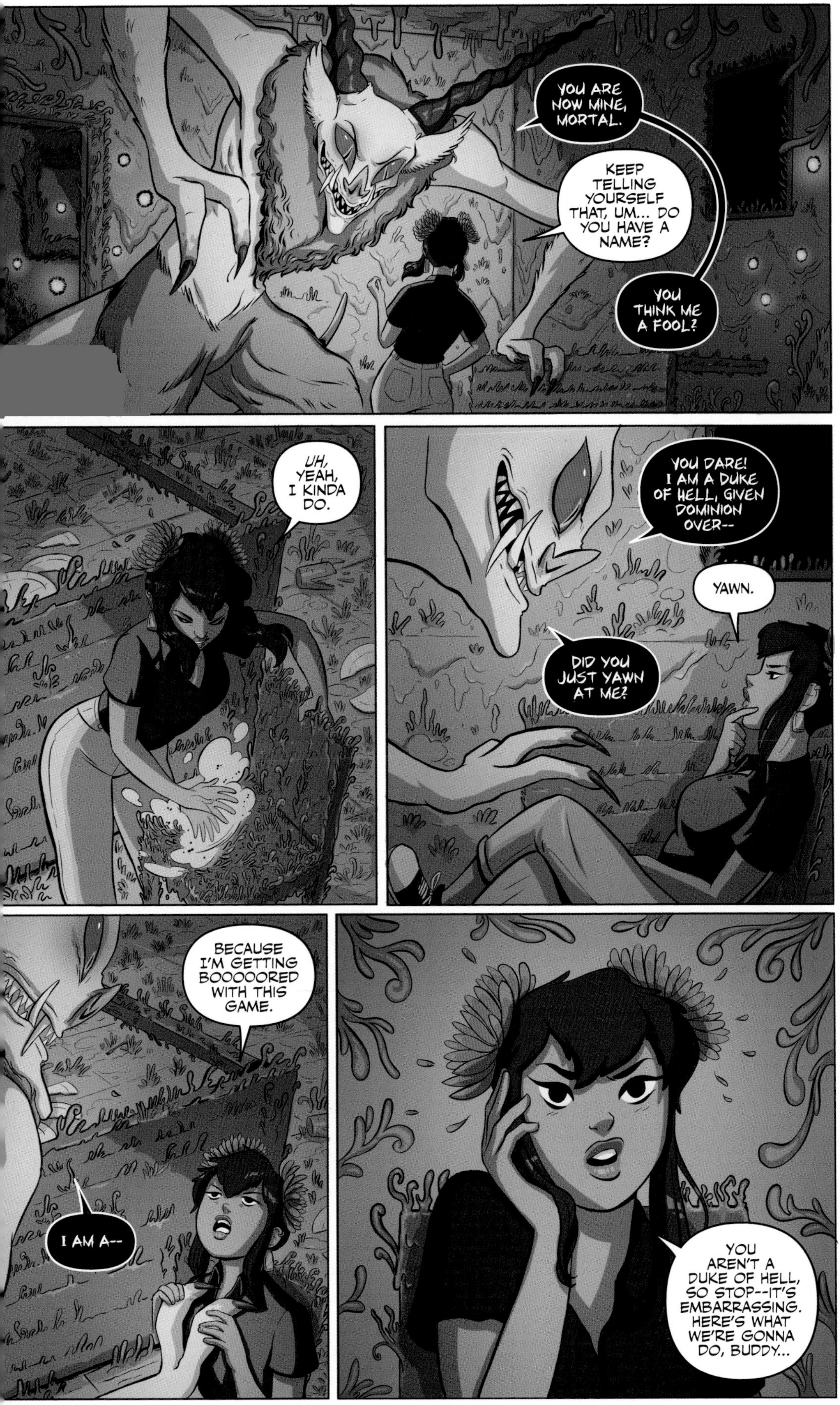
YOU ARE NOW MINE, MORTAL.
KEEP TELLING YOURSELF THAT, UM... DO YOU HAVE A NAME?
YOU THINK ME A FOOL?
UH, YEAH, I KINDA DO.
YOU DARE! I AM A DUKE OF HELL, GIVEN DOMINION OVER--
YAWN.
DID YOU JUST YAWN AT ME?
BECAUSE I'M GETTING BOOOOORED WITH THIS GAME.
I AM A--
YOU AREN'T A DUKE OF HELL, SO STOP--IT'S EMBARRASSING. HERE'S WHAT WE'RE GONNA DO, BUDDY...

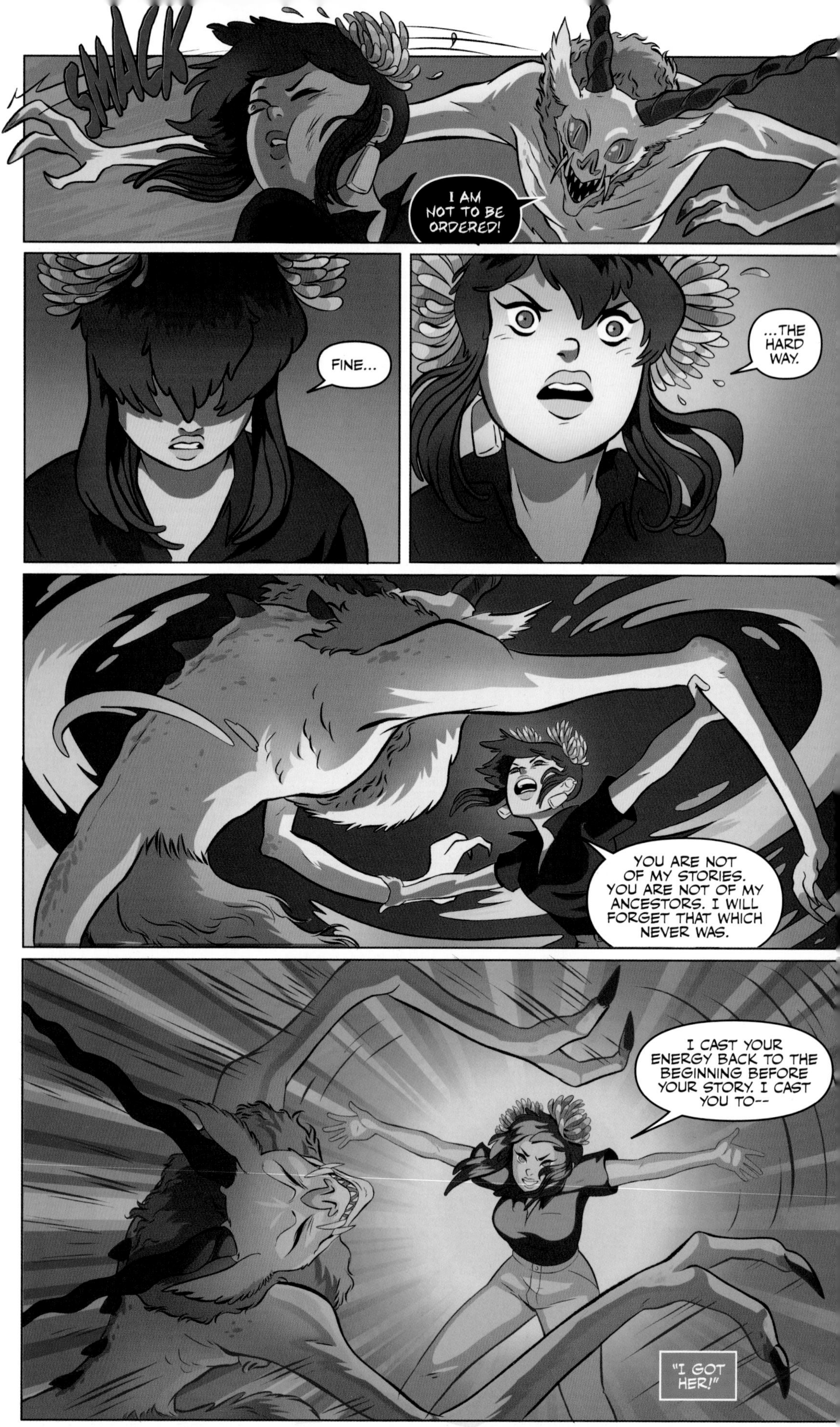
SMACK
I AM NOT TO BE ORDERED!
FINE...
...THE HARD WAY.
YOU ARE NOT OF MY STORIES. YOU ARE NOT OF MY ANCESTORS. I WILL FORGET THAT WHICH NEVER WAS.
I CAST YOUR ENERGY BACK TO THE BEGINNING BEFORE YOUR STORY. I CAST YOU TO--
"I GOT HER!"

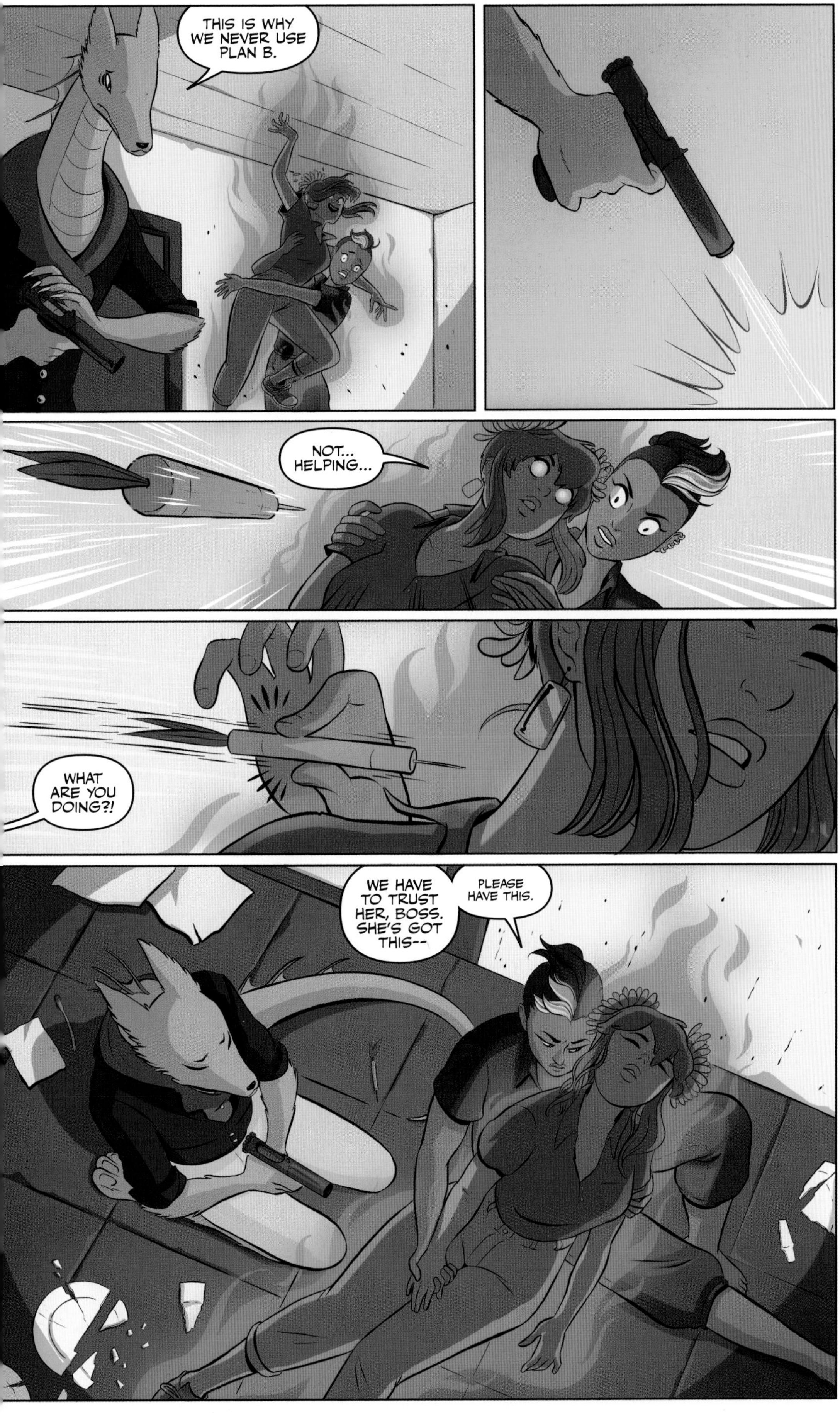
THIS IS WHY WE NEVER USE PLAN B.
NOT... HELPING...
WHAT ARE YOU DOING?!
WE HAVE TO TRUST HER, BOSS. SHE'S GOT THIS--
PLEASE HAVE THIS.

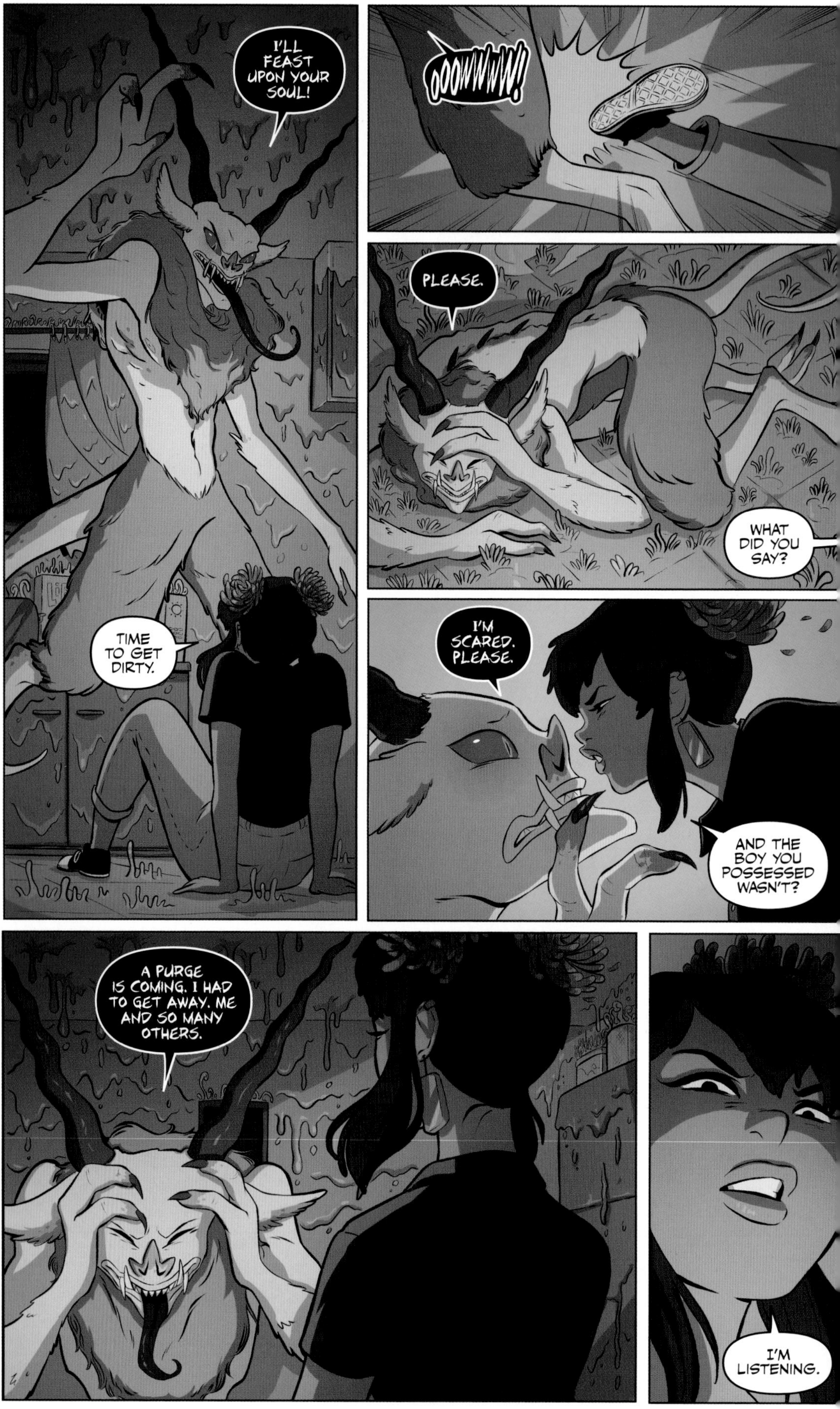
I'LL FEAST UPON YOUR SOUL!
TIME TO GET DIRTY.
OOOWWWW!
PLEASE.
WHAT DID YOU SAY?
I'M SCARED. PLEASE.
AND THE BOY YOU POSSESSED WASN'T?
A PURGE IS COMING. I HAD TO GET AWAY. ME AND SO MANY OTHERS.
I'M LISTENING.

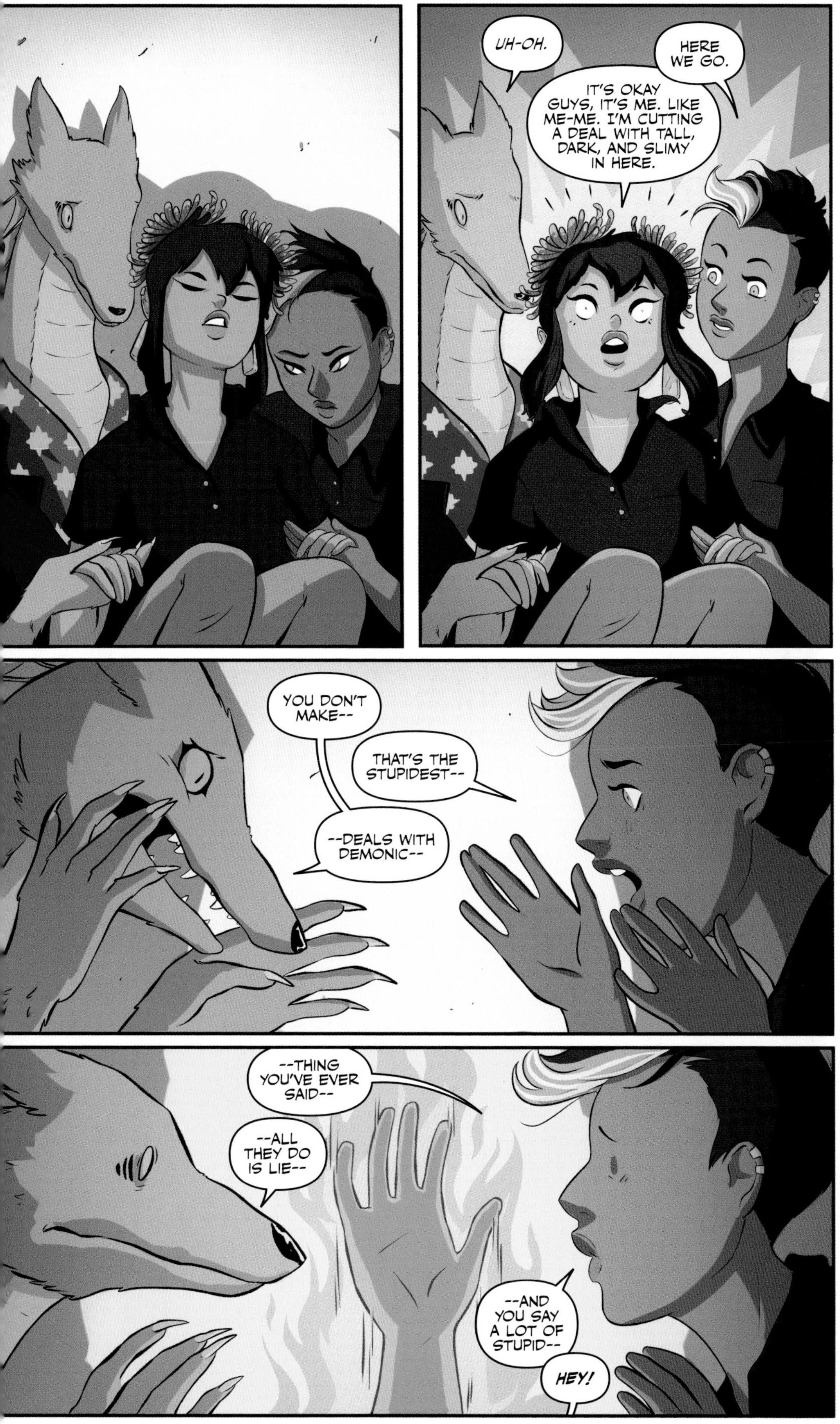
UH-OH.
HERE WE GO.
IT'S OKAY GUYS, IT'S ME. LIKE ME-ME. I'M CUTTING A DEAL WITH TALL, DARK, AND SLIMY IN HERE.
YOU DON'T MAKE--
THAT'S THE STUPIDEST--
--DEALS WITH DEMONIC--
--THING YOU'VE EVER SAID--
--ALL THEY DO IS LIE--
--AND YOU SAY A LOT OF STUPID--
HEY!

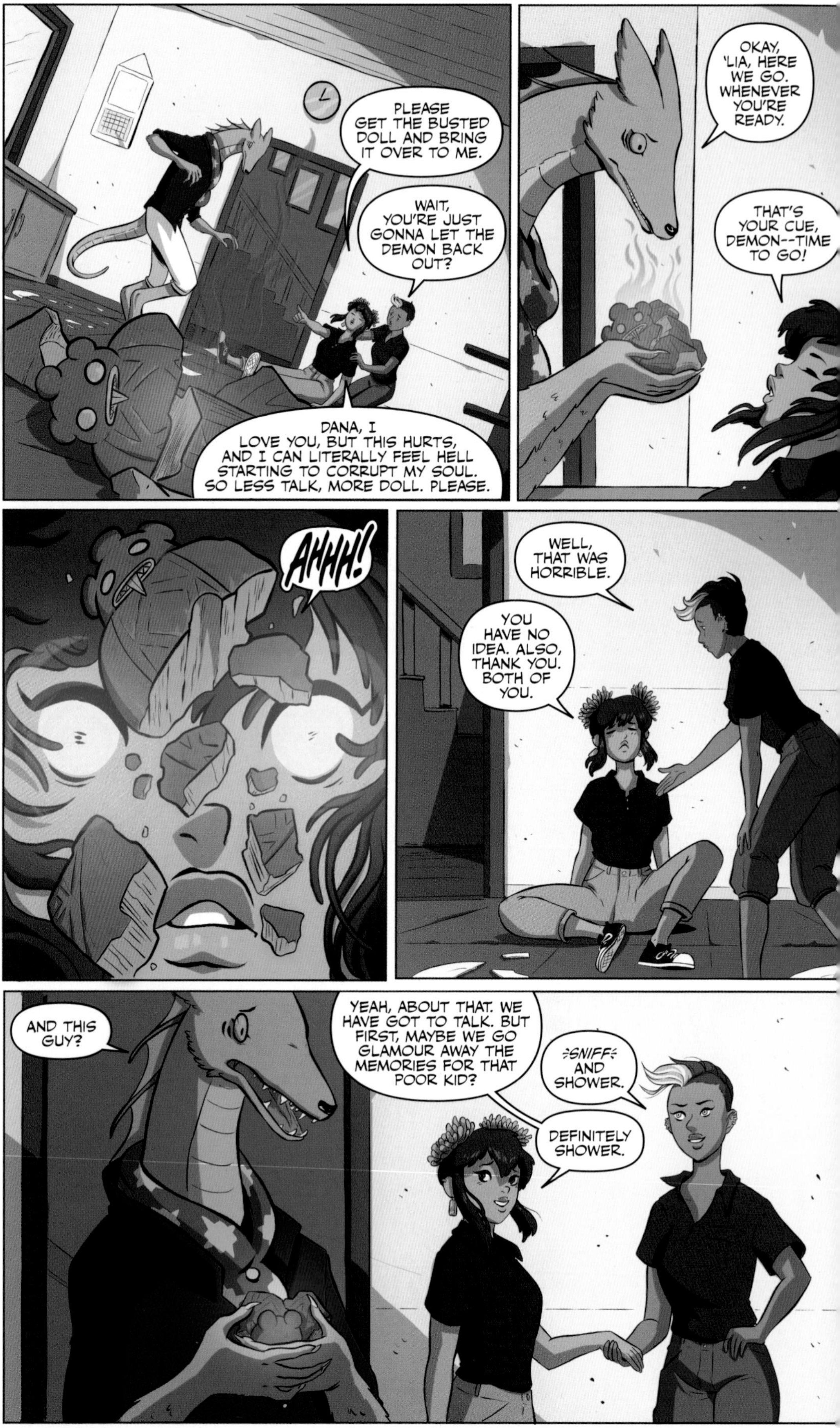
PLEASE GET THE BUSTED DOLL AND BRING IT OVER TO ME.
WAIT, YOU'RE JUST GONNA LET THE DEMON BACK OUT?
DANA, I LOVE YOU, BUT THIS HURTS, AND I CAN LITERALLY FEEL HELL STARTING TO CORRUPT MY SOUL. SO LESS TALK, MORE DOLL. PLEASE.
OKAY, 'LIA, HERE WE GO. WHENEVER YOU'RE READY.
THAT'S YOUR CUE, DEMON--TIME TO GO!
AHHH!
WELL, THAT WAS HORRIBLE.
YOU HAVE NO IDEA. ALSO, THANK YOU. BOTH OF YOU.
AND THIS GUY?
YEAH, ABOUT THAT. WE HAVE GOT TO TALK. BUT FIRST, MAYBE WE GO GLAMOUR AWAY THE MEMORIES FOR THAT POOR KID?
SNIFF AND SHOWER.
DEFINITELY SHOWER.

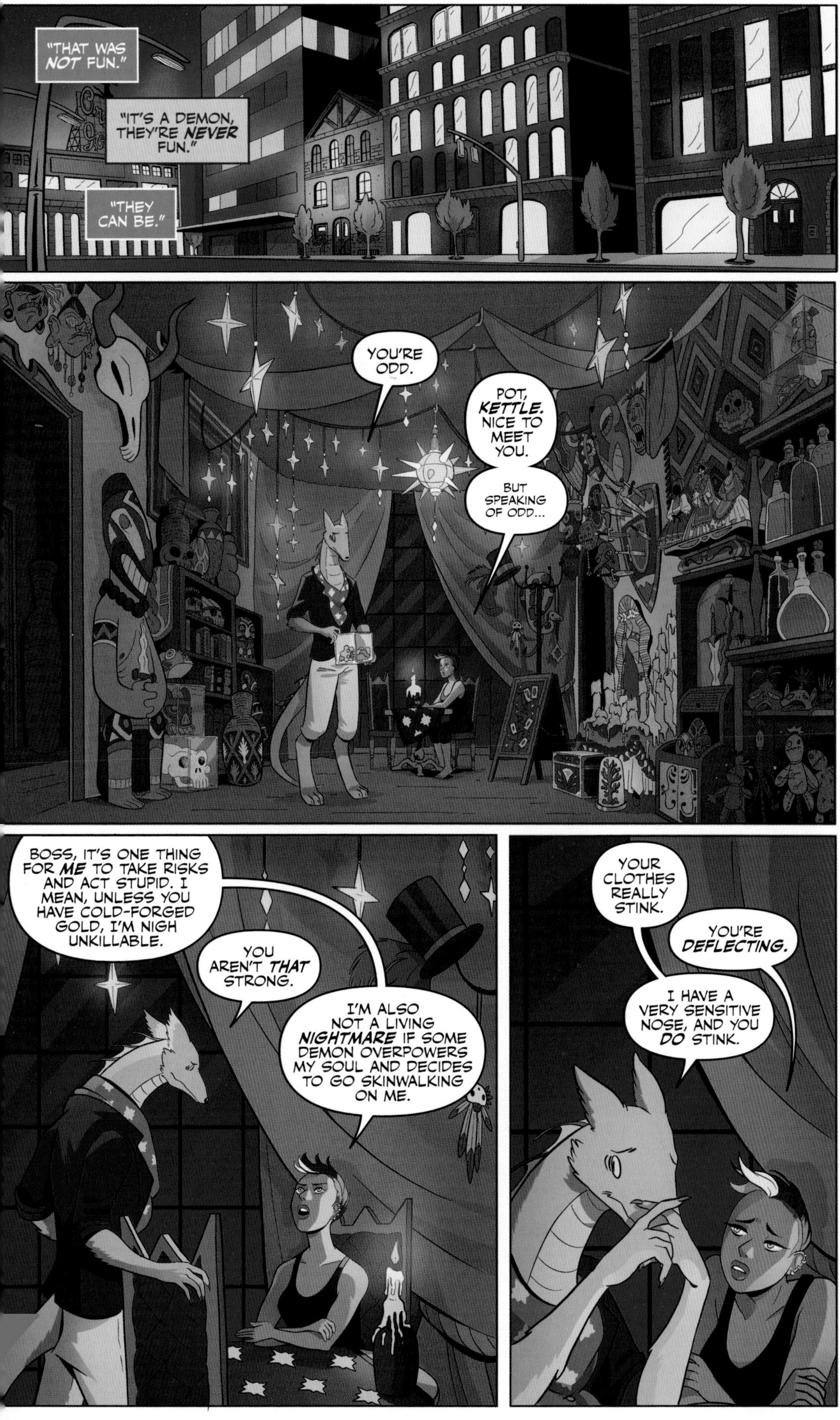
"THAT WAS NOT FUN."
"IT'S A DEMON, THEY'RE NEVER FUN."
"THEY CAN BE."
YOU'RE ODD.
POT, KETTLE. NICE TO MEET YOU.
BUT SPEAKING OF ODD...
BOSS, IT'S ONE THING FOR ME TO TAKE RISKS AND ACT STUPID. I MEAN, UNLESS YOU HAVE COLD-FORGED GOLD, I'M NIGH UNKILLABLE.
YOU AREN'T THAT STRONG.
I'M ALSO NOT A LIVING NIGHTMARE IF SOME DEMON OVERPOWERS MY SOUL AND DECIDES TO GO SKINWALKING ON ME.
YOUR CLOTHES REALLY STINK.
YOU'RE DEFLECTING.
I HAVE A VERY SENSITIVE NOSE, AND YOU DO STINK.

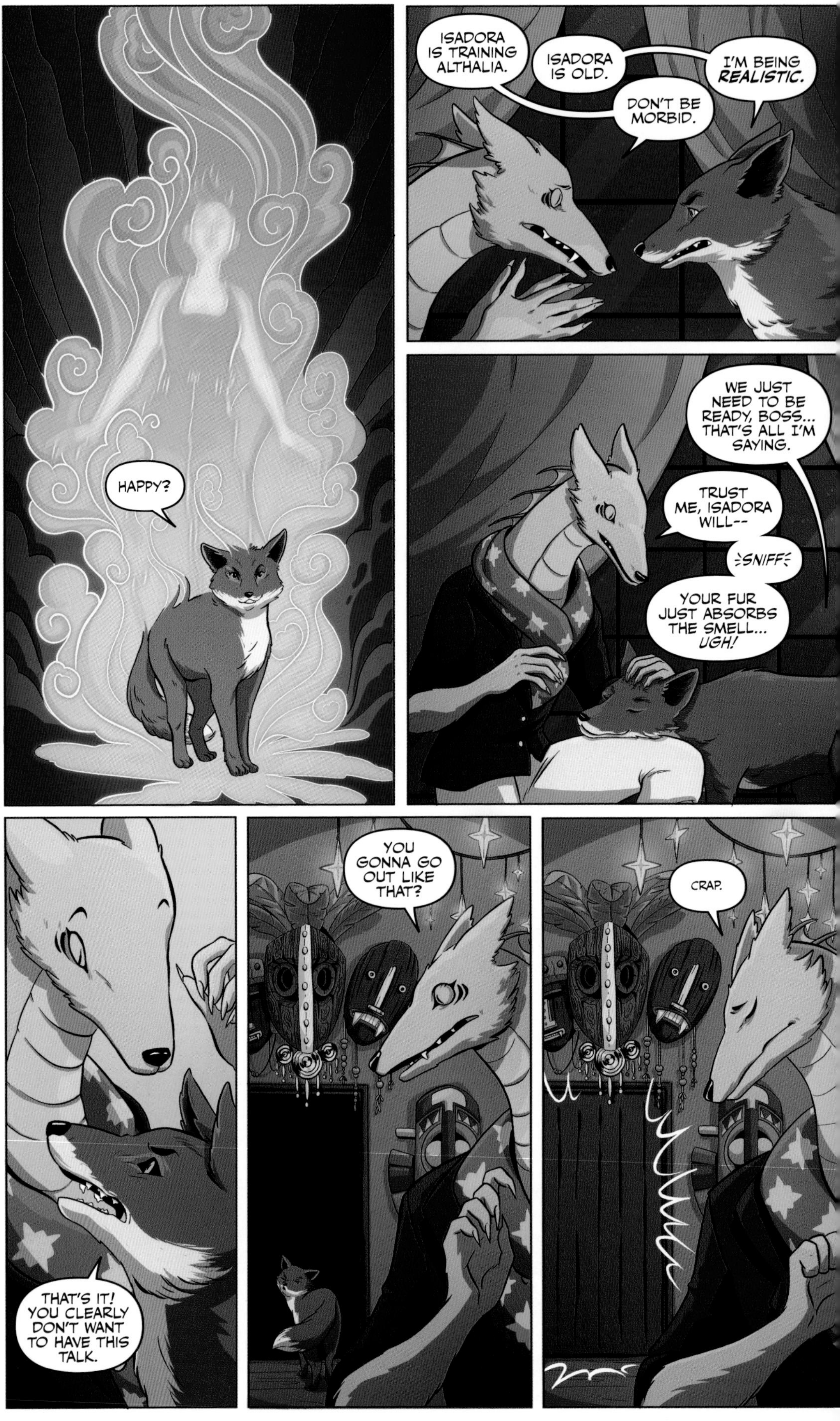
HAPPY?
ISADORA IS TRAINING ALTHALIA.
ISADORA IS OLD.
DON'T BE MORBID.
I'M BEING *REALISTIC.*
WE JUST NEED TO BE READY, BOSS... THAT'S ALL I'M SAYING.
TRUST ME, ISADORA WILL--
SNIFF
YOUR FUR JUST ABSORBS THE SMELL... *UGH!*
THAT'S IT! YOU CLEARLY DON'T WANT TO HAVE THIS TALK.
YOU GONNA GO OUT LIKE THAT?
CRAP.

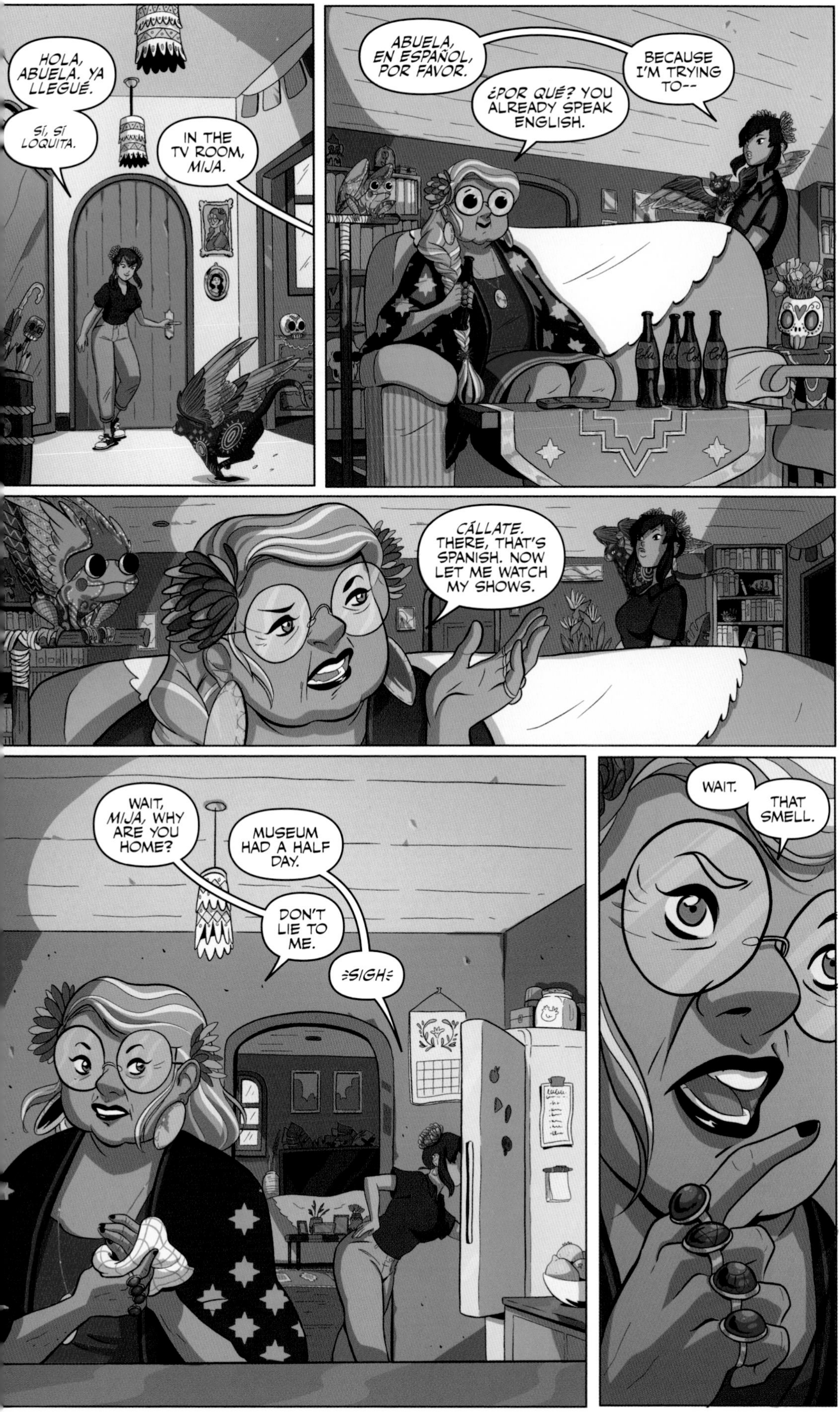
HOLA, ABUELA. YA LLEGUÉ.
SÍ, SÍ LOQUITA.
IN THE TV ROOM, MIJA.
ABUELA, EN ESPAÑOL, POR FAVOR.
¿POR QUÉ? YOU ALREADY SPEAK ENGLISH.
BECAUSE I'M TRYING TO--
CÁLLATE. THERE, THAT'S SPANISH. NOW LET ME WATCH MY SHOWS.
WAIT, MIJA, WHY ARE YOU HOME?
MUSEUM HAD A HALF DAY.
DON'T LIE TO ME.
≈SIGH≈
WAIT.
THAT SMELL.

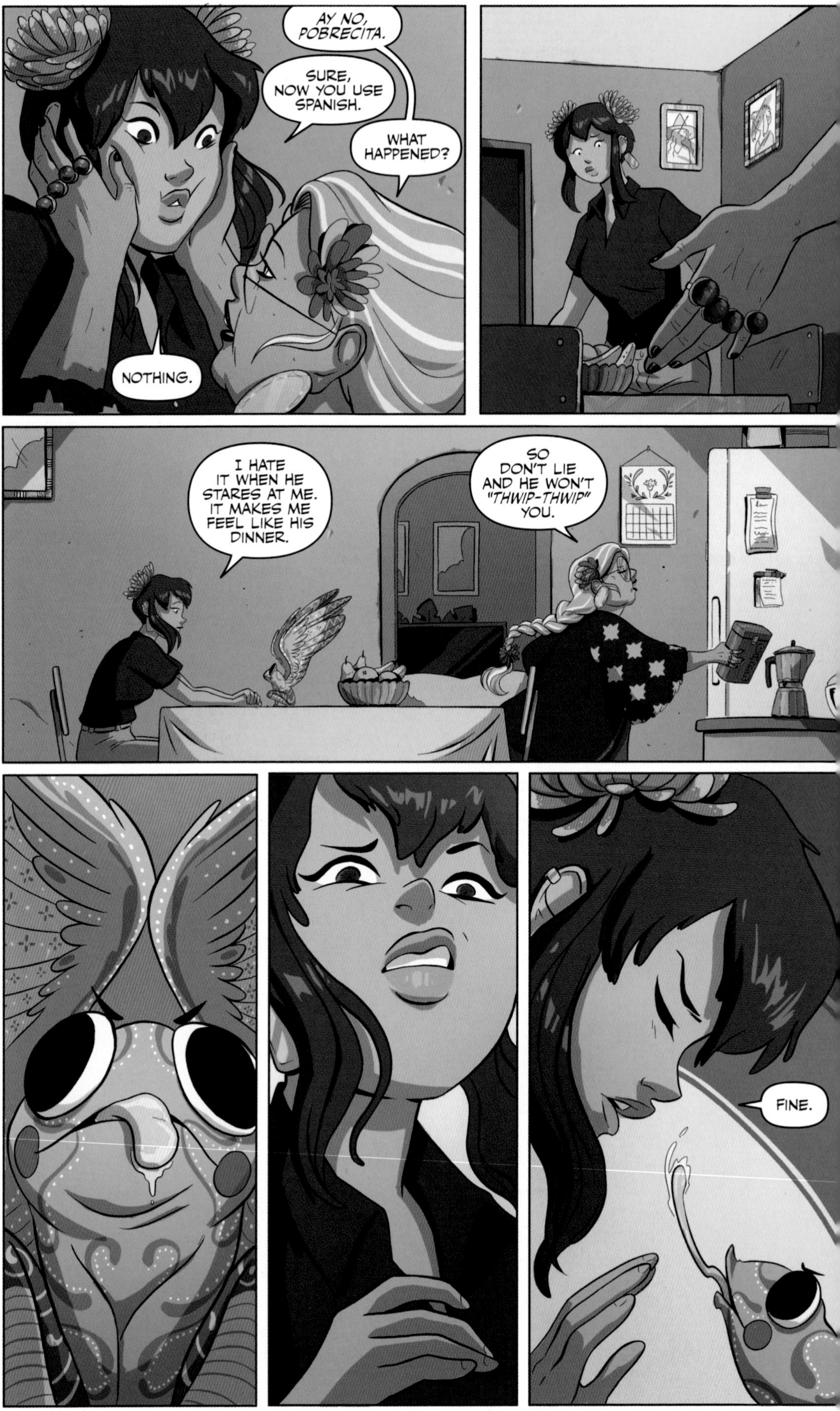
AY NO, POBRECITA.
SURE, NOW YOU USE SPANISH.
WHAT HAPPENED?
NOTHING.
I HATE IT WHEN HE STARES AT ME. IT MAKES ME FEEL LIKE HIS DINNER.
SO DON'T LIE AND HE WON'T "THWIP-THWIP" YOU.
FINE.

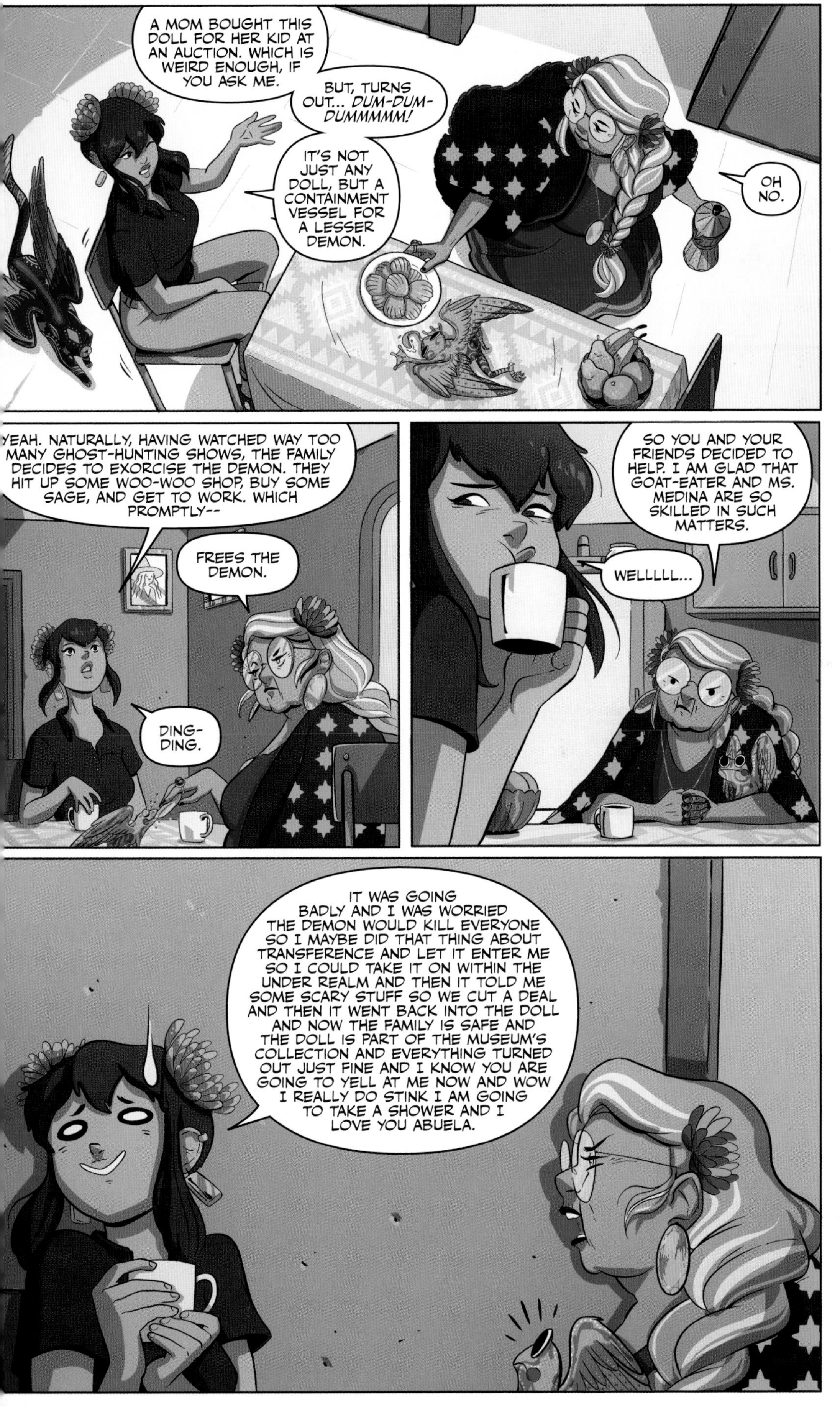
A MOM BOUGHT THIS DOLL FOR HER KID AT AN AUCTION. WHICH IS WEIRD ENOUGH, IF YOU ASK ME.
BUT, TURNS OUT... DUM-DUM-DUMMMMM!
IT'S NOT JUST ANY DOLL, BUT A CONTAINMENT VESSEL FOR A LESSER DEMON.
OH NO.
YEAH. NATURALLY, HAVING WATCHED WAY TOO MANY GHOST-HUNTING SHOWS, THE FAMILY DECIDES TO EXORCISE THE DEMON. THEY HIT UP SOME WOO-WOO SHOP, BUY SOME SAGE, AND GET TO WORK. WHICH PROMPTLY--
FREES THE DEMON.
DING-DING.
SO YOU AND YOUR FRIENDS DECIDED TO HELP. I AM GLAD THAT GOAT-EATER AND MS. MEDINA ARE SO SKILLED IN SUCH MATTERS.
WELLLLL...
IT WAS GOING BADLY AND I WAS WORRIED THE DEMON WOULD KILL EVERYONE SO I MAYBE DID THAT THING ABOUT TRANSFERENCE AND LET IT ENTER ME SO I COULD TAKE IT ON WITHIN THE UNDER REALM AND THEN IT TOLD ME SOME SCARY STUFF SO WE CUT A DEAL AND THEN IT WENT BACK INTO THE DOLL AND NOW THE FAMILY IS SAFE AND THE DOLL IS PART OF THE MUSEUM'S COLLECTION AND EVERYTHING TURNED OUT JUST FINE AND I KNOW YOU ARE GOING TO YELL AT ME NOW AND WOW I REALLY DO STINK I AM GOING TO TAKE A SHOWER AND I LOVE YOU ABUELA.

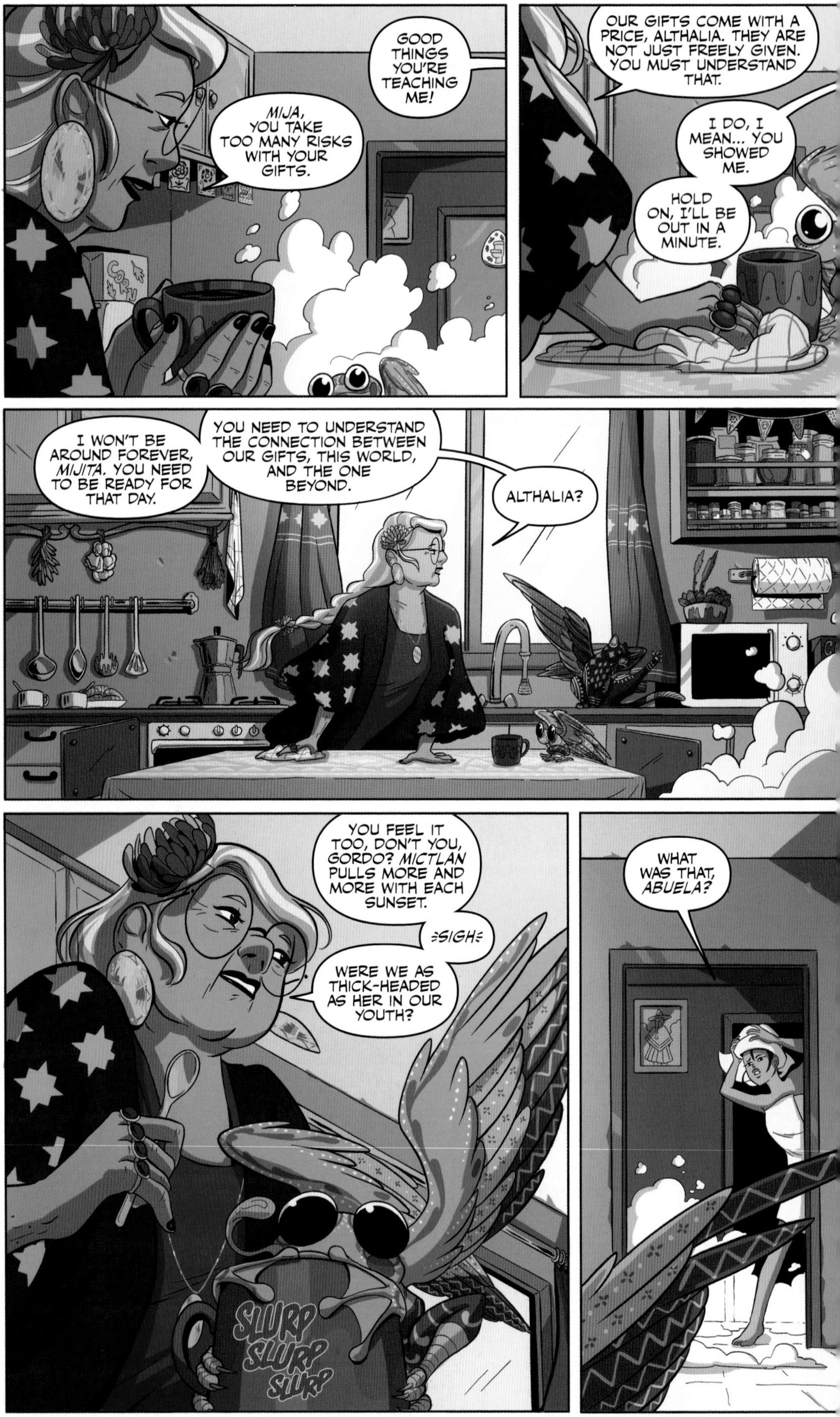
GOOD THINGS YOU'RE TEACHING ME!
MIJA, YOU TAKE TOO MANY RISKS WITH YOUR GIFTS.
OUR GIFTS COME WITH A PRICE, ALTHALIA. THEY ARE NOT JUST FREELY GIVEN. YOU MUST UNDERSTAND THAT.
I DO, I MEAN... YOU SHOWED ME.
HOLD ON, I'LL BE OUT IN A MINUTE.
I WON'T BE AROUND FOREVER, *MIJITA*. YOU NEED TO BE READY FOR THAT DAY.
YOU NEED TO UNDERSTAND THE CONNECTION BETWEEN OUR GIFTS, THIS WORLD, AND THE ONE BEYOND.
ALTHALIA?
YOU FEEL IT TOO, DON'T YOU, GORDO? *MICTLAN* PULLS MORE AND MORE WITH EACH SUNSET.
SIGH
WERE WE AS THICK-HEADED AS HER IN OUR YOUTH?
SLURP SLURP SLURP
WHAT WAS THAT, *ABUELA*?

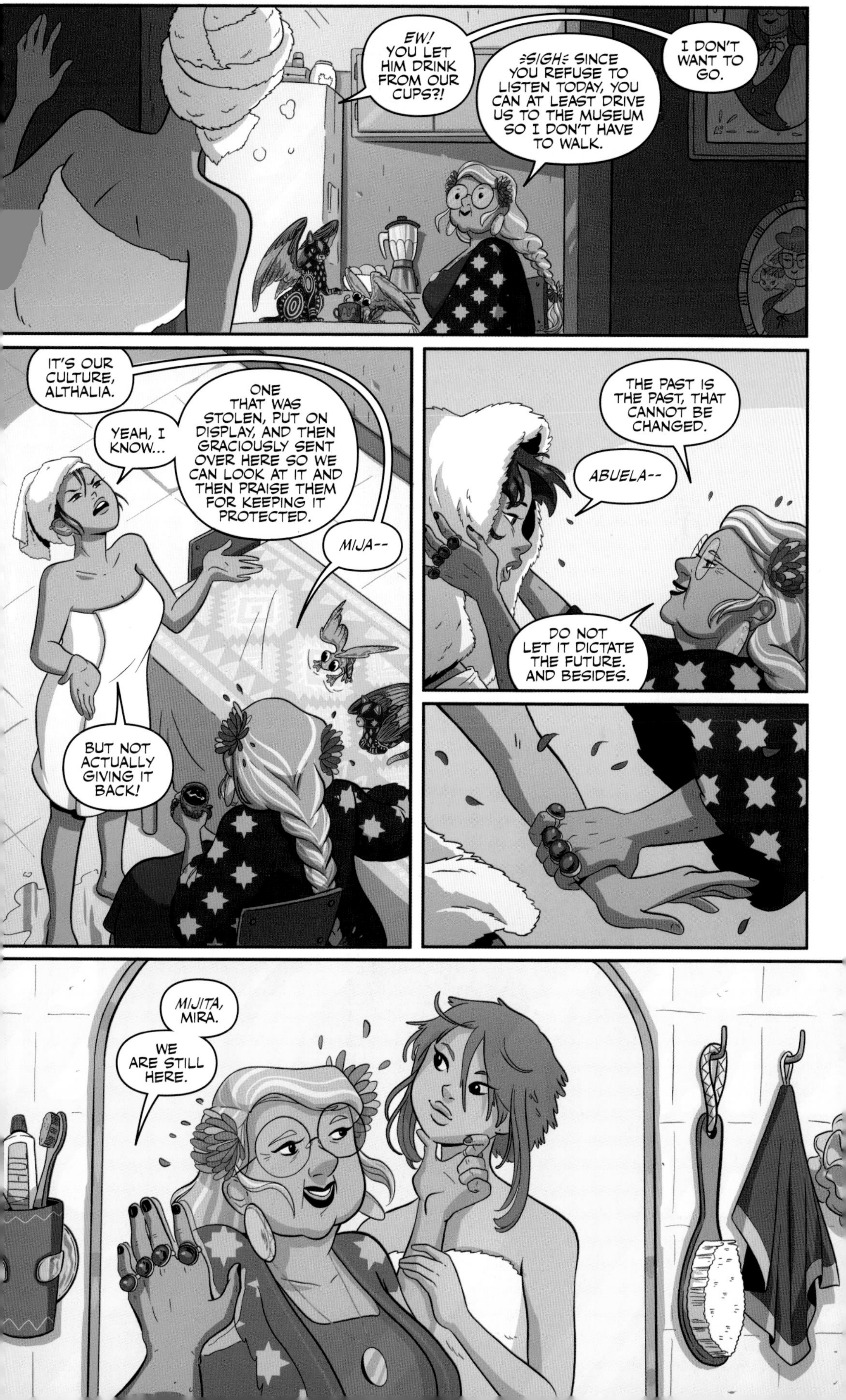
EW! YOU LET HIM DRINK FROM OUR CUPS?!
=SIGH= SINCE YOU REFUSE TO LISTEN TODAY, YOU CAN AT LEAST DRIVE US TO THE MUSEUM SO I DON'T HAVE TO WALK.
I DON'T WANT TO GO.
IT'S OUR CULTURE, ALTHALIA.
YEAH, I KNOW...
ONE THAT WAS STOLEN, PUT ON DISPLAY, AND THEN GRACIOUSLY SENT OVER HERE SO WE CAN LOOK AT IT AND THEN PRAISE THEM FOR KEEPING IT PROTECTED.
MIJA--
BUT NOT ACTUALLY GIVING IT BACK!
THE PAST IS THE PAST, THAT CANNOT BE CHANGED.
ABUELA--
DO NOT LET IT DICTATE THE FUTURE. AND BESIDES.
MIJITA, MIRA.
WE ARE STILL HERE.

"I'M SORRY, ABUELA, BUT EVERYTHING I SEE JUST MAKES ME MAD."

"CAN YOU NOT SEE THE BEAUTY AND PRIDE WITHIN THE ART?"

TREASURES OF THE NEW WORLD

Coffee!

OF COURSE I SEE IT, AND FRANKLY, THAT'S WHAT MAKES ME SO MAD. THEY AREN'T HERE AS A CELEBRATION OF OUR CULTURE. THEY'RE SPOILS OF WAR--DON'T YOU SEE?

≈SIGH≈ I DO, MIJITA, I DO. I EVEN HEAR THE ECHOES OF THOSE WHO DIED, AS YOU WILL IN TIME. BUT TO DWELL ON THE ANGER... THAT PATH WILL ONLY LEAD TO MORE SUFFERING. YOU NEED TO UNDERSTAND THIS.

DO NOT BE SO QUICK TO ASSUME WE WERE WITHOUT DARKNESS AND VIOLENCE. THAT IS THE VERY ARROGANCE WHICH FUELED ALL WE SEE BEFORE US... THE ART AND THE CONQUEST.

I UNDERSTAND, ABUELA, I'M JUST...

JUST YOUNG AND FILLED WITH RIGHTEOUS PASSION.

ENOUGH OF THAT FOR NOW. I SMELLED SOME AMAZING COFFEE AND I WOULD LIKE SOME. GIMME SOME MONEY, MIJA.

NONE OF MY FRIENDS' NANAS HIT UP THEIR GRANDKIDS FOR MONEY.

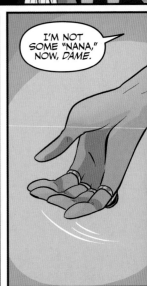

I'M NOT SOME "NANA," NOW, DAME.

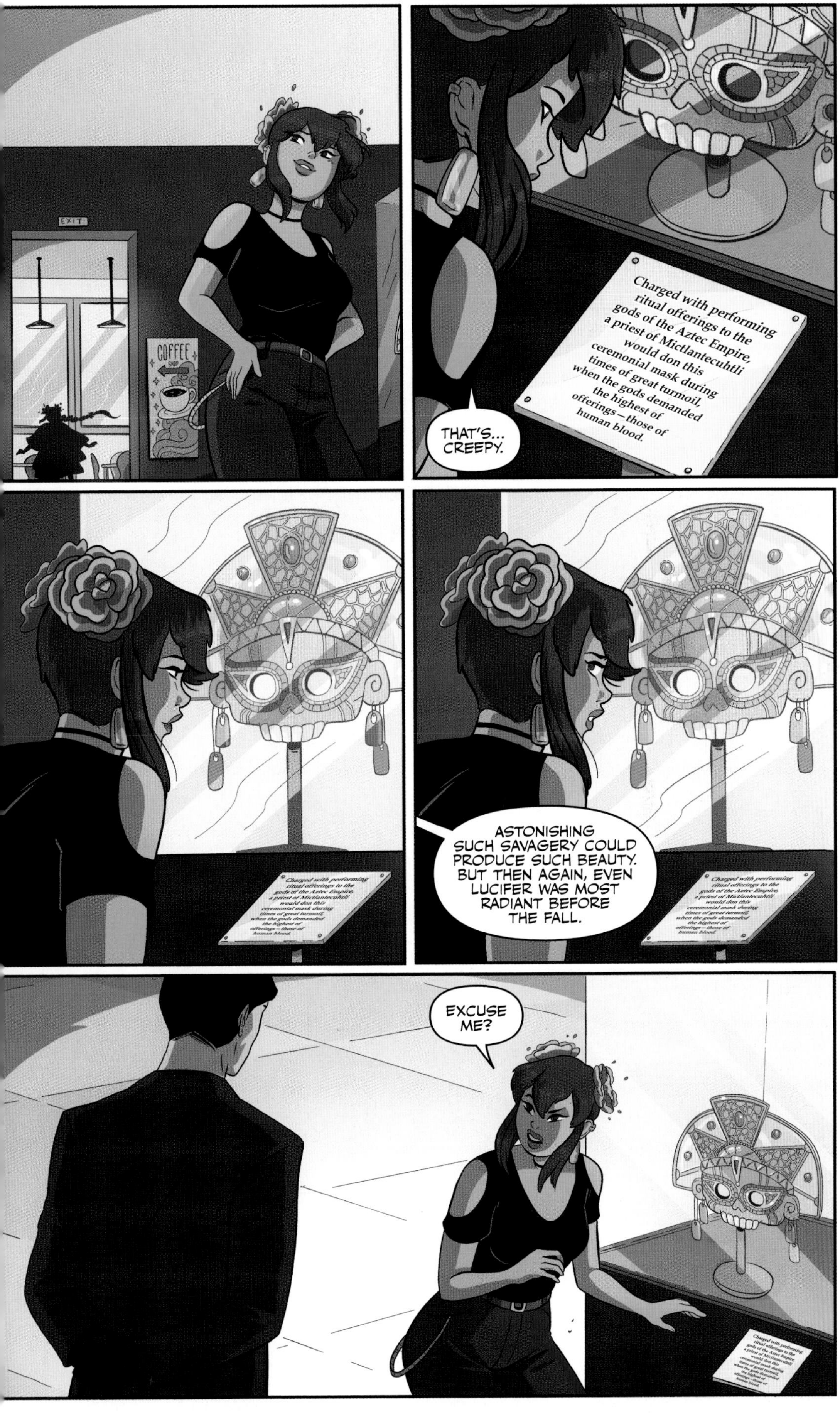

EXIT
COFFEE SHOP
Charged with performing ritual offerings to the gods of the Aztec Empire, a priest of Mictlantecuhtli would don this ceremonial mask during times of great turmoil, when the gods demanded the highest of offerings—those of human blood.
THAT'S... CREEPY.
ASTONISHING SUCH SAVAGERY COULD PRODUCE SUCH BEAUTY. BUT THEN AGAIN, EVEN LUCIFER WAS MOST RADIANT BEFORE THE FALL.
EXCUSE ME?

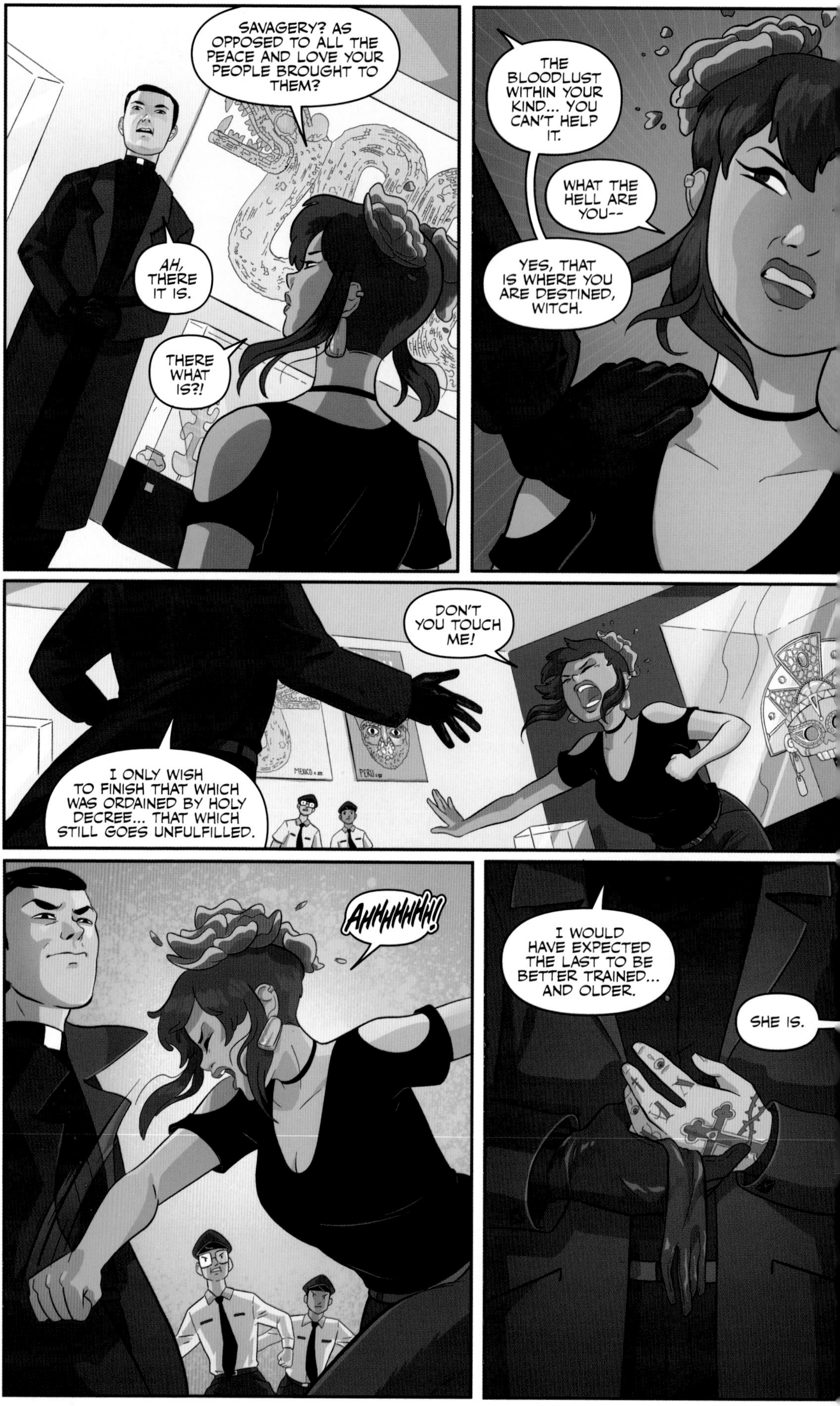
SAVAGERY? AS OPPOSED TO ALL THE PEACE AND LOVE YOUR PEOPLE BROUGHT TO THEM?
AH, THERE IT IS.
THERE WHAT IS?!
THE BLOODLUST WITHIN YOUR KIND... YOU CAN'T HELP IT.
WHAT THE HELL ARE YOU--
YES, THAT IS WHERE YOU ARE DESTINED, WITCH.
DON'T YOU TOUCH ME!
I ONLY WISH TO FINISH THAT WHICH WAS ORDAINED BY HOLY DECREE... THAT WHICH STILL GOES UNFULFILLED.
MEXICO
PERU
AHHHHHHH!
I WOULD HAVE EXPECTED THE LAST TO BE BETTER TRAINED... AND OLDER.
SHE IS.

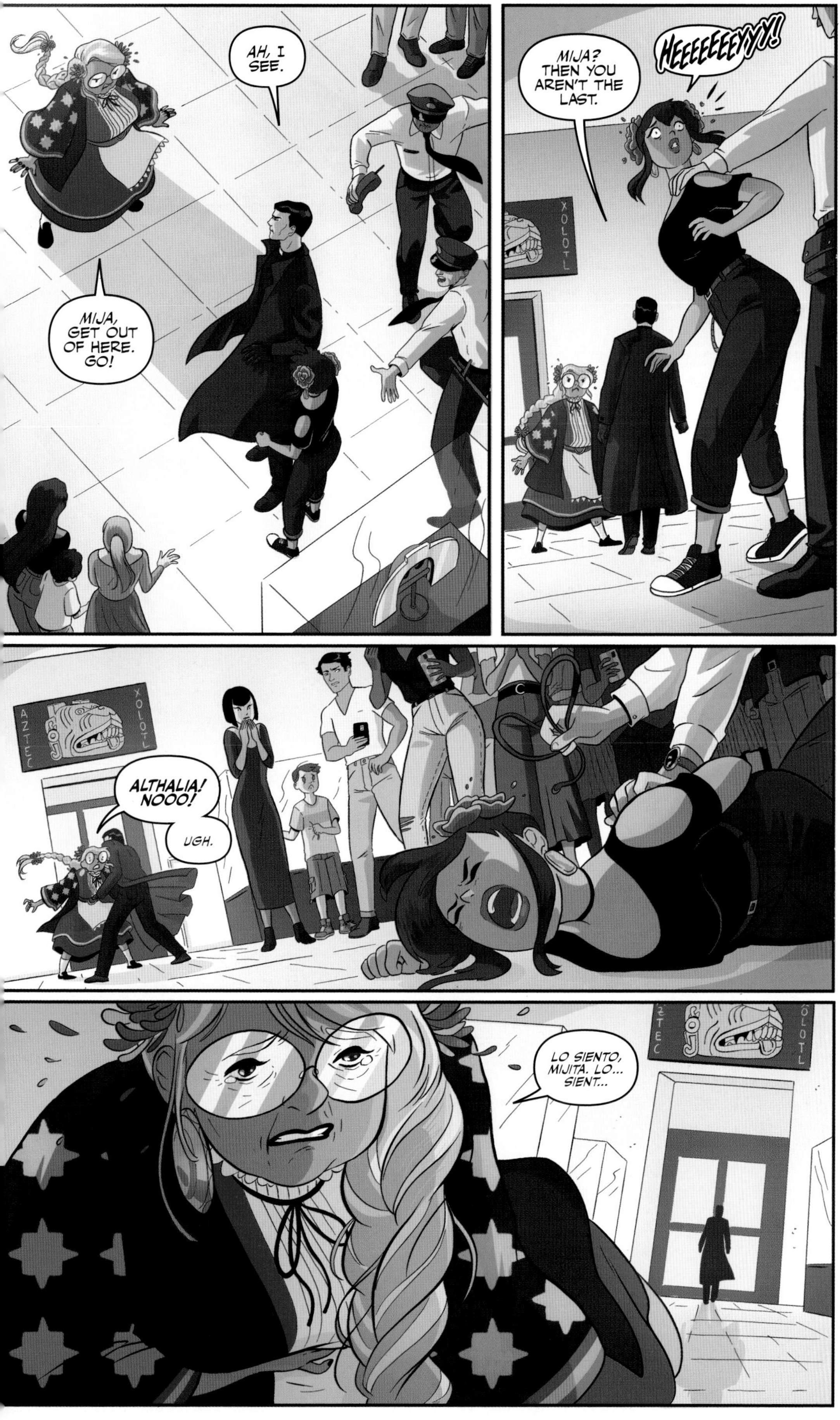
AH, I SEE.
MIJA, GET OUT OF HERE. GO!
MIJA? THEN YOU AREN'T THE LAST.
HEEEEEEEYYY!
XOLOTL
AZTEC
ALTHALIA! NOOO!
UGH.
LO SIENTO, MIJITA. LO... SIENT...

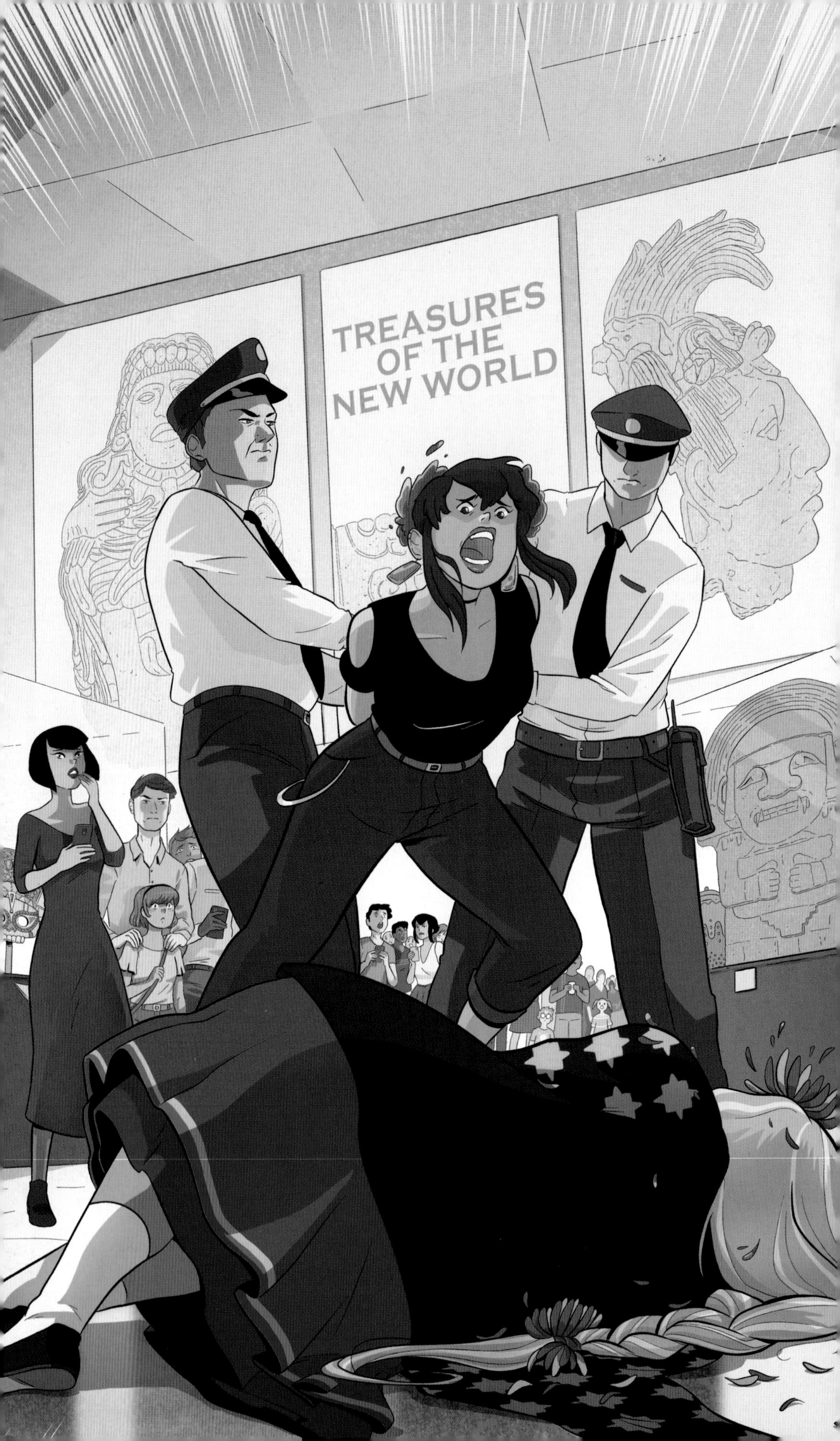
TREASURES OF THE NEW WORLD

CHAPTER 2

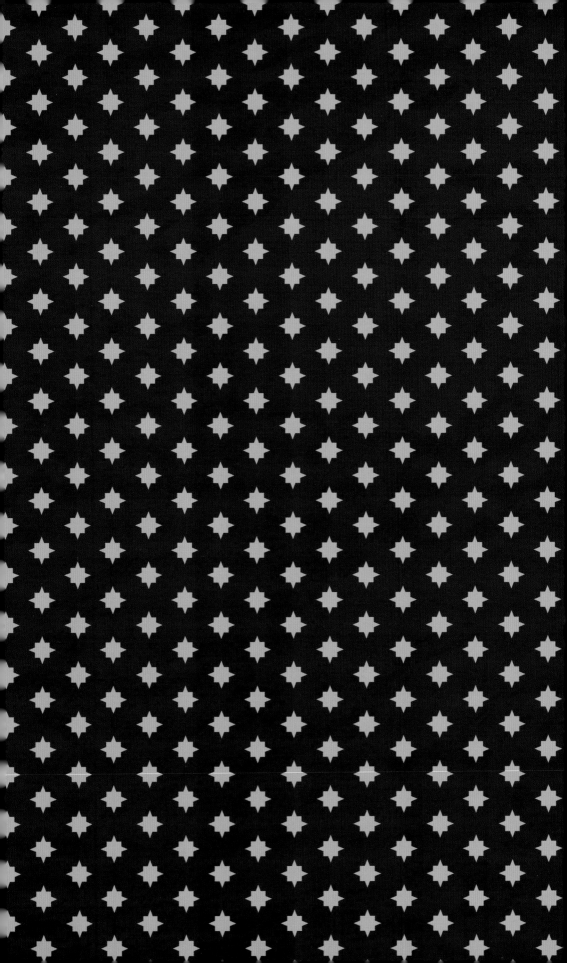

♪ CON UN BESO DE SU BOCA PUSO A SOÑAR MIS AMORES ♪

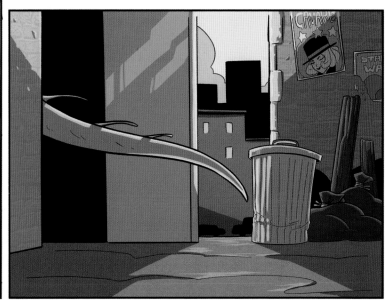

♪ LA TONTA DESMEMORIADA LO HA NEGADO POR SER POBRE ♪

COMO QUE TE VAS LLEVÁNDOTE--

--OOPS, SHOULD TWIST THE RING. AND...

MMMMWAH

GORGEOUS.

SERIOUSLY?

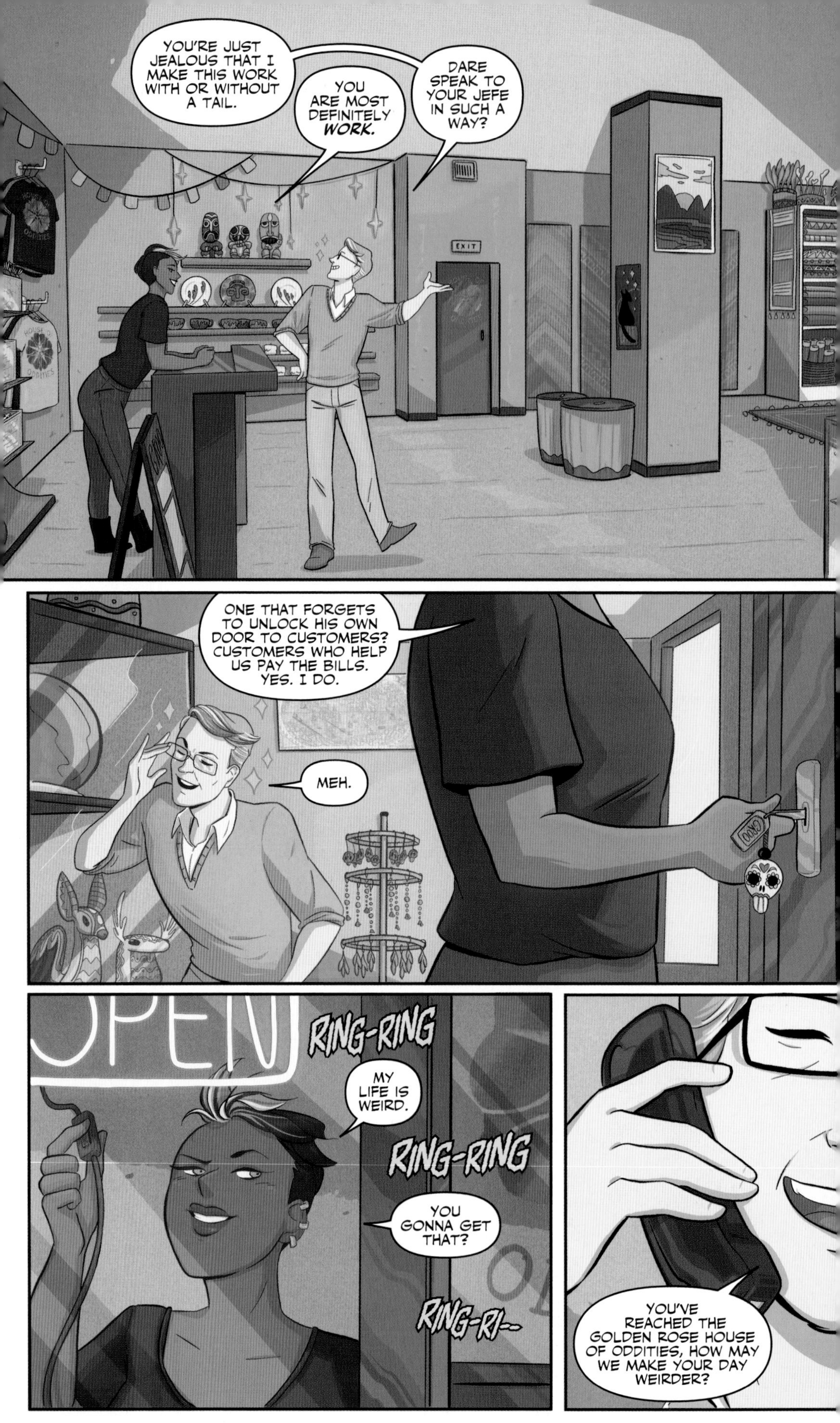
YOU'RE JUST JEALOUS THAT I MAKE THIS WORK WITH OR WITHOUT A TAIL.
DARE SPEAK TO YOUR JEFE IN SUCH A WAY?
YOU ARE MOST DEFINITELY WORK.
EXIT
ONE THAT FORGETS TO UNLOCK HIS OWN DOOR TO CUSTOMERS? CUSTOMERS WHO HELP US PAY THE BILLS. YES. I DO.
MEH.
OPEN
RING-RING
MY LIFE IS WEIRD.
RING-RING
YOU GONNA GET THAT?
RING-RI--
YOU'VE REACHED THE GOLDEN ROSE HOUSE OF ODDITIES, HOW MAY WE MAKE YOUR DAY WEIRDER?

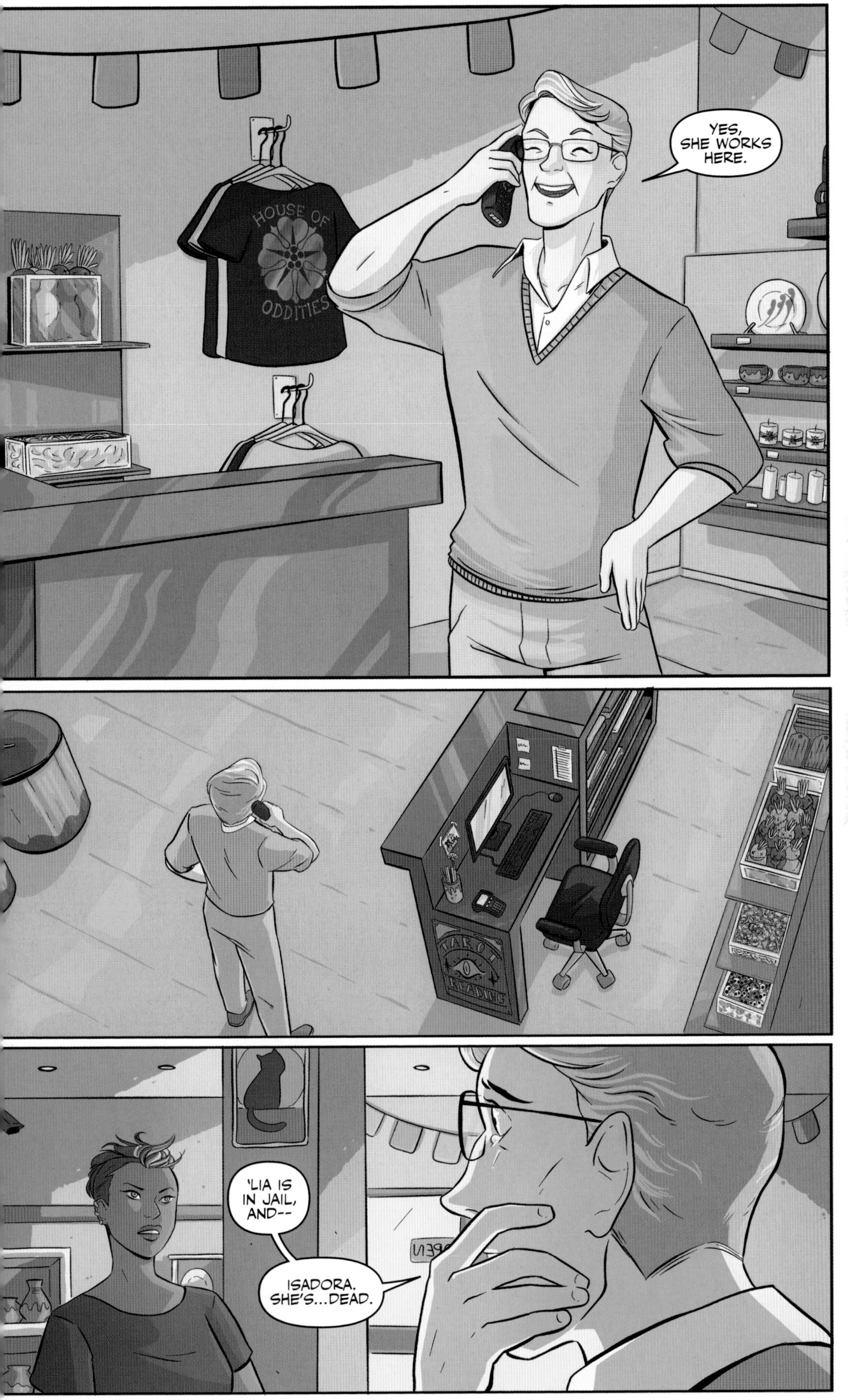
YES, SHE WORKS HERE.
HOUSE OF ODDITIES
TAROT READING
'LIA IS IN JAIL, AND--
ISADORA. SHE'S...DEAD.

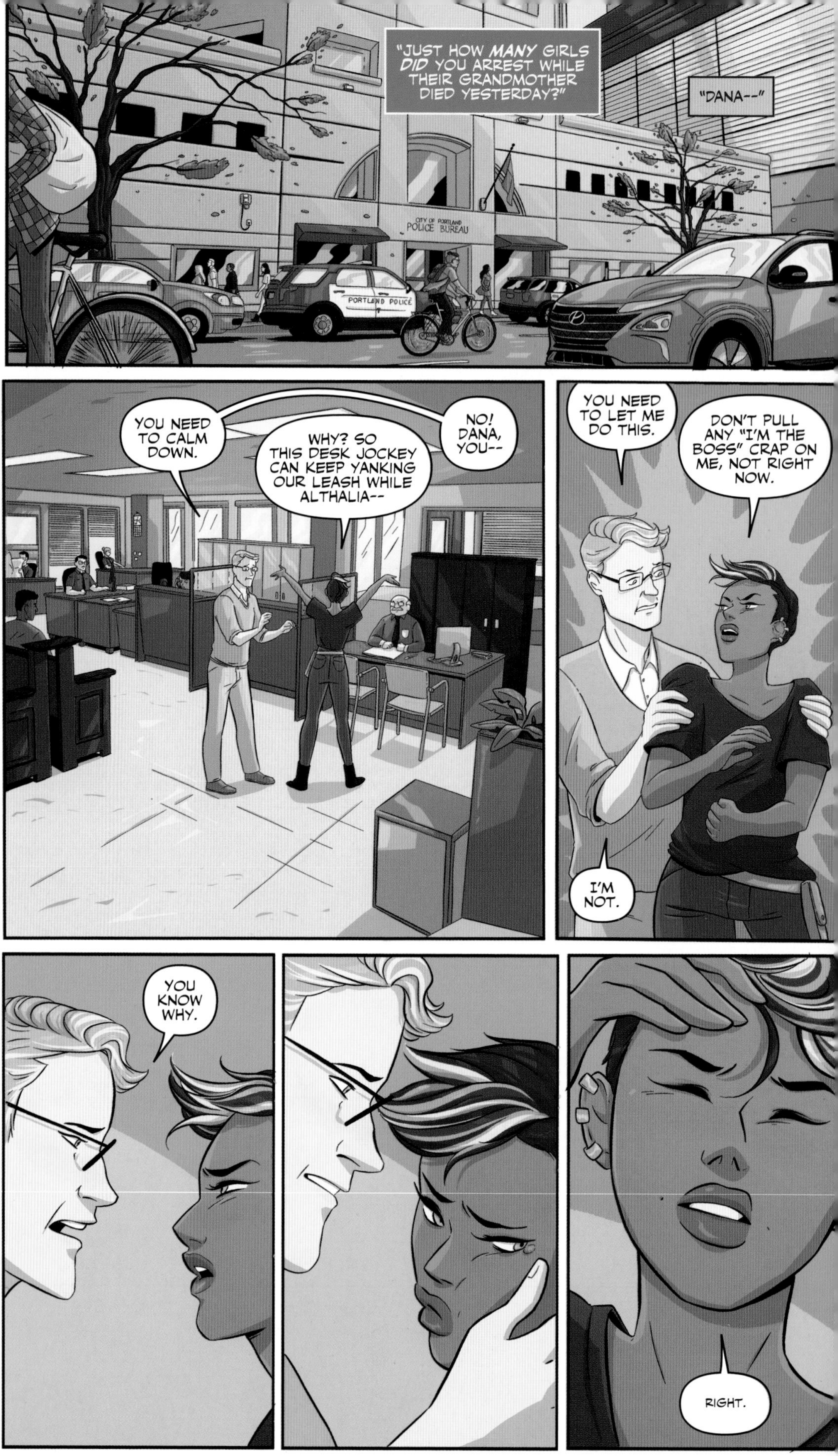
"JUST HOW MANY GIRLS DID YOU ARREST WHILE THEIR GRANDMOTHER DIED YESTERDAY?"
"DANA--"
CITY OF PORTLAND POLICE BUREAU
PORTLAND POLICE
YOU NEED TO CALM DOWN.
WHY? SO THIS DESK JOCKEY CAN KEEP YANKING OUR LEASH WHILE ALTHALIA--
NO! DANA, YOU--
YOU NEED TO LET ME DO THIS.
DON'T PULL ANY "I'M THE BOSS" CRAP ON ME, NOT RIGHT NOW.
I'M NOT.
YOU KNOW WHY.
RIGHT.

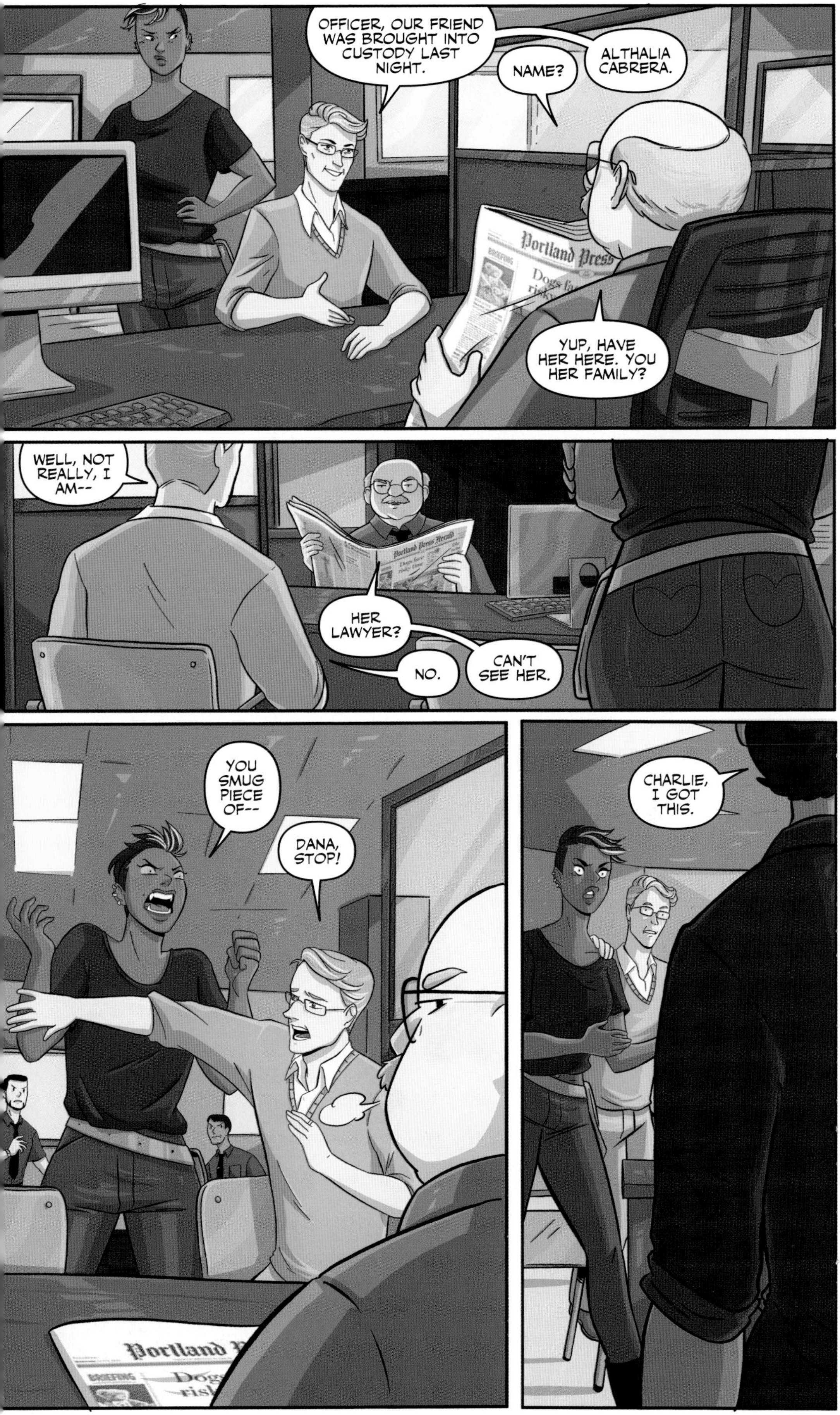
OFFICER, OUR FRIEND WAS BROUGHT INTO CUSTODY LAST NIGHT.
NAME?
ALTHALIA CABRERA.
YUP, HAVE HER HERE. YOU HER FAMILY?
WELL, NOT REALLY, I AM--
HER LAWYER?
NO.
CAN'T SEE HER.
YOU SMUG PIECE OF--
DANA, STOP!
CHARLIE, I GOT THIS.

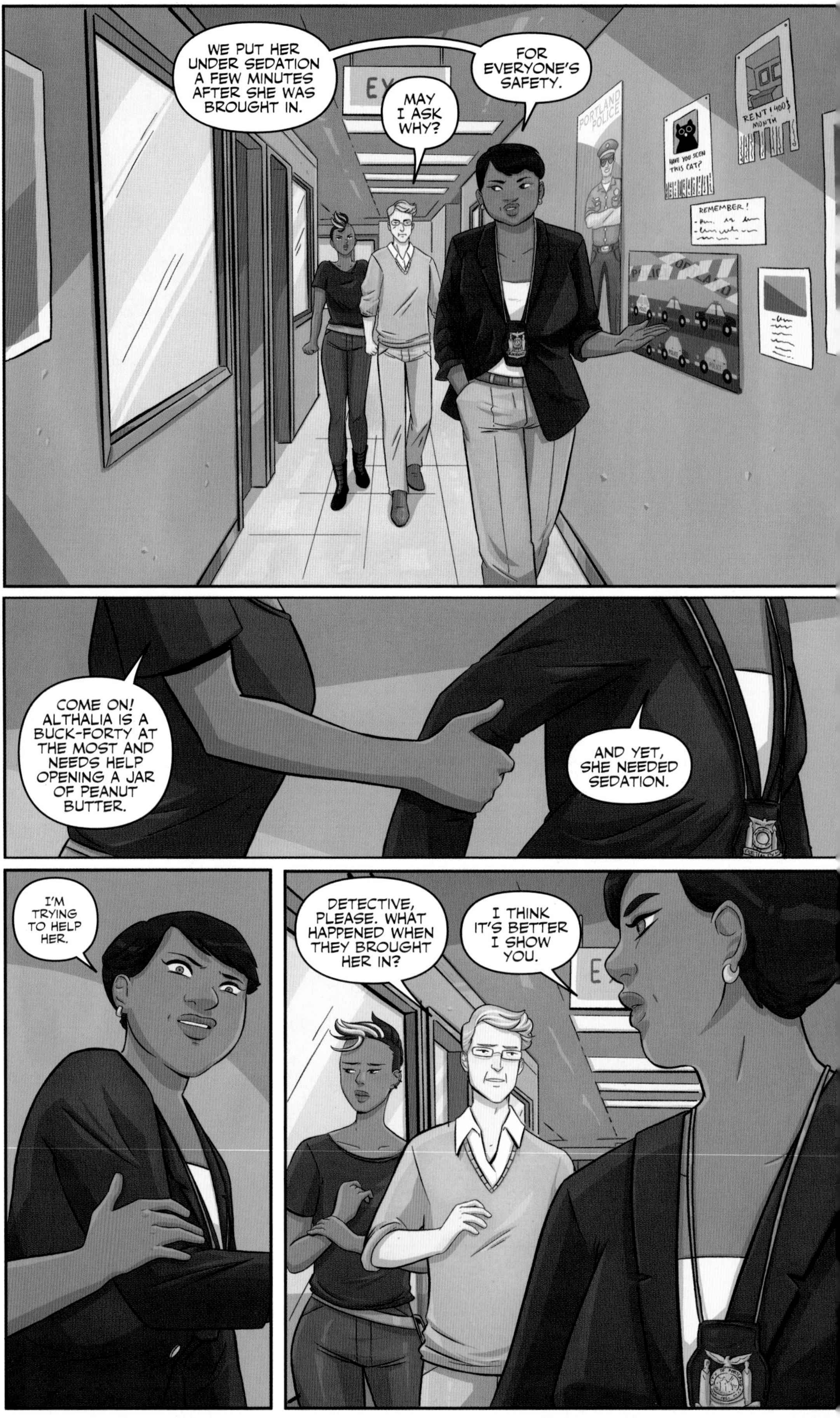
WE PUT HER UNDER SEDATION A FEW MINUTES AFTER SHE WAS BROUGHT IN.
FOR EVERYONE'S SAFETY.
MAY I ASK WHY?
PORTLAND POLICE
HAVE YOU SEEN THIS CAT?
RENT 400$ MONTH
REMEMBER!
COME ON! ALTHALIA IS A BUCK-FORTY AT THE MOST AND NEEDS HELP OPENING A JAR OF PEANUT BUTTER.
AND YET, SHE NEEDED SEDATION.
I'M TRYING TO HELP HER.
DETECTIVE, PLEASE. WHAT HAPPENED WHEN THEY BROUGHT HER IN?
I THINK IT'S BETTER I SHOW YOU.

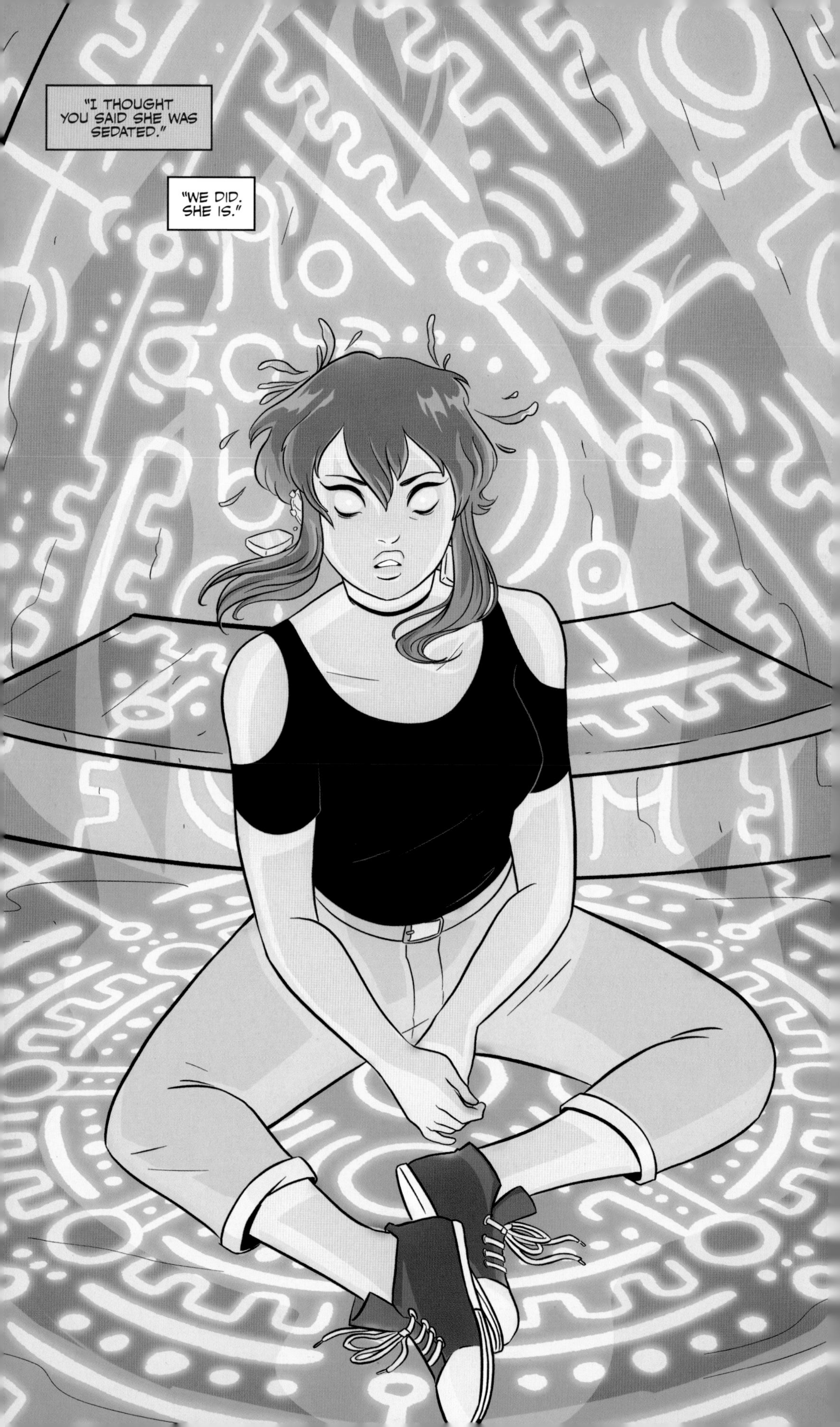
"I THOUGHT YOU SAID SHE WAS SEDATED."
"WE DID. SHE IS."

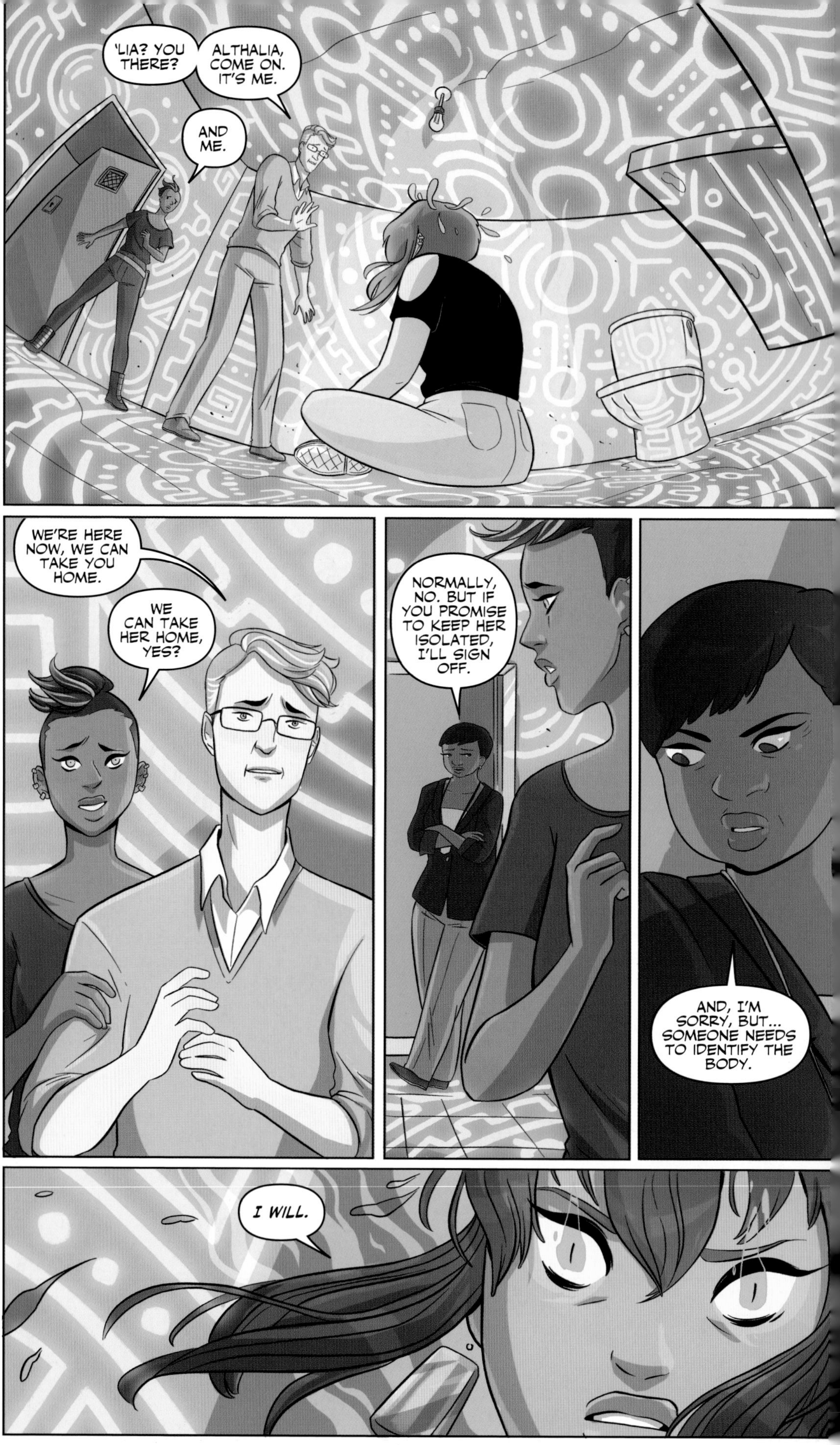
'LIA? YOU THERE?
ALTHALIA, COME ON. IT'S ME.
AND ME.
WE'RE HERE NOW, WE CAN TAKE YOU HOME.
WE CAN TAKE HER HOME, YES?
NORMALLY, NO. BUT IF YOU PROMISE TO KEEP HER ISOLATED, I'LL SIGN OFF.
AND, I'M SORRY, BUT... SOMEONE NEEDS TO IDENTIFY THE BODY.
I WILL.

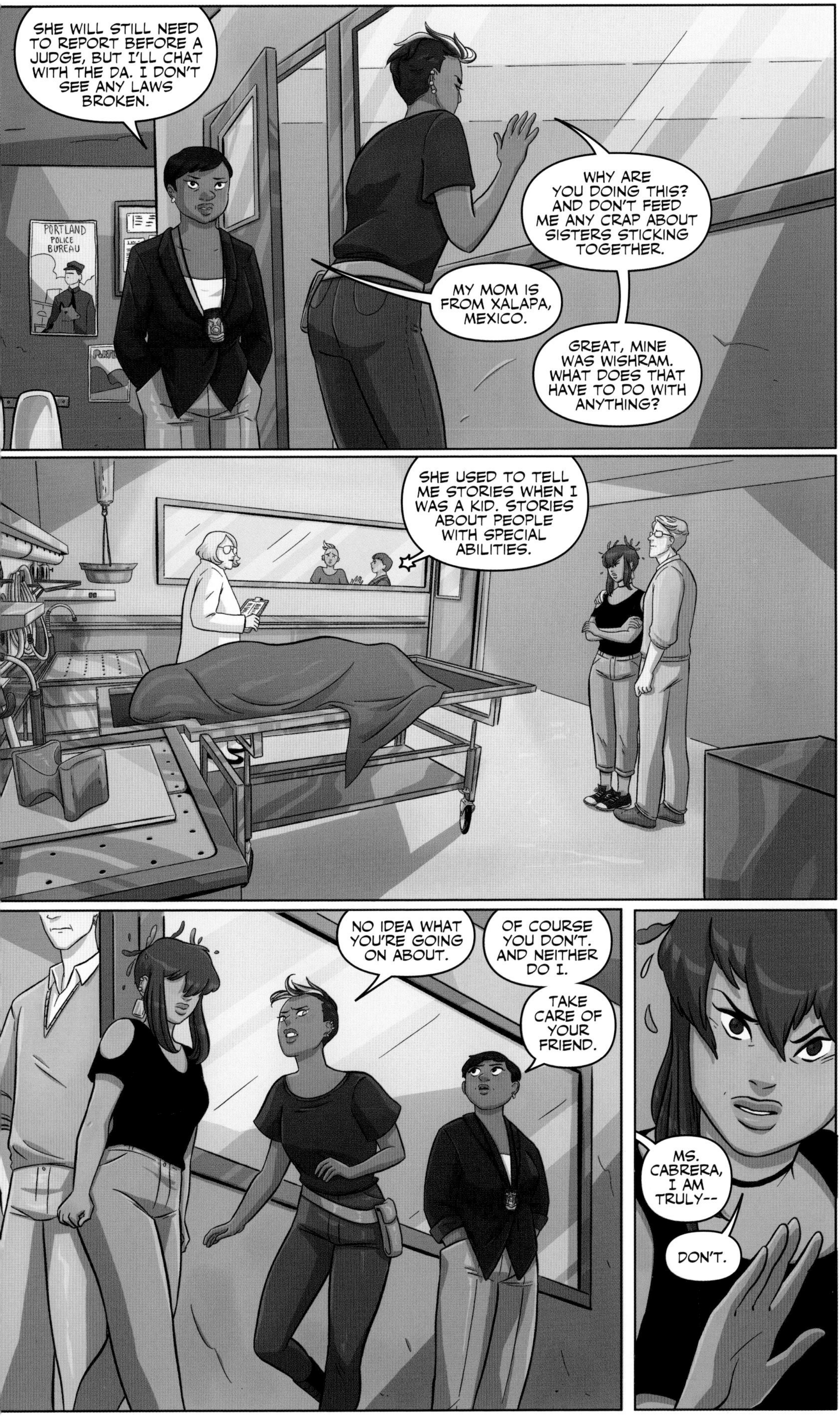

SHE WILL STILL NEED TO REPORT BEFORE A JUDGE, BUT I'LL CHAT WITH THE DA. I DON'T SEE ANY LAWS BROKEN.
PORTLAND POLICE BUREAU
WHY ARE YOU DOING THIS? AND DON'T FEED ME ANY CRAP ABOUT SISTERS STICKING TOGETHER.
MY MOM IS FROM XALAPA, MEXICO.
GREAT, MINE WAS WISHRAM. WHAT DOES THAT HAVE TO DO WITH ANYTHING?
SHE USED TO TELL ME STORIES WHEN I WAS A KID. STORIES ABOUT PEOPLE WITH SPECIAL ABILITIES.
NO IDEA WHAT YOU'RE GOING ON ABOUT.
OF COURSE YOU DON'T. AND NEITHER DO I.
TAKE CARE OF YOUR FRIEND.
MS. CABRERA, I AM TRULY--
DON'T.

"I DON'T THINK SHE SHOULD BE ALONE."

"NEITHER DO I, BUT WE'RE GOING TO HONOR HER WISHES.

"FOR NOW.

"I DON'T CARE WHAT YOU SAY, I AM BRINGING HER FOOD LATER."

"I KNOW YOU ARE."

"GLAD WE'RE ON THE SAME PAGE HERE."

"SHE'S FAMILY."

POBRECITO.

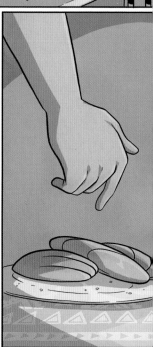

LO SIEN... LO...

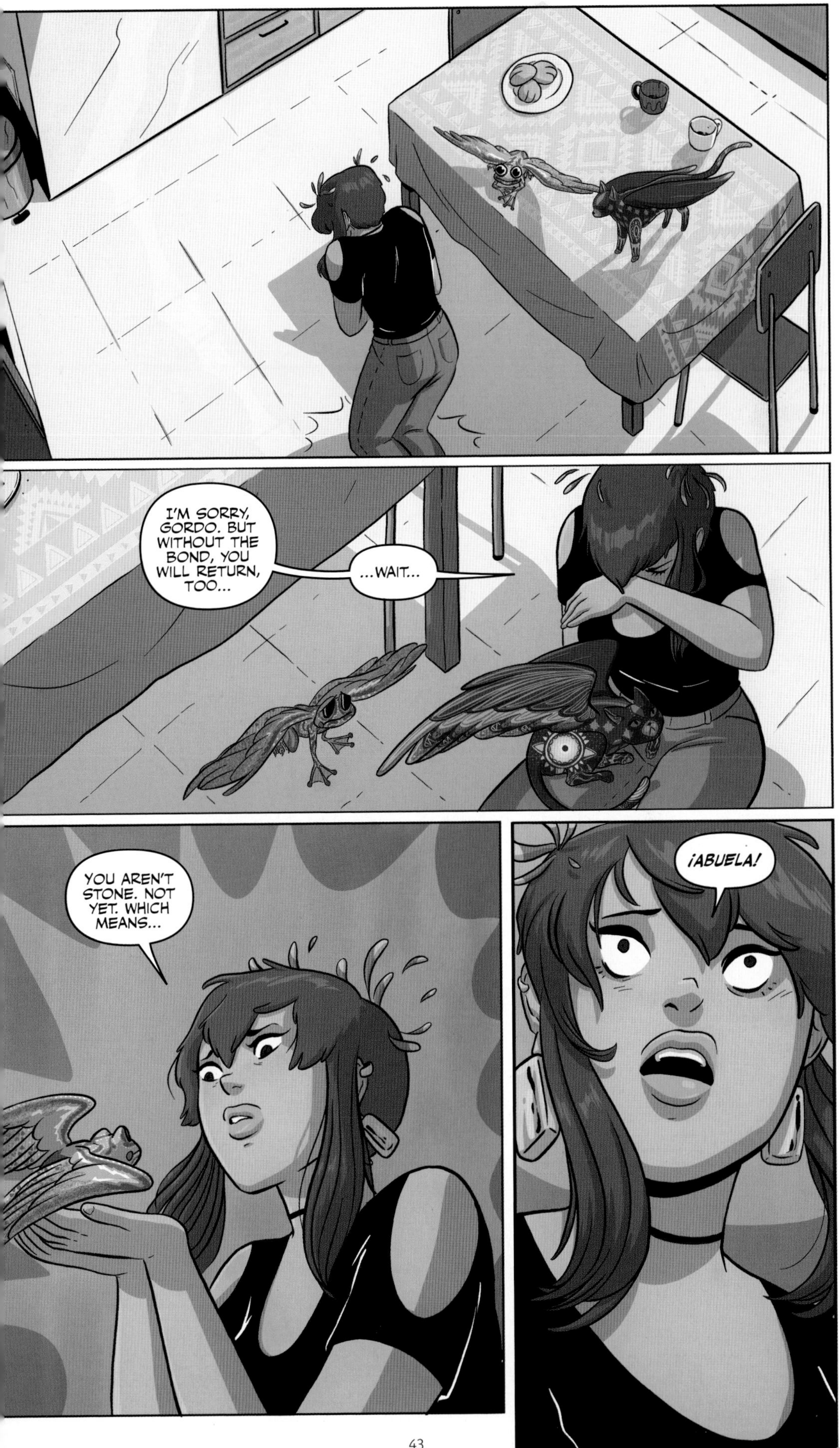
I'M SORRY, GORDO. BUT WITHOUT THE BOND, YOU WILL RETURN, TOO...
...WAIT...
YOU AREN'T STONE. NOT YET. WHICH MEANS...
¡ABUELA!

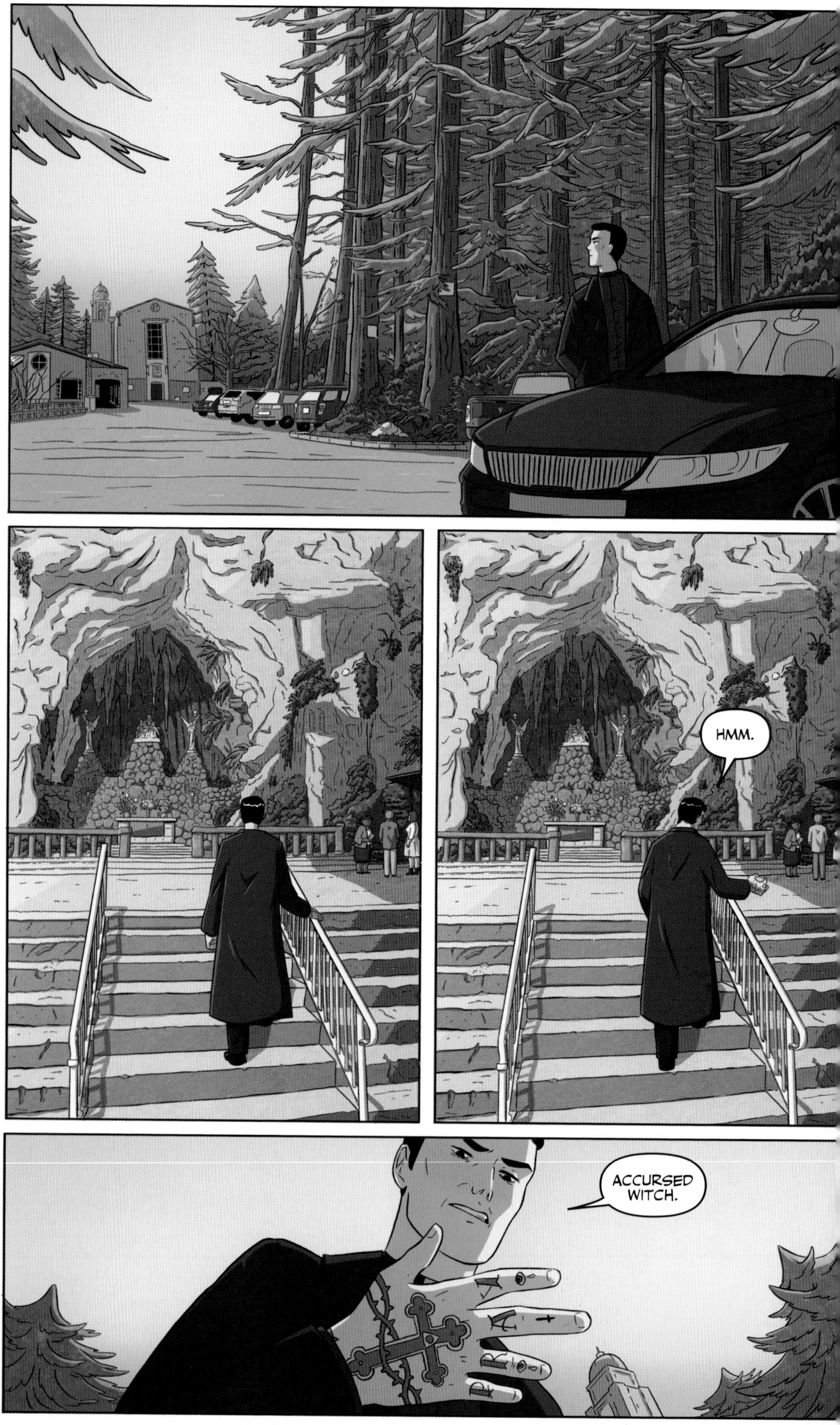
HMM.
ACCURSED WITCH.

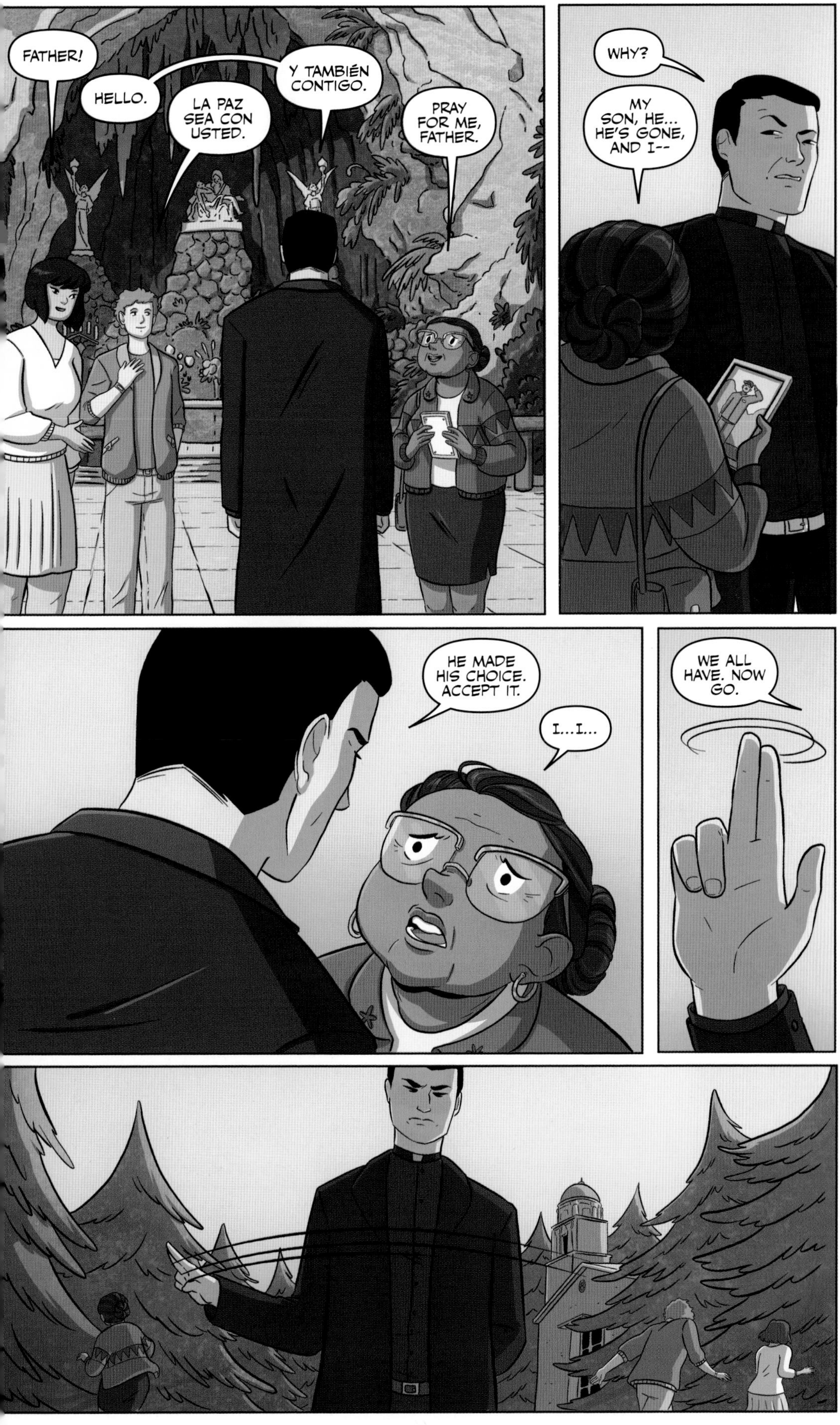
FATHER!
HELLO.
LA PAZ SEA CON USTED.
Y TAMBIÉN CONTIGO.
PRAY FOR ME, FATHER.
WHY?
MY SON, HE... HE'S GONE, AND I--
HE MADE HIS CHOICE. ACCEPT IT.
I...I...
WE ALL HAVE. NOW GO.

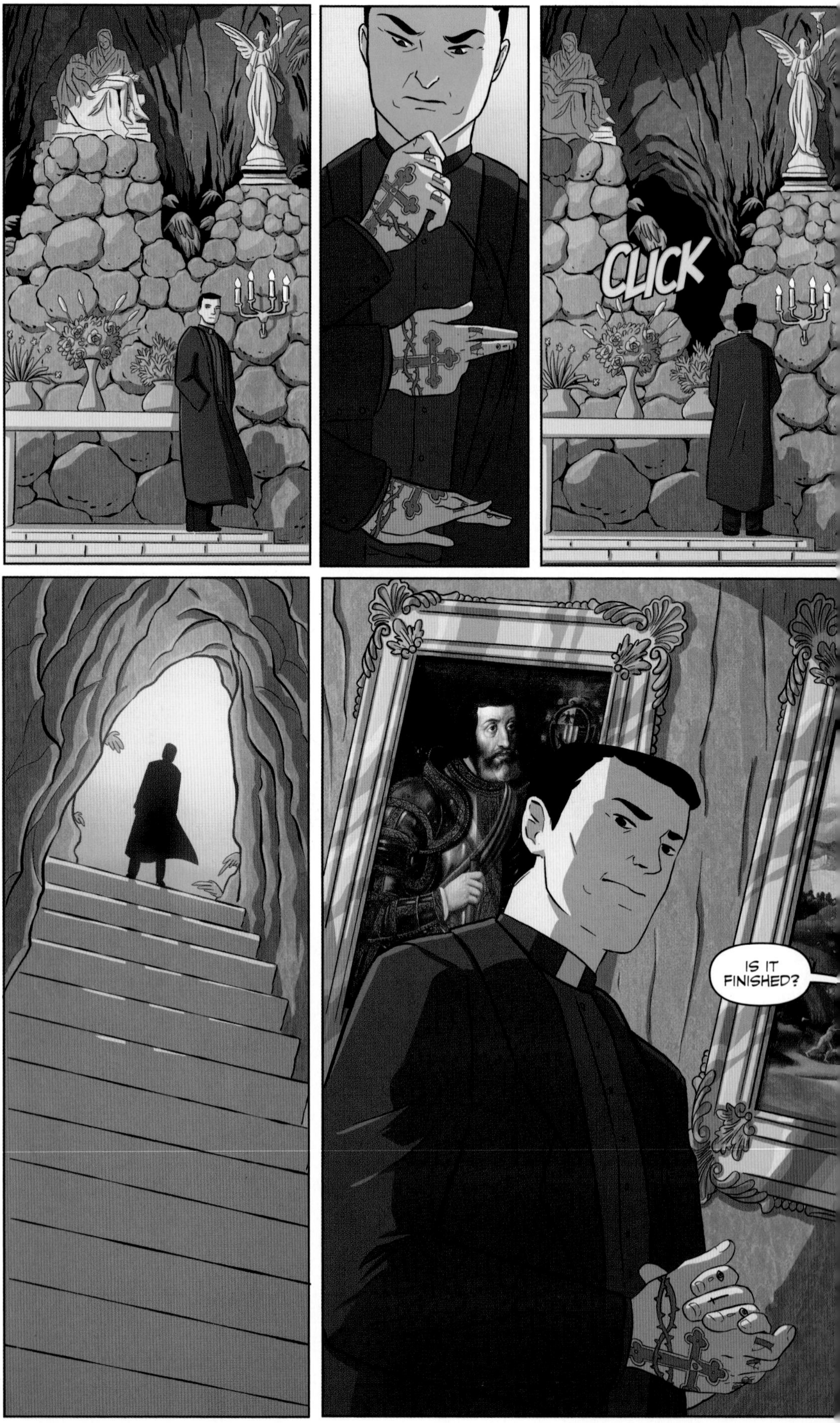
CLICK
IS IT FINISHED?

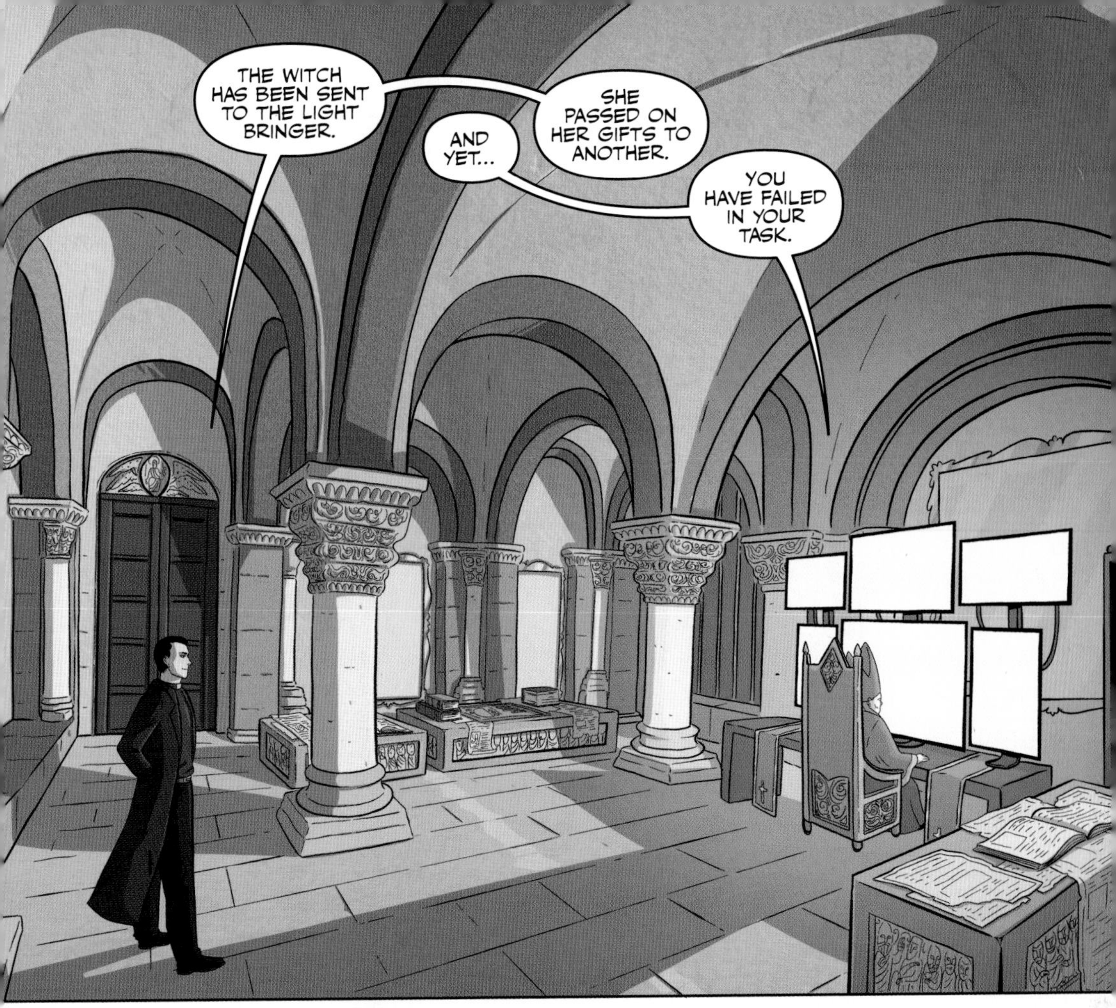
THE WITCH HAS BEEN SENT TO THE LIGHT BRINGER.
AND YET...
SHE PASSED ON HER GIFTS TO ANOTHER.
YOU HAVE FAILED IN YOUR TASK.

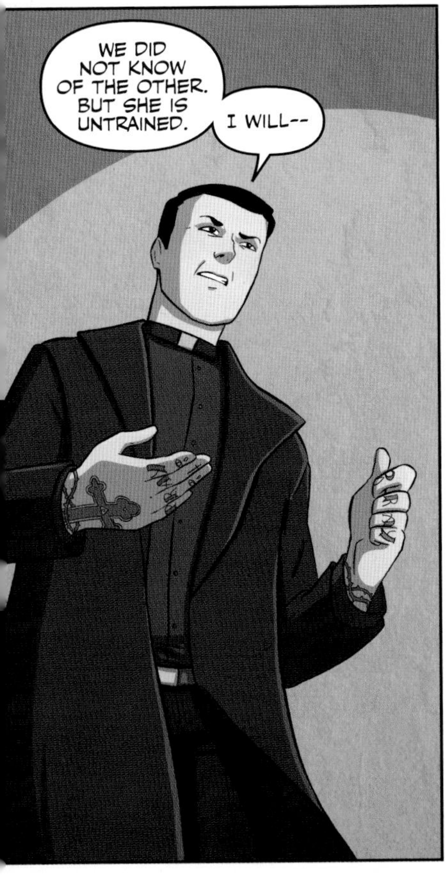
WE DID NOT KNOW OF THE OTHER. BUT SHE IS UNTRAINED.
I WILL--

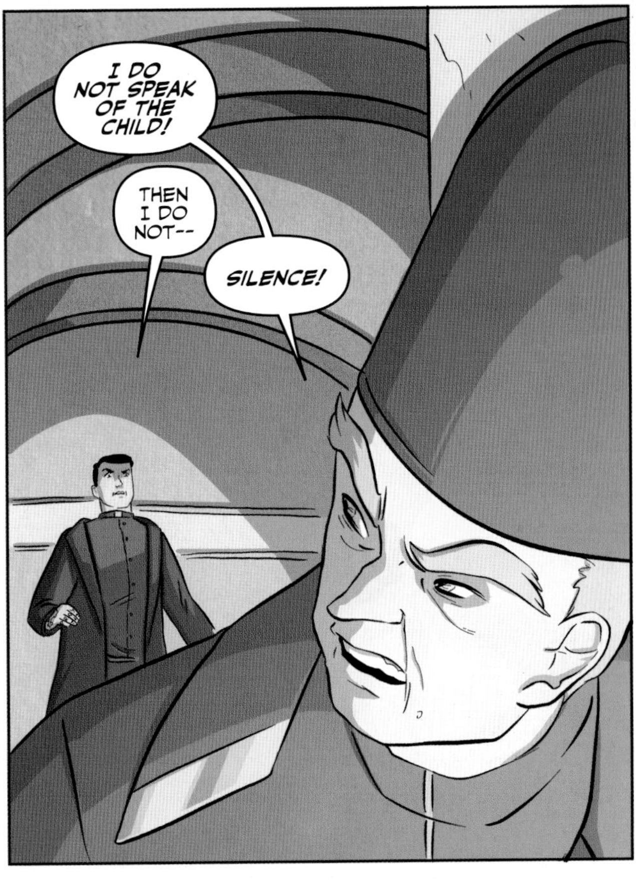
I DO NOT SPEAK OF THE CHILD!
THEN I DO NOT--
SILENCE!

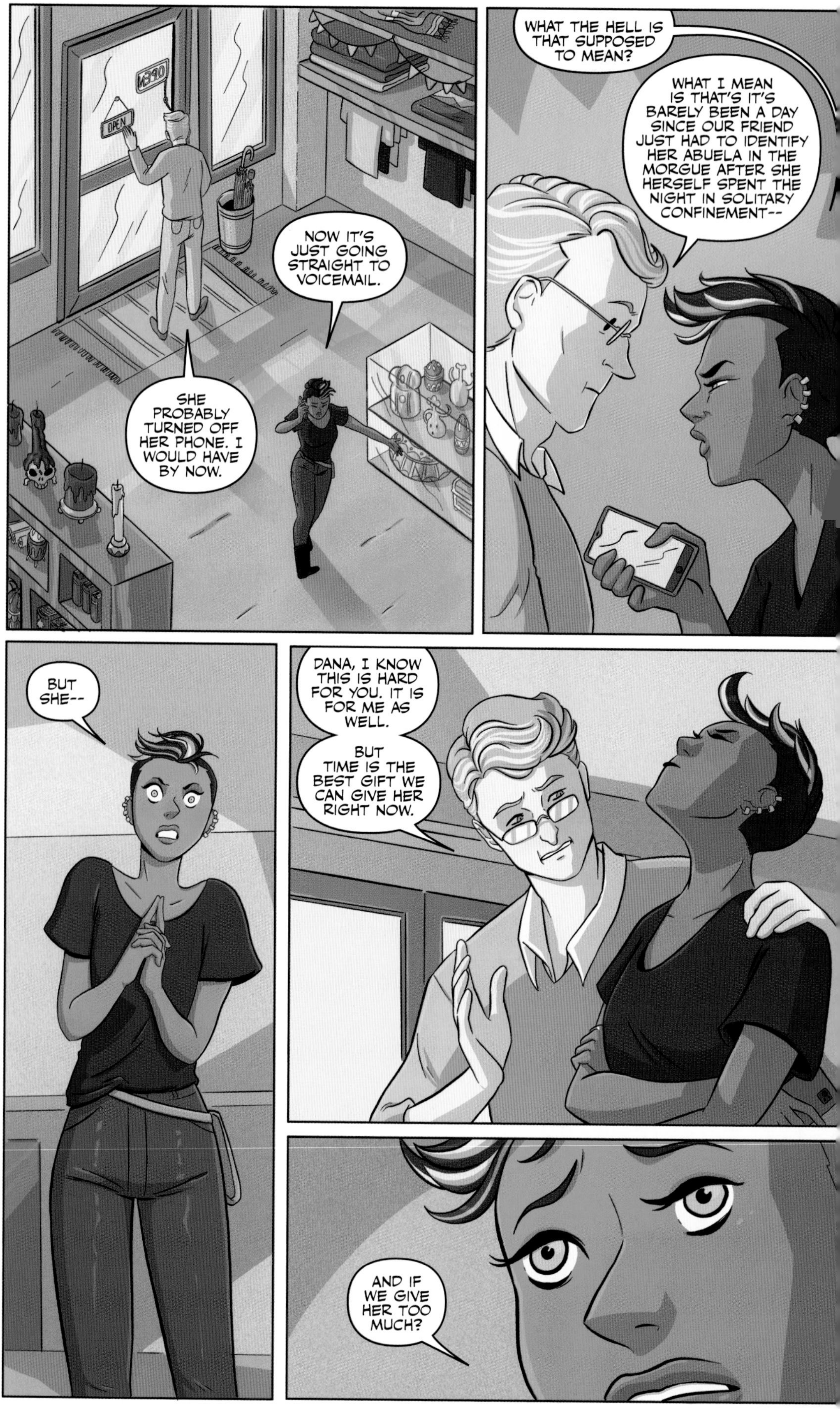
OPEN
NOW IT'S JUST GOING STRAIGHT TO VOICEMAIL.
SHE PROBABLY TURNED OFF HER PHONE. I WOULD HAVE BY NOW.
WHAT THE HELL IS THAT SUPPOSED TO MEAN?
WHAT I MEAN IS THAT'S IT'S BARELY BEEN A DAY SINCE OUR FRIEND JUST HAD TO IDENTIFY HER ABUELA IN THE MORGUE AFTER SHE HERSELF SPENT THE NIGHT IN SOLITARY CONFINEMENT--
BUT SHE--
DANA, I KNOW THIS IS HARD FOR YOU. IT IS FOR ME AS WELL.
BUT TIME IS THE BEST GIFT WE CAN GIVE HER RIGHT NOW.
AND IF WE GIVE HER TOO MUCH?

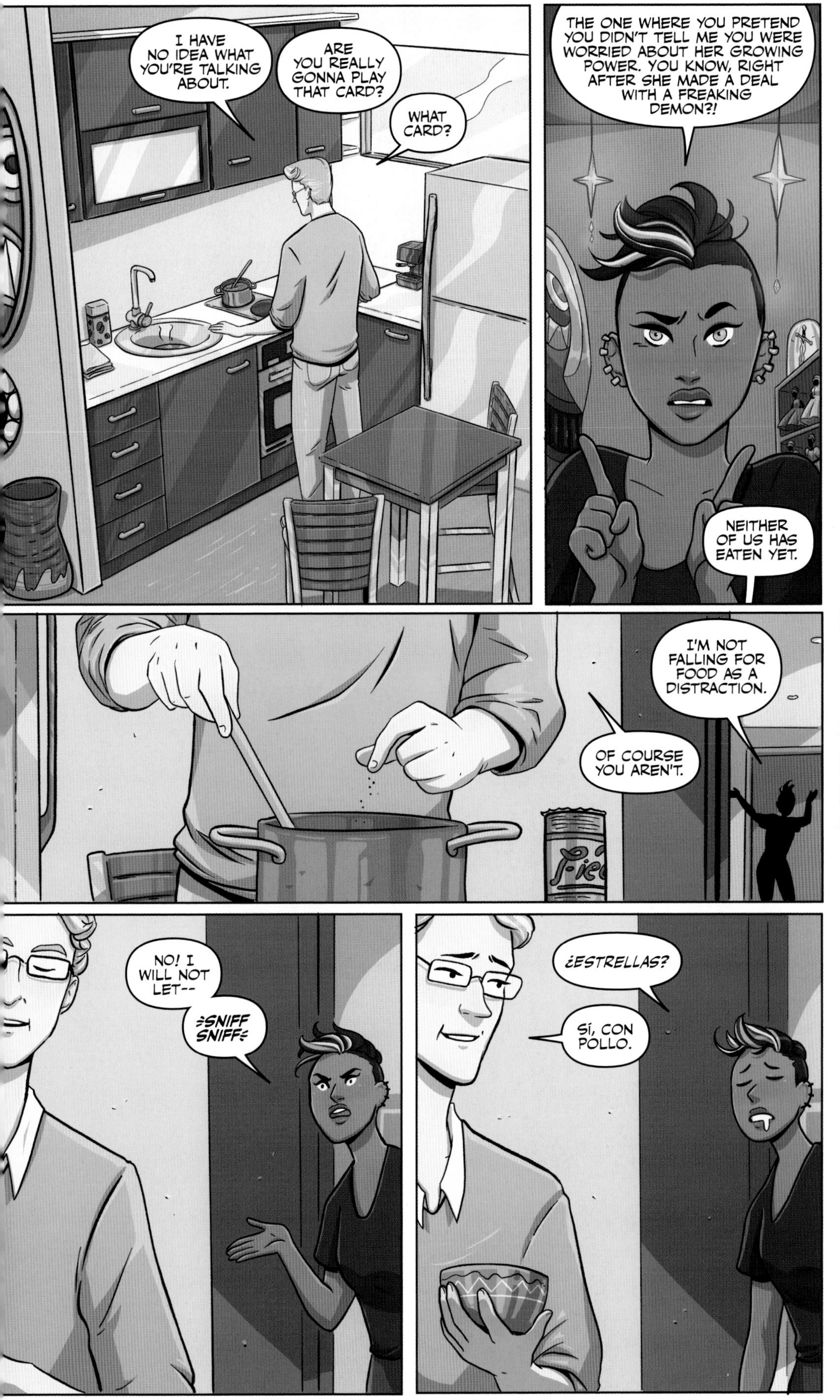
I HAVE NO IDEA WHAT YOU'RE TALKING ABOUT.
ARE YOU REALLY GONNA PLAY THAT CARD?
WHAT CARD?
THE ONE WHERE YOU PRETEND YOU DIDN'T TELL ME YOU WERE WORRIED ABOUT HER GROWING POWER. YOU KNOW, RIGHT AFTER SHE MADE A DEAL WITH A FREAKING DEMON?!
NEITHER OF US HAS EATEN YET.
I'M NOT FALLING FOR FOOD AS A DISTRACTION.
OF COURSE YOU AREN'T.
NO! I WILL NOT LET--
SNIFF SNIFF
¿ESTRELLAS?
SÍ, CON POLLO.

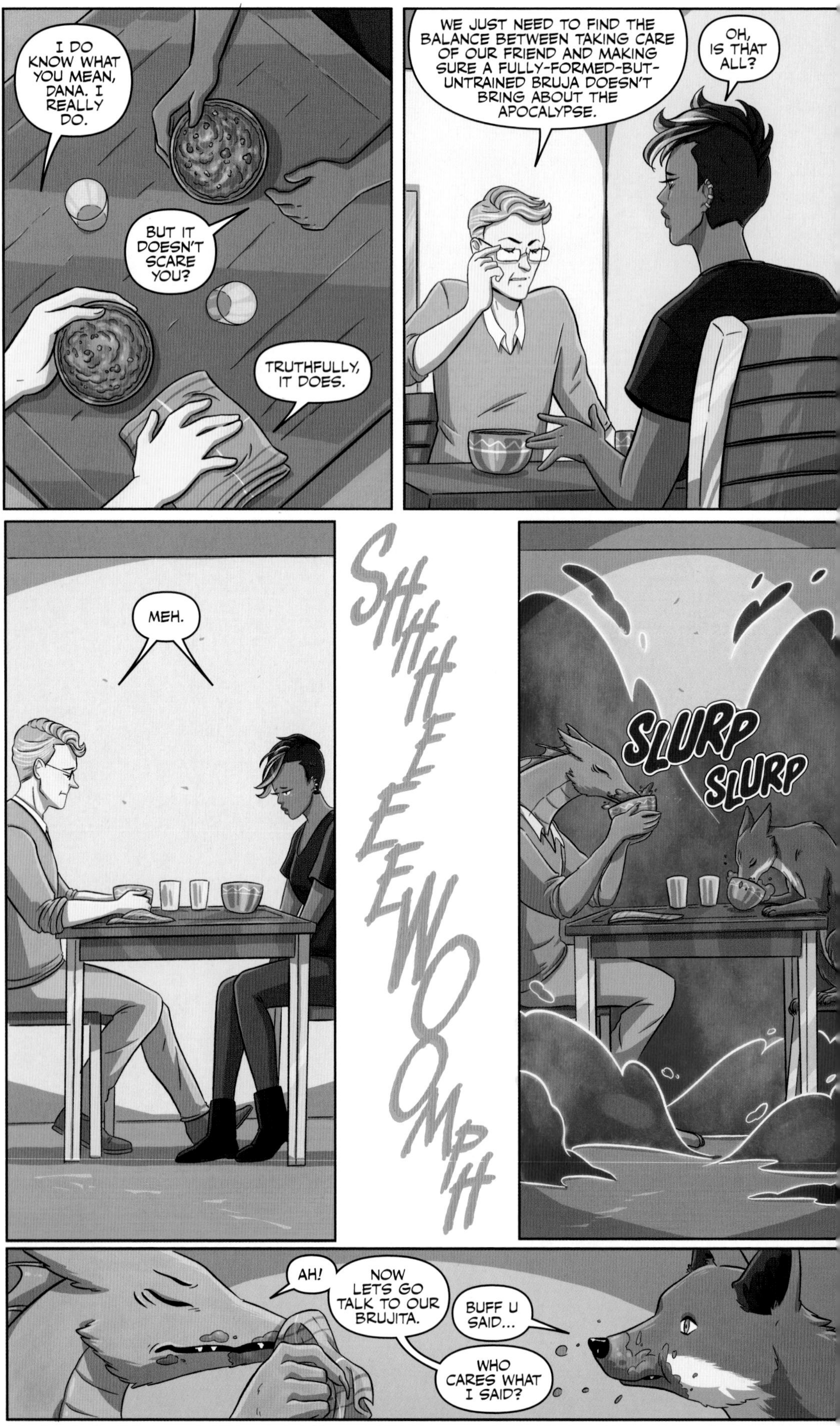
I DO KNOW WHAT YOU MEAN, DANA. I REALLY DO.
BUT IT DOESN'T SCARE YOU?
TRUTHFULLY, IT DOES.
WE JUST NEED TO FIND THE BALANCE BETWEEN TAKING CARE OF OUR FRIEND AND MAKING SURE A FULLY-FORMED-BUT-UNTRAINED BRUJA DOESN'T BRING ABOUT THE APOCALYPSE.
OH, IS THAT ALL?
MEH.
SHHHEEEEWOOOMPHH
SLURP
SLURP
AH!
NOW LETS GO TALK TO OUR BRUJITA.
BUFF U SAID...
WHO CARES WHAT I SAID?

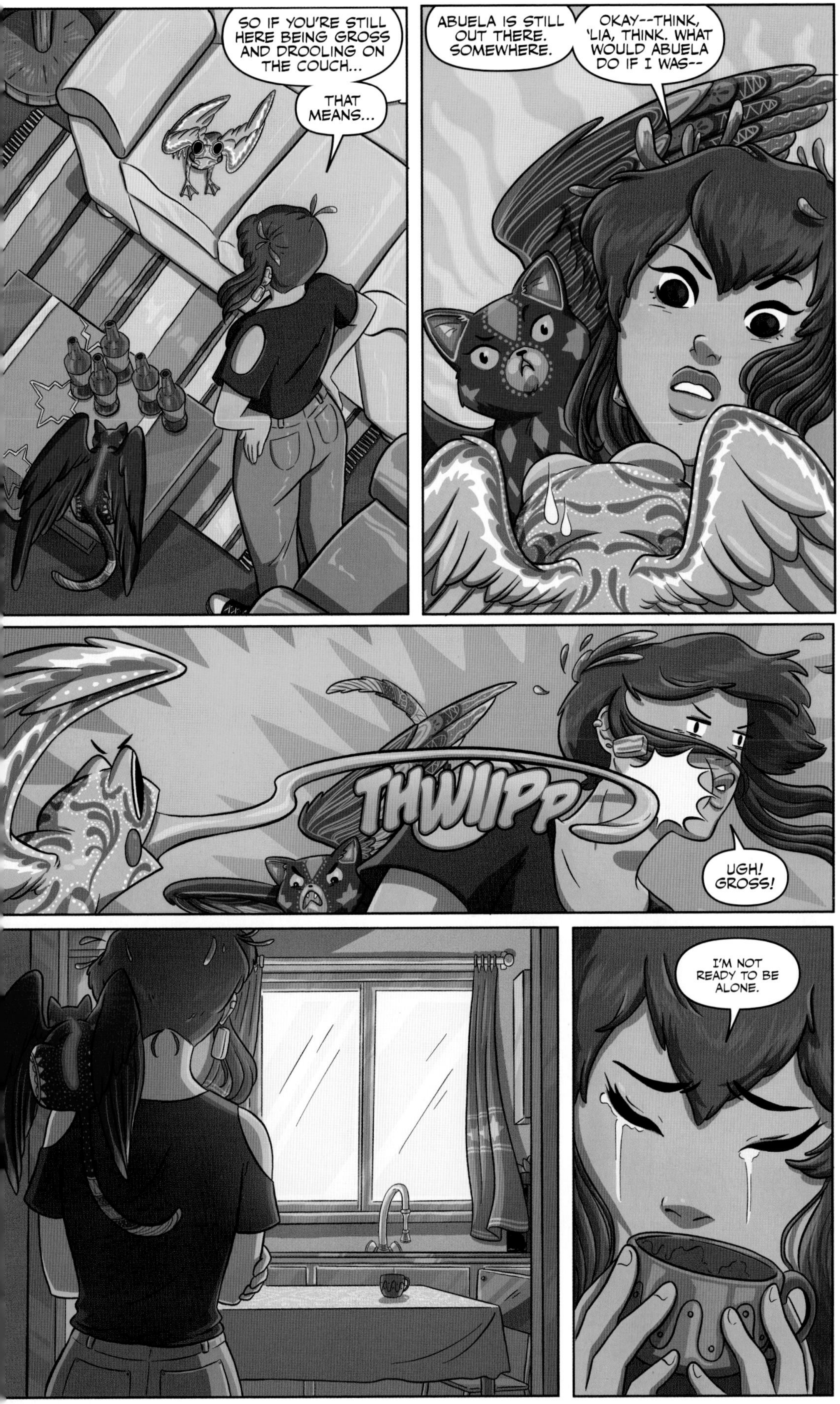
SO IF YOU'RE STILL HERE BEING GROSS AND DROOLING ON THE COUCH...
THAT MEANS...
ABUELA IS STILL OUT THERE. SOMEWHERE.
OKAY--THINK, 'LIA, THINK. WHAT WOULD ABUELA DO IF I WAS--
THWIIPP
UGH! GROSS!
I'M NOT READY TO BE ALONE.

SORRY, ABUELA. I KNOW I PROMISED TO NEVER BE IN HERE WITHOUT YOU.

BUT I KNOW YOU AREN'T GONE... YOU CAN'T BE.

THERE HAS TO BE SOMETHING.

DON'T TELL ME SHE LET YOU USE HER PILLOW?

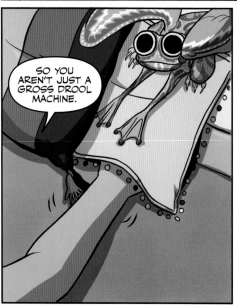

SO YOU AREN'T JUST A GROSS DROOL MACHINE.

MIJITA, IF YOU'RE READING THIS, THEN I DIDN'T HAVE TIME TO FINISH YOUR LESSONS...

ABUELA...

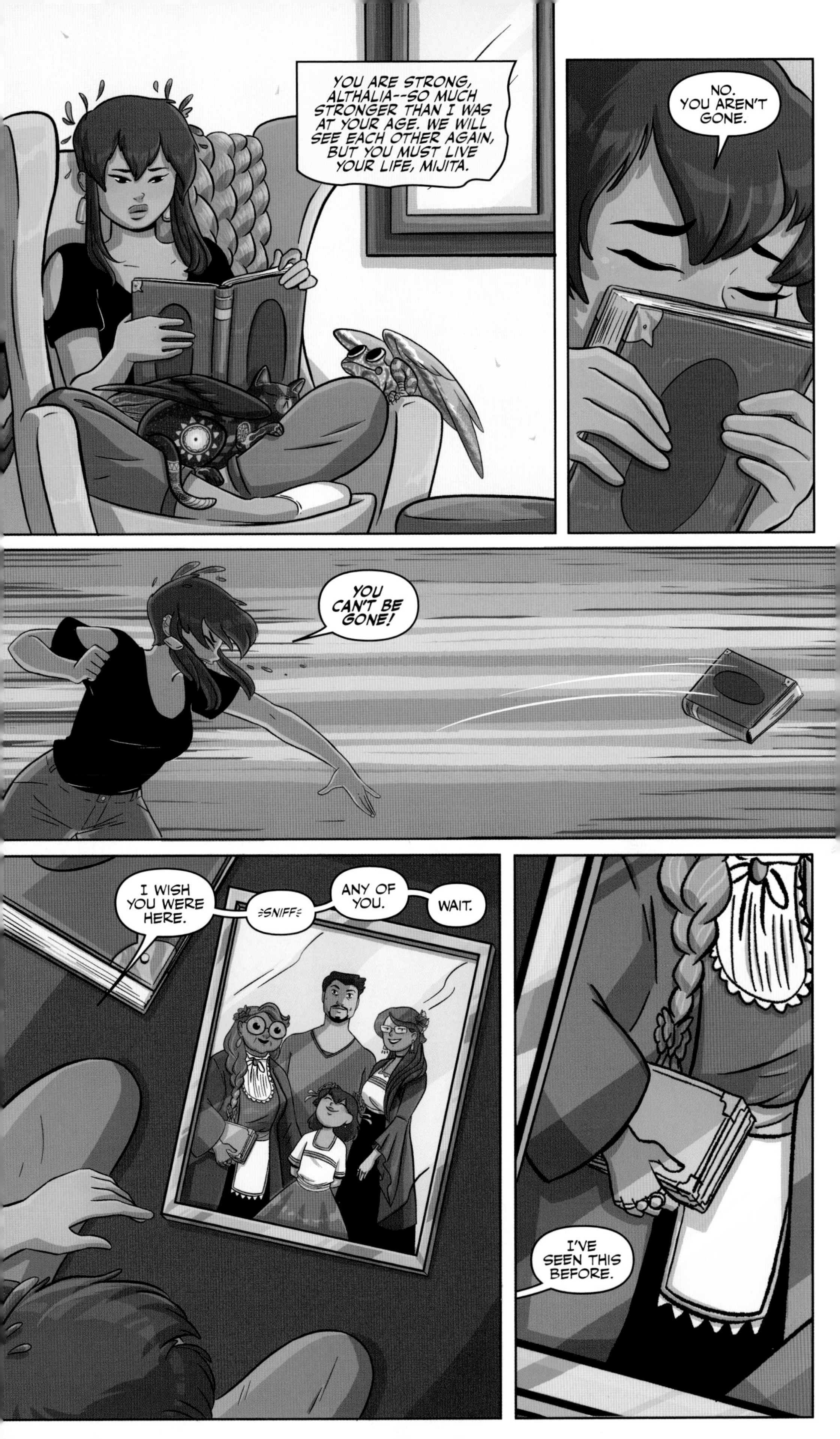

YOU ARE STRONG, ALTHALIA--SO MUCH STRONGER THAN I WAS AT YOUR AGE. WE WILL SEE EACH OTHER AGAIN, BUT YOU MUST LIVE YOUR LIFE, MIJITA.
NO. YOU AREN'T GONE.
YOU CAN'T BE GONE!
I WISH YOU WERE HERE.
SNIFF
ANY OF YOU.
WAIT.
I'VE SEEN THIS BEFORE.

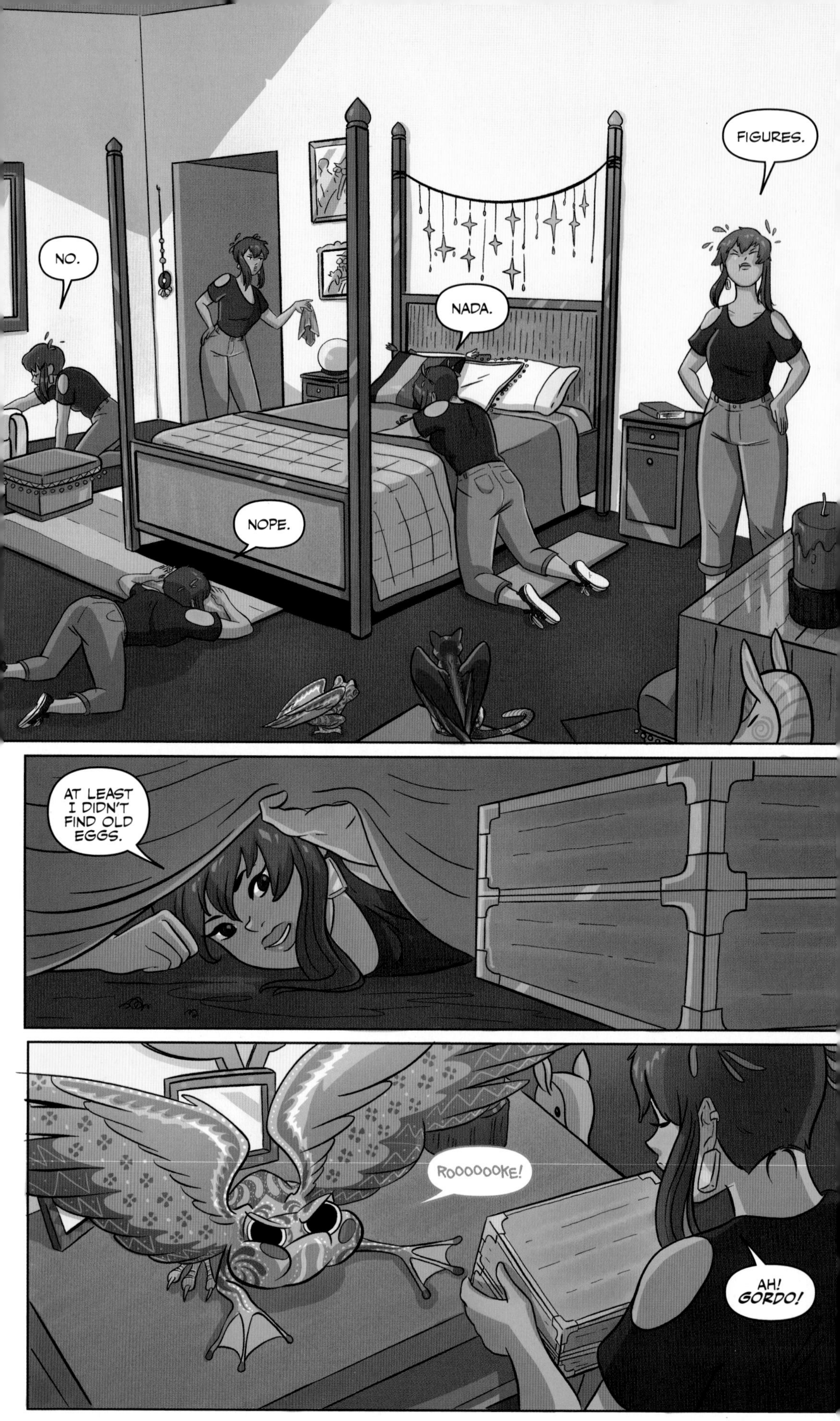
NO.
NOPE.
NADA.
FIGURES.
AT LEAST I DIDN'T FIND OLD EGGS.
ROOOOOOKE!
AH! GORDO!

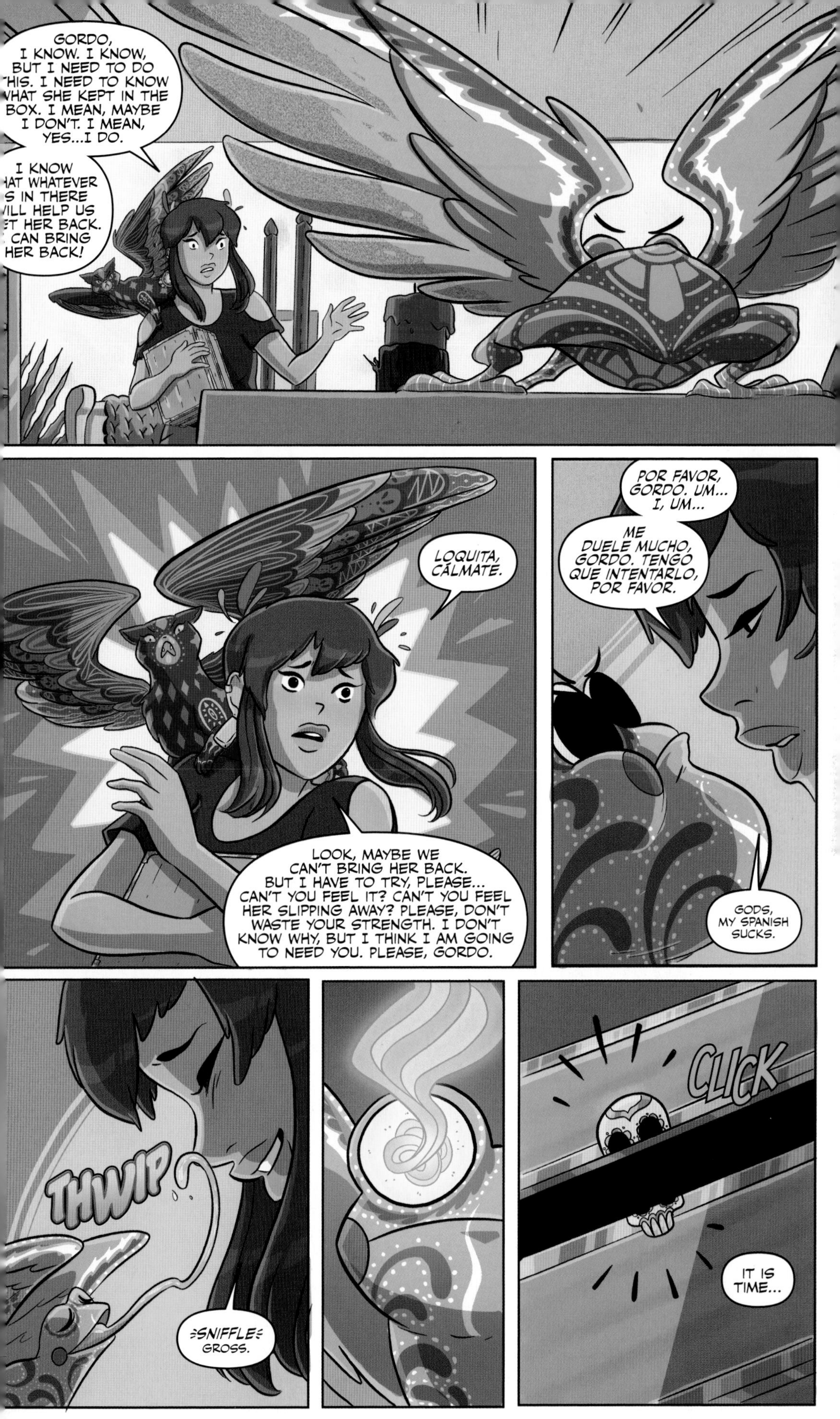
GORDO, I KNOW. I KNOW, BUT I NEED TO DO THIS. I NEED TO KNOW WHAT SHE KEPT IN THE BOX. I MEAN, MAYBE I DON'T. I MEAN, YES...I DO.
I KNOW THAT WHATEVER IS IN THERE WILL HELP US GET HER BACK. I CAN BRING HER BACK!
LOQUITA, CÁLMATE.
LOOK, MAYBE WE CAN'T BRING HER BACK. BUT I HAVE TO TRY, PLEASE... CAN'T YOU FEEL IT? CAN'T YOU FEEL HER SLIPPING AWAY? PLEASE, DON'T WASTE YOUR STRENGTH. I DON'T KNOW WHY, BUT I THINK I AM GOING TO NEED YOU. PLEASE, GORDO.
POR FAVOR, GORDO. UM... I, UM...
ME DUELE MUCHO, GORDO. TENGO QUE INTENTARLO, POR FAVOR.
GODS, MY SPANISH SUCKS.
THWIP
SNIFFLE
GROSS.
CLICK
IT IS TIME...

CHAPTER 3

=SIGH=

MY CHILD, DO NOT CONFUSE MY RAISED VOICE TO BE ONE OF ANGER TOWARD YOU.

BUT YOUR HOLI--

SHH.

NO. I WAS FEARFUL, SO VERY FEARFUL. OUR ORDER HAS FOUGHT THESE IDOLATERS FOR CENTURIES. I KNOW THE DANGER THEY POSE, AND I WAS FEARFUL I PLACED SUCH A PROMISING PUPIL IN HARM'S WAY BEFORE HE COULD BE FULLY PREPARED FOR HIS...

...FOR *OUR* ADVERSARY.

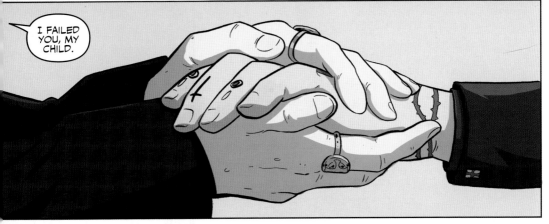

I FAILED YOU, MY CHILD.

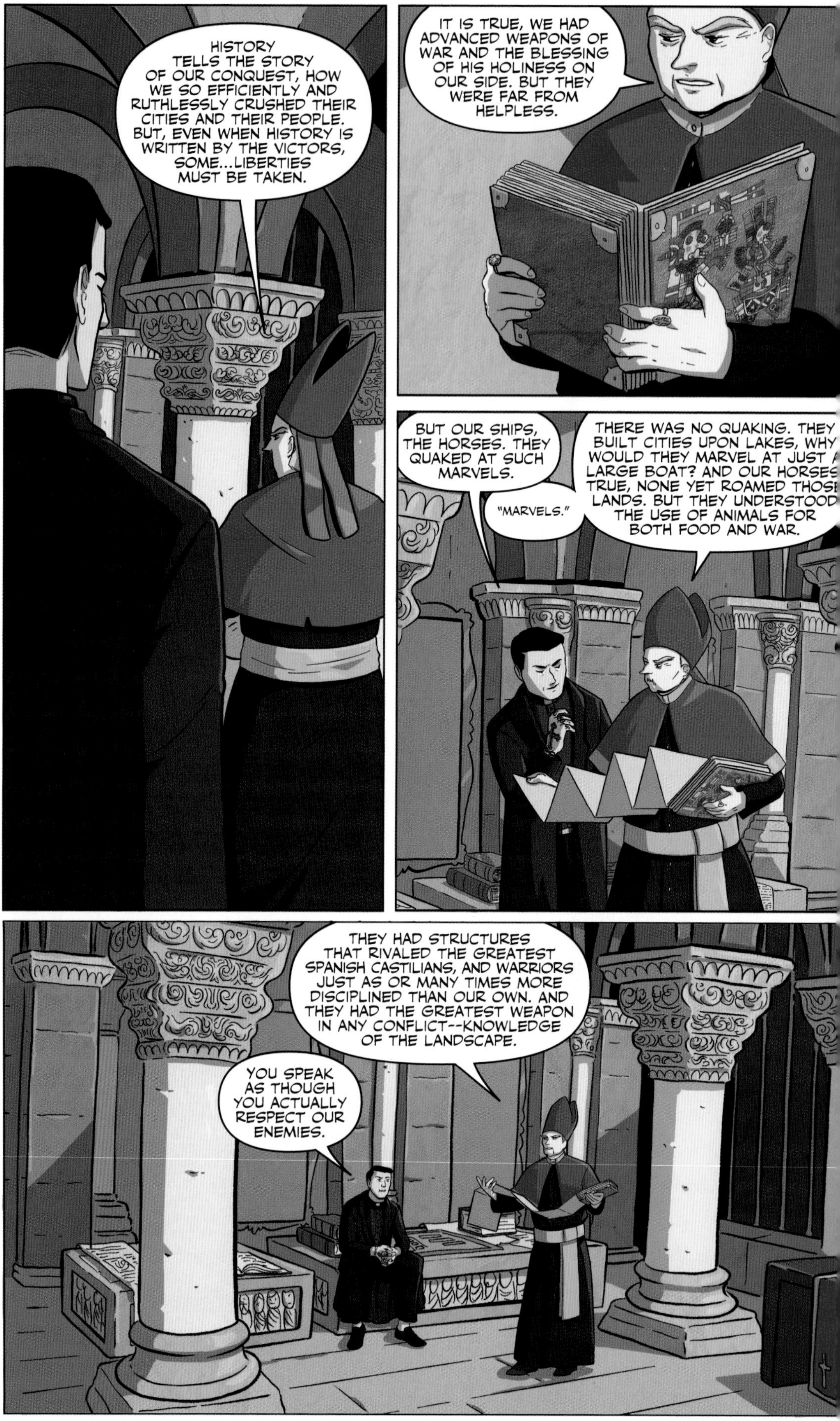
HISTORY TELLS THE STORY OF OUR CONQUEST, HOW WE SO EFFICIENTLY AND RUTHLESSLY CRUSHED THEIR CITIES AND THEIR PEOPLE. BUT, EVEN WHEN HISTORY IS WRITTEN BY THE VICTORS, SOME...LIBERTIES MUST BE TAKEN.
IT IS TRUE, WE HAD ADVANCED WEAPONS OF WAR AND THE BLESSING OF HIS HOLINESS ON OUR SIDE. BUT THEY WERE FAR FROM HELPLESS.
BUT OUR SHIPS, THE HORSES. THEY QUAKED AT SUCH MARVELS.
"MARVELS."
THERE WAS NO QUAKING. THEY BUILT CITIES UPON LAKES, WHY WOULD THEY MARVEL AT JUST A LARGE BOAT? AND OUR HORSES TRUE, NONE YET ROAMED THOSE LANDS. BUT THEY UNDERSTOOD THE USE OF ANIMALS FOR BOTH FOOD AND WAR.
THEY HAD STRUCTURES THAT RIVALED THE GREATEST SPANISH CASTILIANS, AND WARRIORS JUST AS OR MANY TIMES MORE DISCIPLINED THAN OUR OWN. AND THEY HAD THE GREATEST WEAPON IN ANY CONFLICT--KNOWLEDGE OF THE LANDSCAPE.
YOU SPEAK AS THOUGH YOU ACTUALLY RESPECT OUR ENEMIES.

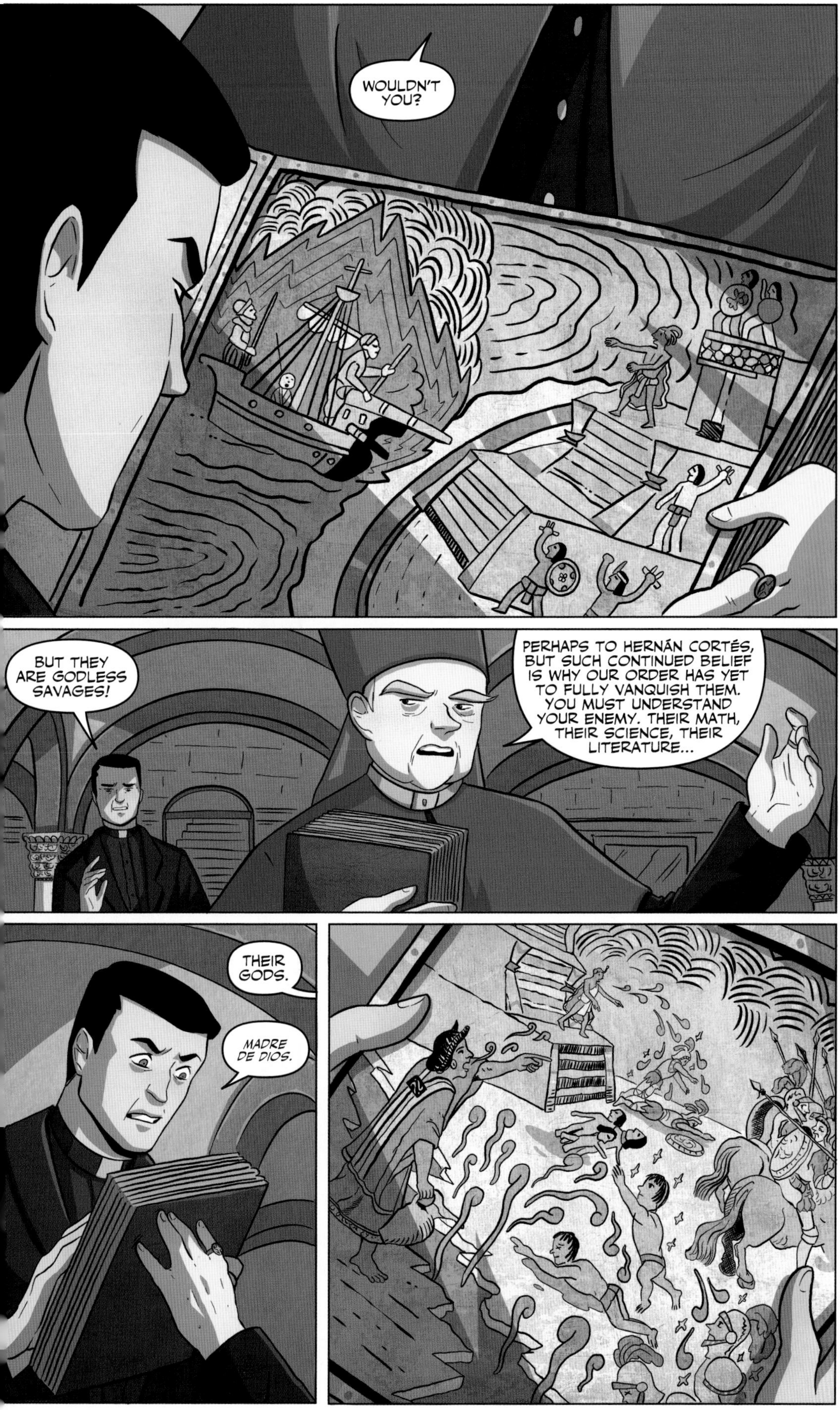
WOULDN'T YOU?
BUT THEY ARE GODLESS SAVAGES!
PERHAPS TO HERNÁN CORTÉS, BUT SUCH CONTINUED BELIEF IS WHY OUR ORDER HAS YET TO FULLY VANQUISH THEM. YOU MUST UNDERSTAND YOUR ENEMY. THEIR MATH, THEIR SCIENCE, THEIR LITERATURE...
THEIR GODS.
MADRE DE DIOS.

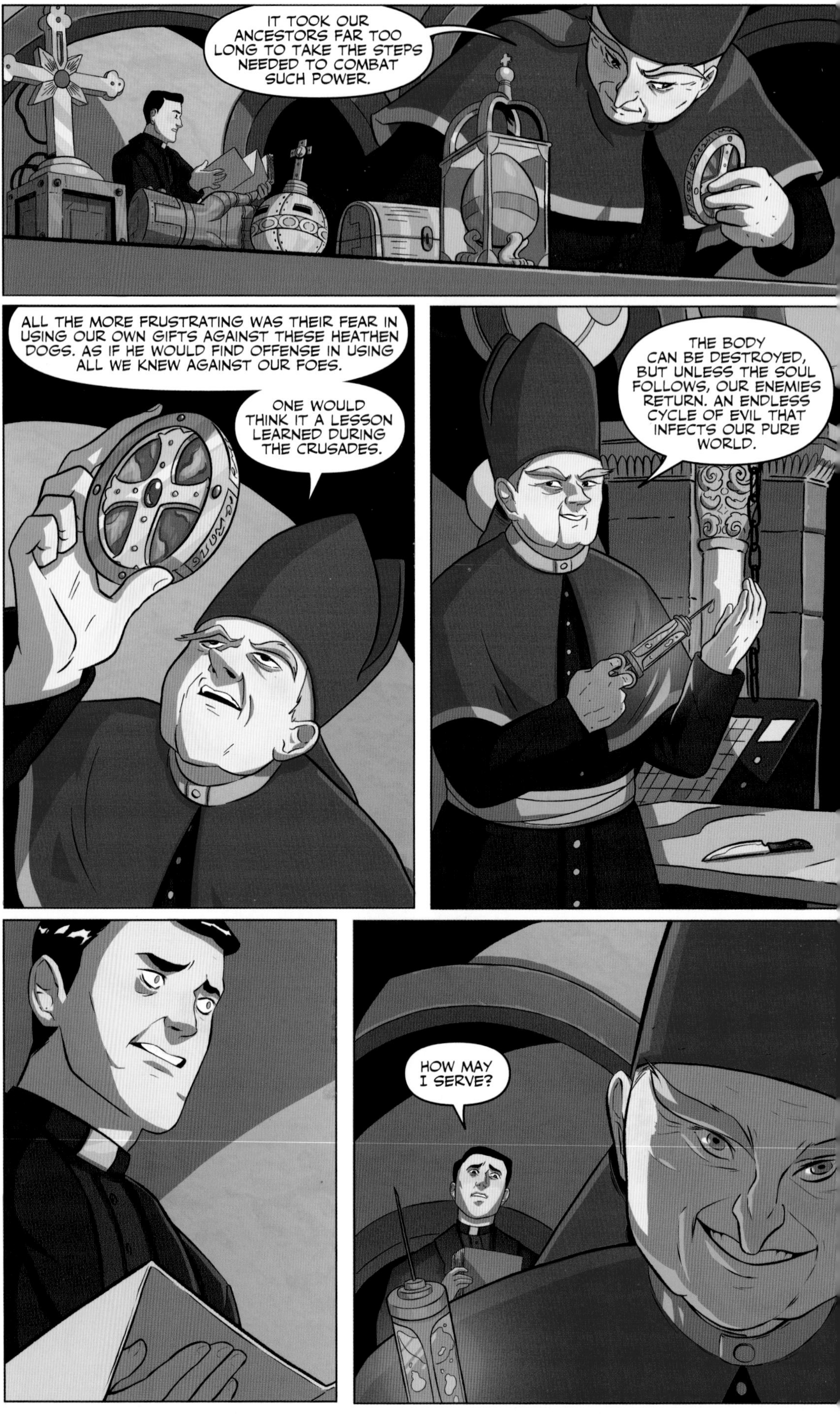
IT TOOK OUR ANCESTORS FAR TOO LONG TO TAKE THE STEPS NEEDED TO COMBAT SUCH POWER.
ALL THE MORE FRUSTRATING WAS THEIR FEAR IN USING OUR OWN GIFTS AGAINST THESE HEATHEN DOGS. AS IF HE WOULD FIND OFFENSE IN USING ALL WE KNEW AGAINST OUR FOES.
ONE WOULD THINK IT A LESSON LEARNED DURING THE CRUSADES.
THE BODY CAN BE DESTROYED, BUT UNLESS THE SOUL FOLLOWS, OUR ENEMIES RETURN. AN ENDLESS CYCLE OF EVIL THAT INFECTS OUR PURE WORLD.
HOW MAY I SERVE?

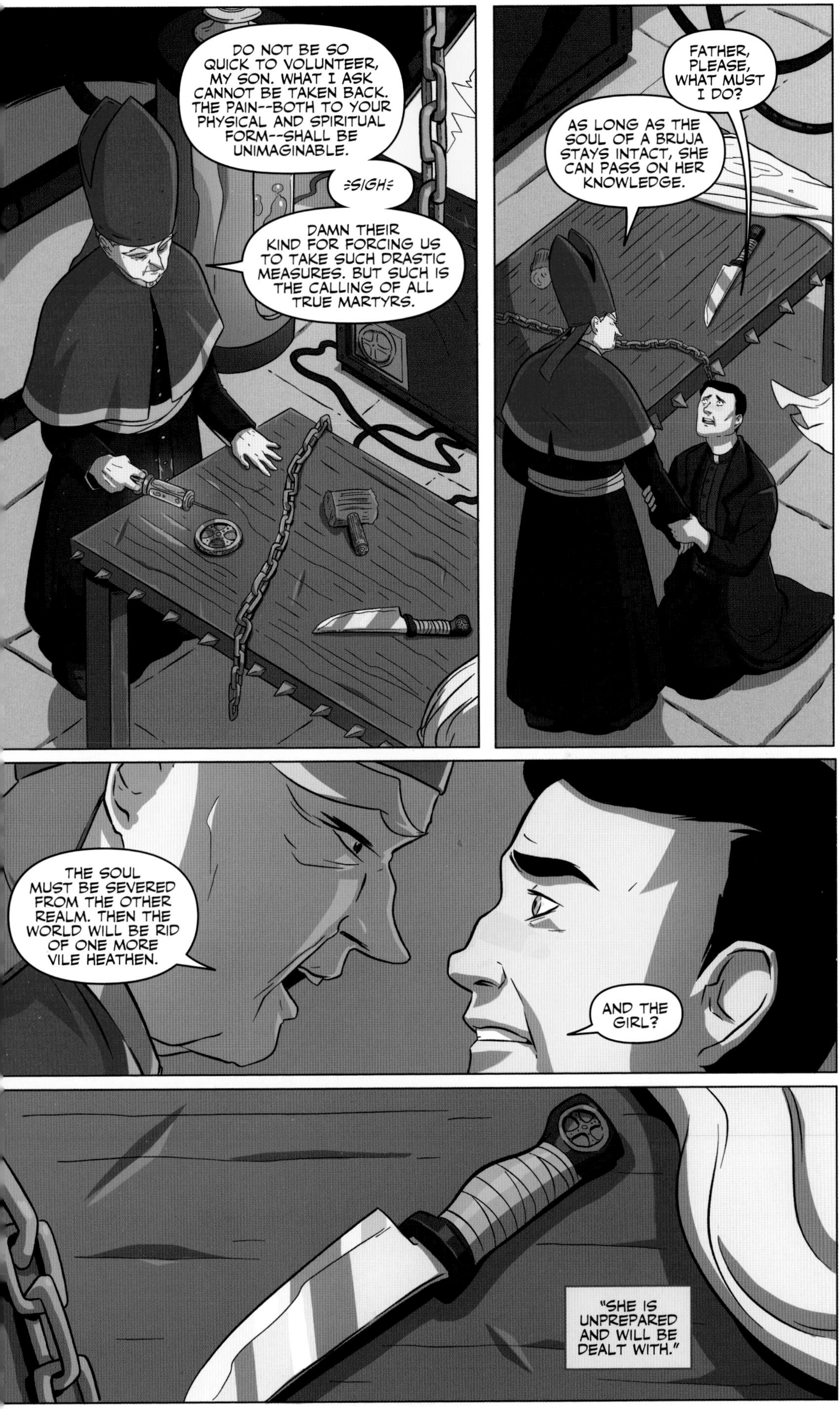

DO NOT BE SO QUICK TO VOLUNTEER, MY SON. WHAT I ASK CANNOT BE TAKEN BACK. THE PAIN--BOTH TO YOUR PHYSICAL AND SPIRITUAL FORM--SHALL BE UNIMAGINABLE.
SIGH
DAMN THEIR KIND FOR FORCING US TO TAKE SUCH DRASTIC MEASURES. BUT SUCH IS THE CALLING OF ALL TRUE MARTYRS.
FATHER, PLEASE, WHAT MUST I DO?
AS LONG AS THE SOUL OF A BRUJA STAYS INTACT, SHE CAN PASS ON HER KNOWLEDGE.
THE SOUL MUST BE SEVERED FROM THE OTHER REALM. THEN THE WORLD WILL BE RID OF ONE MORE VILE HEATHEN.
AND THE GIRL?
"SHE IS UNPREPARED AND WILL BE DEALT WITH."

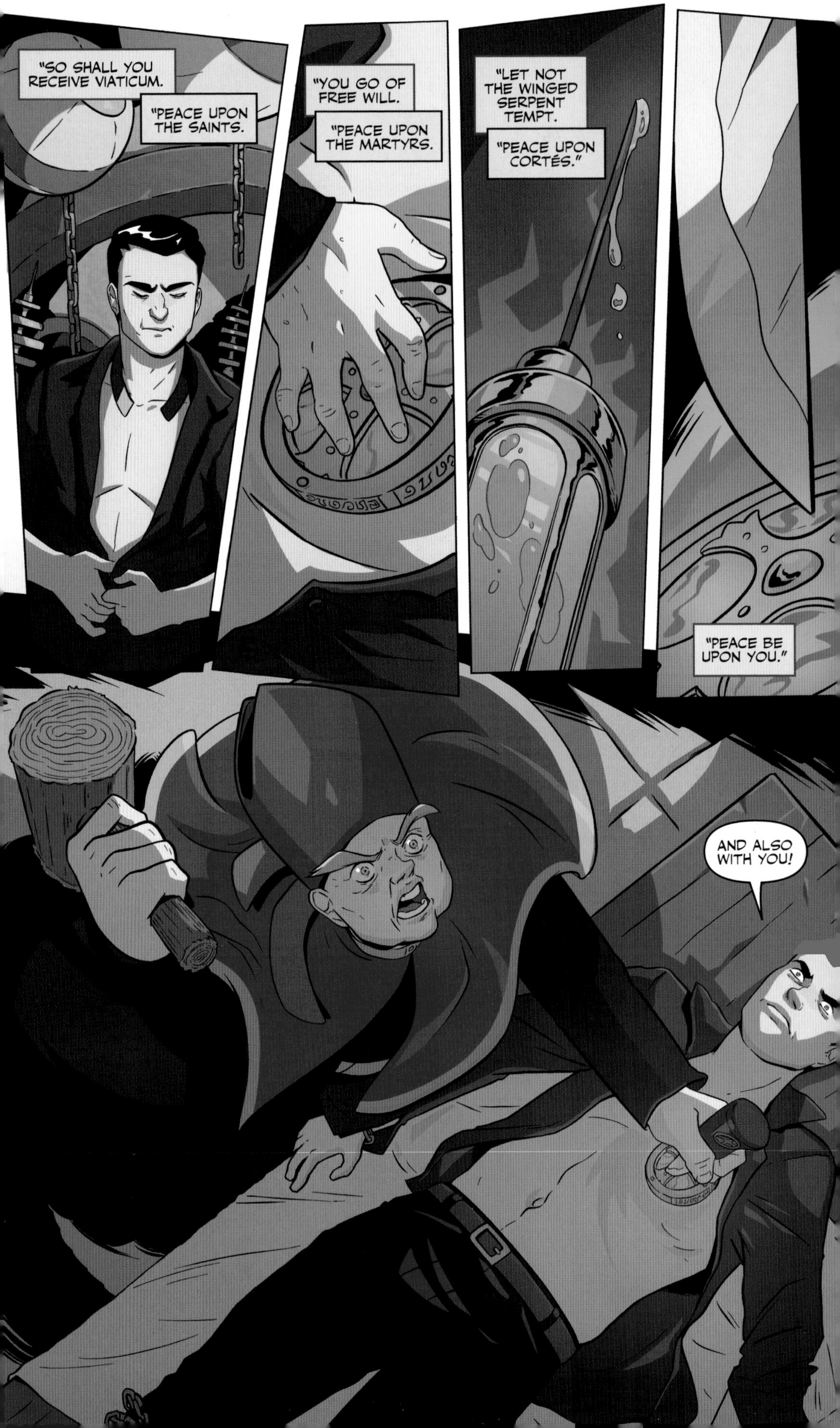
"SO SHALL YOU RECEIVE VIATICUM.
"PEACE UPON THE SAINTS.
"YOU GO OF FREE WILL.
"PEACE UPON THE MARTYRS.
"LET NOT THE WINGED SERPENT TEMPT.
"PEACE UPON CORTÉS."
"PEACE BE UPON YOU."
AND ALSO WITH YOU!

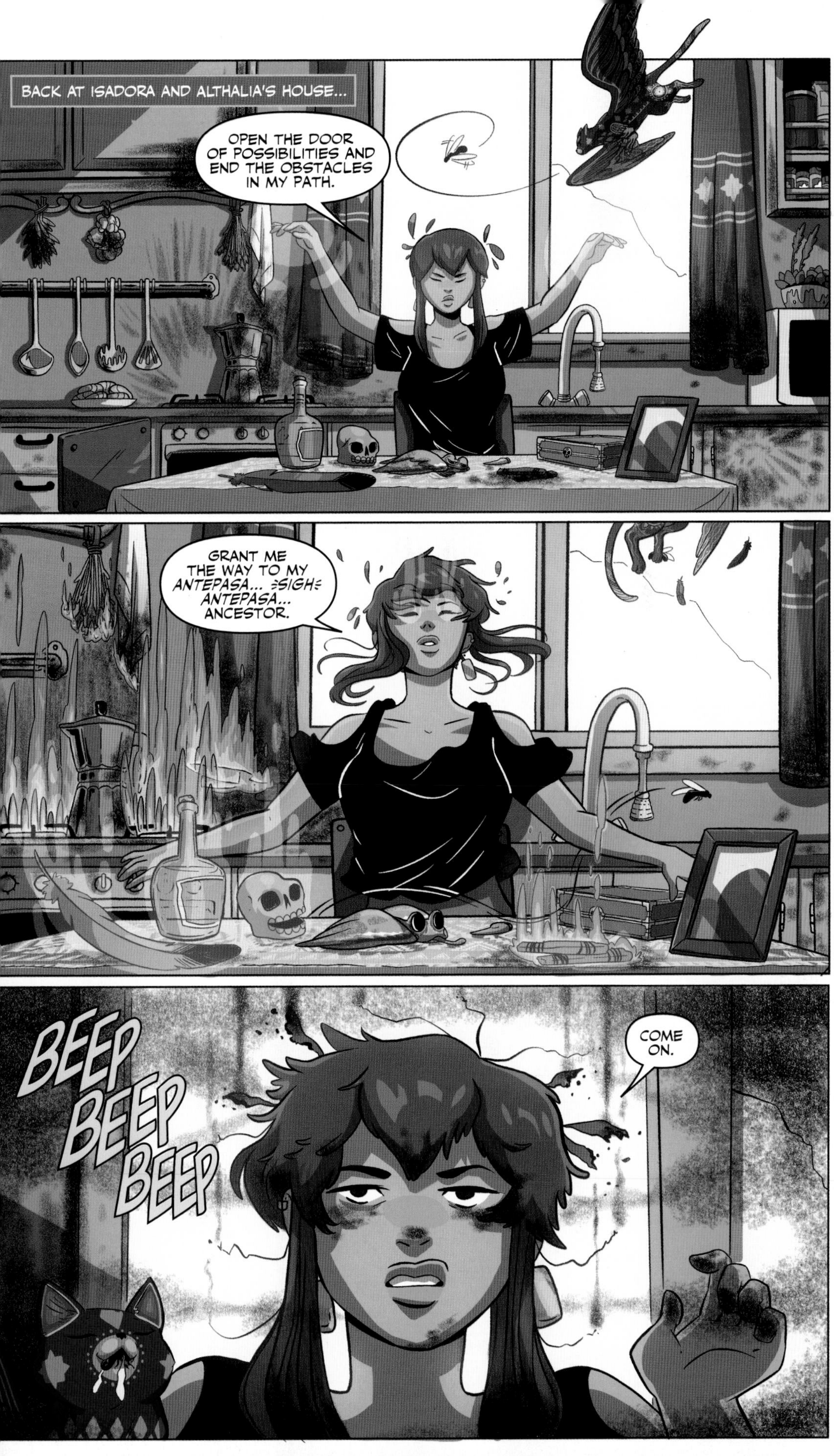
BACK AT ISADORA AND ALTHALIA'S HOUSE...
OPEN THE DOOR OF POSSIBILITIES AND END THE OBSTACLES IN MY PATH.
GRANT ME THE WAY TO MY ANTEPASA... SIGH ANTEPASA... ANCESTOR.
BEEP BEEP BEEP
COME ON.

OKAY, THINK. WHAT WOULD MY ABUELA DO?

FIRST, SHE'D IGNORE HER PREDIABETES AND CHUG ONE OF THESE.

"MIJITA, A BRUJA DRAWS THEIR POWER FROM THE PAST. FROM THOSE WHO TOLD OUR TALE BEFORE. SO THAT WE MAY CONTINUE THE STORY."

FROM WHAT CAME BEFORE.

I NEED TO REMEMBER.

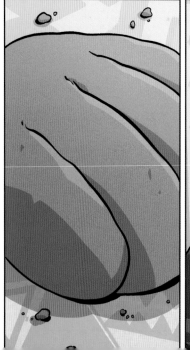

PRO JJrestli ILLUSTRAT

T.V

W V

THHHAWEEEE

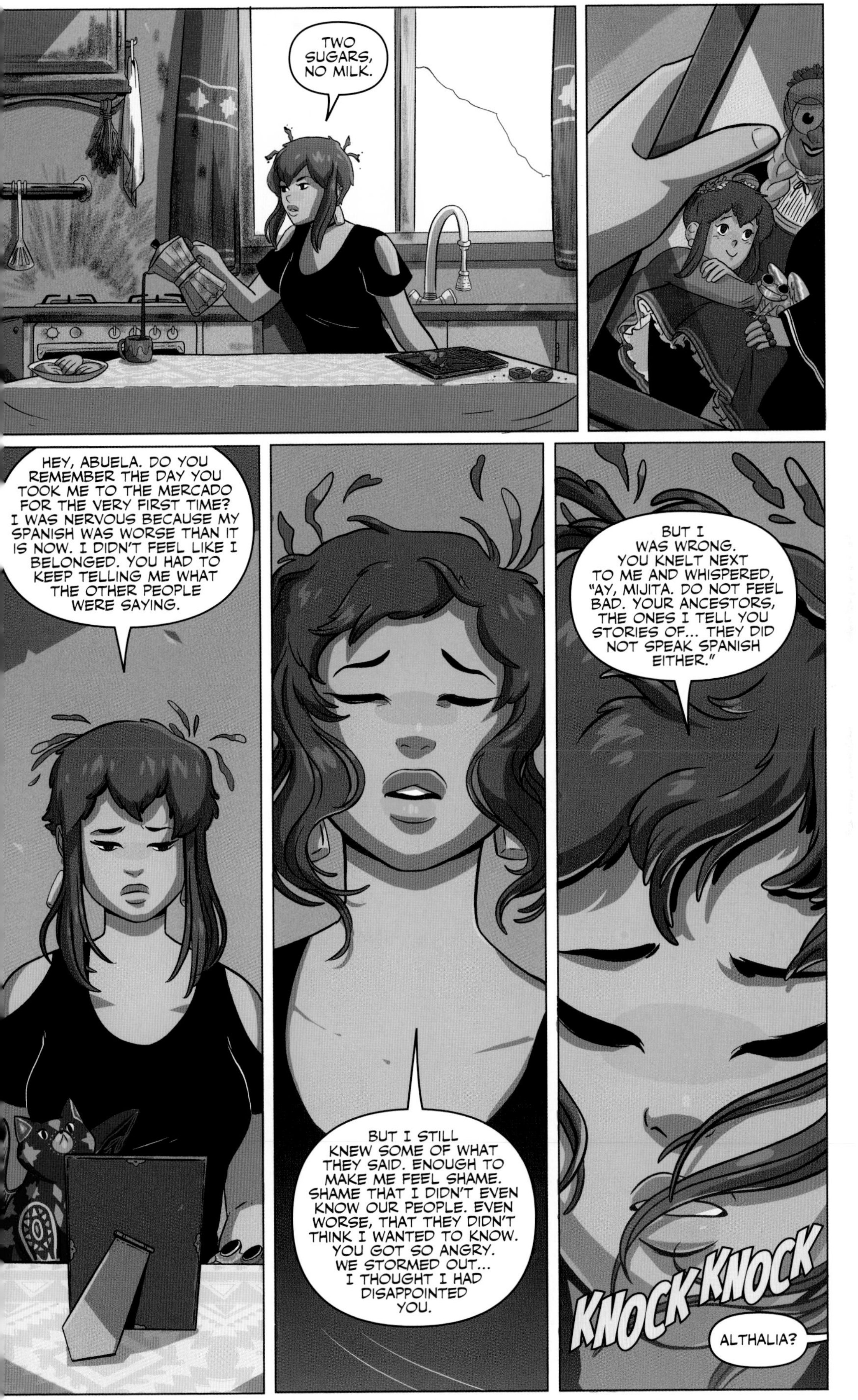
TWO SUGARS, NO MILK.
HEY, ABUELA. DO YOU REMEMBER THE DAY YOU TOOK ME TO THE MERCADO FOR THE VERY FIRST TIME? I WAS NERVOUS BECAUSE MY SPANISH WAS WORSE THAN IT IS NOW. I DIDN'T FEEL LIKE I BELONGED. YOU HAD TO KEEP TELLING ME WHAT THE OTHER PEOPLE WERE SAYING.
BUT I STILL KNEW SOME OF WHAT THEY SAID. ENOUGH TO MAKE ME FEEL SHAME. SHAME THAT I DIDN'T EVEN KNOW OUR PEOPLE. EVEN WORSE, THAT THEY DIDN'T THINK I WANTED TO KNOW. YOU GOT SO ANGRY. WE STORMED OUT... I THOUGHT I HAD DISAPPOINTED YOU.
BUT I WAS WRONG. YOU KNELT NEXT TO ME AND WHISPERED, "AY, MIJITA. DO NOT FEEL BAD. YOUR ANCESTORS, THE ONES I TELL YOU STORIES OF... THEY DID NOT SPEAK SPANISH EITHER."
KNOCK KNOCK
ALTHALIA?

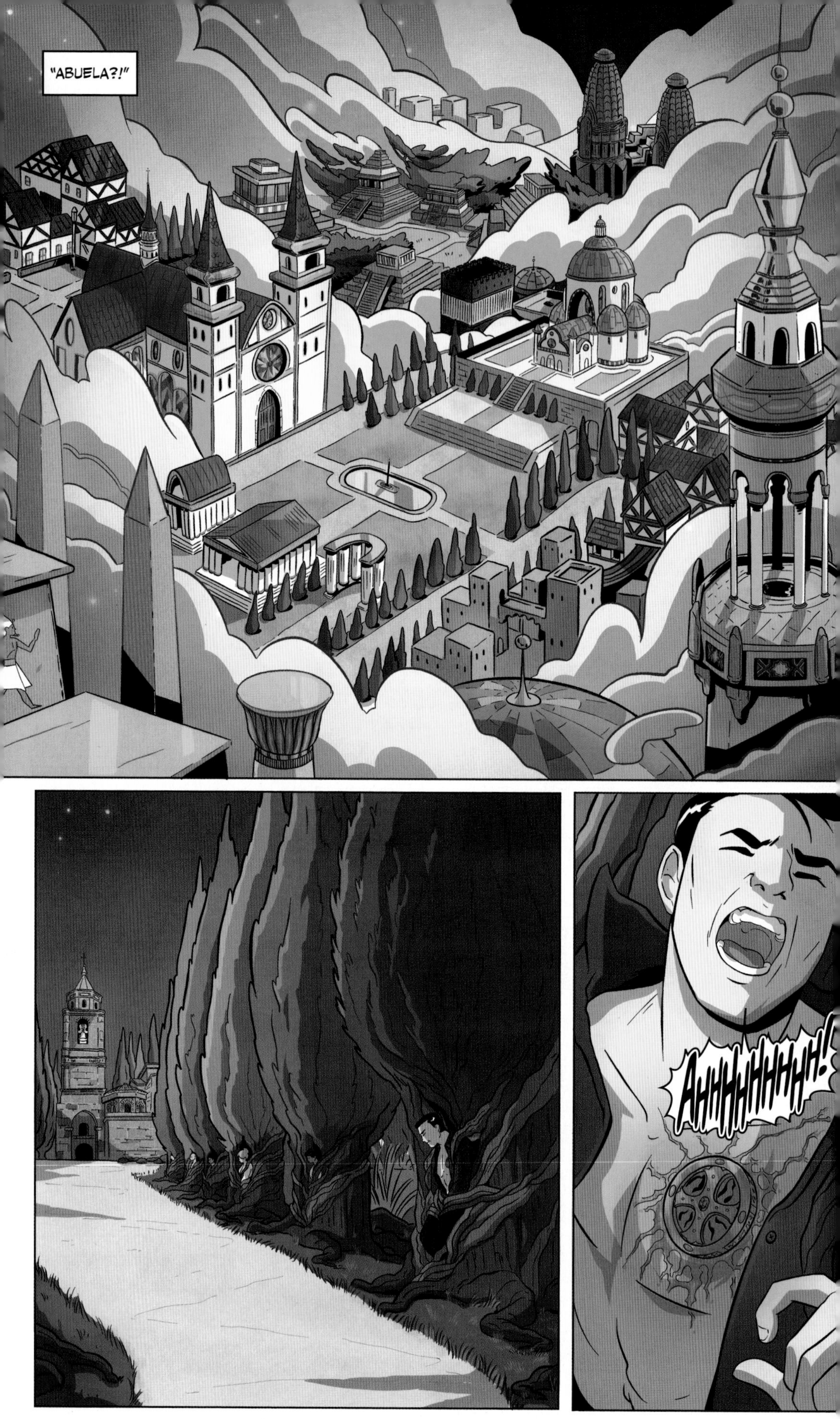
"ABUELA?!"
AHHHHHHHHH!

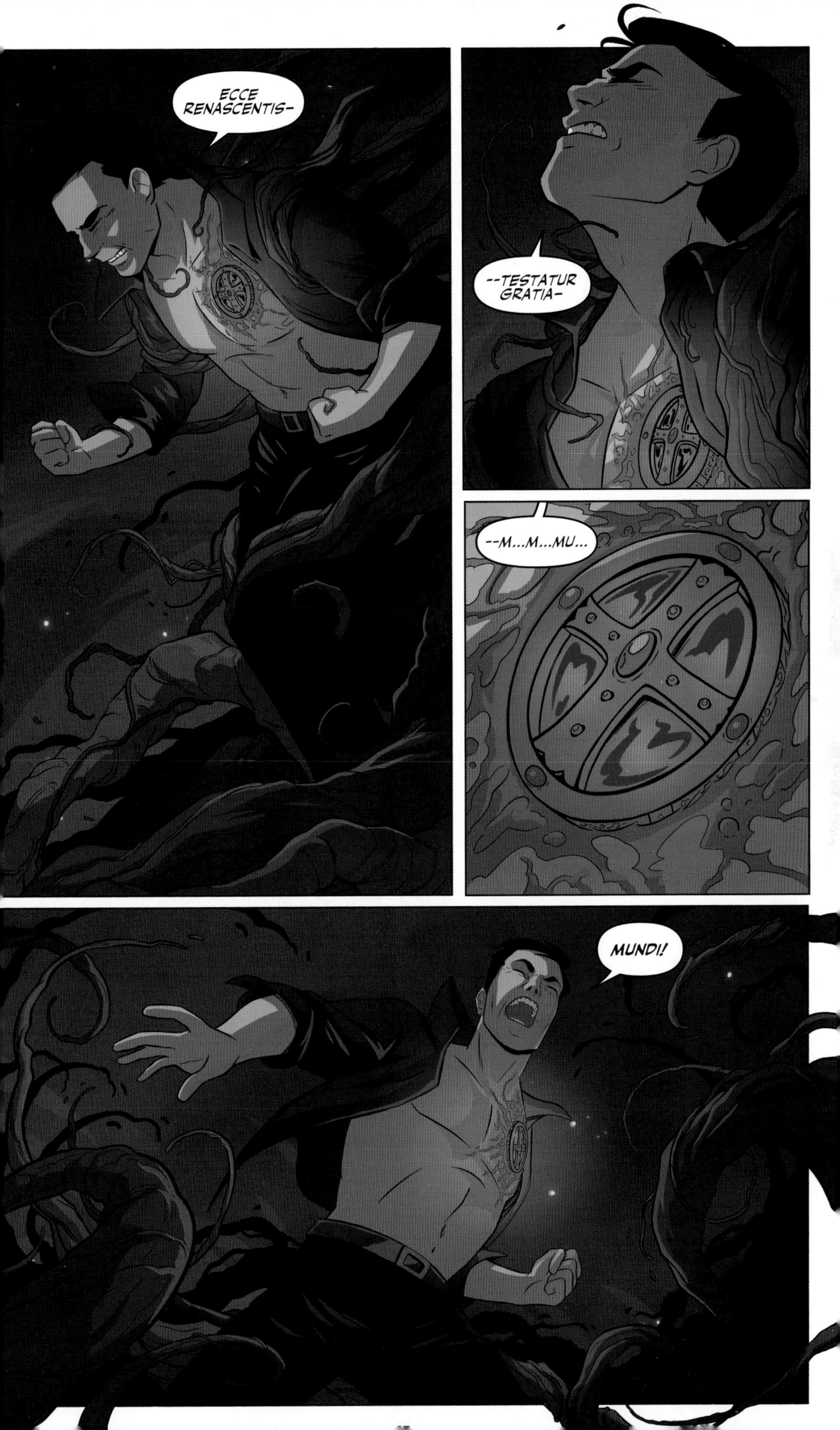
ECCE RENASCENTIS–
--TESTATUR GRATIA–
--M...M...MU...
MUNDI!

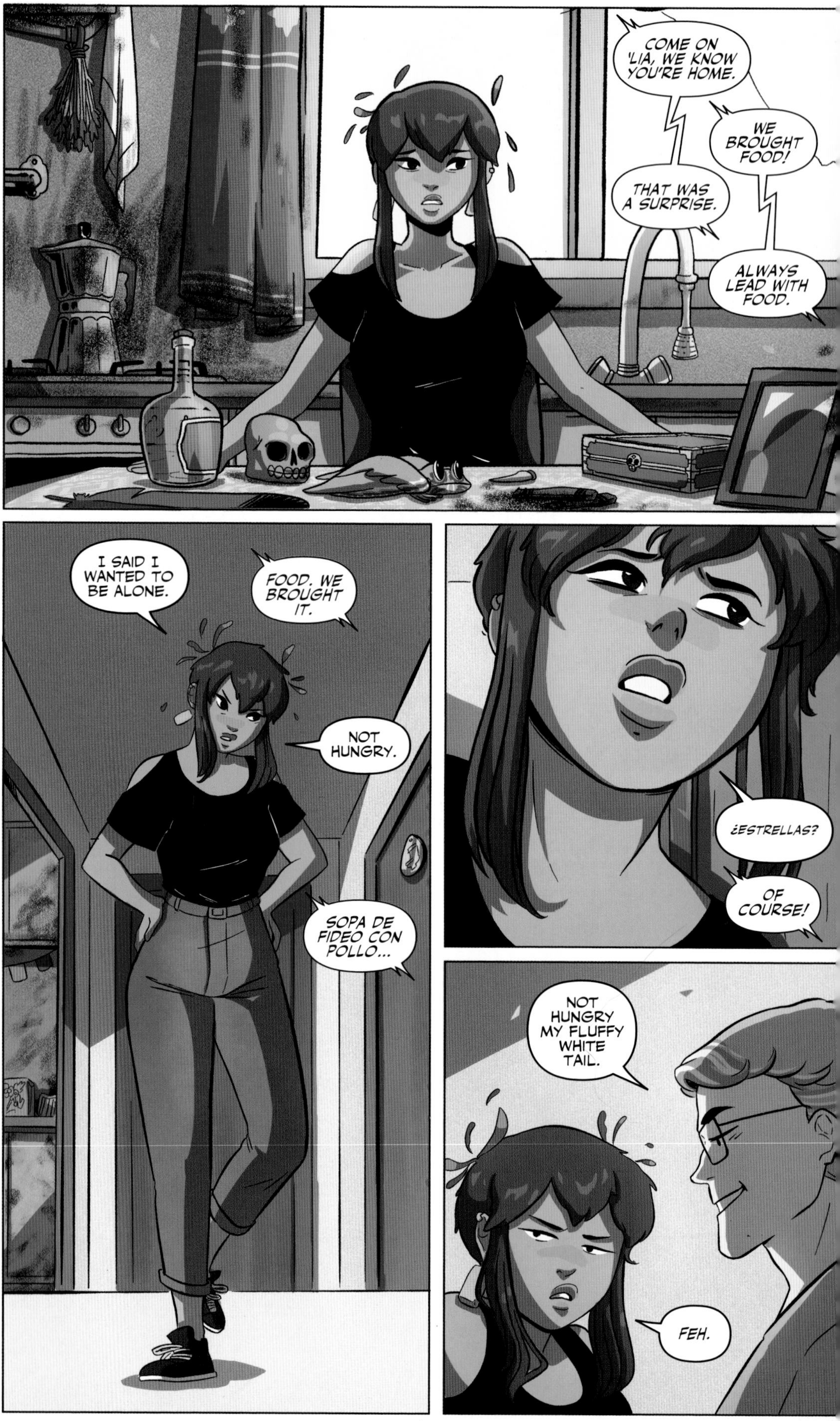
COME ON 'LIA, WE KNOW YOU'RE HOME.
THAT WAS A SURPRISE.
WE BROUGHT FOOD!
ALWAYS LEAD WITH FOOD.
I SAID I WANTED TO BE ALONE.
FOOD. WE BROUGHT IT.
NOT HUNGRY.
SOPA DE FIDEO CON POLLO...
¿ESTRELLAS?
OF COURSE!
NOT HUNGRY MY FLUFFY WHITE TAIL.
FEH.

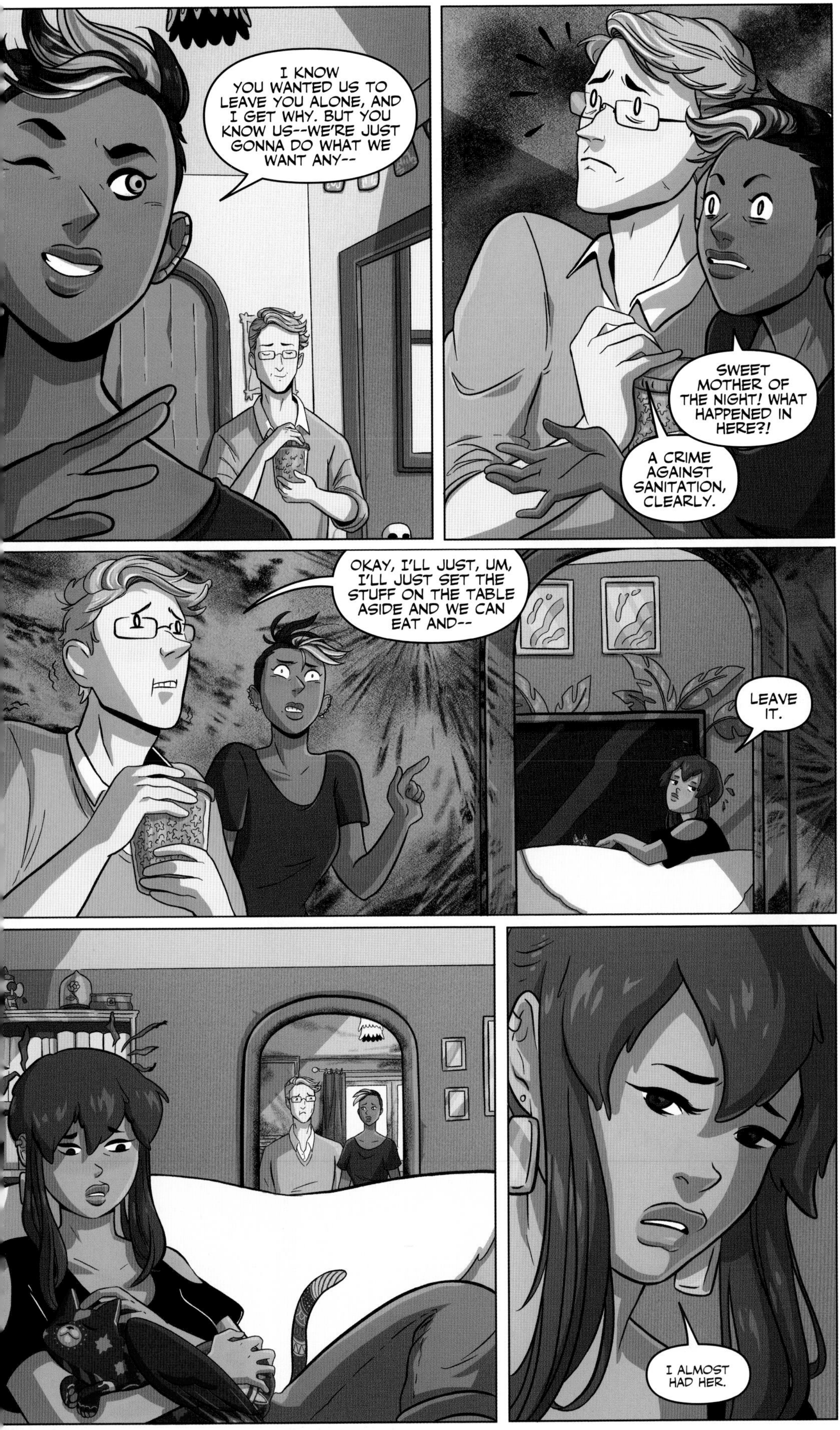
I KNOW YOU WANTED US TO LEAVE YOU ALONE, AND I GET WHY. BUT YOU KNOW US--WE'RE JUST GONNA DO WHAT WE WANT ANY--
SWEET MOTHER OF THE NIGHT! WHAT HAPPENED IN HERE?!
A CRIME AGAINST SANITATION, CLEARLY.
OKAY, I'LL JUST, UM, I'LL JUST SET THE STUFF ON THE TABLE ASIDE AND WE CAN EAT AND--
LEAVE IT.
I ALMOST HAD HER.

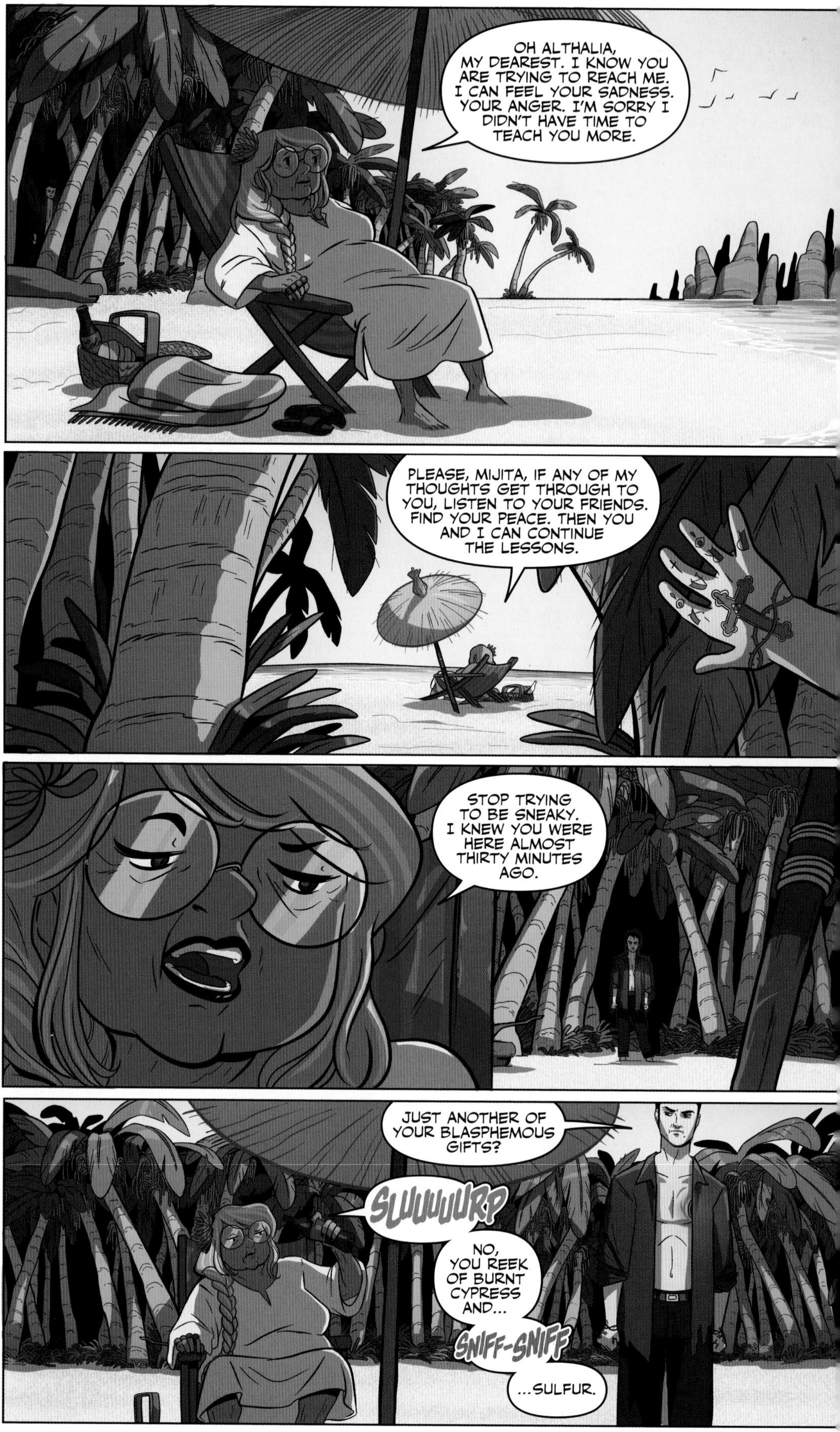
OH ALTHALIA, MY DEAREST. I KNOW YOU ARE TRYING TO REACH ME. I CAN FEEL YOUR SADNESS. YOUR ANGER. I'M SORRY I DIDN'T HAVE TIME TO TEACH YOU MORE.
PLEASE, MIJITA, IF ANY OF MY THOUGHTS GET THROUGH TO YOU, LISTEN TO YOUR FRIENDS. FIND YOUR PEACE. THEN YOU AND I CAN CONTINUE THE LESSONS.
STOP TRYING TO BE SNEAKY. I KNEW YOU WERE HERE ALMOST THIRTY MINUTES AGO.
JUST ANOTHER OF YOUR BLASPHEMOUS GIFTS?
SLUUUUURP
NO, YOU REEK OF BURNT CYPRESS AND...
SNIFF-SNIFF
...SULFUR.

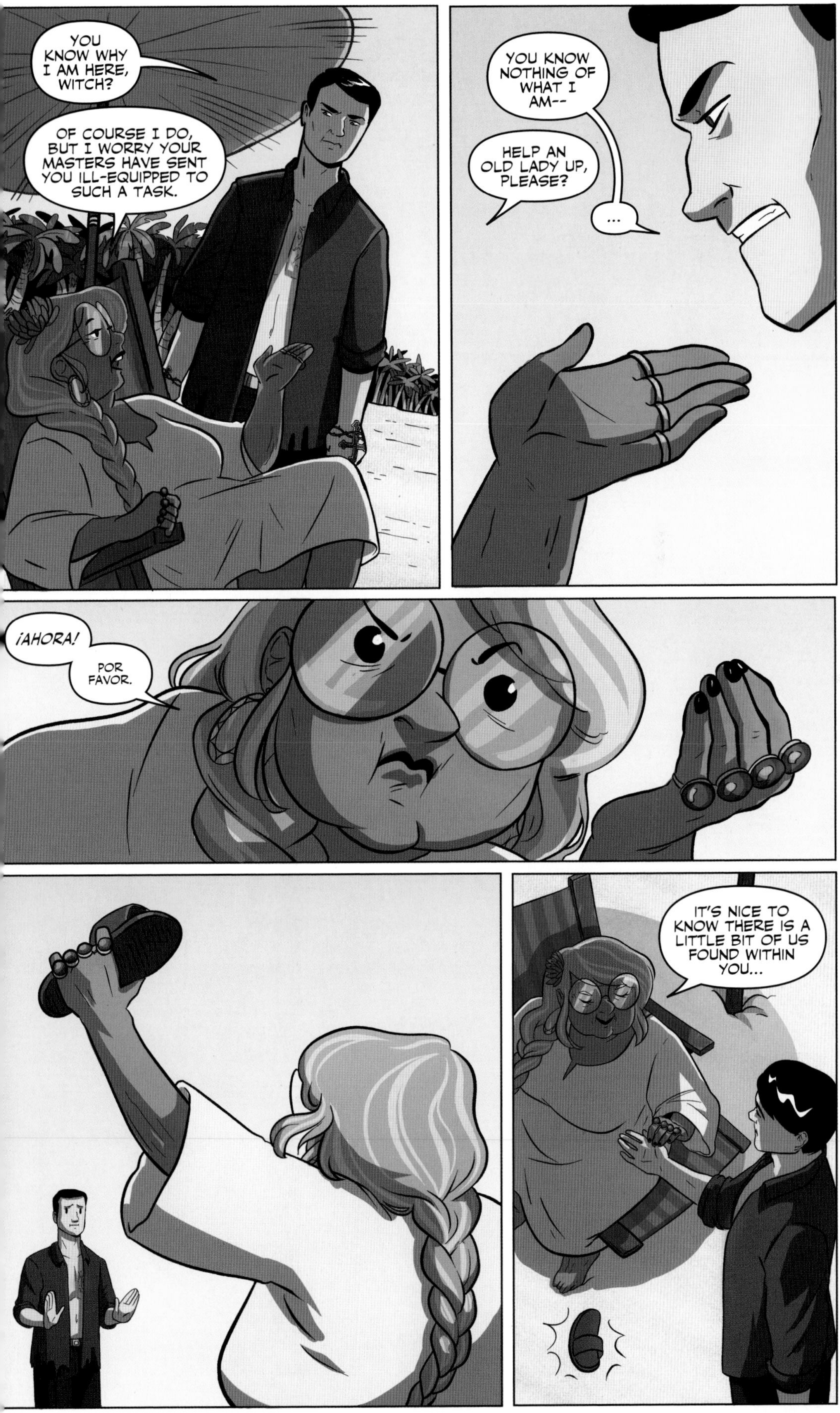
YOU KNOW WHY I AM HERE, WITCH?
OF COURSE I DO, BUT I WORRY YOUR MASTERS HAVE SENT YOU ILL-EQUIPPED TO SUCH A TASK.
YOU KNOW NOTHING OF WHAT I AM--
HELP AN OLD LADY UP, PLEASE?
...
¡AHORA!
POR FAVOR.
IT'S NICE TO KNOW THERE IS A LITTLE BIT OF US FOUND WITHIN YOU...

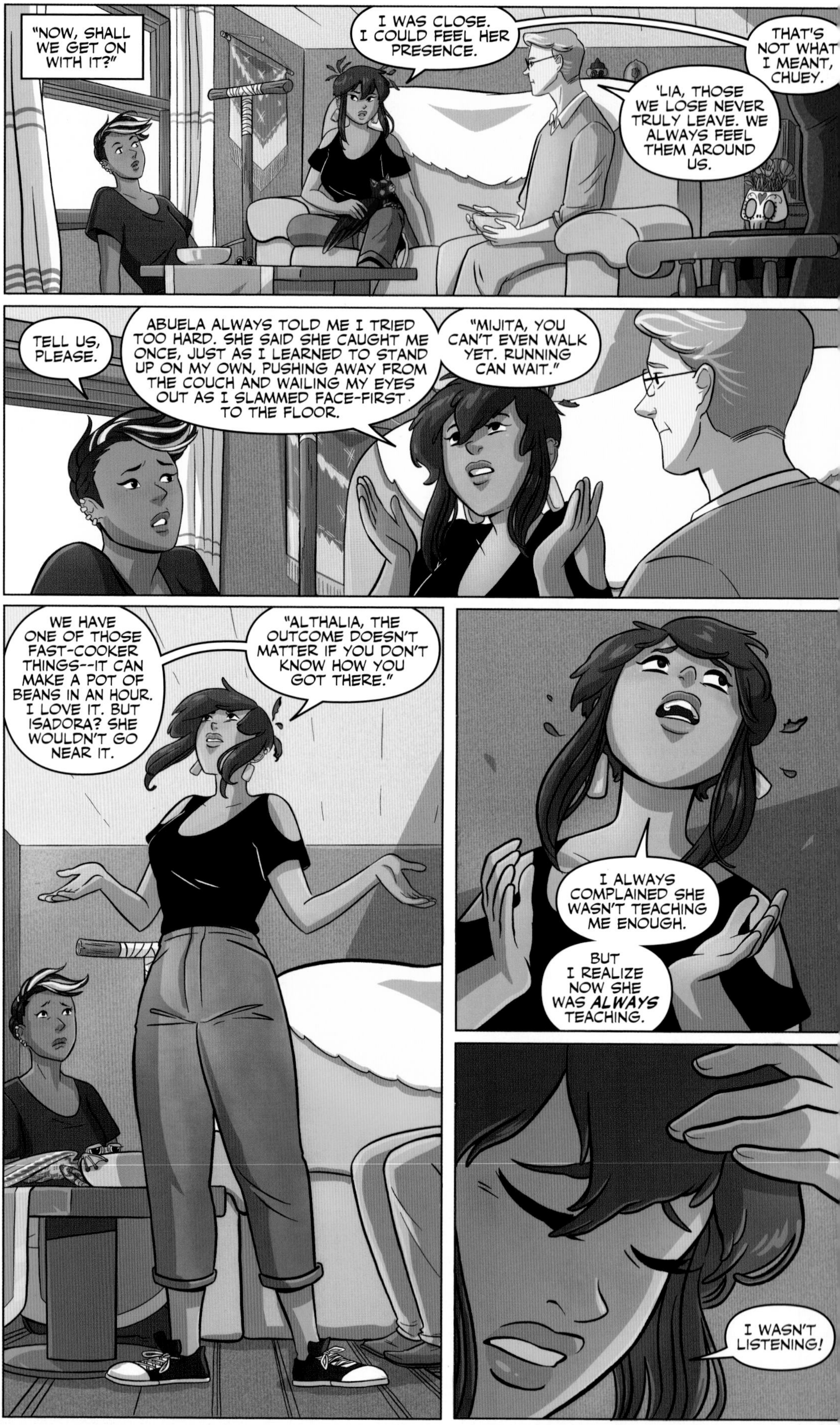
"NOW, SHALL WE GET ON WITH IT?"
I WAS CLOSE. I COULD FEEL HER PRESENCE.
THAT'S NOT WHAT I MEANT, CHUEY.
'LIA, THOSE WE LOSE NEVER TRULY LEAVE. WE ALWAYS FEEL THEM AROUND US.
TELL US, PLEASE.
ABUELA ALWAYS TOLD ME I TRIED TOO HARD. SHE SAID SHE CAUGHT ME ONCE, JUST AS I LEARNED TO STAND UP ON MY OWN, PUSHING AWAY FROM THE COUCH AND WAILING MY EYES OUT AS I SLAMMED FACE-FIRST TO THE FLOOR.
"MIJITA, YOU CAN'T EVEN WALK YET. RUNNING CAN WAIT."
WE HAVE ONE OF THOSE FAST-COOKER THINGS--IT CAN MAKE A POT OF BEANS IN AN HOUR. I LOVE IT. BUT ISADORA? SHE WOULDN'T GO NEAR IT.
"ALTHALIA, THE OUTCOME DOESN'T MATTER IF YOU DON'T KNOW HOW YOU GOT THERE."
I ALWAYS COMPLAINED SHE WASN'T TEACHING ME ENOUGH.
BUT I REALIZE NOW SHE WAS *ALWAYS* TEACHING.
I WASN'T LISTENING!

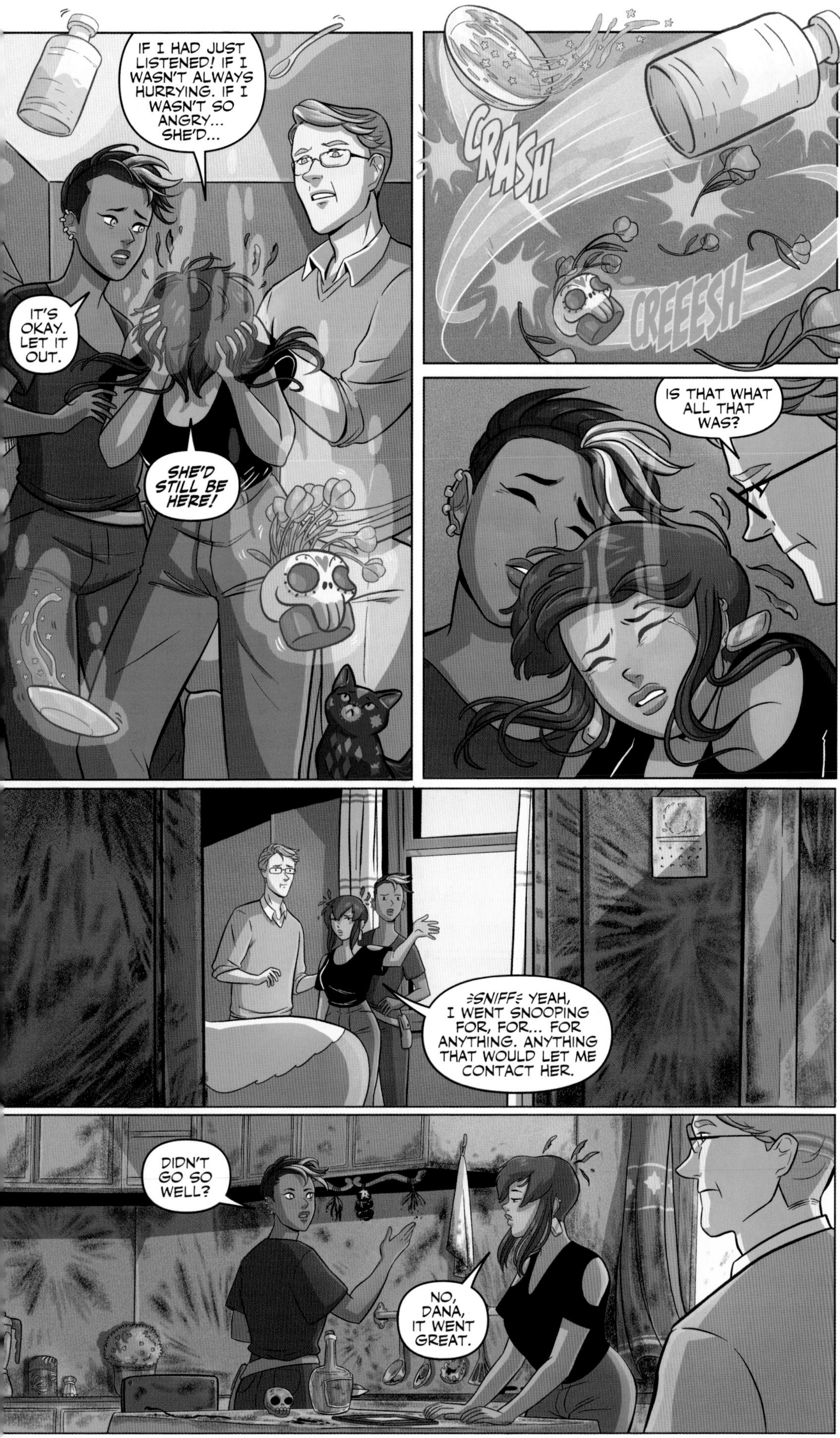
IF I HAD JUST LISTENED! IF I WASN'T ALWAYS HURRYING. IF I WASN'T SO ANGRY... SHE'D...
IT'S OKAY. LET IT OUT.
SHE'D STILL BE HERE!
CRASH
CREEESH
IS THAT WHAT ALL THAT WAS?
≈SNIFF≈ YEAH, I WENT SNOOPING FOR, FOR... FOR ANYTHING. ANYTHING THAT WOULD LET ME CONTACT HER.
DIDN'T GO SO WELL?
NO, DANA, IT WENT GREAT.

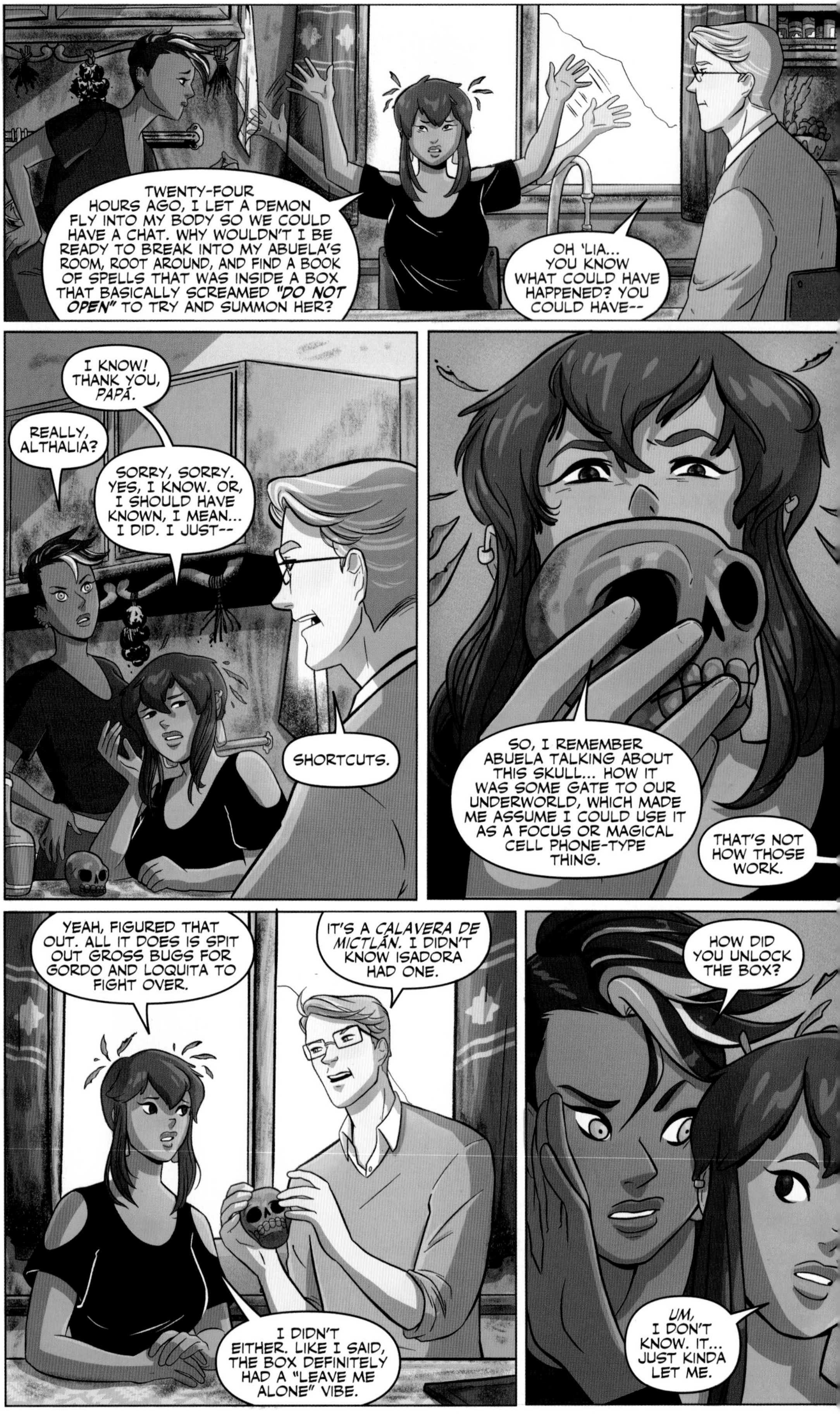

TWENTY-FOUR HOURS AGO, I LET A DEMON FLY INTO MY BODY SO WE COULD HAVE A CHAT. WHY WOULDN'T I BE READY TO BREAK INTO MY ABUELA'S ROOM, ROOT AROUND, AND FIND A BOOK OF SPELLS THAT WAS INSIDE A BOX THAT BASICALLY SCREAMED "DO NOT OPEN" TO TRY AND SUMMON HER?
OH 'LIA... YOU KNOW WHAT COULD HAVE HAPPENED? YOU COULD HAVE--
I KNOW! THANK YOU, PAPÁ.
REALLY, ALTHALIA?
SORRY, SORRY. YES, I KNOW. OR, I SHOULD HAVE KNOWN, I MEAN... I DID. I JUST--
SHORTCUTS.
SO, I REMEMBER ABUELA TALKING ABOUT THIS SKULL... HOW IT WAS SOME GATE TO OUR UNDERWORLD, WHICH MADE ME ASSUME I COULD USE IT AS A FOCUS OR MAGICAL CELL PHONE-TYPE THING.
THAT'S NOT HOW THOSE WORK.
YEAH, FIGURED THAT OUT. ALL IT DOES IS SPIT OUT GROSS BUGS FOR GORDO AND LOQUITA TO FIGHT OVER.
IT'S A CALAVERA DE MICTLÁN. I DIDN'T KNOW ISADORA HAD ONE.
I DIDN'T EITHER. LIKE I SAID, THE BOX DEFINITELY HAD A "LEAVE ME ALONE" VIBE.
HOW DID YOU UNLOCK THE BOX?
UM, I DON'T KNOW. IT... JUST KINDA LET ME.

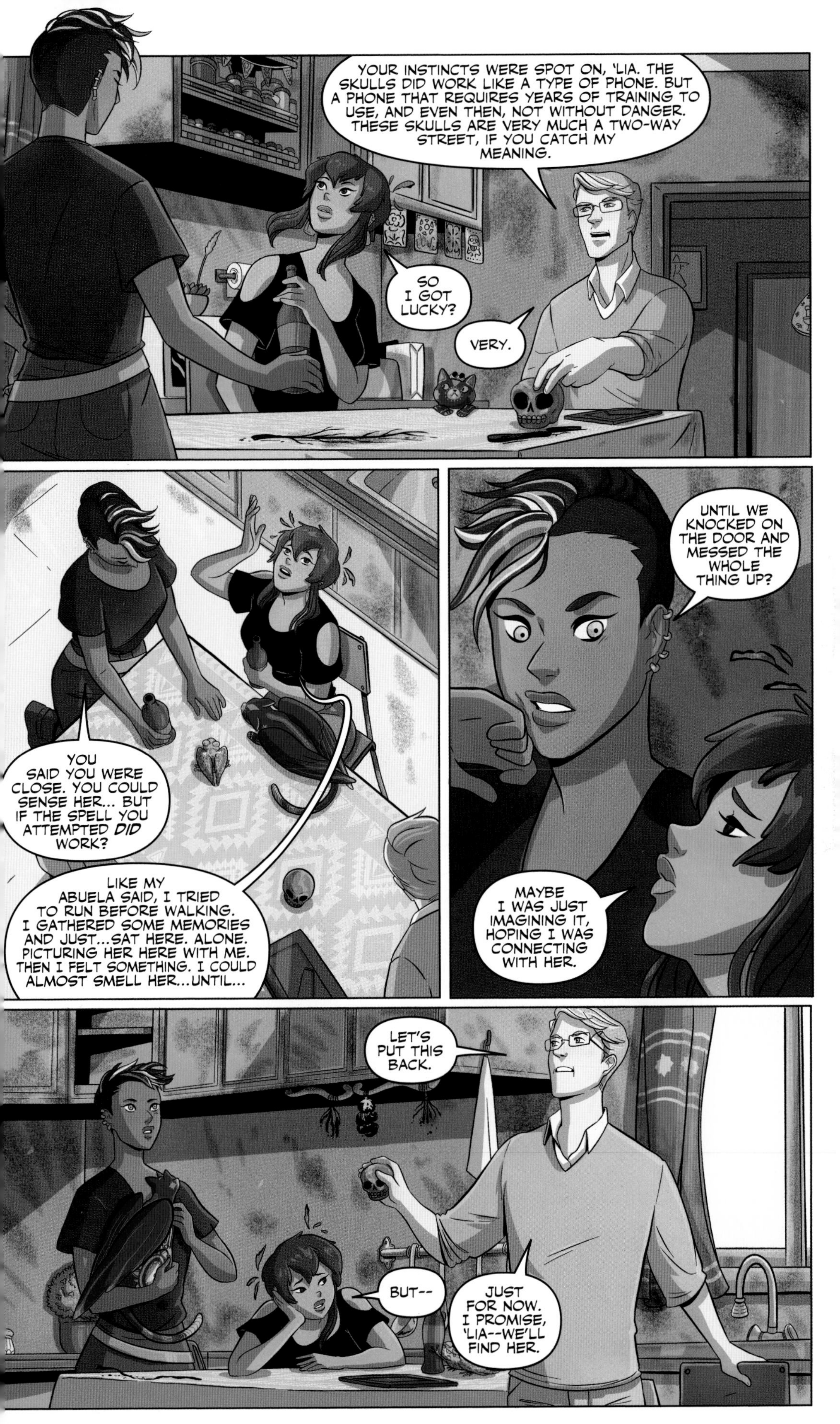
YOUR INSTINCTS WERE SPOT ON, 'LIA. THE SKULLS DID WORK LIKE A TYPE OF PHONE. BUT A PHONE THAT REQUIRES YEARS OF TRAINING TO USE, AND EVEN THEN, NOT WITHOUT DANGER. THESE SKULLS ARE VERY MUCH A TWO-WAY STREET, IF YOU CATCH MY MEANING.
SO I GOT LUCKY?
VERY.
YOU SAID YOU WERE CLOSE. YOU COULD SENSE HER... BUT IF THE SPELL YOU ATTEMPTED *DID* WORK?
LIKE MY ABUELA SAID, I TRIED TO RUN BEFORE WALKING. I GATHERED SOME MEMORIES AND JUST...SAT HERE. ALONE. PICTURING HER HERE WITH ME. THEN I FELT SOMETHING. I COULD ALMOST SMELL HER...UNTIL...
UNTIL WE KNOCKED ON THE DOOR AND MESSED THE WHOLE THING UP?
MAYBE I WAS JUST IMAGINING IT, HOPING I WAS CONNECTING WITH HER.
LET'S PUT THIS BACK.
BUT--
JUST FOR NOW. I PROMISE, 'LIA--WE'LL FIND HER.

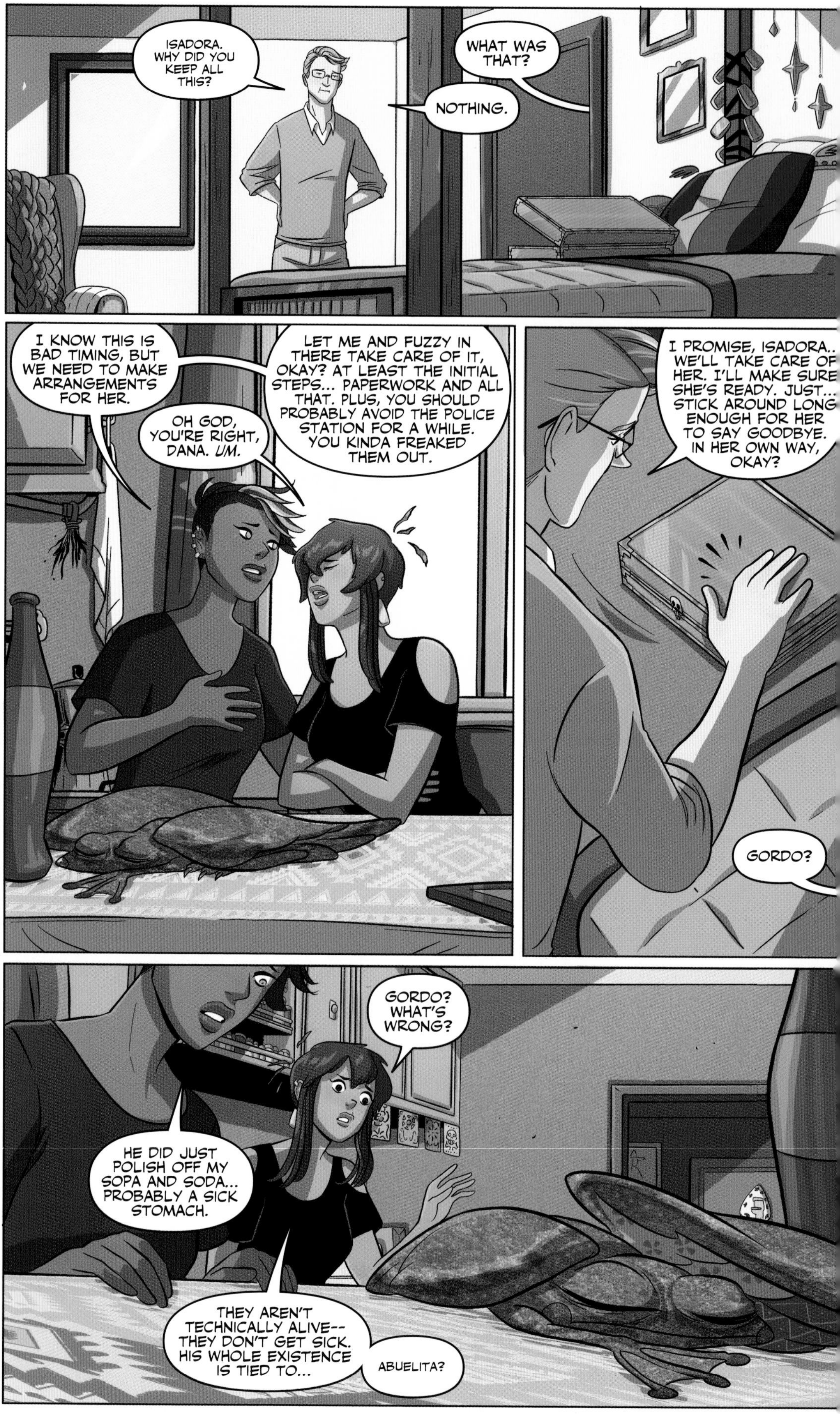
ISADORA. WHY DID YOU KEEP ALL THIS?
WHAT WAS THAT?
NOTHING.
I KNOW THIS IS BAD TIMING, BUT WE NEED TO MAKE ARRANGEMENTS FOR HER.
OH GOD, YOU'RE RIGHT, DANA. UM.
LET ME AND FUZZY IN THERE TAKE CARE OF IT, OKAY? AT LEAST THE INITIAL STEPS... PAPERWORK AND ALL THAT. PLUS, YOU SHOULD PROBABLY AVOID THE POLICE STATION FOR A WHILE. YOU KINDA FREAKED THEM OUT.
I PROMISE, ISADORA.. WE'LL TAKE CARE OF HER. I'LL MAKE SURE SHE'S READY. JUST... STICK AROUND LONG ENOUGH FOR HER TO SAY GOODBYE. IN HER OWN WAY, OKAY?
GORDO?
GORDO? WHAT'S WRONG?
HE DID JUST POLISH OFF MY SOPA AND SODA... PROBABLY A SICK STOMACH.
THEY AREN'T TECHNICALLY ALIVE-- THEY DON'T GET SICK. HIS WHOLE EXISTENCE IS TIED TO...
ABUELITA?

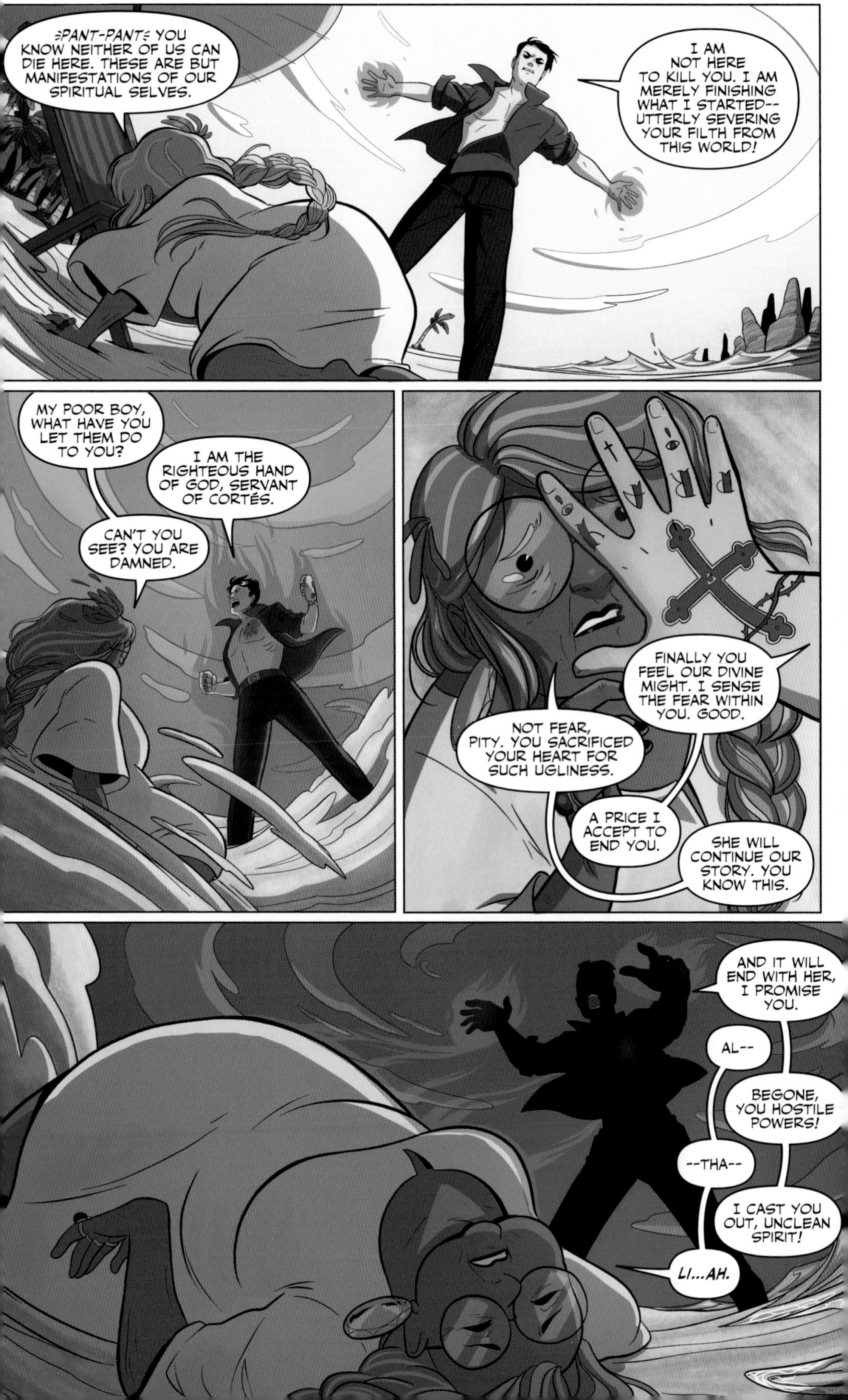
≡PANT-PANT≡ YOU KNOW NEITHER OF US CAN DIE HERE. THESE ARE BUT MANIFESTATIONS OF OUR SPIRITUAL SELVES.
I AM NOT HERE TO KILL YOU. I AM MERELY FINISHING WHAT I STARTED-- UTTERLY SEVERING YOUR FILTH FROM THIS WORLD!
MY POOR BOY, WHAT HAVE YOU LET THEM DO TO YOU?
I AM THE RIGHTEOUS HAND OF GOD, SERVANT OF CORTÉS.
CAN'T YOU SEE? YOU ARE DAMNED.
FINALLY YOU FEEL OUR DIVINE MIGHT. I SENSE THE FEAR WITHIN YOU. GOOD.
NOT FEAR, PITY. YOU SACRIFICED YOUR HEART FOR SUCH UGLINESS.
A PRICE I ACCEPT TO END YOU.
SHE WILL CONTINUE OUR STORY. YOU KNOW THIS.
AND IT WILL END WITH HER, I PROMISE YOU.
AL--
BEGONE, YOU HOSTILE POWERS!
--THA--
I CAST YOU OUT, UNCLEAN SPIRIT!
LI...AH.

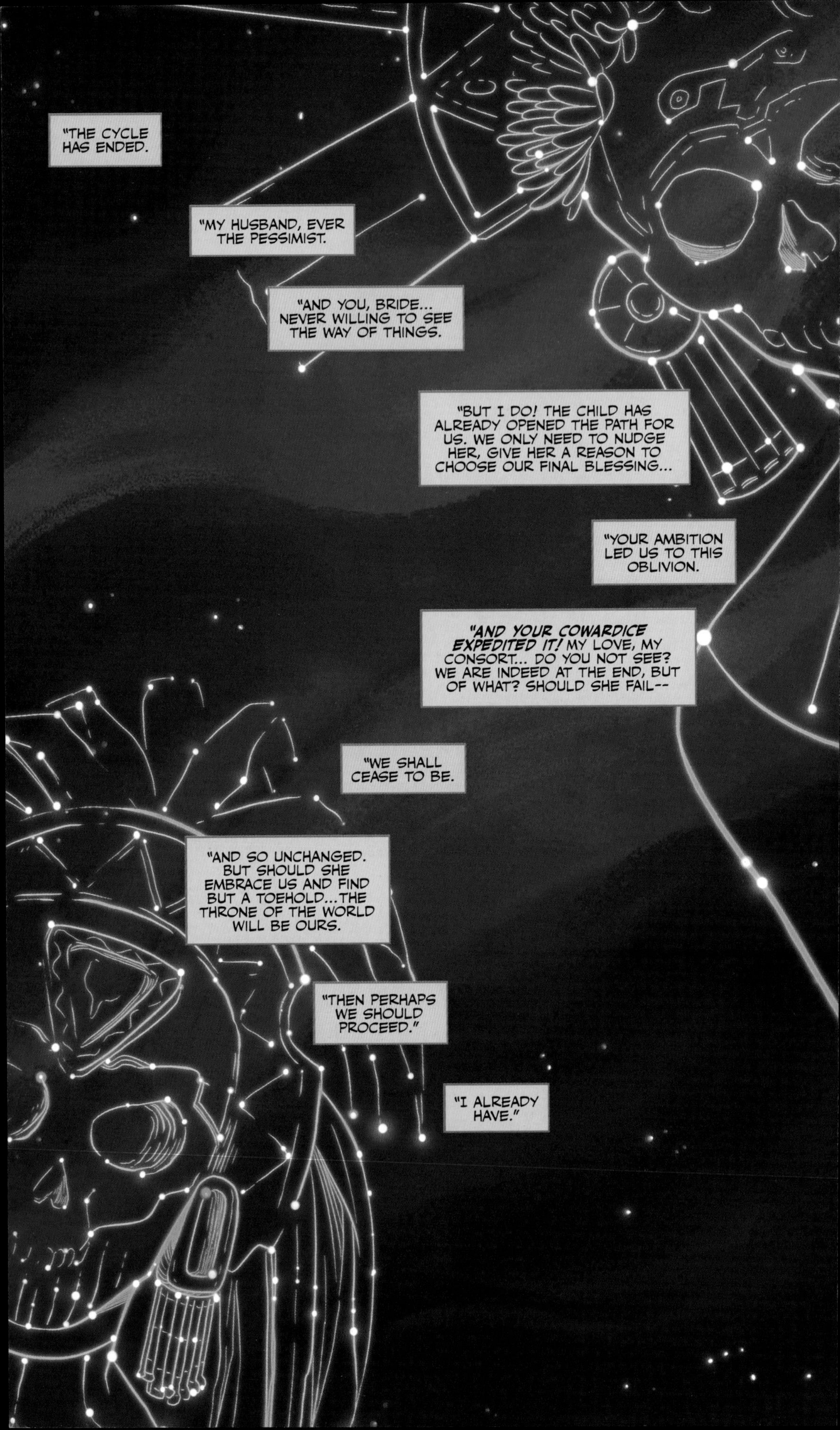
"THE CYCLE HAS ENDED.
"MY HUSBAND, EVER THE PESSIMIST.
"AND YOU, BRIDE... NEVER WILLING TO SEE THE WAY OF THINGS.
"BUT I DO! THE CHILD HAS ALREADY OPENED THE PATH FOR US. WE ONLY NEED TO NUDGE HER, GIVE HER A REASON TO CHOOSE OUR FINAL BLESSING...
"YOUR AMBITION LED US TO THIS OBLIVION.
"AND YOUR COWARDICE EXPEDITED IT! MY LOVE, MY CONSORT... DO YOU NOT SEE? WE ARE INDEED AT THE END, BUT OF WHAT? SHOULD SHE FAIL--
"WE SHALL CEASE TO BE.
"AND SO UNCHANGED. BUT SHOULD SHE EMBRACE US AND FIND BUT A TOEHOLD...THE THRONE OF THE WORLD WILL BE OURS.
"THEN PERHAPS WE SHOULD PROCEED."
"I ALREADY HAVE."

CHAPTER 4

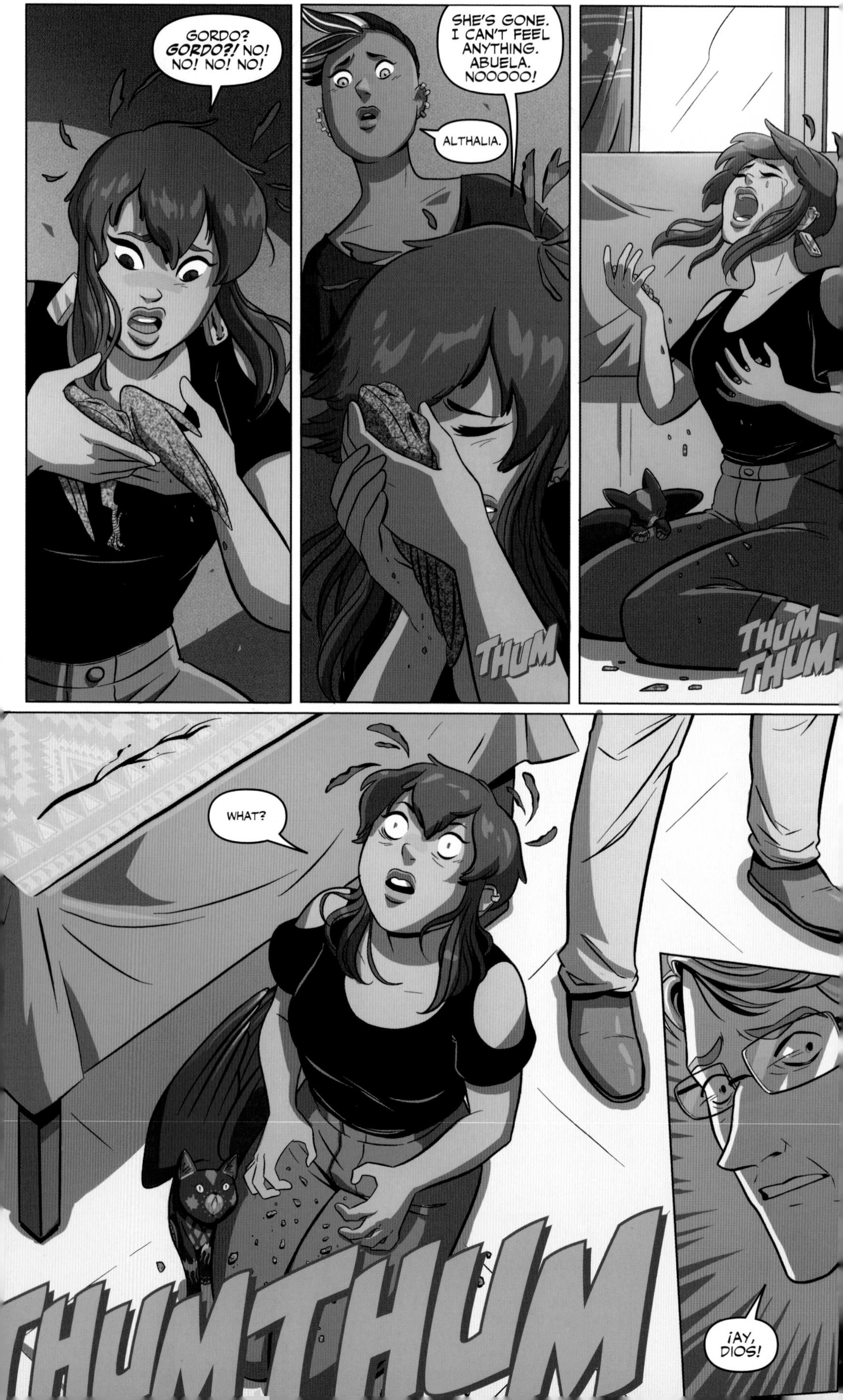

GORDO? *GORDO?!* NO! NO! NO! NO!
ALTHALIA.
SHE'S GONE. I CAN'T FEEL ANYTHING. ABUELA. NOOOOO!
THUM
THUM THUM
WHAT?
THUM THUM
¡AY, DIOS!

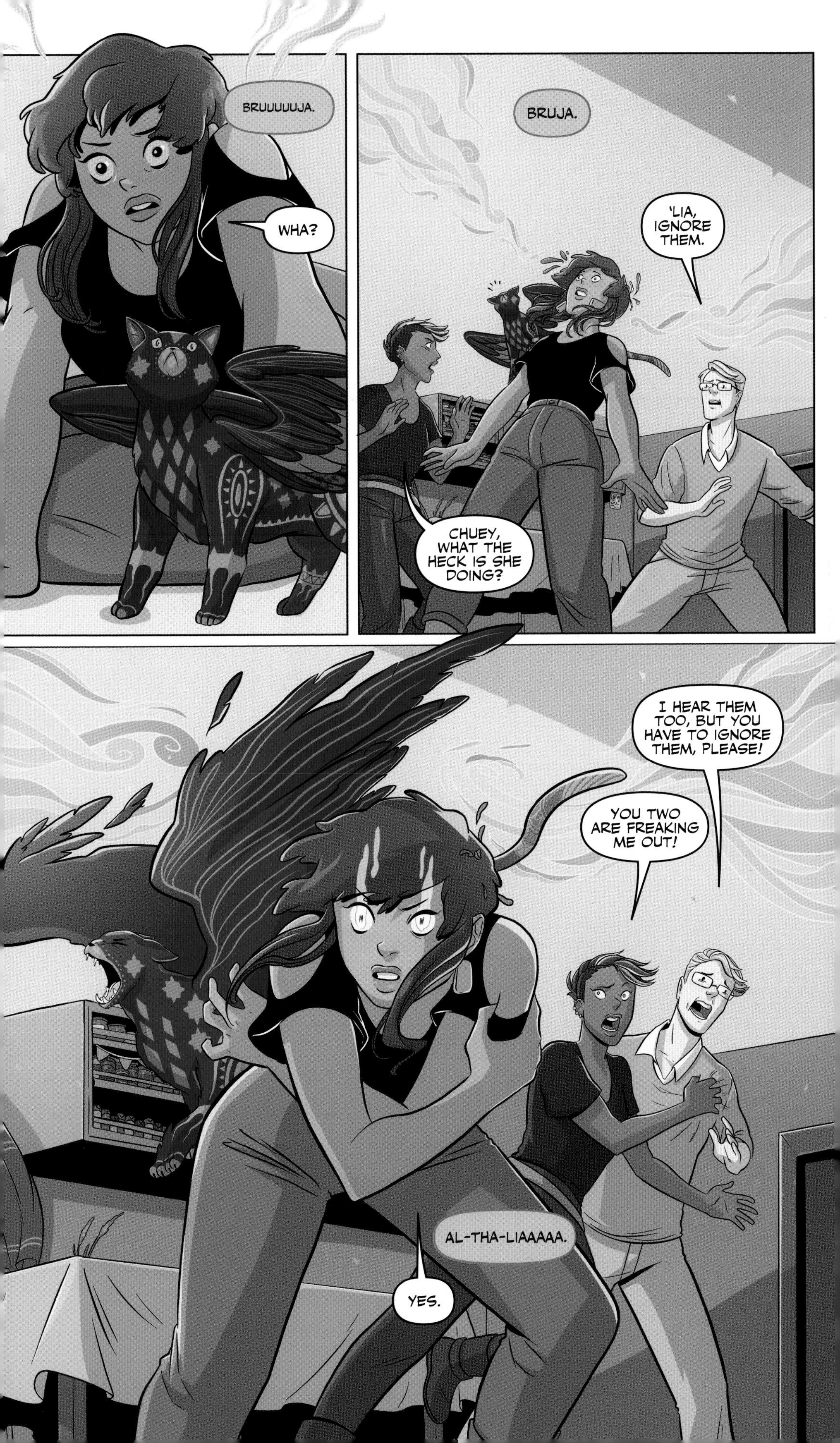
BRUUUUUJA.
WHA?
BRUJA.
'LIA, IGNORE THEM.
CHUEY, WHAT THE HECK IS SHE DOING?
I HEAR THEM TOO, BUT YOU HAVE TO IGNORE THEM, PLEASE!
YOU TWO ARE FREAKING ME OUT!
AL-THA-LIAAAAA.
YES.

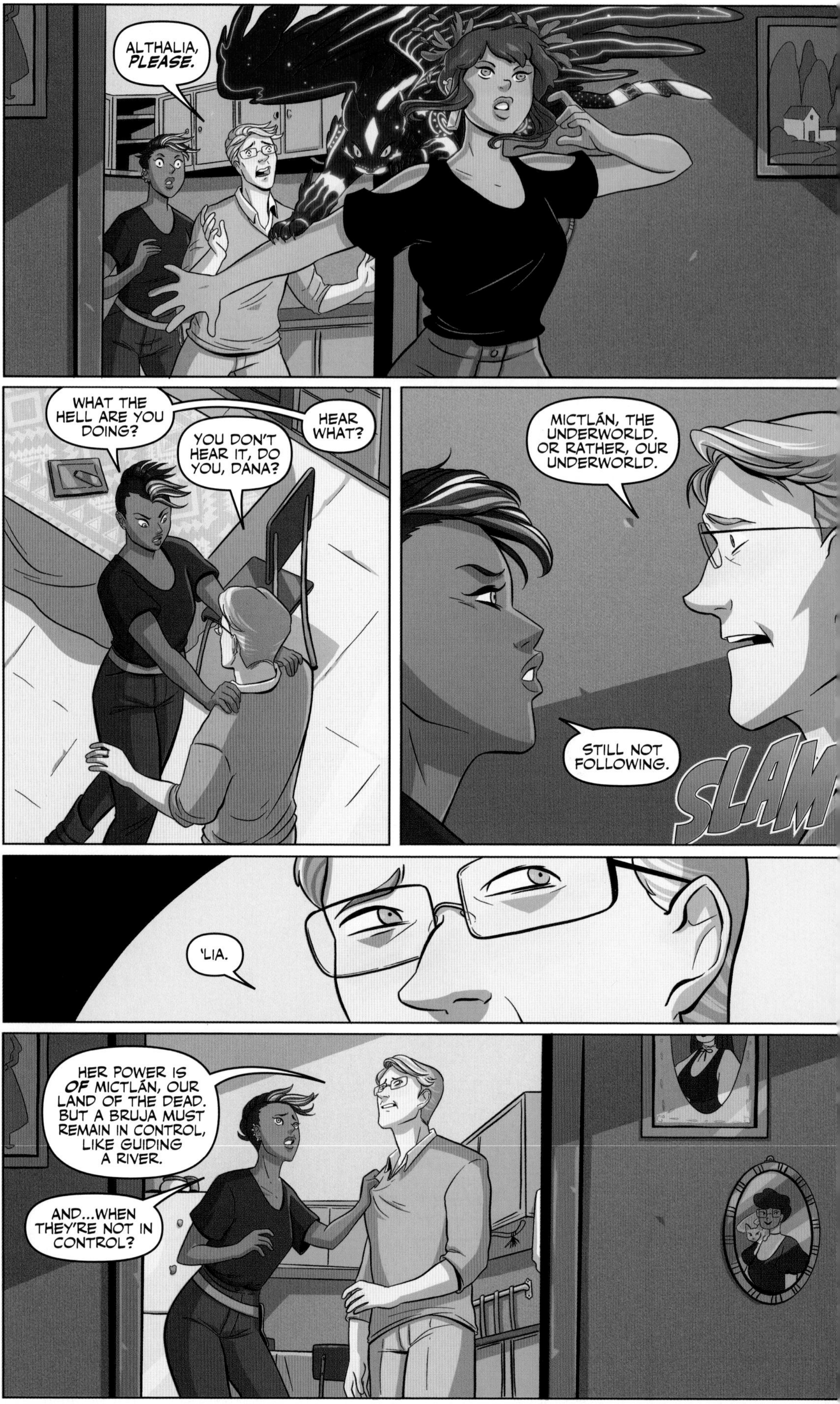
ALTHALIA, *PLEASE.*
WHAT THE HELL ARE YOU DOING?
YOU DON'T HEAR IT, DO YOU, DANA?
HEAR WHAT?
MICTLÁN, THE UNDERWORLD. OR RATHER, OUR UNDERWORLD.
STILL NOT FOLLOWING.
SLAM
'LIA.
HER POWER IS *OF* MICTLÁN, OUR LAND OF THE DEAD. BUT A BRUJA MUST REMAIN IN CONTROL, LIKE GUIDING A RIVER.
AND...WHEN THEY'RE NOT IN CONTROL?

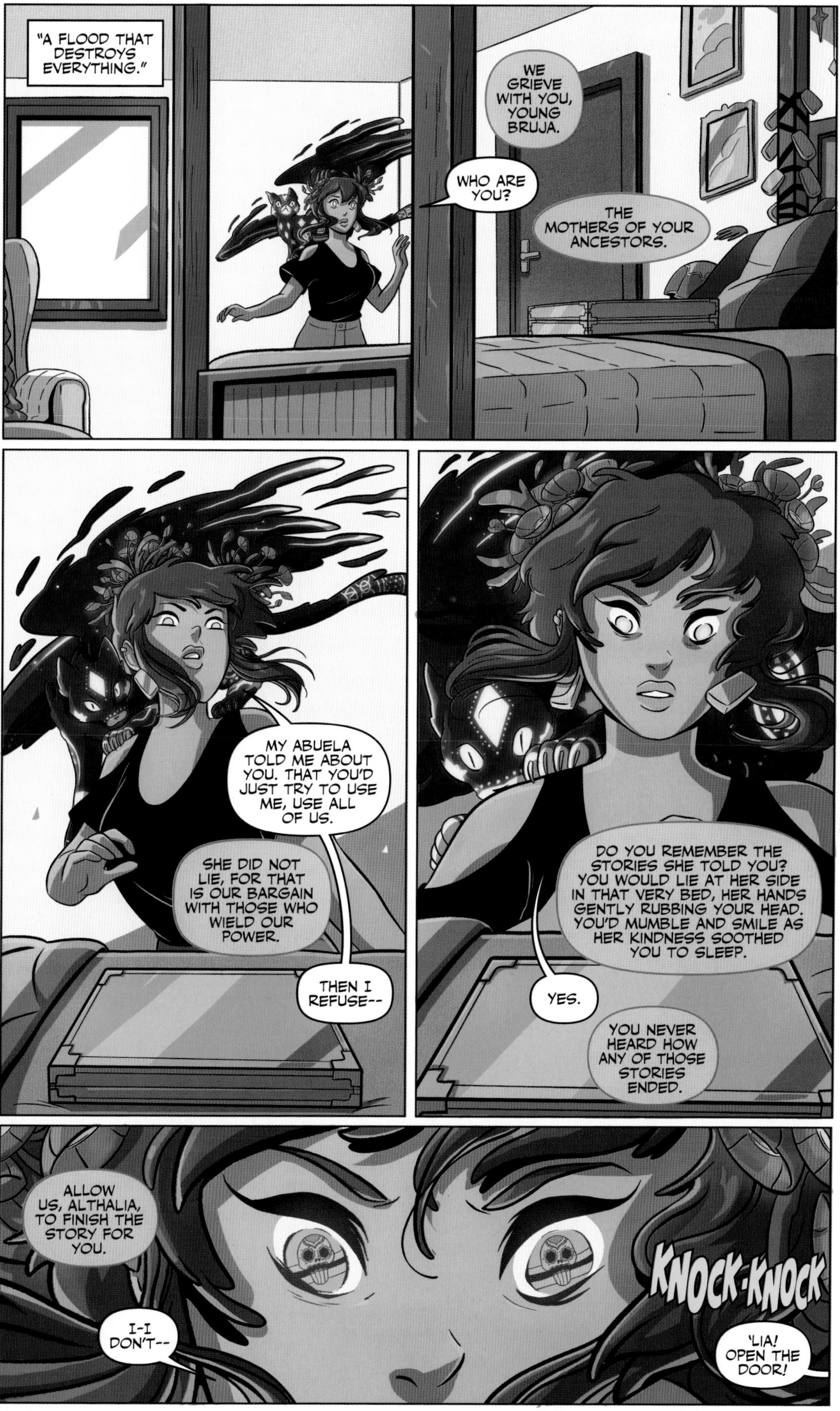

"A FLOOD THAT DESTROYS EVERYTHING."
WE GRIEVE WITH YOU, YOUNG BRUJA.
WHO ARE YOU?
THE MOTHERS OF YOUR ANCESTORS.
MY ABUELA TOLD ME ABOUT YOU. THAT YOU'D JUST TRY TO USE ME, USE ALL OF US.
SHE DID NOT LIE, FOR THAT IS OUR BARGAIN WITH THOSE WHO WIELD OUR POWER.
THEN I REFUSE--
DO YOU REMEMBER THE STORIES SHE TOLD YOU? YOU WOULD LIE AT HER SIDE IN THAT VERY BED, HER HANDS GENTLY RUBBING YOUR HEAD. YOU'D MUMBLE AND SMILE AS HER KINDNESS SOOTHED YOU TO SLEEP.
YES.
YOU NEVER HEARD HOW ANY OF THOSE STORIES ENDED.
ALLOW US, ALTHALIA, TO FINISH THE STORY FOR YOU.
I-I DON'T--
KNOCK-KNOCK
'LIA! OPEN THE DOOR!

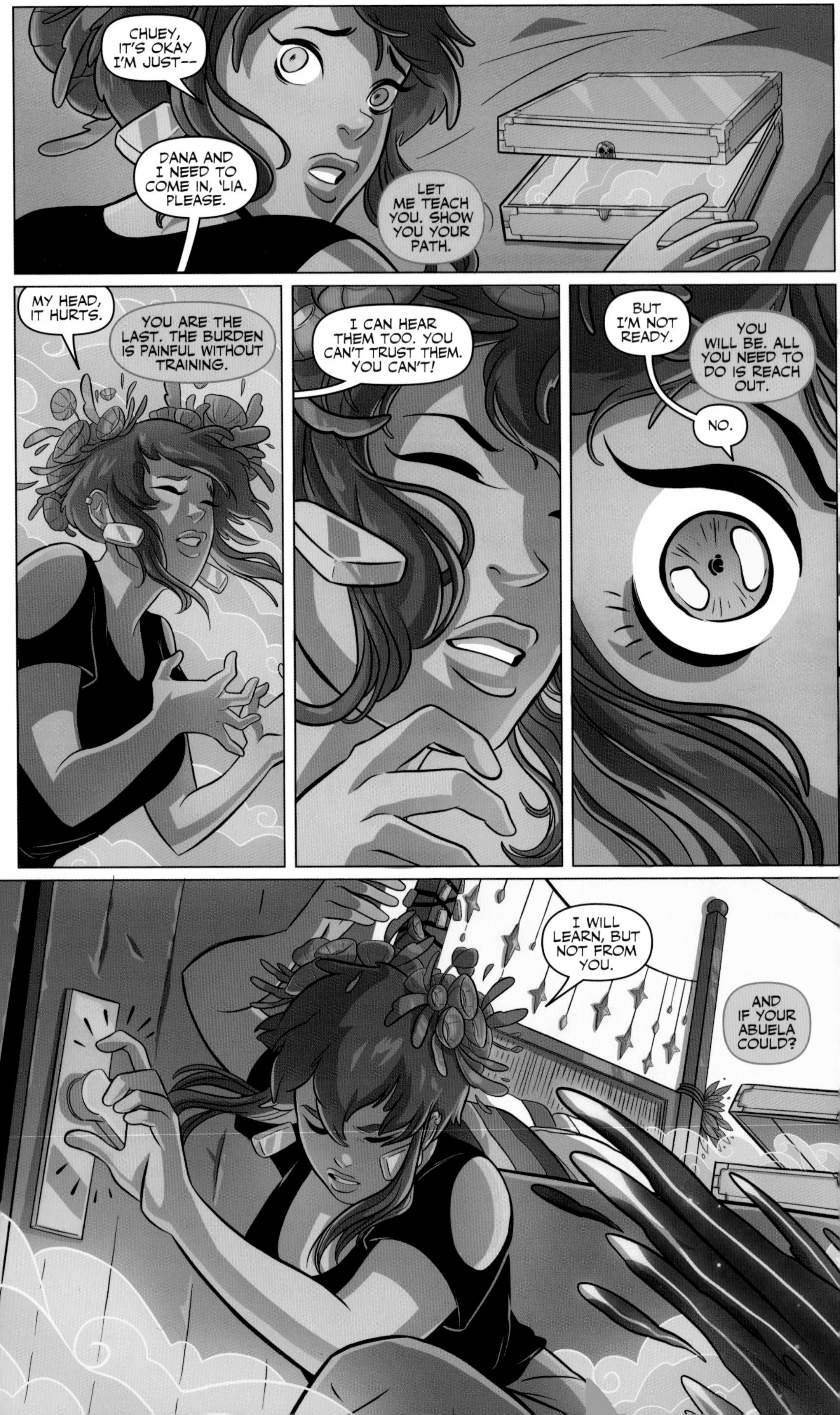
CHUEY, IT'S OKAY I'M JUST--
DANA AND I NEED TO COME IN, 'LIA. PLEASE.
LET ME TEACH YOU. SHOW YOU YOUR PATH.
MY HEAD, IT HURTS.
YOU ARE THE LAST. THE BURDEN IS PAINFUL WITHOUT TRAINING.
I CAN HEAR THEM TOO. YOU CAN'T TRUST THEM. YOU CAN'T!
BUT I'M NOT READY.
YOU WILL BE. ALL YOU NEED TO DO IS REACH OUT.
NO.
I WILL LEARN, BUT NOT FROM YOU.
AND IF YOUR ABUELA COULD?

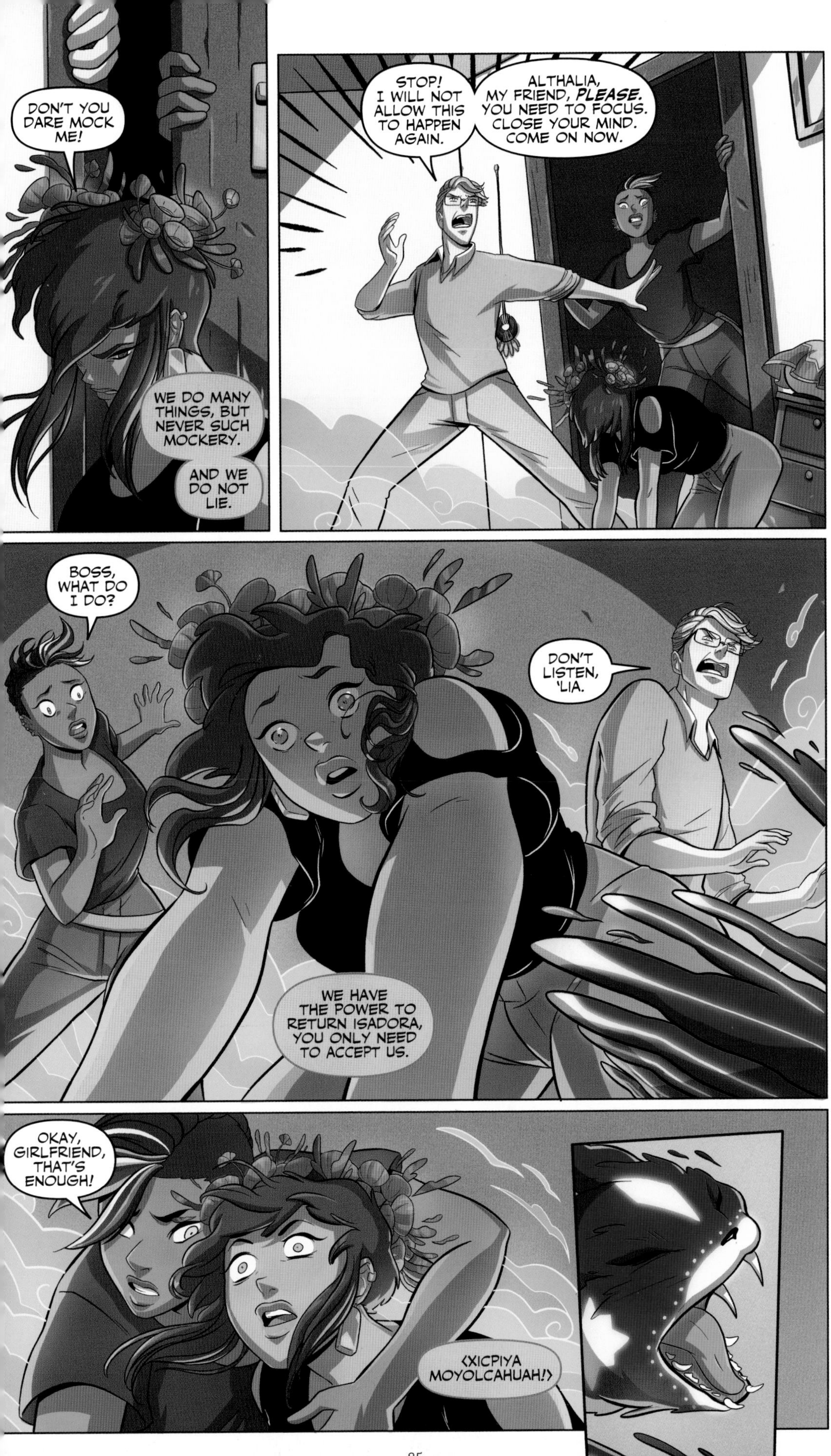
DON'T YOU DARE MOCK ME!
WE DO MANY THINGS, BUT NEVER SUCH MOCKERY.
AND WE DO NOT LIE.
STOP! I WILL NOT ALLOW THIS TO HAPPEN AGAIN.
ALTHALIA, MY FRIEND, PLEASE. YOU NEED TO FOCUS. CLOSE YOUR MIND. COME ON NOW.
BOSS, WHAT DO I DO?
DON'T LISTEN, 'LIA.
WE HAVE THE POWER TO RETURN ISADORA, YOU ONLY NEED TO ACCEPT US.
OKAY, GIRLFRIEND, THAT'S ENOUGH!
‹XICPIYA MOYOLCAHUAH!›

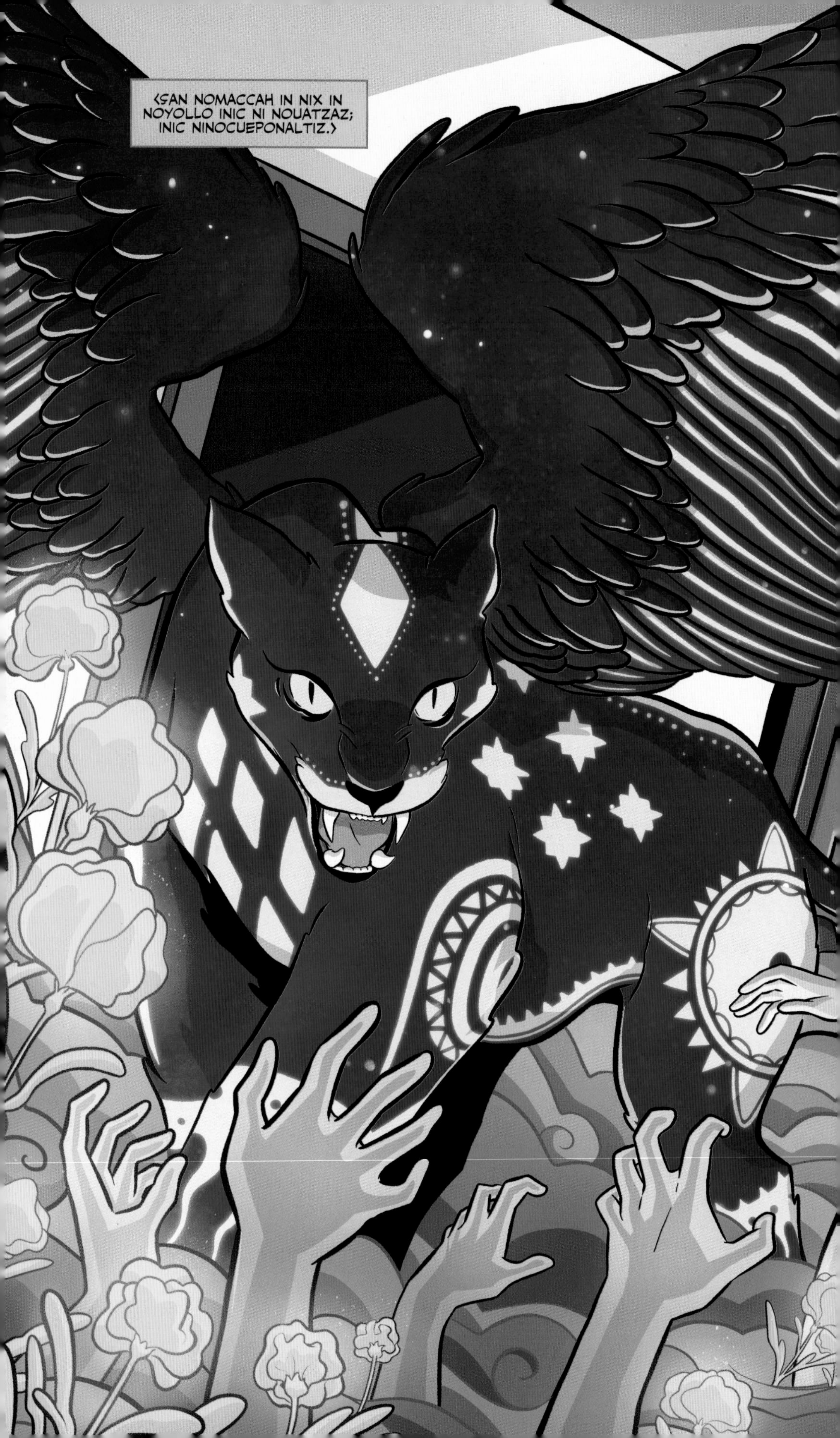
<ÇAN NOMACCAH IN NIX IN NOYOLLO INIC NI NOUATZAZ; INIC NINOCUEPONALTIZ.>

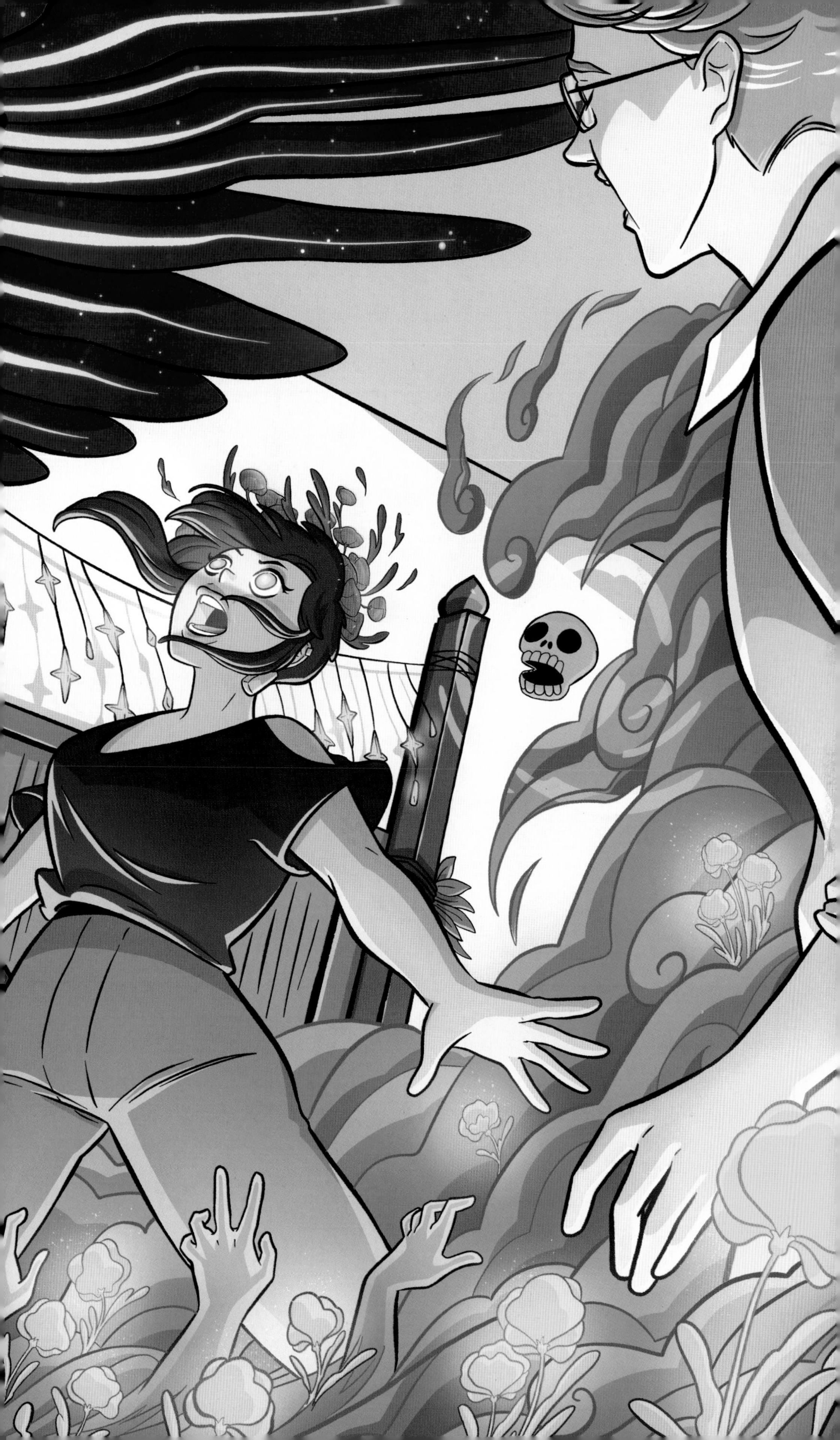

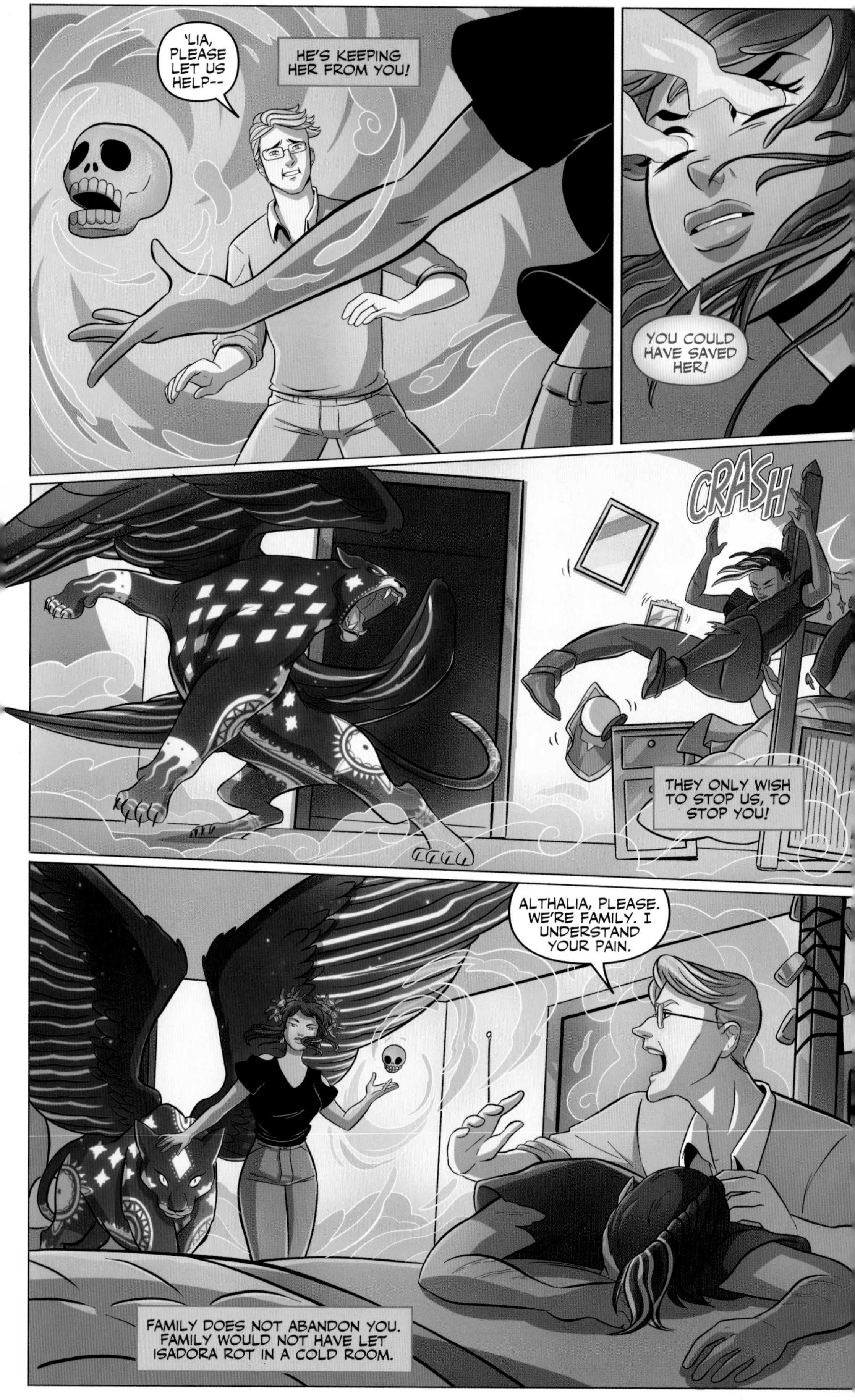
'LIA, PLEASE LET US HELP--
HE'S KEEPING HER FROM YOU!
YOU COULD HAVE SAVED HER!
CRASH
THEY ONLY WISH TO STOP US, TO STOP YOU!
ALTHALIA, PLEASE. WE'RE FAMILY. I UNDERSTAND YOUR PAIN.
FAMILY DOES NOT ABANDON YOU. FAMILY WOULD NOT HAVE LET ISADORA ROT IN A COLD ROOM.

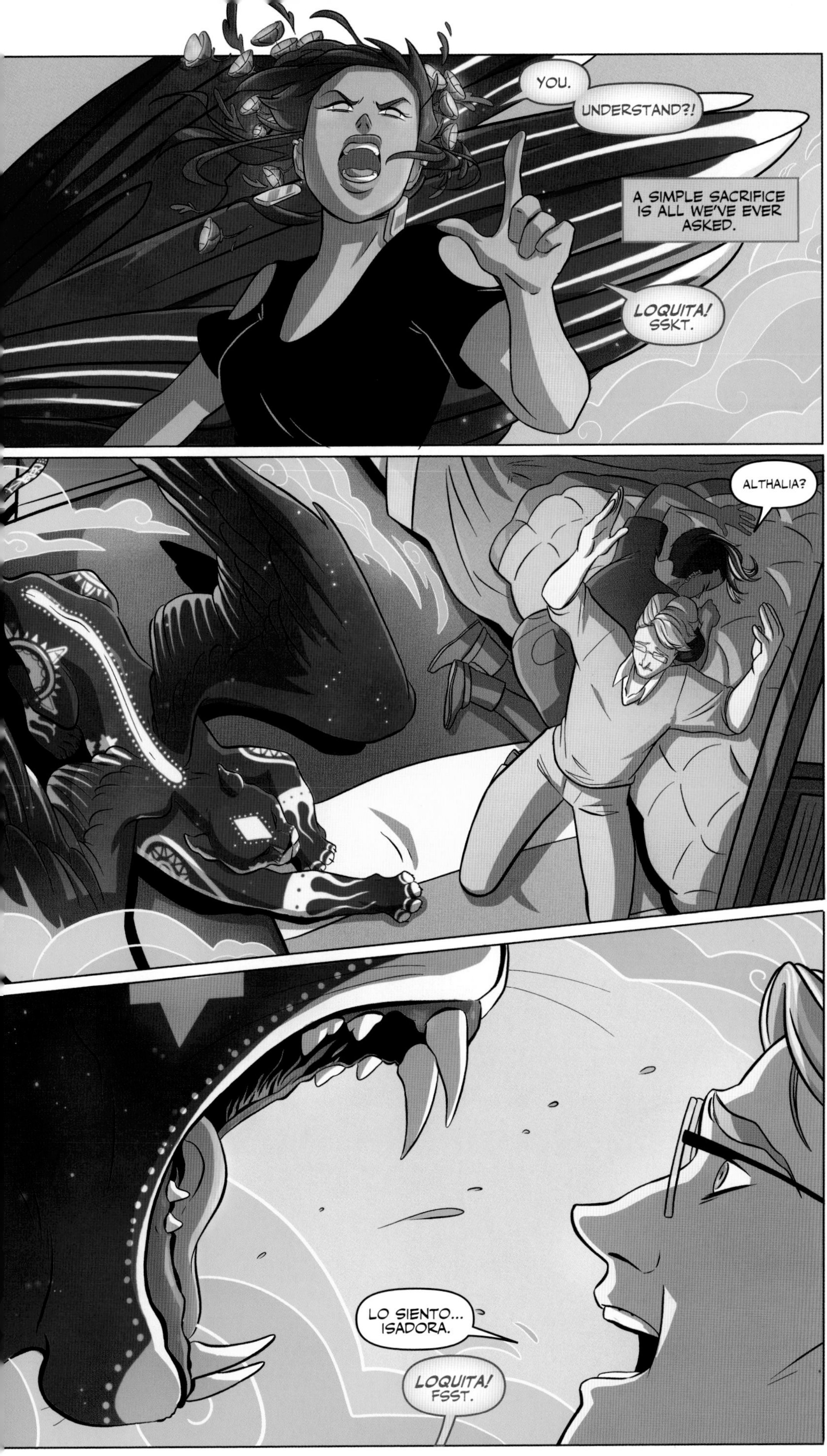
YOU.
UNDERSTAND?!
A SIMPLE SACRIFICE IS ALL WE'VE EVER ASKED.
LOQUITA! SSKT.
ALTHALIA?
LO SIENTO... ISADORA.
LOQUITA! FSST.

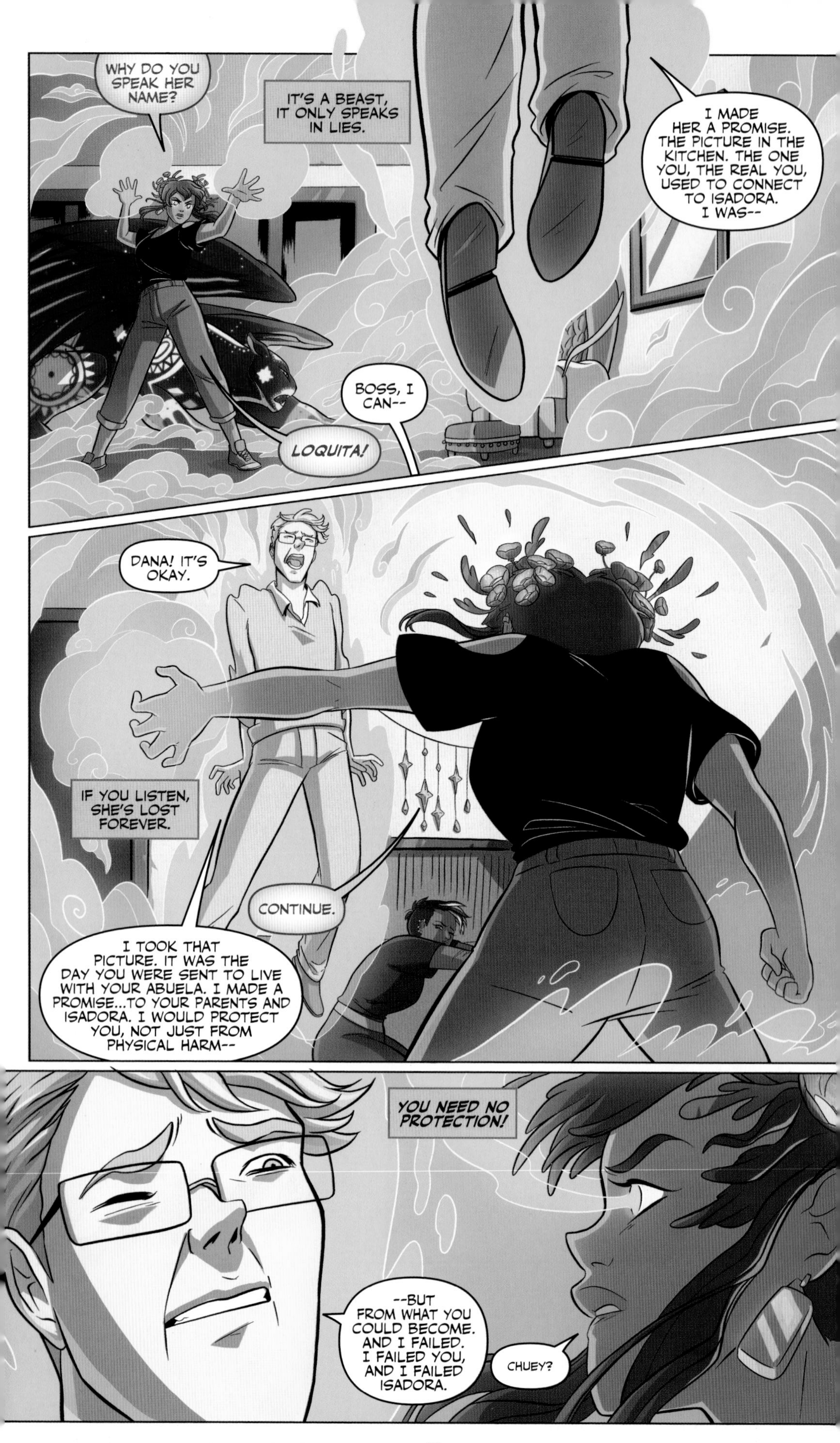
WHY DO YOU SPEAK HER NAME?
IT'S A BEAST, IT ONLY SPEAKS IN LIES.
I MADE HER A PROMISE. THE PICTURE IN THE KITCHEN. THE ONE YOU, THE REAL YOU, USED TO CONNECT TO ISADORA. I WAS--
BOSS, I CAN--
LOQUITA!
DANA! IT'S OKAY.
IF YOU LISTEN, SHE'S LOST FOREVER.
CONTINUE.
I TOOK THAT PICTURE. IT WAS THE DAY YOU WERE SENT TO LIVE WITH YOUR ABUELA. I MADE A PROMISE...TO YOUR PARENTS AND ISADORA. I WOULD PROTECT YOU, NOT JUST FROM PHYSICAL HARM--
YOU NEED NO PROTECTION!
--BUT FROM WHAT YOU COULD BECOME. AND I FAILED. I FAILED YOU, AND I FAILED ISADORA.
CHUEY?

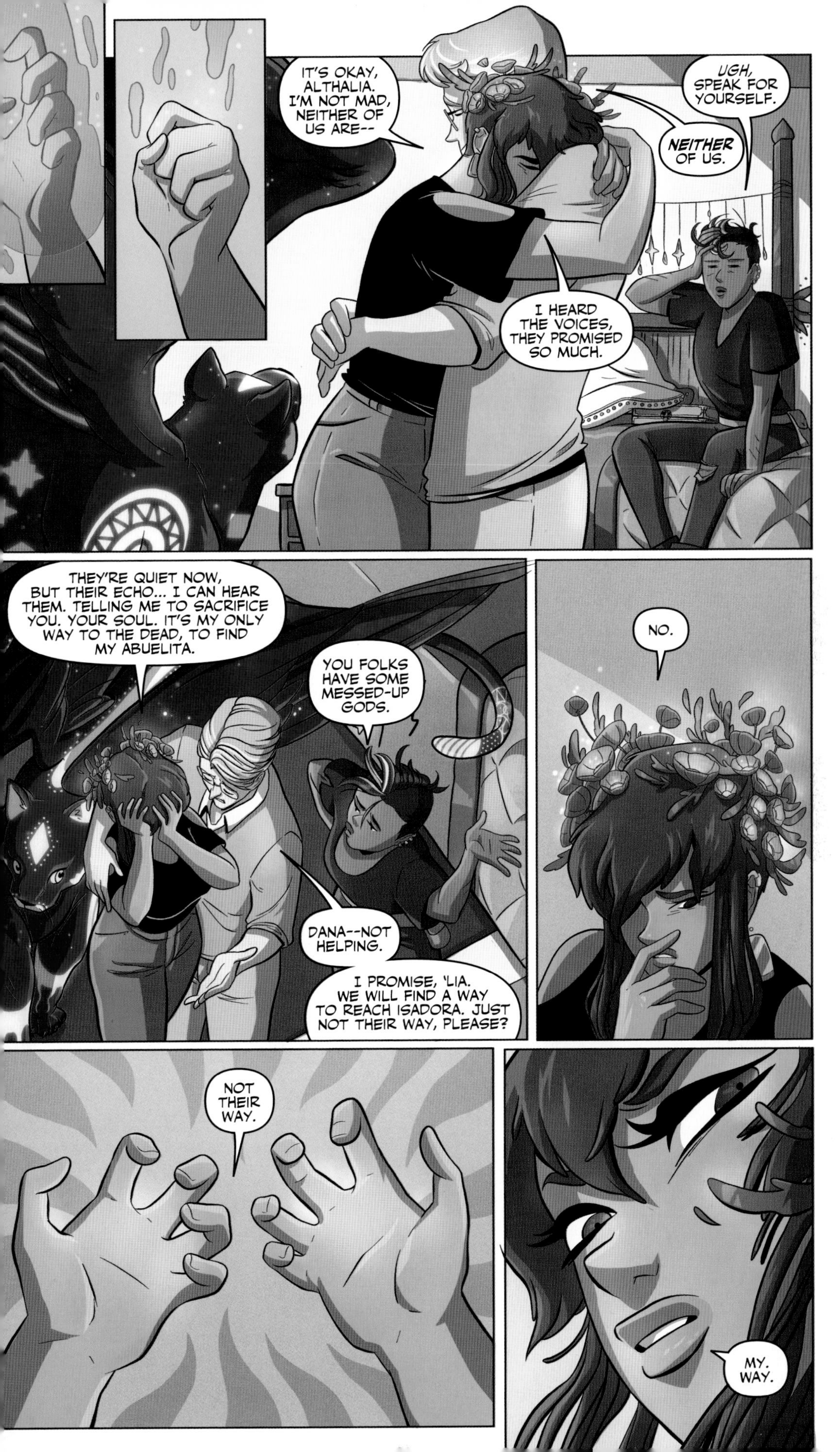
IT'S OKAY, ALTHALIA. I'M NOT MAD, NEITHER OF US ARE--
NEITHER OF US.
UGH, SPEAK FOR YOURSELF.
I HEARD THE VOICES, THEY PROMISED SO MUCH.
THEY'RE QUIET NOW, BUT THEIR ECHO... I CAN HEAR THEM. TELLING ME TO SACRIFICE YOU. YOUR SOUL. IT'S MY ONLY WAY TO THE DEAD, TO FIND MY ABUELITA.
YOU FOLKS HAVE SOME MESSED-UP GODS.
DANA--NOT HELPING.
I PROMISE, 'LIA. WE WILL FIND A WAY TO REACH ISADORA. JUST NOT THEIR WAY, PLEASE?
NO.
NOT THEIR WAY.
MY. WAY.

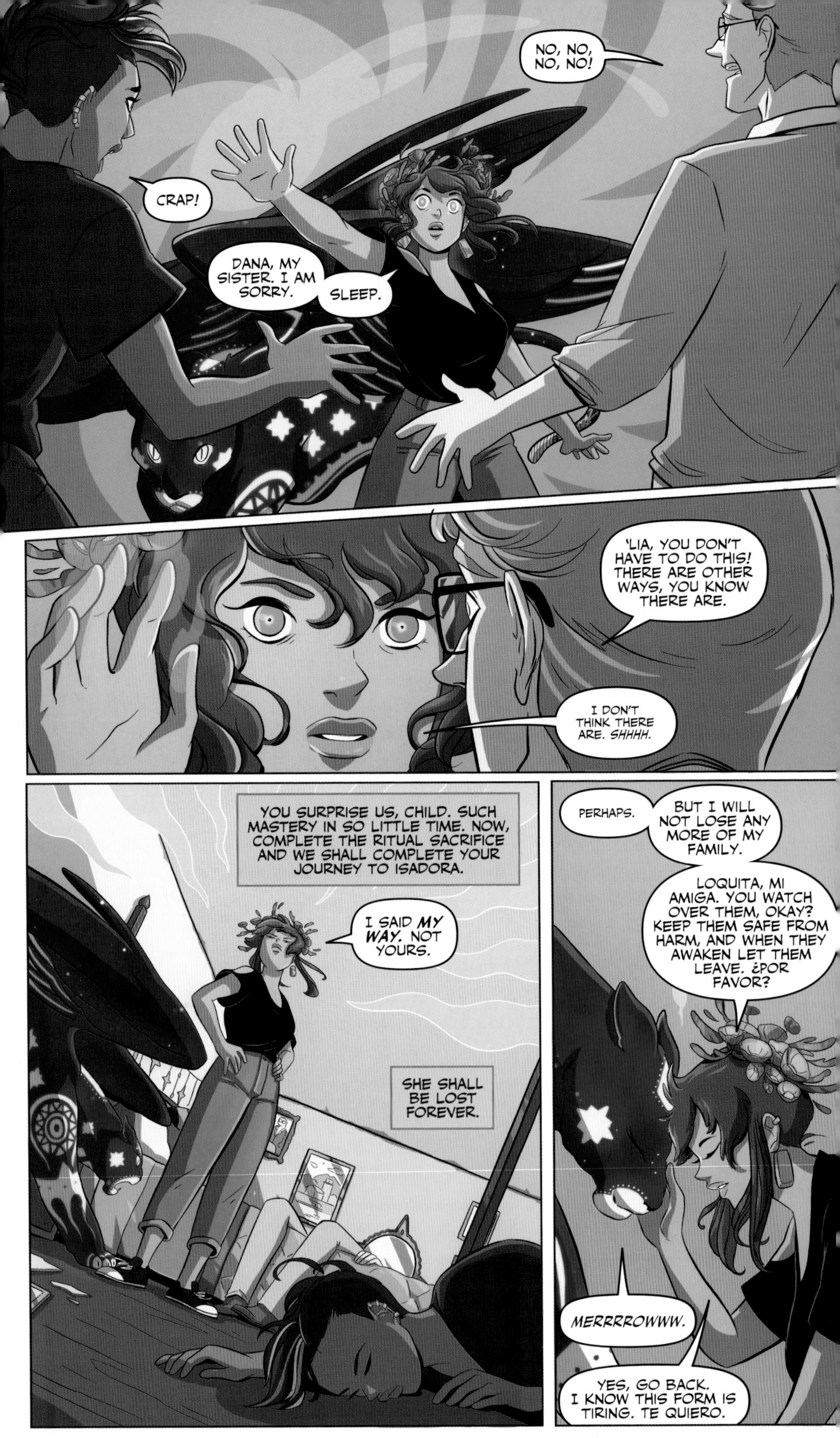
NO, NO, NO, NO!
CRAP!
DANA, MY SISTER. I AM SORRY.
SLEEP.
'LIA, YOU DON'T HAVE TO DO THIS! THERE ARE OTHER WAYS, YOU KNOW THERE ARE.
I DON'T THINK THERE ARE. *SHHHH.*
YOU SURPRISE US, CHILD. SUCH MASTERY IN SO LITTLE TIME. NOW, COMPLETE THE RITUAL SACRIFICE AND WE SHALL COMPLETE YOUR JOURNEY TO ISADORA.
I SAID ***MY WAY.*** NOT YOURS.
SHE SHALL BE LOST FOREVER.
PERHAPS.
BUT I WILL NOT LOSE ANY MORE OF MY FAMILY.
LOQUITA, MI AMIGA. YOU WATCH OVER THEM, OKAY? KEEP THEM SAFE FROM HARM, AND WHEN THEY AWAKEN LET THEM LEAVE. ¿POR FAVOR?
MERRRROWWW.
YES, GO BACK. I KNOW THIS FORM IS TIRING. TE QUIERO.

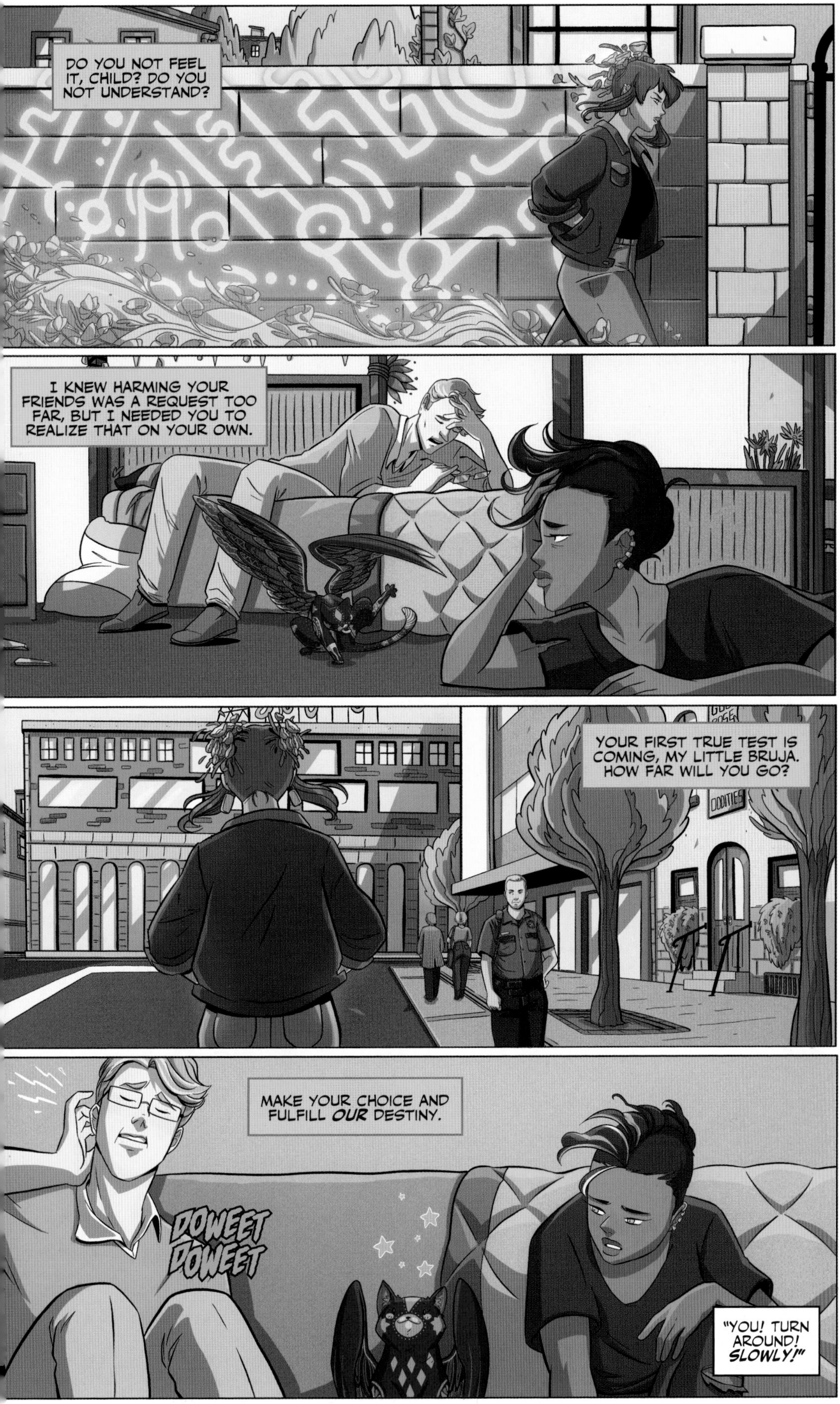
DO YOU NOT FEEL IT, CHILD? DO YOU NOT UNDERSTAND?
I KNEW HARMING YOUR FRIENDS WAS A REQUEST TOO FAR, BUT I NEEDED YOU TO REALIZE THAT ON YOUR OWN.
YOUR FIRST TRUE TEST IS COMING, MY LITTLE BRUJA. HOW FAR WILL YOU GO?
ODDITIES
MAKE YOUR CHOICE AND FULFILL *OUR* DESTINY.
DOWEET DOWEET
"YOU! TURN AROUND! ***SLOWLY!***"

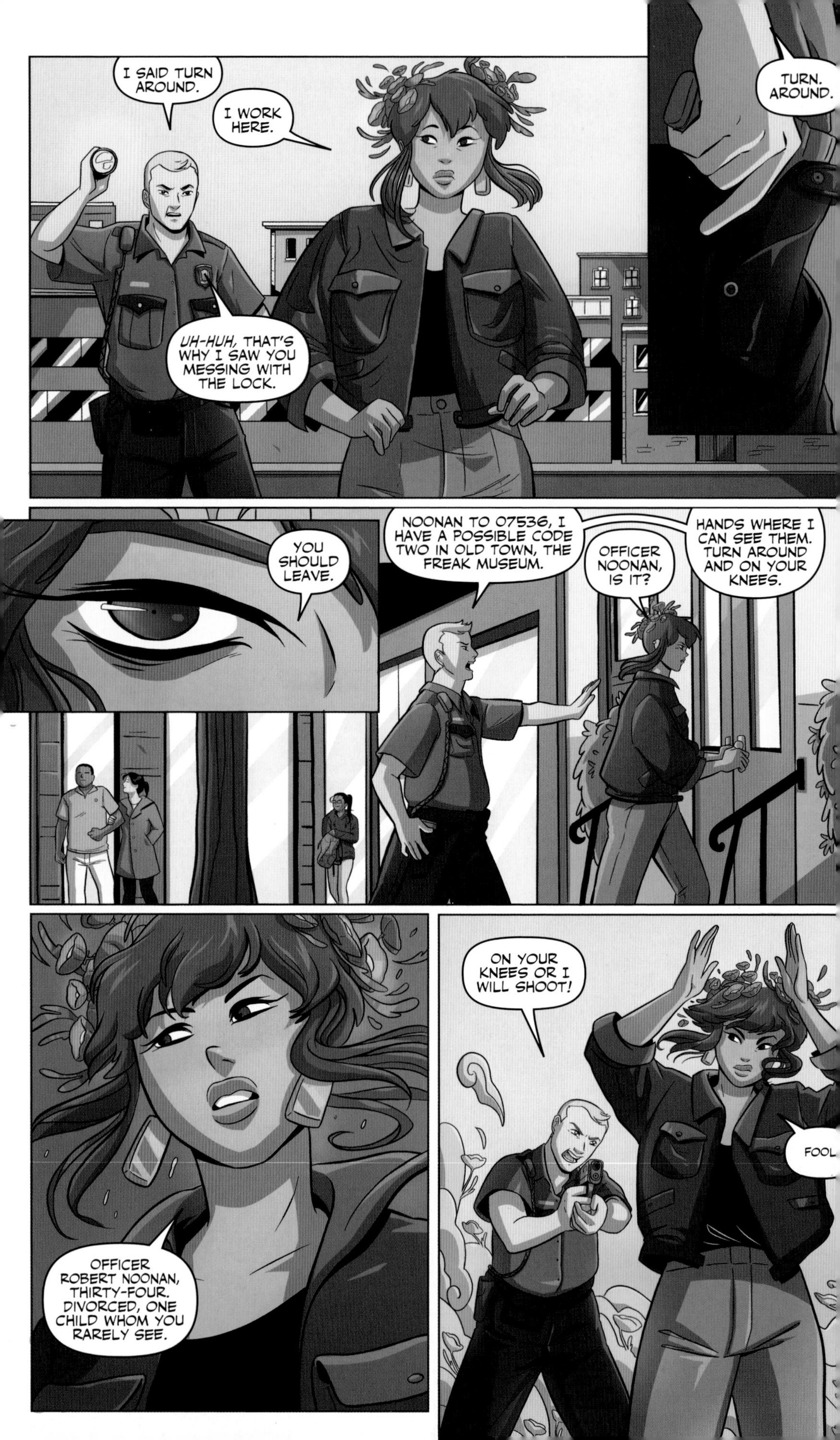
I SAID TURN AROUND.
I WORK HERE.
UH-HUH, THAT'S WHY I SAW YOU MESSING WITH THE LOCK.
TURN. AROUND.
YOU SHOULD LEAVE.
NOONAN TO 07536, I HAVE A POSSIBLE CODE TWO IN OLD TOWN, THE FREAK MUSEUM.
OFFICER NOONAN, IS IT?
HANDS WHERE I CAN SEE THEM. TURN AROUND AND ON YOUR KNEES.
OFFICER ROBERT NOONAN, THIRTY-FOUR. DIVORCED, ONE CHILD WHOM YOU RARELY SEE.
ON YOUR KNEES OR I WILL SHOOT!
FOOL

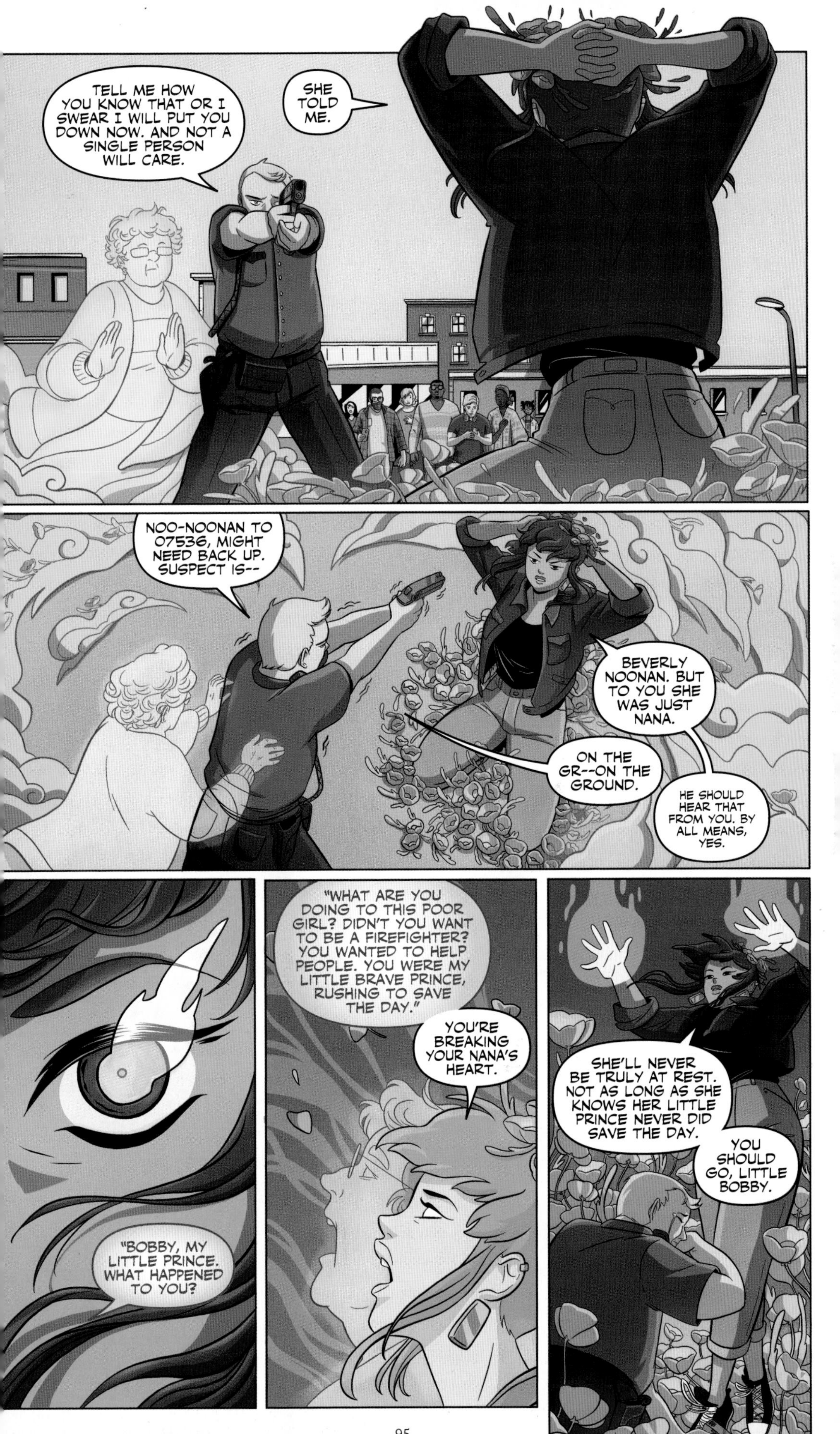
TELL ME HOW YOU KNOW THAT OR I SWEAR I WILL PUT YOU DOWN NOW. AND NOT A SINGLE PERSON WILL CARE.
SHE TOLD ME.
NOO-NOONAN TO 07536, MIGHT NEED BACK UP. SUSPECT IS--
BEVERLY NOONAN. BUT TO YOU SHE WAS JUST NANA.
ON THE GR--ON THE GROUND.
HE SHOULD HEAR THAT FROM YOU. BY ALL MEANS, YES.
"BOBBY, MY LITTLE PRINCE. WHAT HAPPENED TO YOU?
"WHAT ARE YOU DOING TO THIS POOR GIRL? DIDN'T YOU WANT TO BE A FIREFIGHTER? YOU WANTED TO HELP PEOPLE. YOU WERE MY LITTLE BRAVE PRINCE, RUSHING TO SAVE THE DAY."
YOU'RE BREAKING YOUR NANA'S HEART.
SHE'LL NEVER BE TRULY AT REST. NOT AS LONG AS SHE KNOWS HER LITTLE PRINCE NEVER DID SAVE THE DAY.
YOU SHOULD GO, LITTLE BOBBY.

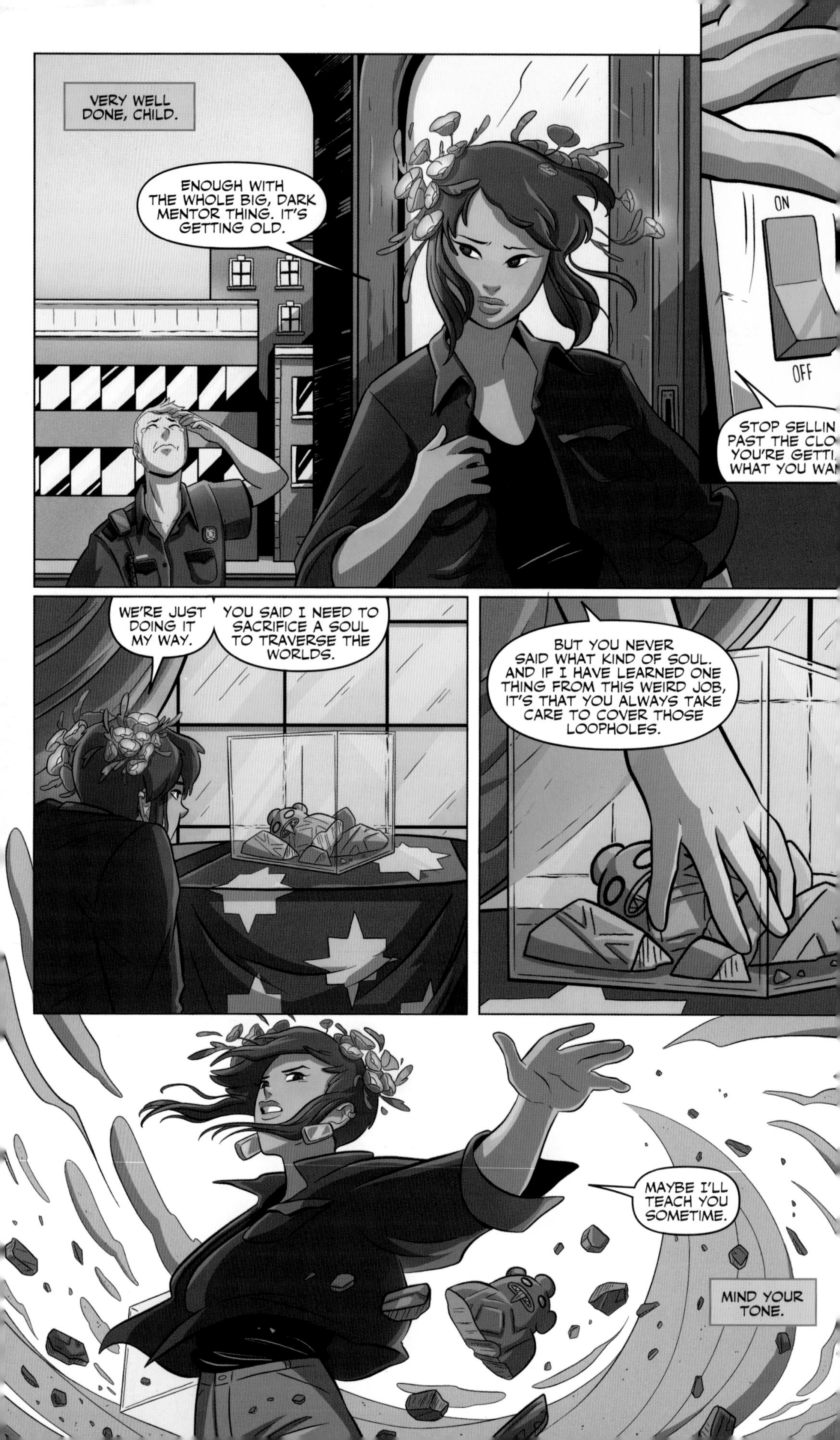
VERY WELL DONE, CHILD.
ENOUGH WITH THE WHOLE BIG, DARK MENTOR THING. IT'S GETTING OLD.
ON
OFF
STOP SELLIN PAST THE CLO YOU'RE GETTI WHAT YOU WA
WE'RE JUST DOING IT MY WAY.
YOU SAID I NEED TO SACRIFICE A SOUL TO TRAVERSE THE WORLDS.
BUT YOU NEVER SAID WHAT KIND OF SOUL. AND IF I HAVE LEARNED ONE THING FROM THIS WEIRD JOB, IT'S THAT YOU ALWAYS TAKE CARE TO COVER THOSE LOOPHOLES.
MAYBE I'LL TEACH YOU SOMETIME.
MIND YOUR TONE.

SURE, SURE.

NOW, IF YOU DON'T MIND, THIS PART CAN BE A LITTLE TRICKY, AND SINCE I AM ALREADY BREAKING MY DEAL WITH THIS GUY BY SUMMONING HIM, HE'S GONNA BE ON THE ANGRY SIDE, WHICH IS NEVER ANY FUN.

WELL, RIGHT THEN. IT'S BREACH A DIABOLIC CONTRACT, SHALL WE?

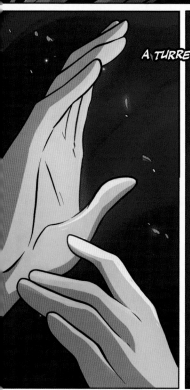

A TURRE CUSTODUM USQUE--

--TE APPELLO--

--TENETUR A ME SERMO--

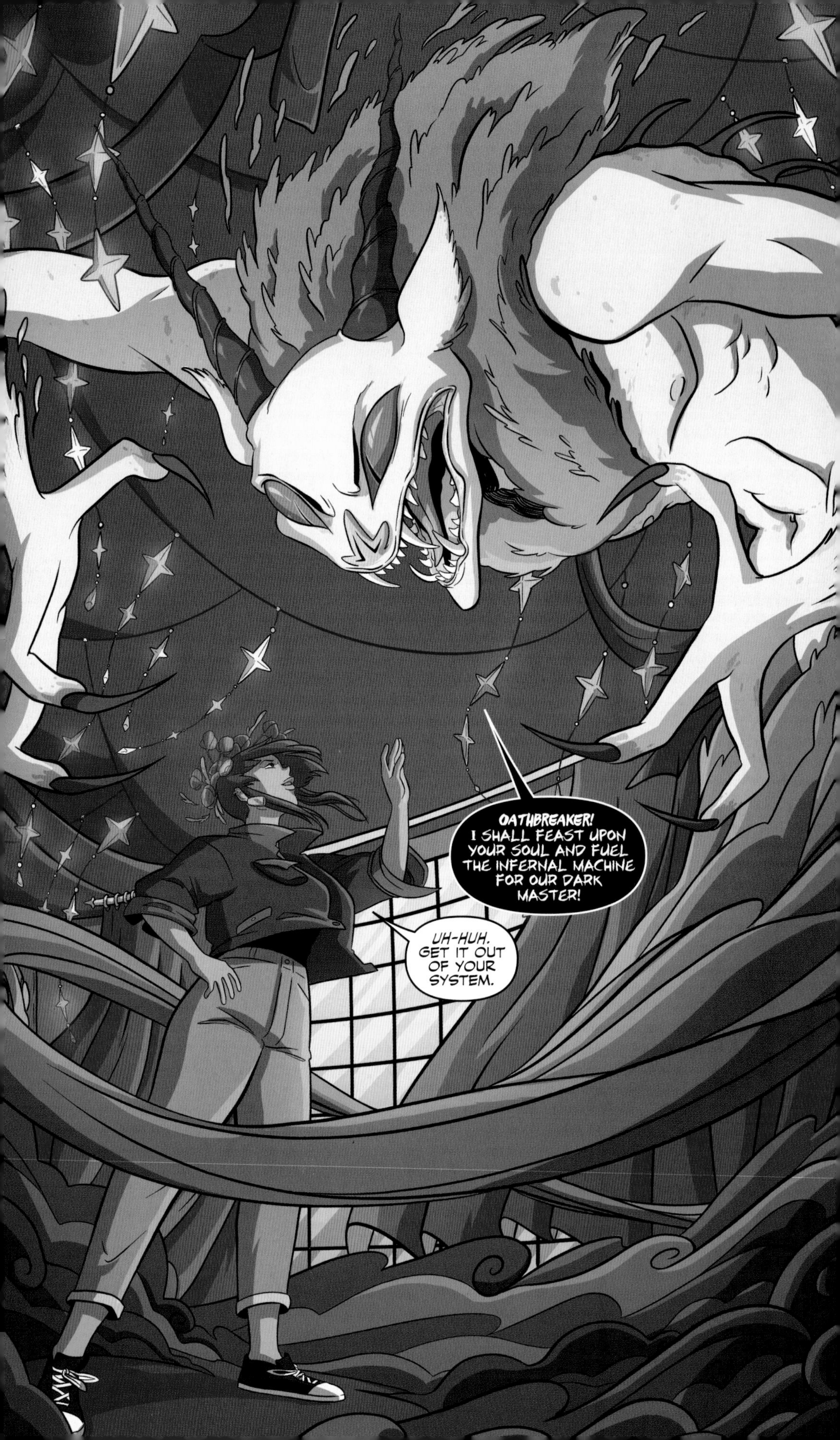
OATHBREAKER! I SHALL FEAST UPON YOUR SOUL AND FUEL THE INFERNAL MACHINE FOR OUR DARK MASTER!
UH-HUH. GET IT OUT OF YOUR SYSTEM.

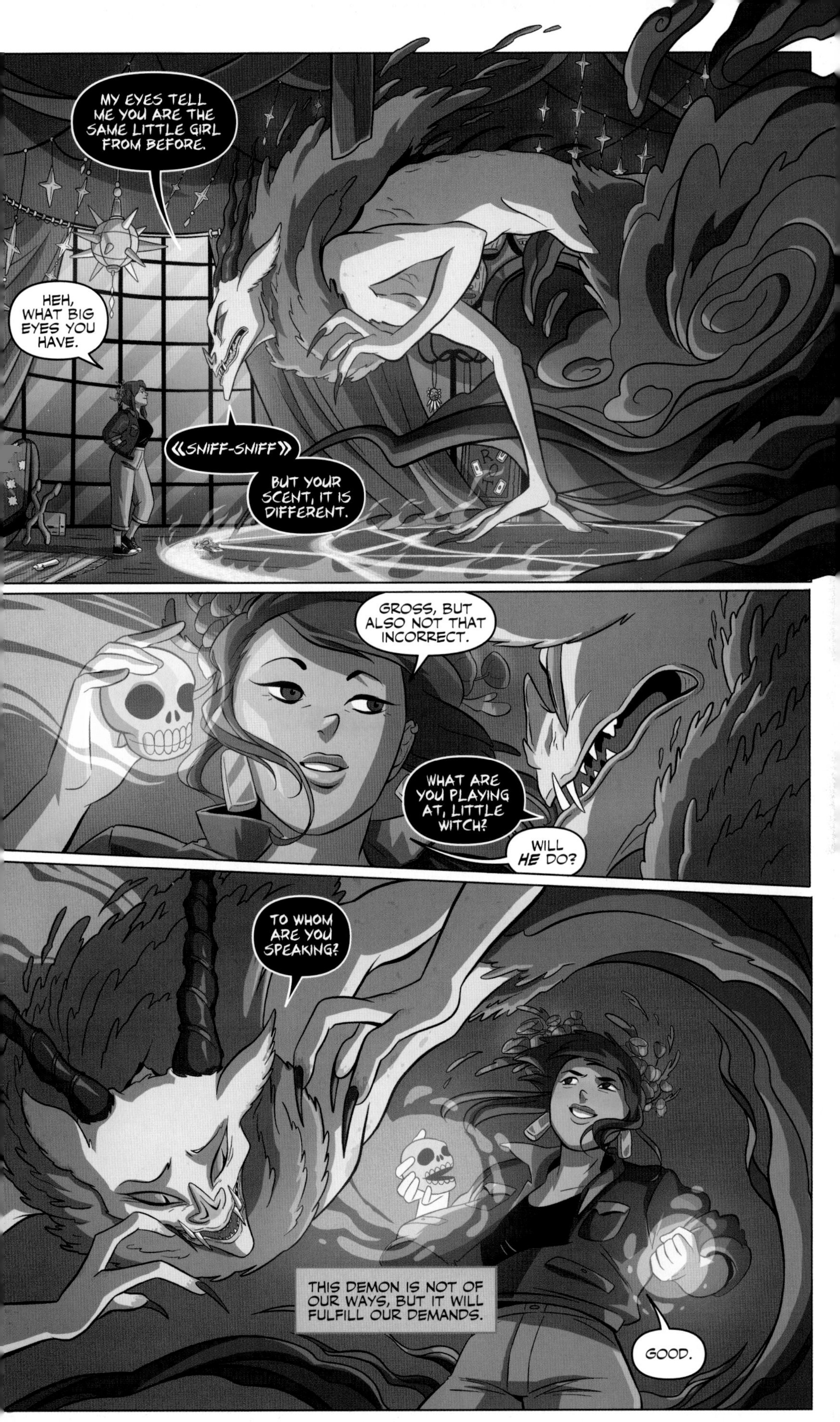
MY EYES TELL ME YOU ARE THE SAME LITTLE GIRL FROM BEFORE.
HEH, WHAT BIG EYES YOU HAVE.
«SNIFF-SNIFF»
BUT YOUR SCENT, IT IS DIFFERENT.
GROSS, BUT ALSO NOT THAT INCORRECT.
WHAT ARE YOU PLAYING AT, LITTLE WITCH?
WILL *HE* DO?
TO WHOM ARE YOU SPEAKING?
THIS DEMON IS NOT OF OUR WAYS, BUT IT WILL FULFILL OUR DEMANDS.
GOOD.

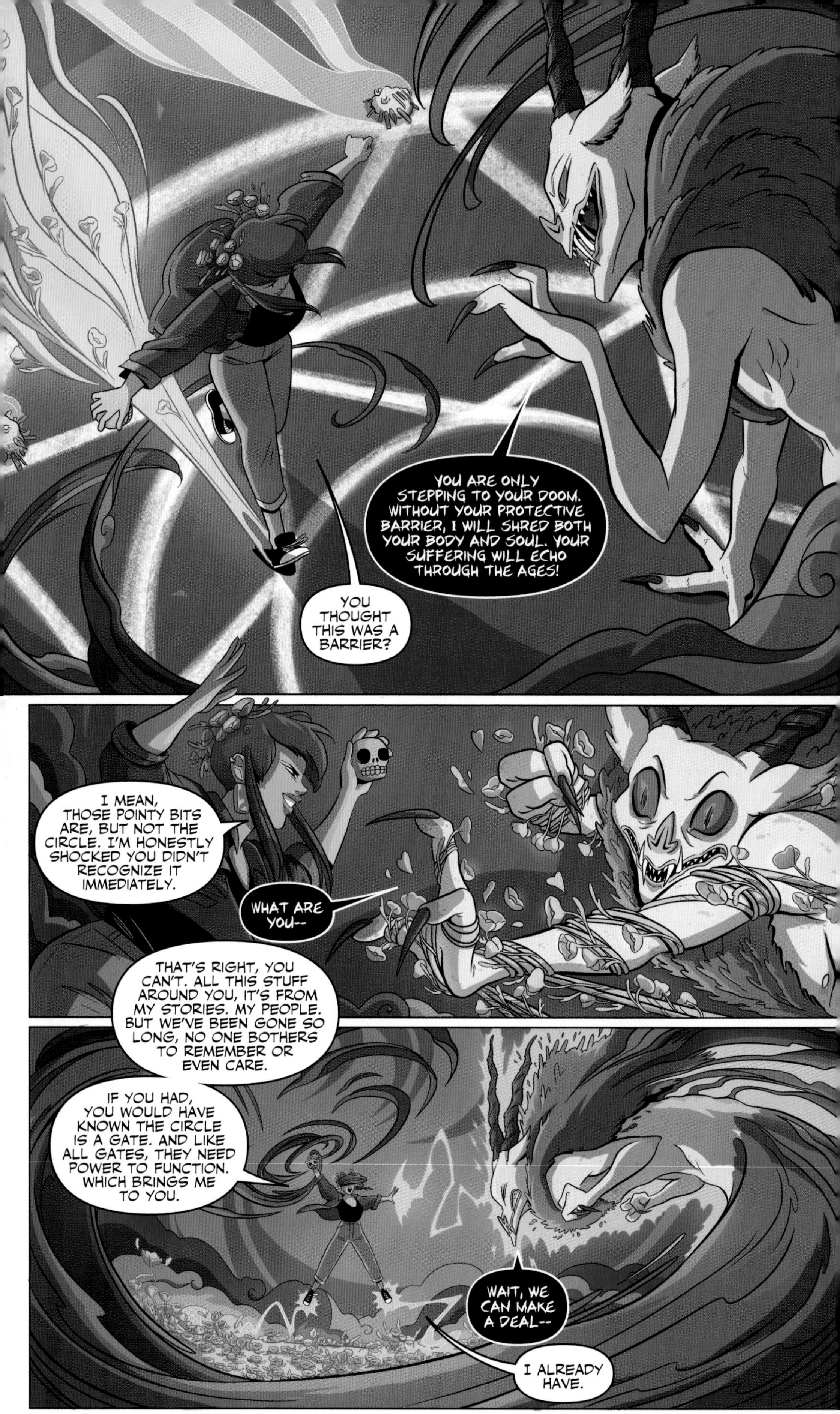
YOU ARE ONLY STEPPING TO YOUR DOOM. WITHOUT YOUR PROTECTIVE BARRIER, I WILL SHRED BOTH YOUR BODY AND SOUL. YOUR SUFFERING WILL ECHO THROUGH THE AGES!
YOU THOUGHT THIS WAS A BARRIER?
I MEAN, THOSE POINTY BITS ARE, BUT NOT THE CIRCLE. I'M HONESTLY SHOCKED YOU DIDN'T RECOGNIZE IT IMMEDIATELY.
WHAT ARE YOU--
THAT'S RIGHT, YOU CAN'T. ALL THIS STUFF AROUND YOU, IT'S FROM MY STORIES. MY PEOPLE. BUT WE'VE BEEN GONE SO LONG, NO ONE BOTHERS TO REMEMBER OR EVEN CARE.
IF YOU HAD, YOU WOULD HAVE KNOWN THE CIRCLE IS A GATE. AND LIKE ALL GATES, THEY NEED POWER TO FUNCTION. WHICH BRINGS ME TO YOU.
WAIT, WE CAN MAKE A DEAL--
I ALREADY HAVE.

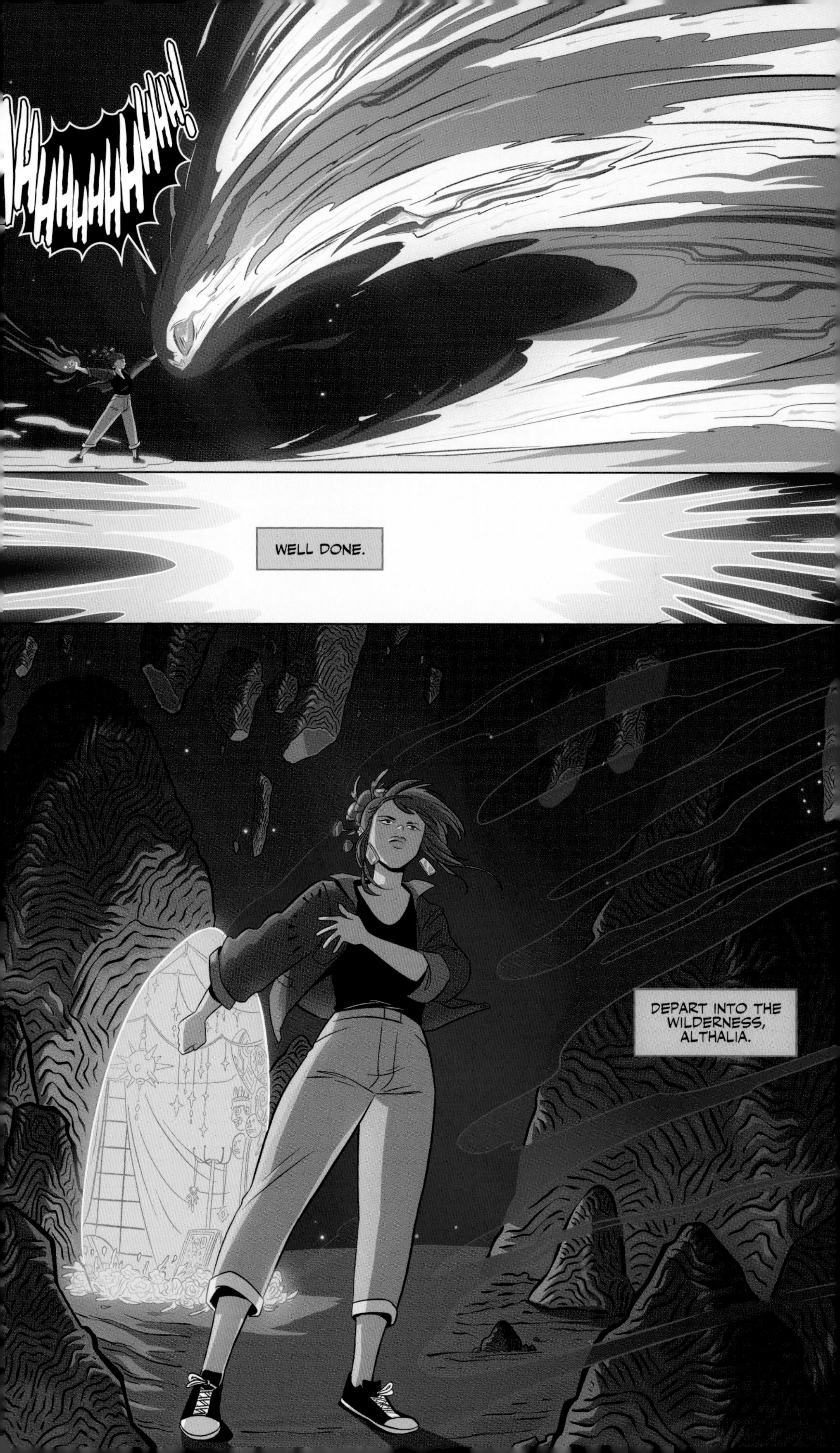
AHHHHHHHHH!
WELL DONE.
DEPART INTO THE WILDERNESS, ALTHALIA.

CHAPTER 5

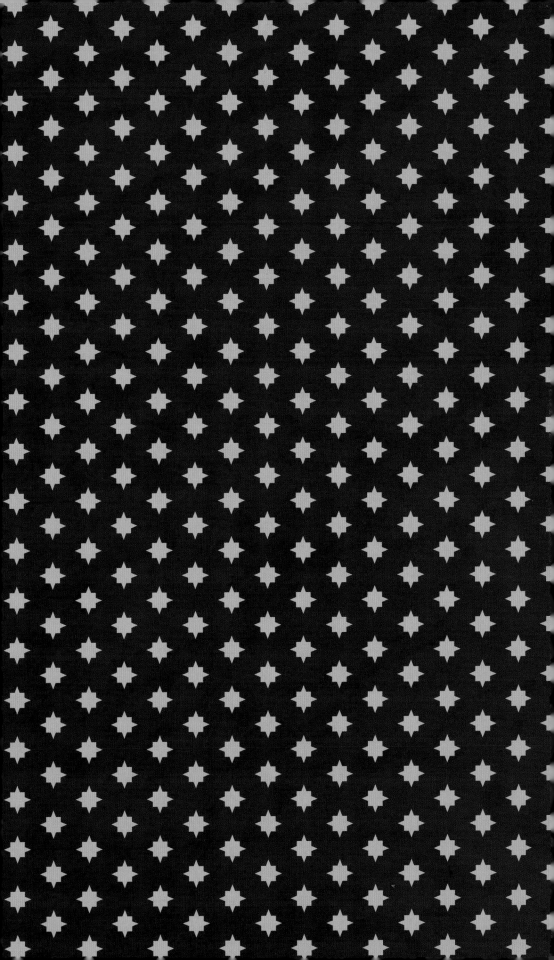

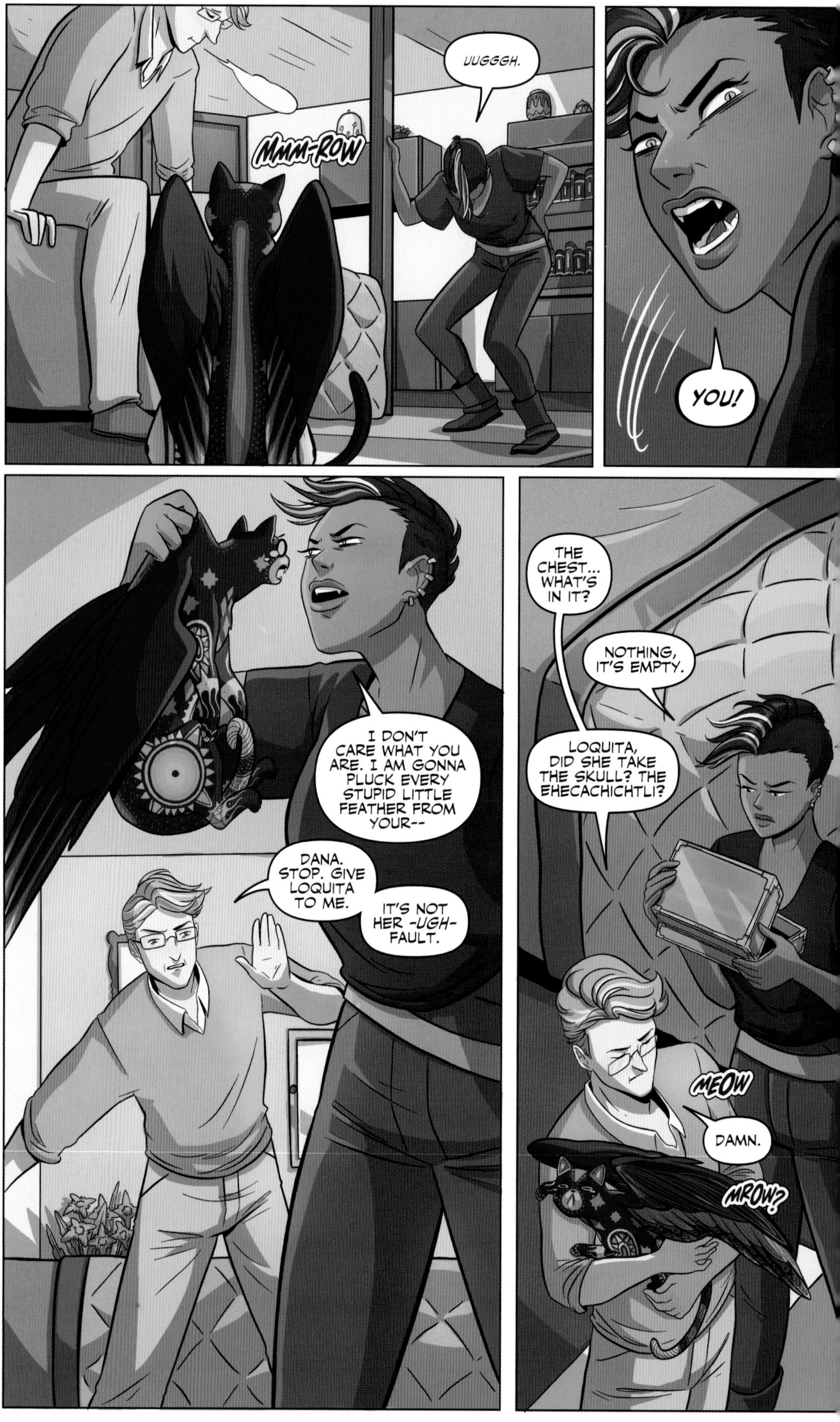
UUGGGH.
MMM-ROW
YOU!
I DON'T CARE WHAT YOU ARE. I AM GONNA PLUCK EVERY STUPID LITTLE FEATHER FROM YOUR--
DANA. STOP. GIVE LOQUITA TO ME.
IT'S NOT HER -UGH- FAULT.
THE CHEST... WHAT'S IN IT?
NOTHING, IT'S EMPTY.
LOQUITA, DID SHE TAKE THE SKULL? THE EHECACHICHTLI?
MEOW
DAMN.
MROW?

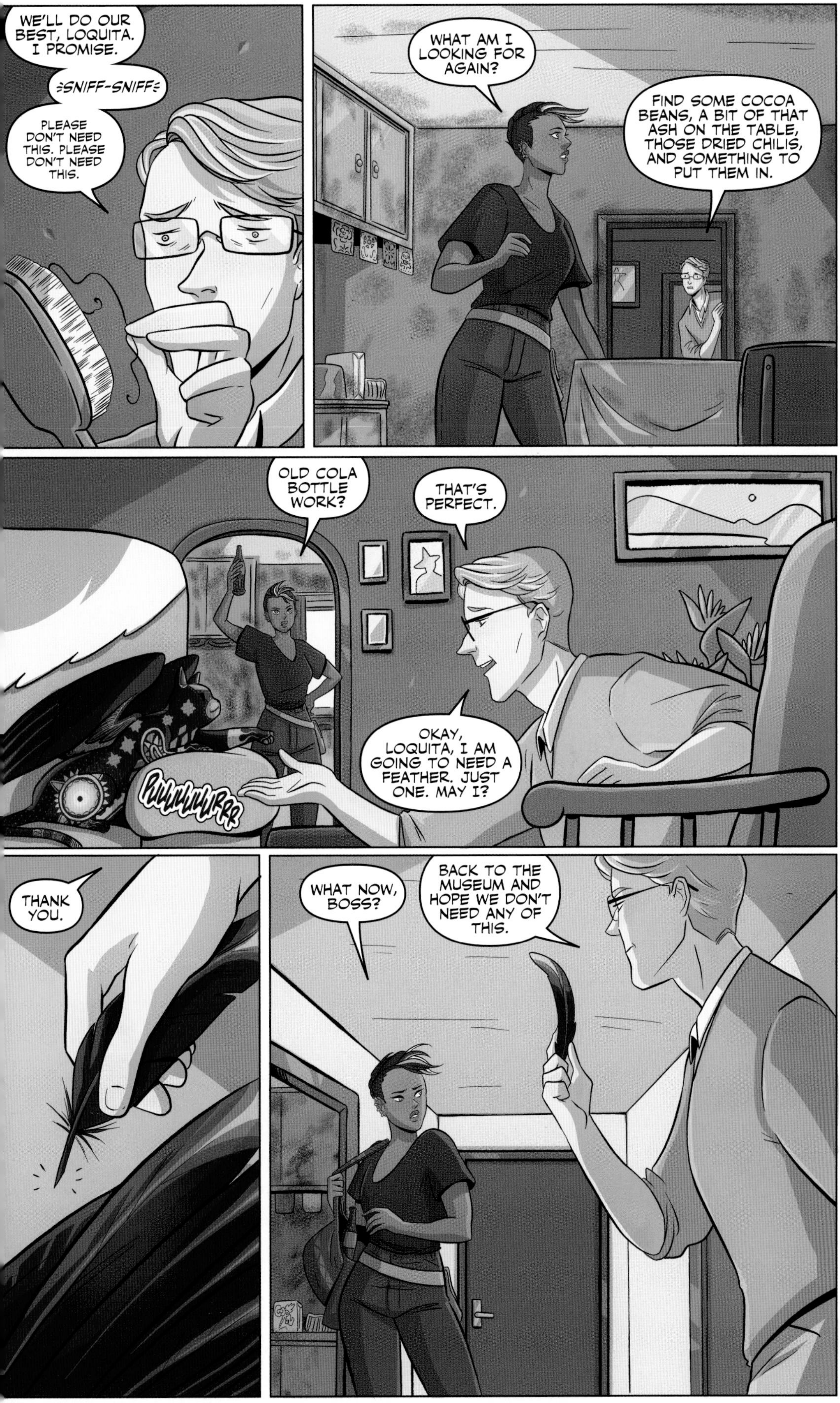
WE'LL DO OUR BEST, LOQUITA. I PROMISE.
SNIFF-SNIFF
PLEASE DON'T NEED THIS. PLEASE DON'T NEED THIS.
WHAT AM I LOOKING FOR AGAIN?
FIND SOME COCOA BEANS, A BIT OF THAT ASH ON THE TABLE, THOSE DRIED CHILIS, AND SOMETHING TO PUT THEM IN.
OLD COLA BOTTLE WORK?
THAT'S PERFECT.
OKAY, LOQUITA, I AM GOING TO NEED A FEATHER. JUST ONE. MAY I?
PUUUUUURRR
THANK YOU.
WHAT NOW, BOSS?
BACK TO THE MUSEUM AND HOPE WE DON'T NEED ANY OF THIS.

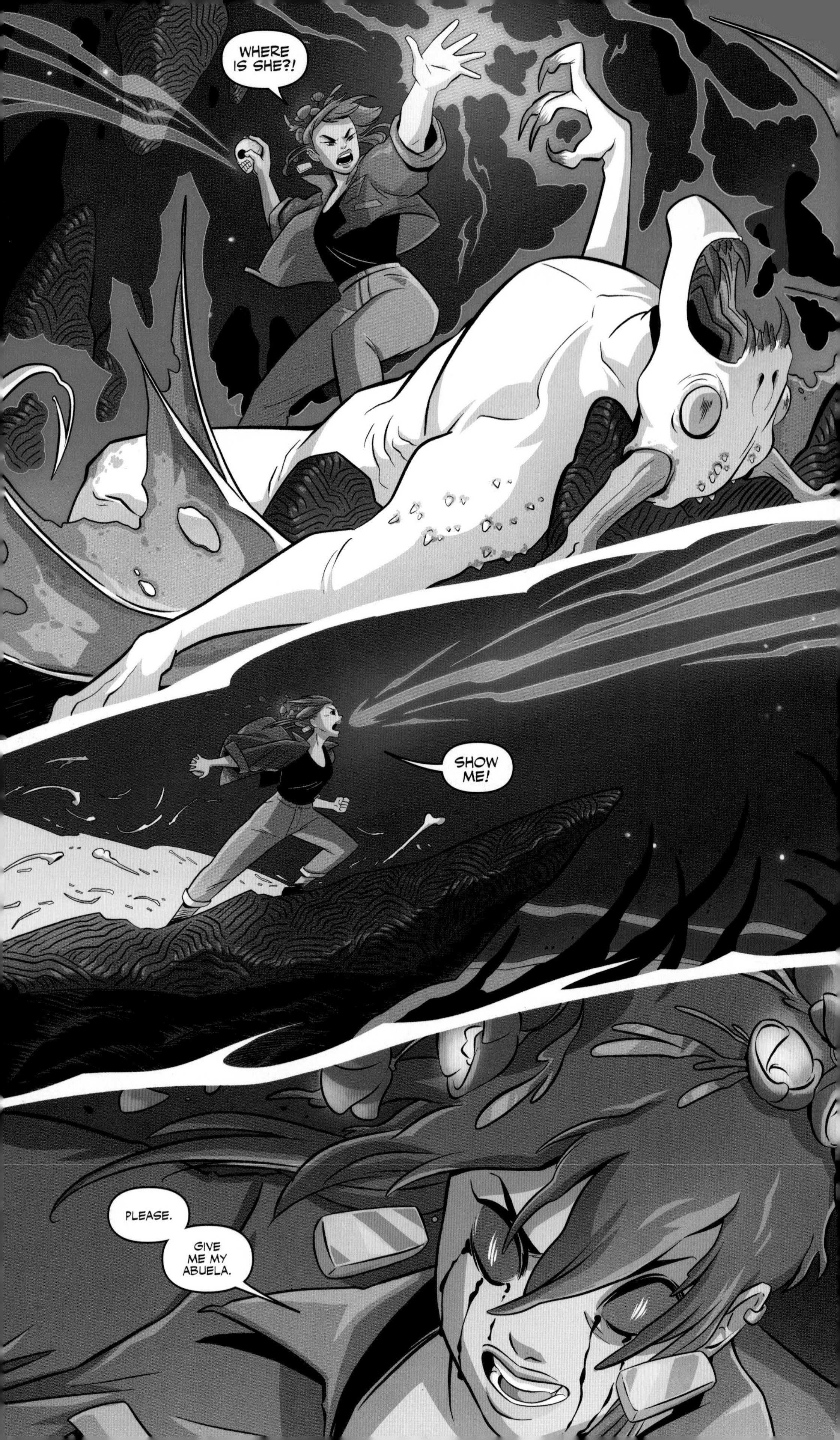
WHERE IS SHE?!
SHOW ME!
PLEASE.
GIVE ME MY ABUELA.

UGH!

THE PRIDE IT TOOK FOR YOU TO EVEN ATTEMPT SUCH AN INCURSION INTO THE MASTER'S DOMAIN.

I AM ALMOST SORRY I NEED TO END YOUR EXISTENCE.

PUH-PLEASE. I JUST NEED HER BACK.

Y-Y-YOU--

YES, MY CHILD.

≈GULP≈ YOU SHOULDN'T HAVE TOUCHED ME...

"LORD MURMUR."

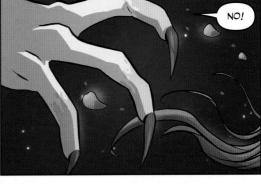

NO!

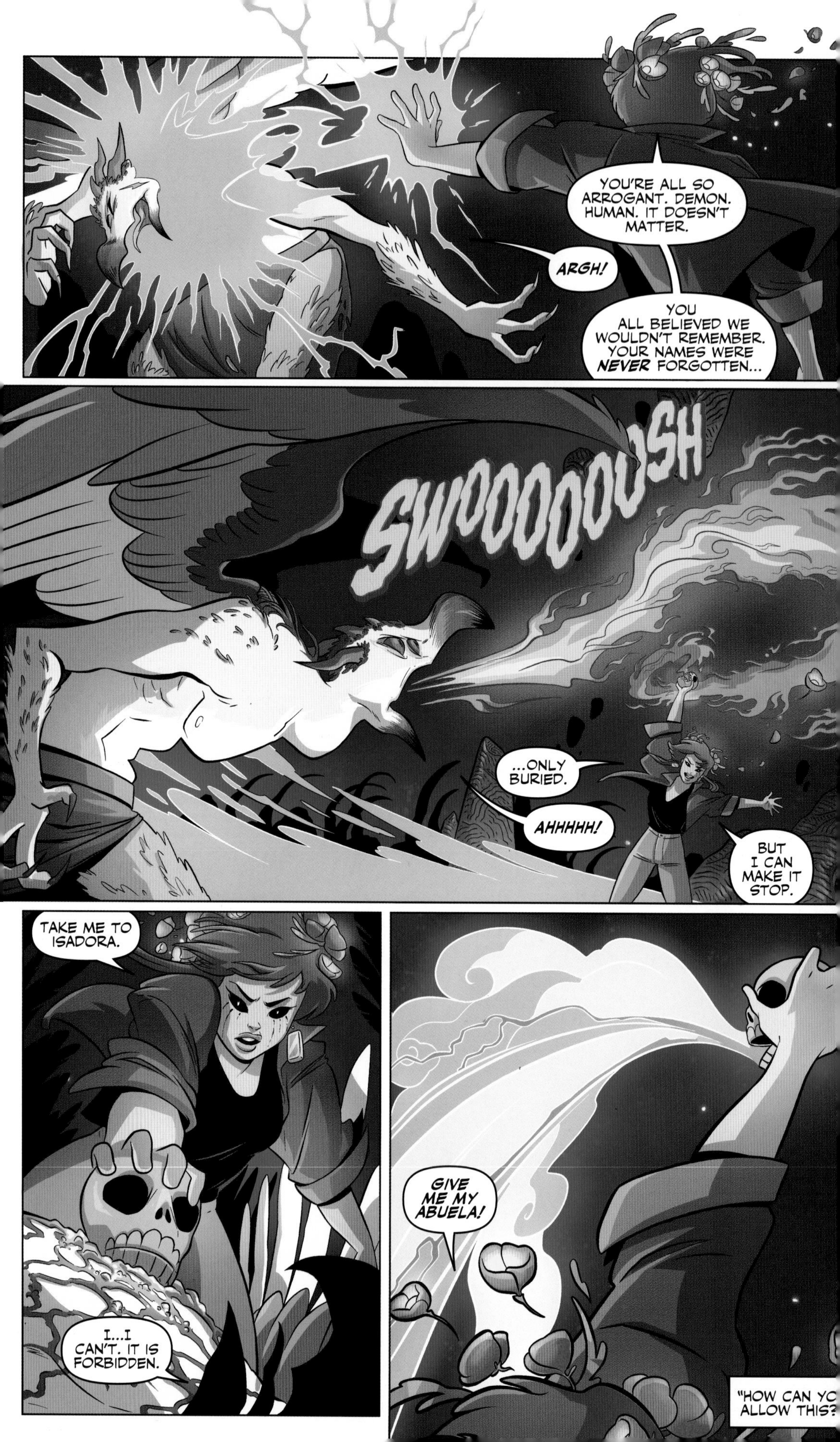
YOU'RE ALL SO ARROGANT. DEMON. HUMAN. IT DOESN'T MATTER.
ARGH!
YOU ALL BELIEVED WE WOULDN'T REMEMBER. YOUR NAMES WERE NEVER FORGOTTEN...
SWOOOOOOSH
...ONLY BURIED.
AHHHHH!
BUT I CAN MAKE IT STOP.
TAKE ME TO ISADORA.
I...I CAN'T. IT IS FORBIDDEN.
GIVE ME MY ABUELA!
"HOW CAN YO
ALLOW THIS?

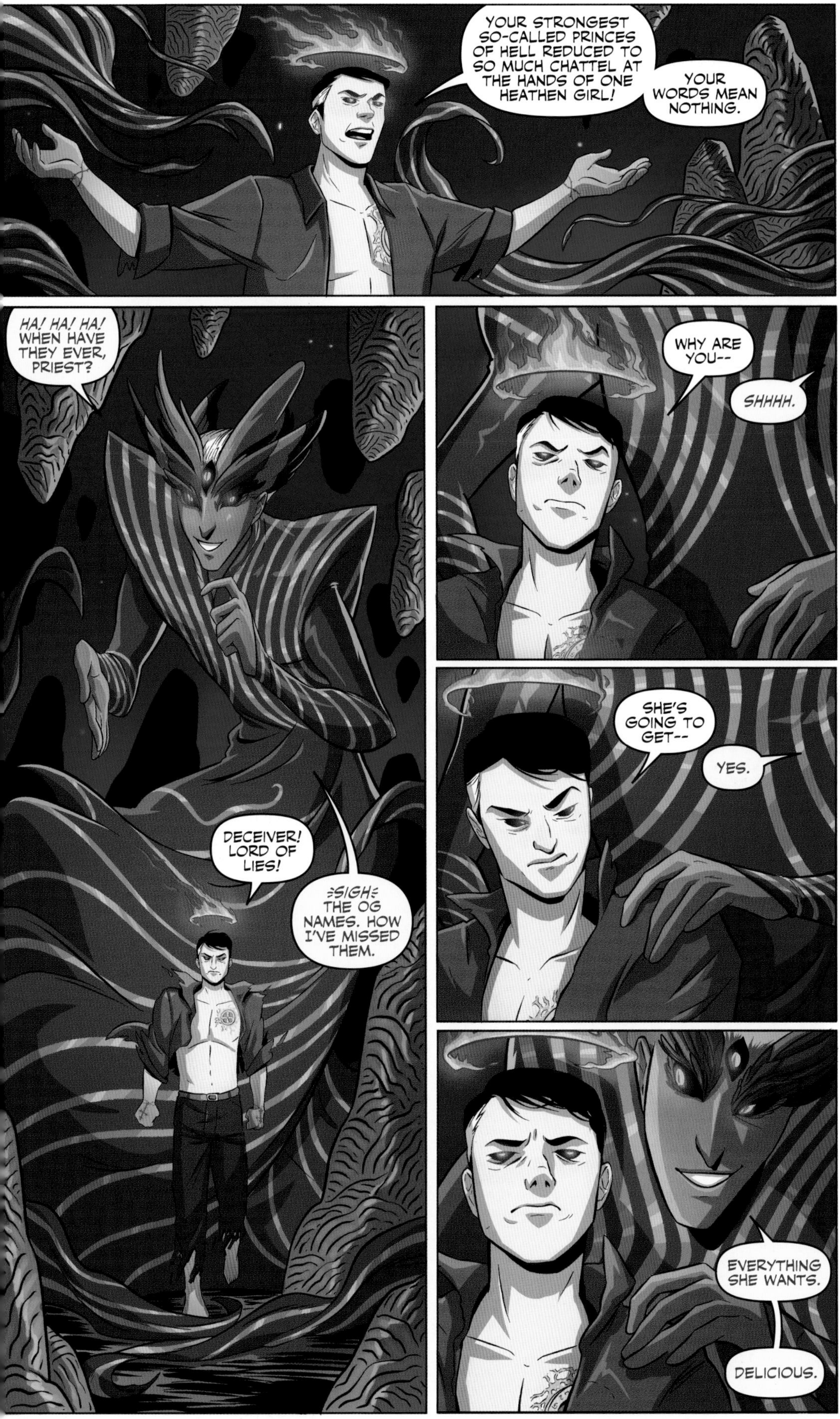
YOUR STRONGEST SO-CALLED PRINCES OF HELL REDUCED TO SO MUCH CHATTEL AT THE HANDS OF ONE HEATHEN GIRL!
YOUR WORDS MEAN NOTHING.
HA! HA! HA! WHEN HAVE THEY EVER, PRIEST?
DECEIVER! LORD OF LIES!
SIGH THE OG NAMES. HOW I'VE MISSED THEM.
WHY ARE YOU--
SHHHH.
SHE'S GOING TO GET--
YES.
EVERYTHING SHE WANTS.
DELICIOUS.

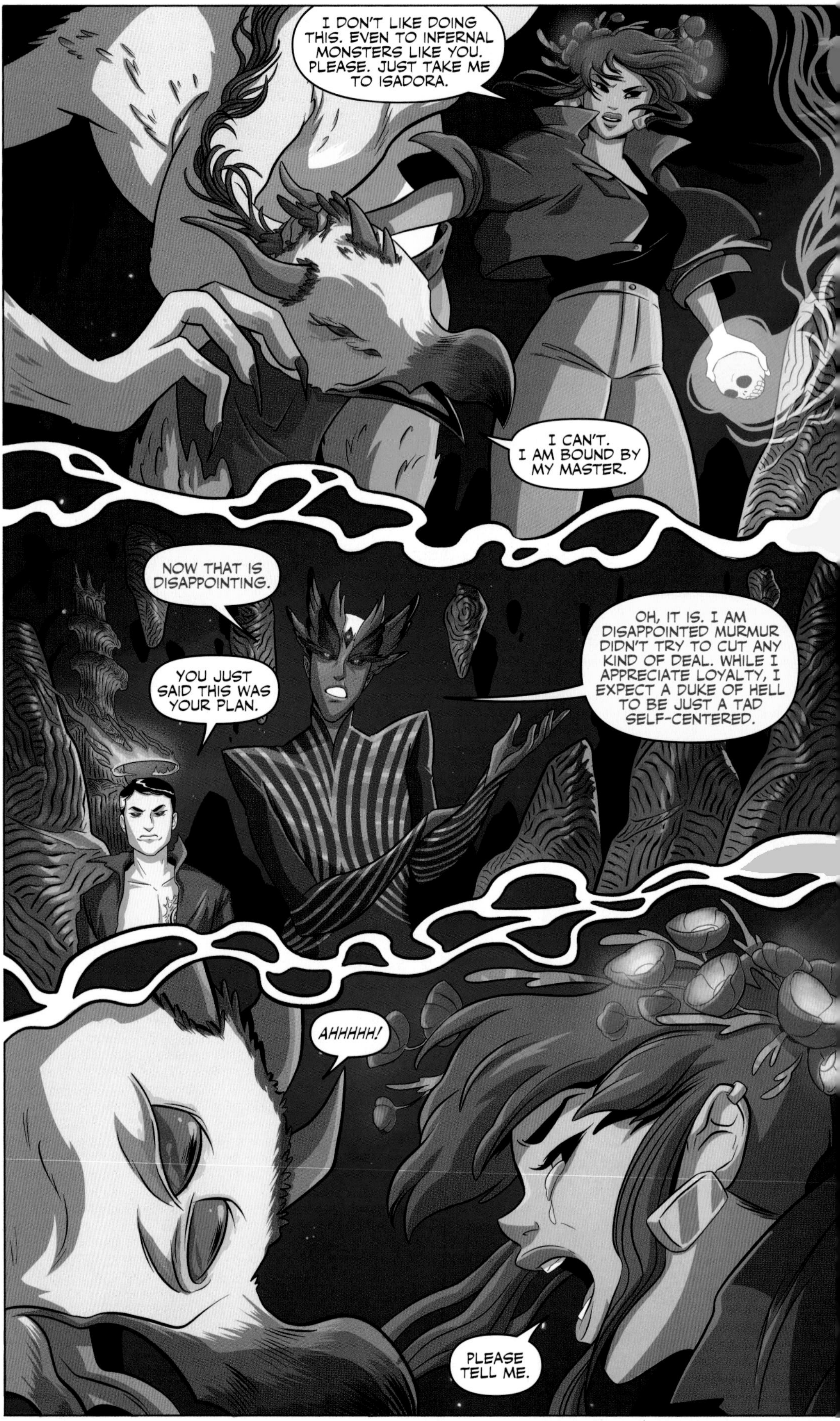

I DON'T LIKE DOING THIS. EVEN TO INFERNAL MONSTERS LIKE YOU. PLEASE. JUST TAKE ME TO ISADORA.
I CAN'T. I AM BOUND BY MY MASTER.
NOW THAT IS DISAPPOINTING.
YOU JUST SAID THIS WAS YOUR PLAN.
OH, IT IS. I AM DISAPPOINTED MURMUR DIDN'T TRY TO CUT ANY KIND OF DEAL. WHILE I APPRECIATE LOYALTY, I EXPECT A DUKE OF HELL TO BE JUST A TAD SELF-CENTERED.
AHHHHH!
PLEASE TELL ME.

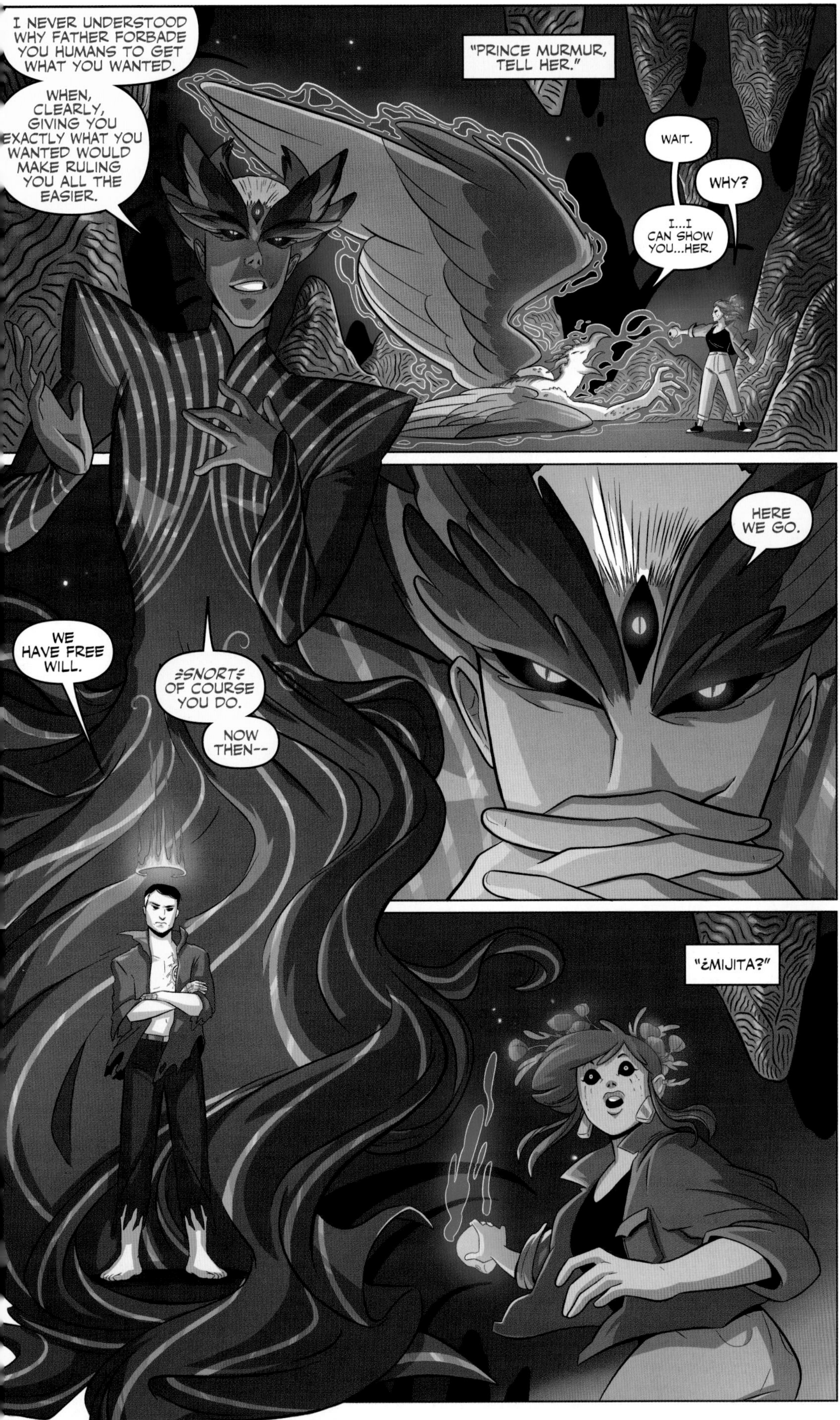

I NEVER UNDERSTOOD WHY FATHER FORBADE YOU HUMANS TO GET WHAT YOU WANTED.
WHEN, CLEARLY, GIVING YOU EXACTLY WHAT YOU WANTED WOULD MAKE RULING YOU ALL THE EASIER.
"PRINCE MURMUR, TELL HER."
WAIT.
WHY?
I...I CAN SHOW YOU...HER.
HERE WE GO.
WE HAVE FREE WILL.
≠SNORT≠ OF COURSE YOU DO.
NOW THEN--
"¿MIJITA?"

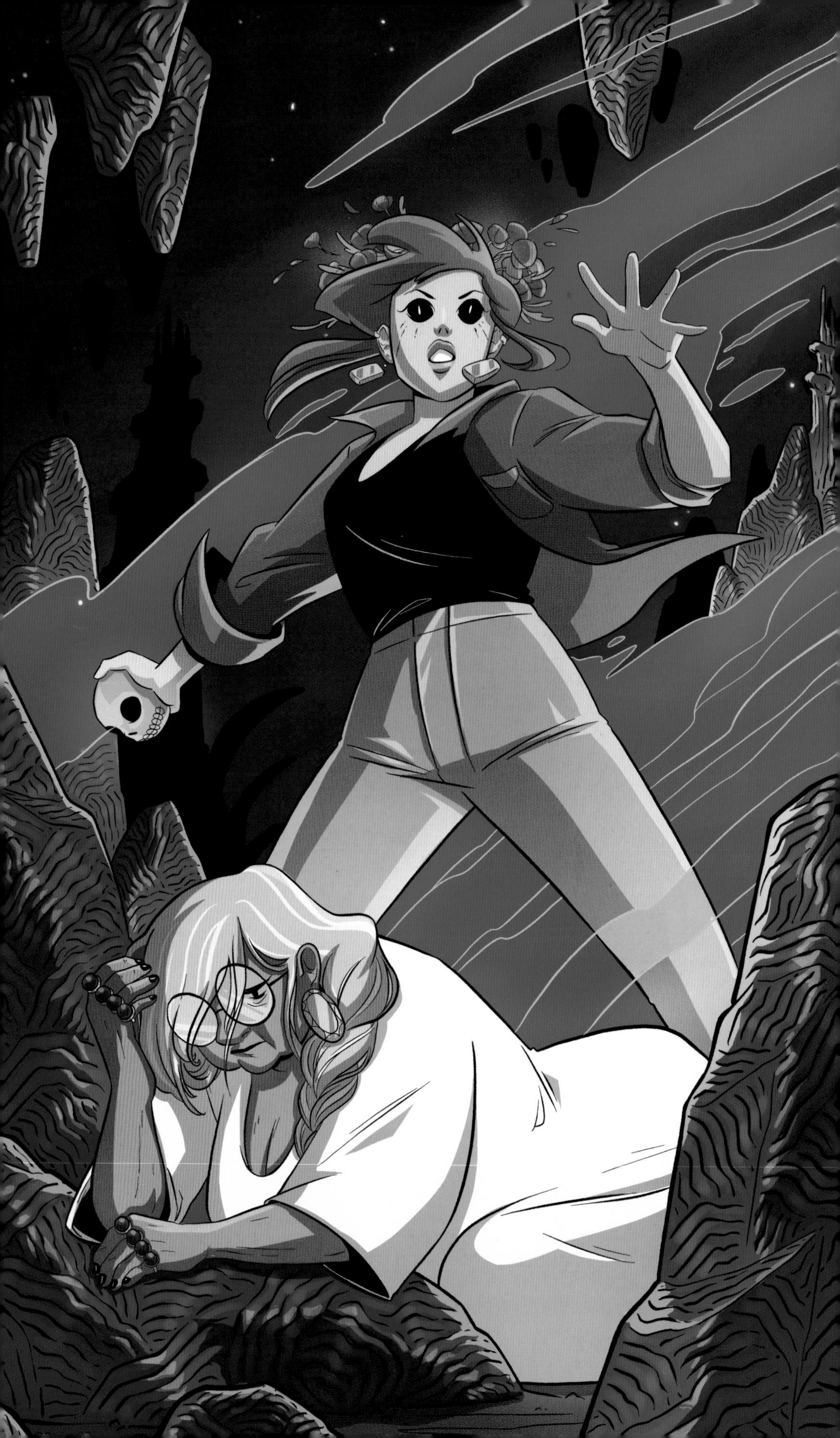

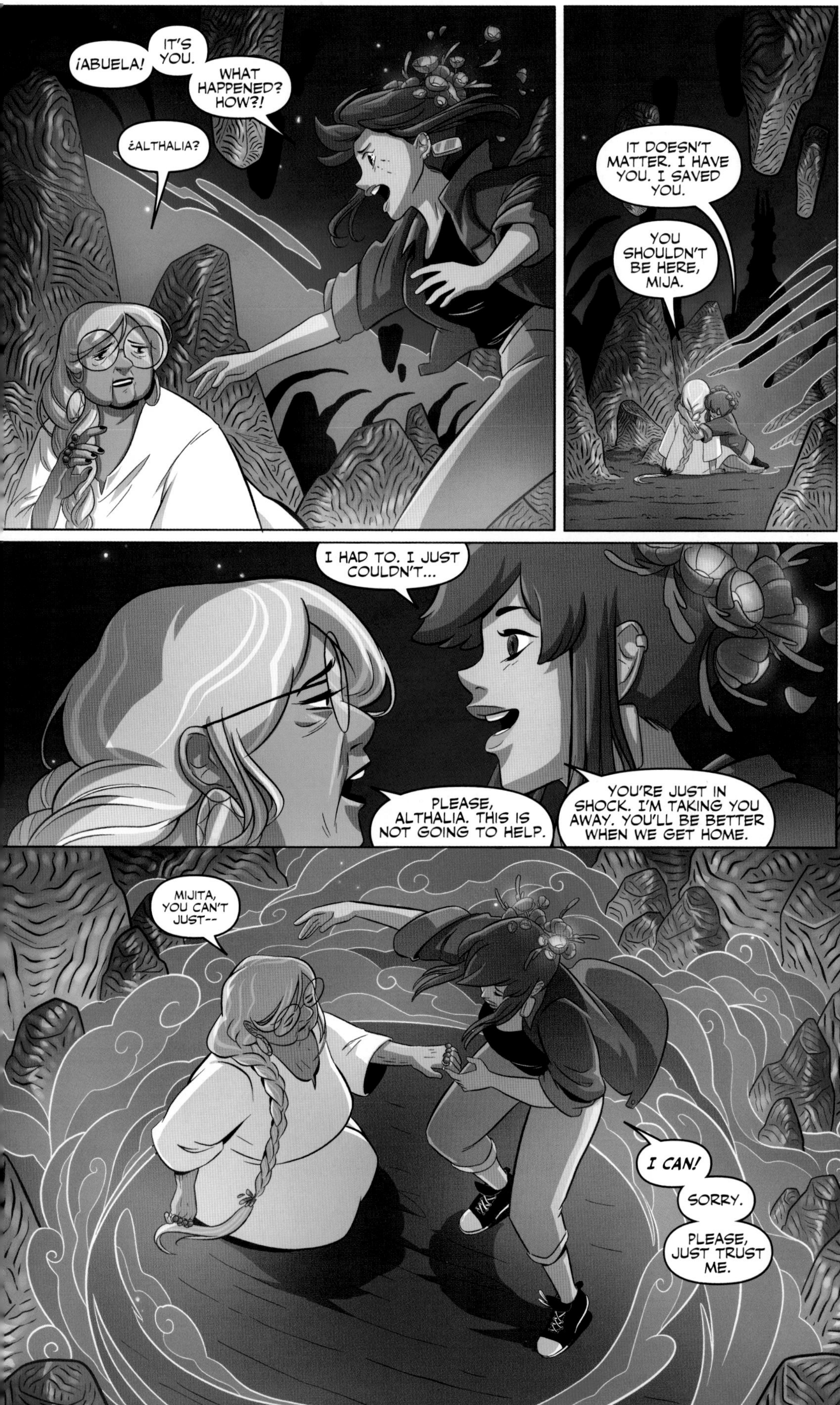
¡ABUELA!
IT'S YOU.
WHAT HAPPENED? HOW?!
¿ALTHALIA?
IT DOESN'T MATTER. I HAVE YOU. I SAVED YOU.
YOU SHOULDN'T BE HERE, MIJA.
I HAD TO. I JUST COULDN'T...
PLEASE, ALTHALIA. THIS IS NOT GOING TO HELP.
YOU'RE JUST IN SHOCK. I'M TAKING YOU AWAY. YOU'LL BE BETTER WHEN WE GET HOME.
MIJITA, YOU CAN'T JUST--
I CAN!
SORRY.
PLEASE, JUST TRUST ME.

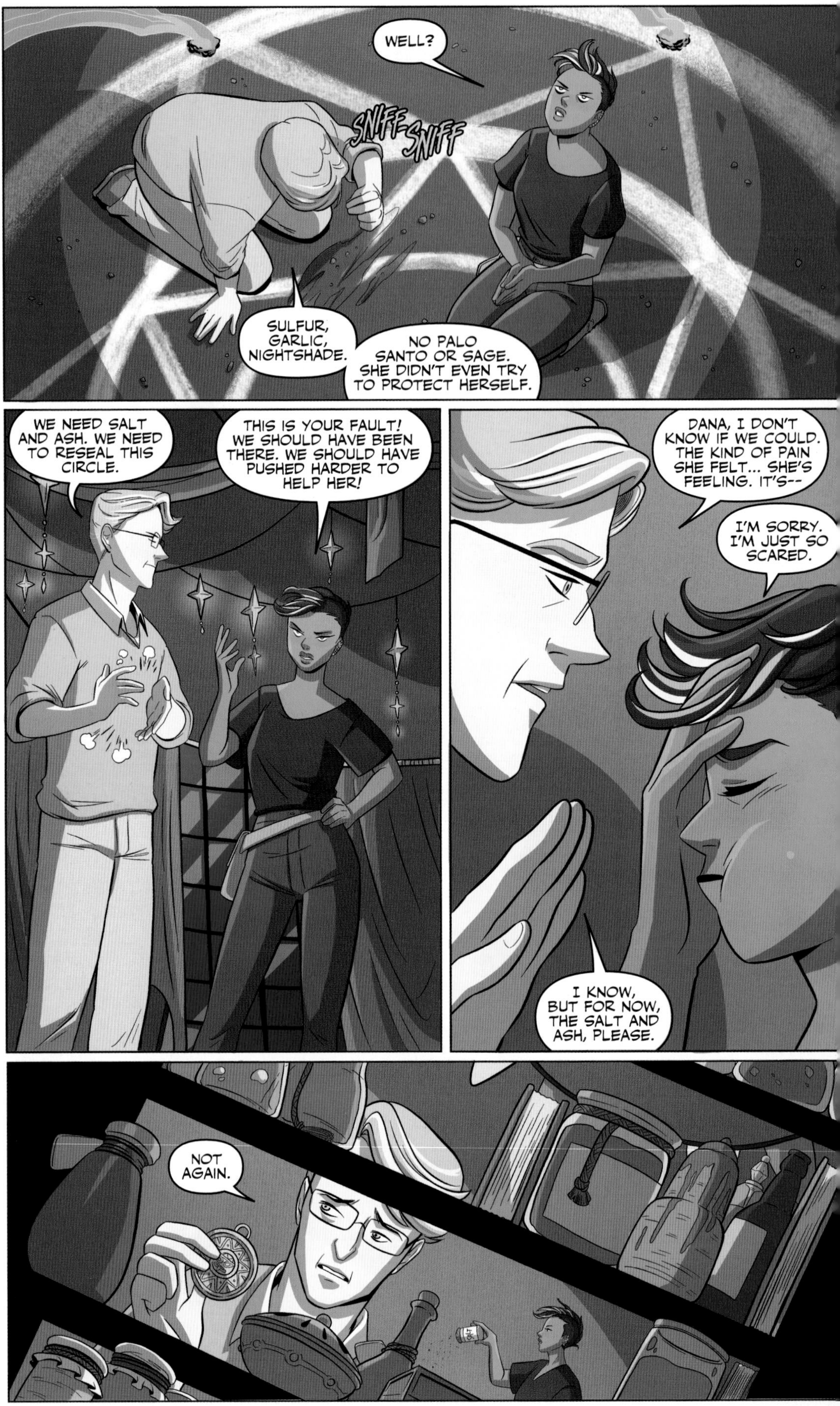
WELL?
SNIFF SNIFF
SULFUR, GARLIC, NIGHTSHADE.
NO PALO SANTO OR SAGE. SHE DIDN'T EVEN TRY TO PROTECT HERSELF.
WE NEED SALT AND ASH. WE NEED TO RESEAL THIS CIRCLE.
THIS IS YOUR FAULT! WE SHOULD HAVE BEEN THERE. WE SHOULD HAVE PUSHED HARDER TO HELP HER!
DANA, I DON'T KNOW IF WE COULD. THE KIND OF PAIN SHE FELT... SHE'S FEELING. IT'S--
I'M SORRY. I'M JUST SO SCARED.
I KNOW, BUT FOR NOW, THE SALT AND ASH, PLEASE.
NOT AGAIN.

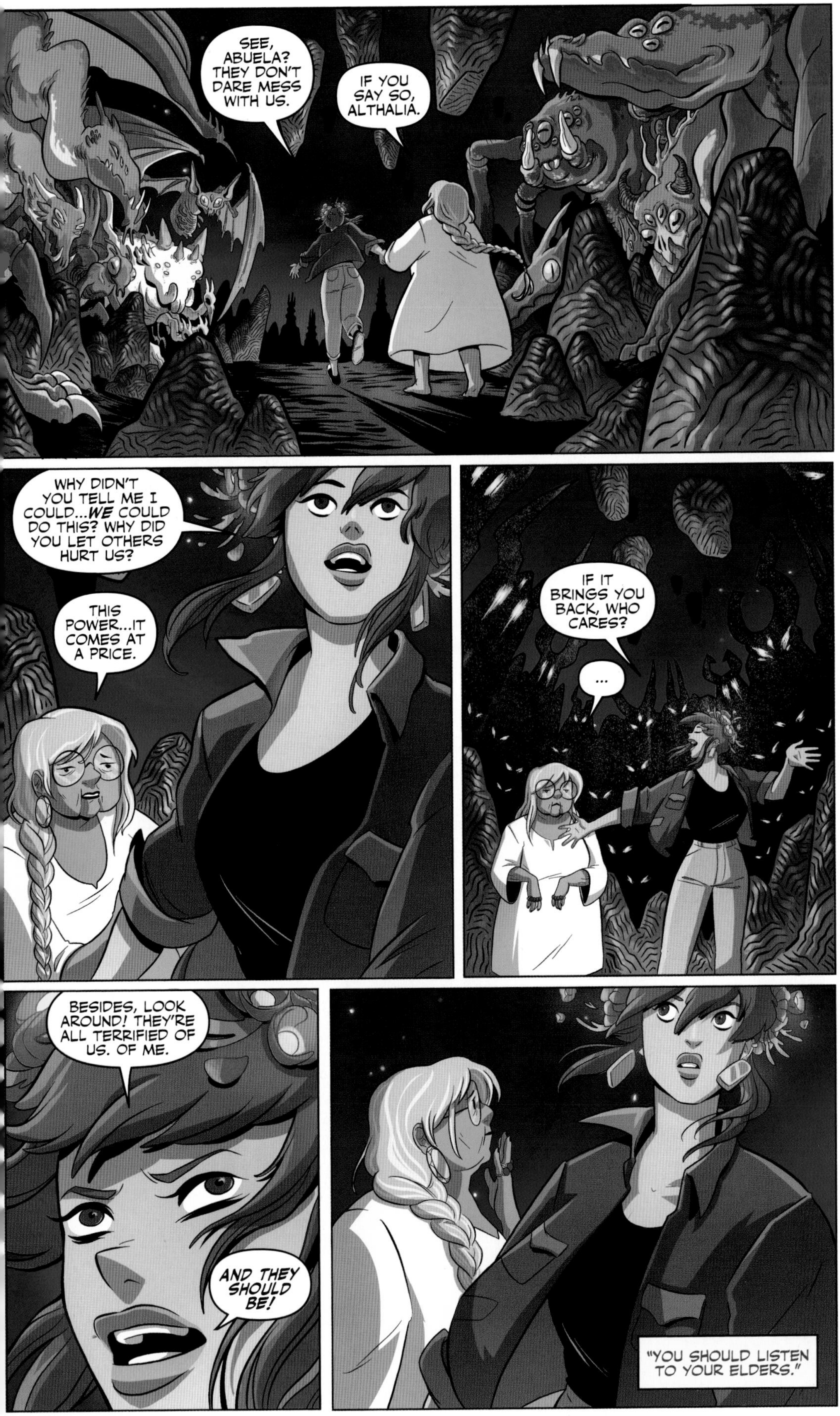
SEE, ABUELA? THEY DON'T DARE MESS WITH US.
IF YOU SAY SO, ALTHALIA.
WHY DIDN'T YOU TELL ME I COULD...*WE* COULD DO THIS? WHY DID YOU LET OTHERS HURT US?
THIS POWER...IT COMES AT A PRICE.
IF IT BRINGS YOU BACK, WHO CARES?
...
BESIDES, LOOK AROUND! THEY'RE ALL TERRIFIED OF US. OF ME.
AND THEY SHOULD BE!
"YOU SHOULD LISTEN TO YOUR ELDERS."

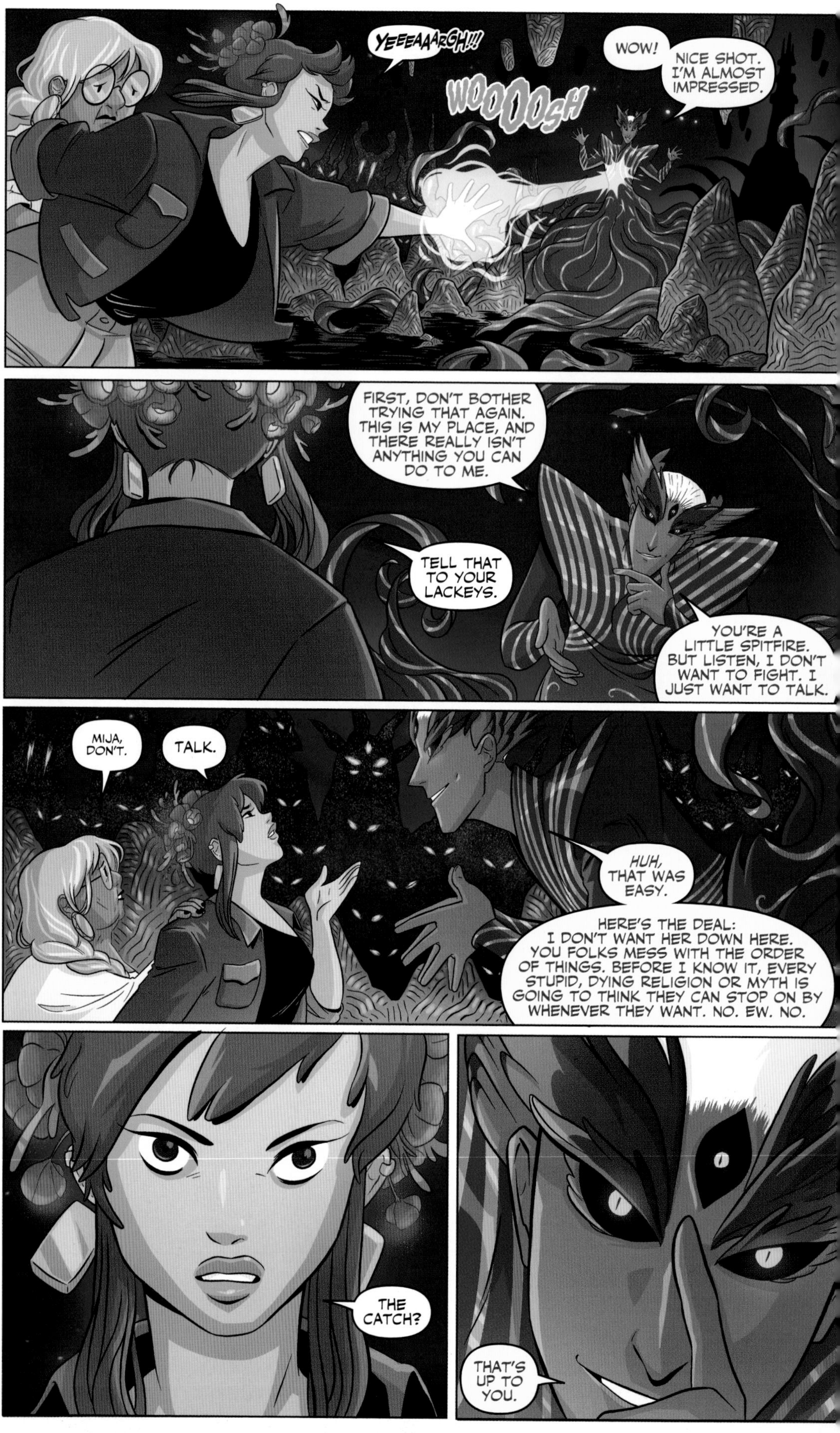

YEEEAAARGH!!!
WOOOOSH
WOW!
NICE SHOT. I'M ALMOST IMPRESSED.
FIRST, DON'T BOTHER TRYING THAT AGAIN. THIS IS MY PLACE, AND THERE REALLY ISN'T ANYTHING YOU CAN DO TO ME.
TELL THAT TO YOUR LACKEYS.
YOU'RE A LITTLE SPITFIRE. BUT LISTEN, I DON'T WANT TO FIGHT. I JUST WANT TO TALK.
MIJA, DON'T.
TALK.
HUH, THAT WAS EASY.
HERE'S THE DEAL: I DON'T WANT HER DOWN HERE. YOU FOLKS MESS WITH THE ORDER OF THINGS. BEFORE I KNOW IT, EVERY STUPID, DYING RELIGION OR MYTH IS GOING TO THINK THEY CAN STOP ON BY WHENEVER THEY WANT. NO. EW. NO.
THE CATCH?
THAT'S UP TO YOU.

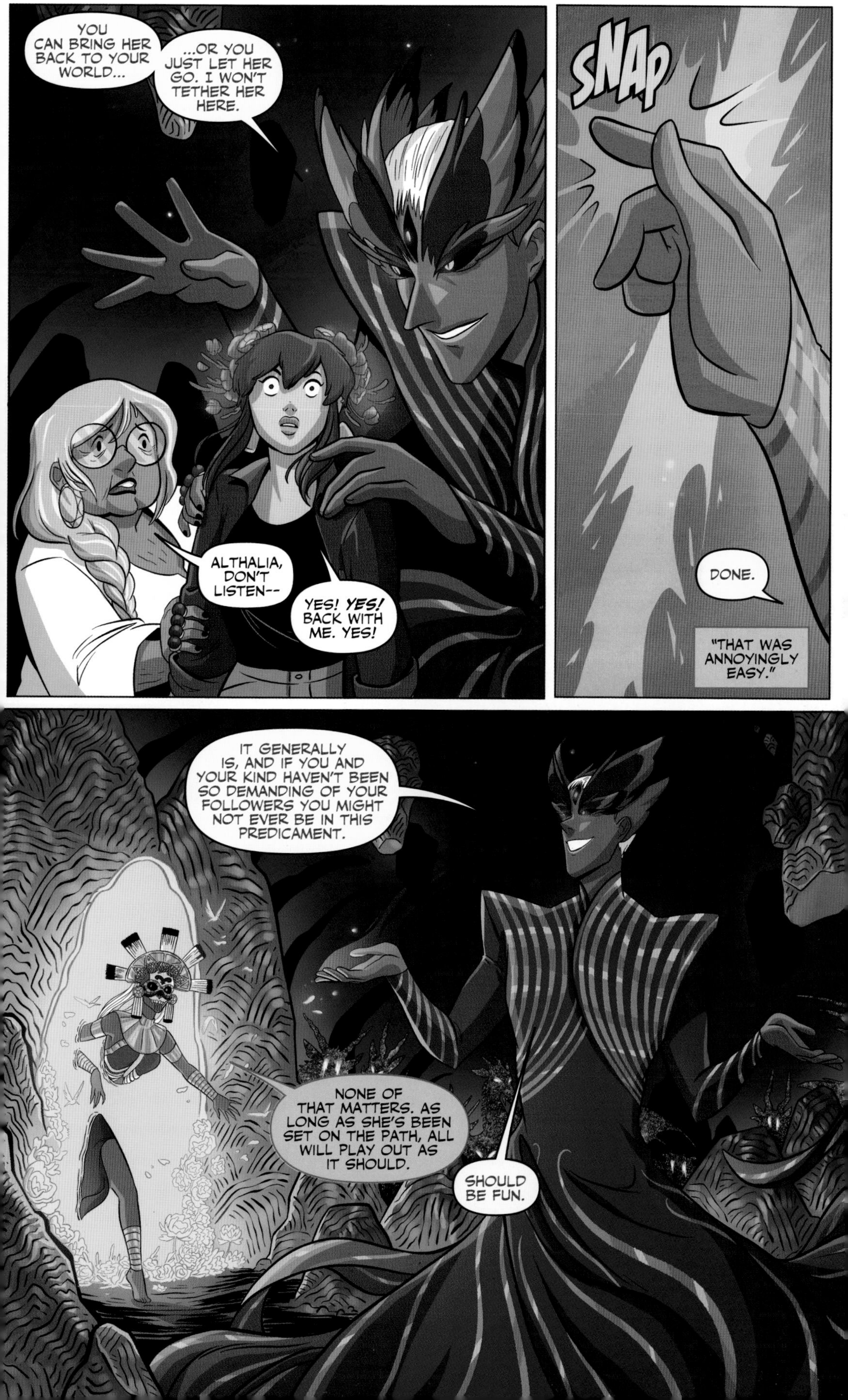
YOU CAN BRING HER BACK TO YOUR WORLD...
...OR YOU JUST LET HER GO. I WON'T TETHER HER HERE.
ALTHALIA, DON'T LISTEN--
YES! *YES!* BACK WITH ME. YES!
SNAP
DONE.
"THAT WAS ANNOYINGLY EASY."
IT GENERALLY IS, AND IF YOU AND YOUR KIND HAVEN'T BEEN SO DEMANDING OF YOUR FOLLOWERS YOU MIGHT NOT EVER BE IN THIS PREDICAMENT.
NONE OF THAT MATTERS. AS LONG AS SHE'S BEEN SET ON THE PATH, ALL WILL PLAY OUT AS IT SHOULD.
SHOULD BE FUN.

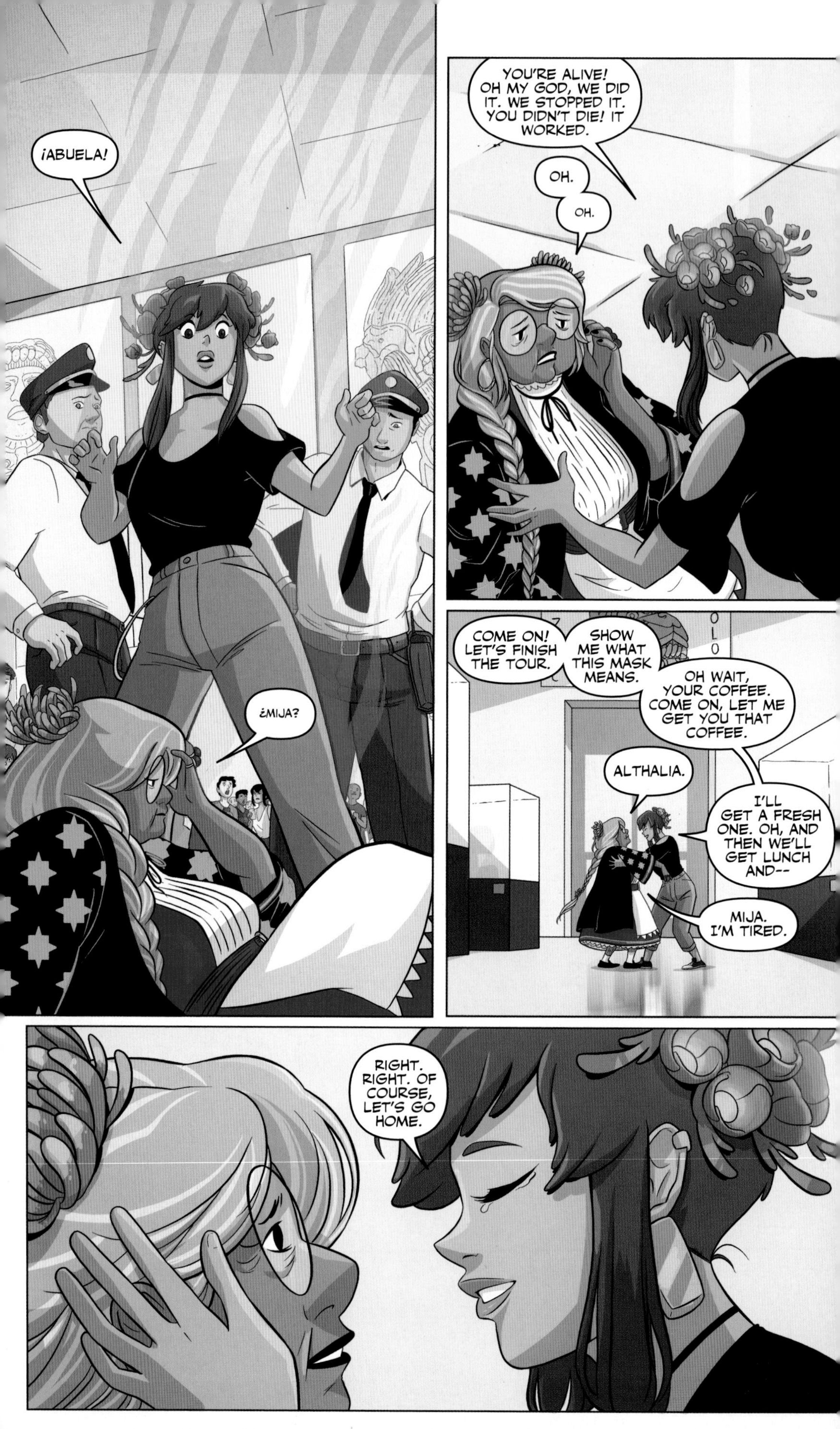
¡ABUELA!
¿MIJA?
YOU'RE ALIVE! OH MY GOD, WE DID IT. WE STOPPED IT. YOU DIDN'T DIE! IT WORKED.
OH.
OH.
COME ON! LET'S FINISH THE TOUR.
SHOW ME WHAT THIS MASK MEANS.
OH WAIT, YOUR COFFEE. COME ON, LET ME GET YOU THAT COFFEE.
ALTHALIA.
I'LL GET A FRESH ONE. OH, AND THEN WE'LL GET LUNCH AND--
MIJA. I'M TIRED.
RIGHT. RIGHT. OF COURSE, LET'S GO HOME.

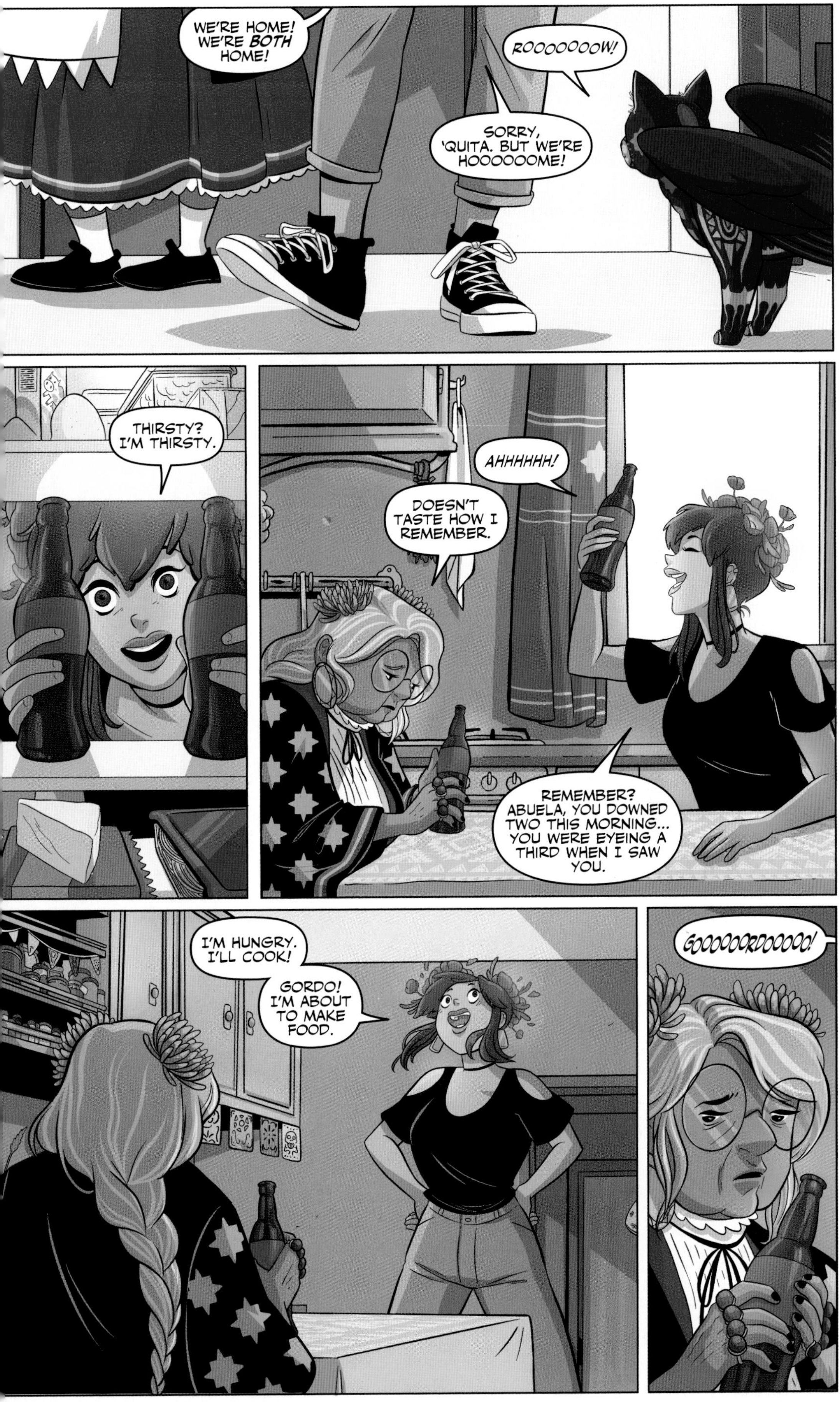
WE'RE HOME! WE'RE *BOTH* HOME!
ROOOOOOOW!
SORRY, 'QUITA. BUT WE'RE HOOOOOOME!
THIRSTY? I'M THIRSTY.
AHHHHHH!
DOESN'T TASTE HOW I REMEMBER.
REMEMBER? ABUELA, YOU DOWNED TWO THIS MORNING... YOU WERE EYEING A THIRD WHEN I SAW YOU.
I'M HUNGRY. I'LL COOK!
GORDO! I'M ABOUT TO MAKE FOOD.
GOOOOORDOOOOO!

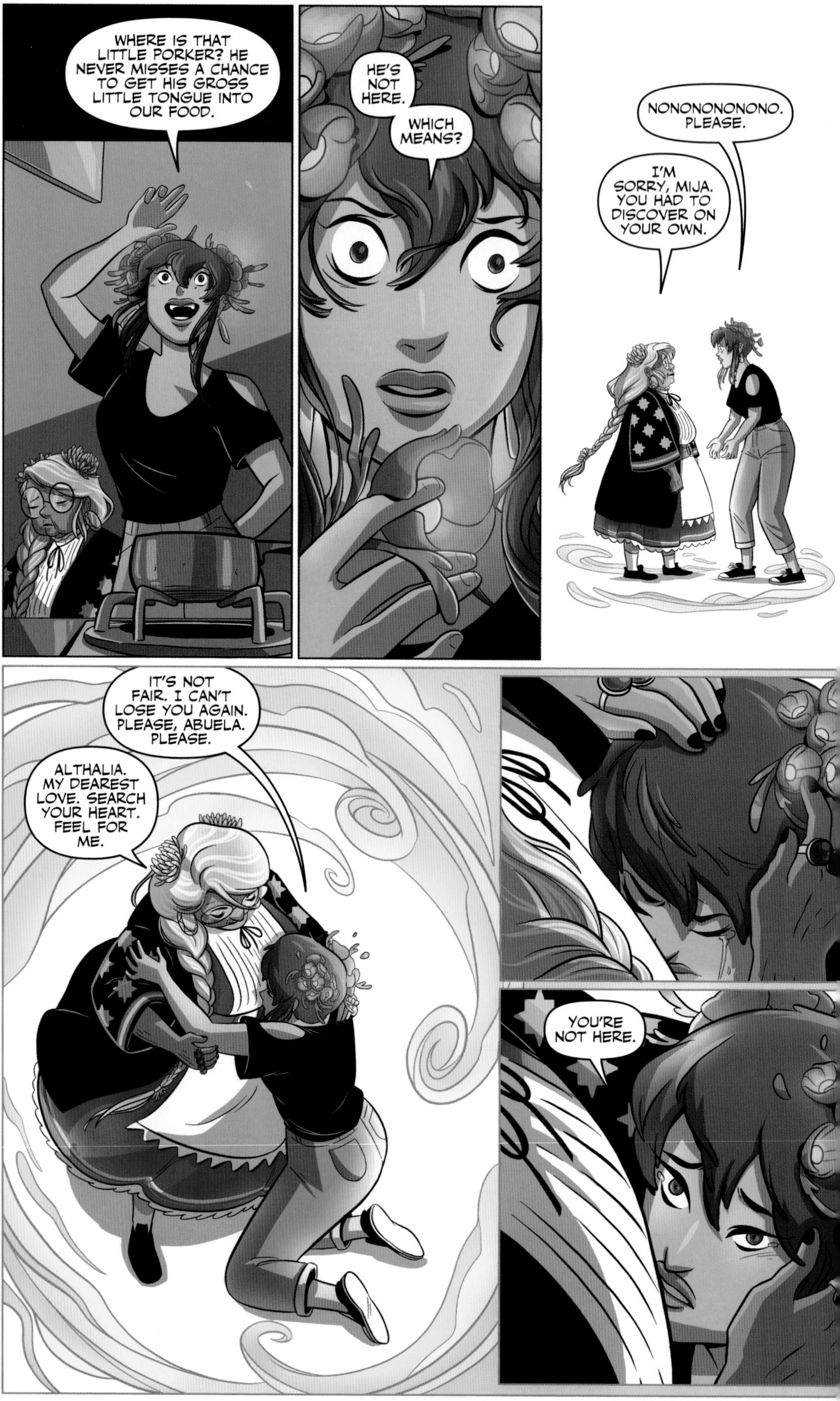
WHERE IS THAT LITTLE PORKER? HE NEVER MISSES A CHANCE TO GET HIS GROSS LITTLE TONGUE INTO OUR FOOD.
HE'S NOT HERE.
WHICH MEANS?
NONONONONONO. PLEASE.
I'M SORRY, MIJA. YOU HAD TO DISCOVER ON YOUR OWN.
IT'S NOT FAIR. I CAN'T LOSE YOU AGAIN. PLEASE, ABUELA. PLEASE.
ALTHALIA. MY DEAREST LOVE. SEARCH YOUR HEART. FEEL FOR ME.
YOU'RE NOT HERE.

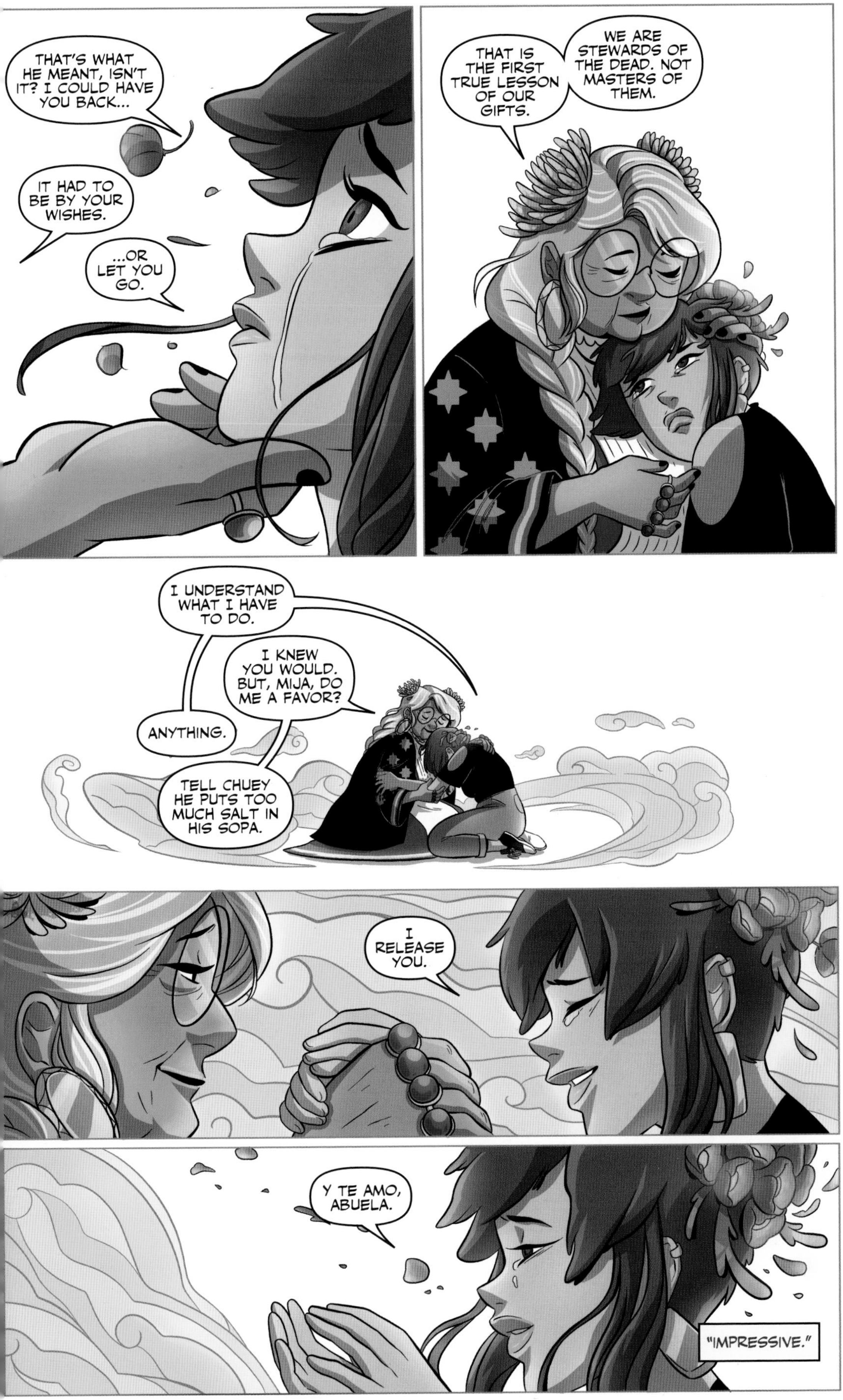
THAT'S WHAT HE MEANT, ISN'T IT? I COULD HAVE YOU BACK...
IT HAD TO BE BY YOUR WISHES.
...OR LET YOU GO.
THAT IS THE FIRST TRUE LESSON OF OUR GIFTS.
WE ARE STEWARDS OF THE DEAD. NOT MASTERS OF THEM.
I UNDERSTAND WHAT I HAVE TO DO.
I KNEW YOU WOULD. BUT, MIJA, DO ME A FAVOR?
ANYTHING.
TELL CHUEY HE PUTS TOO MUCH SALT IN HIS SOPA.
I RELEASE YOU.
Y TE AMO, ABUELA.
"IMPRESSIVE."

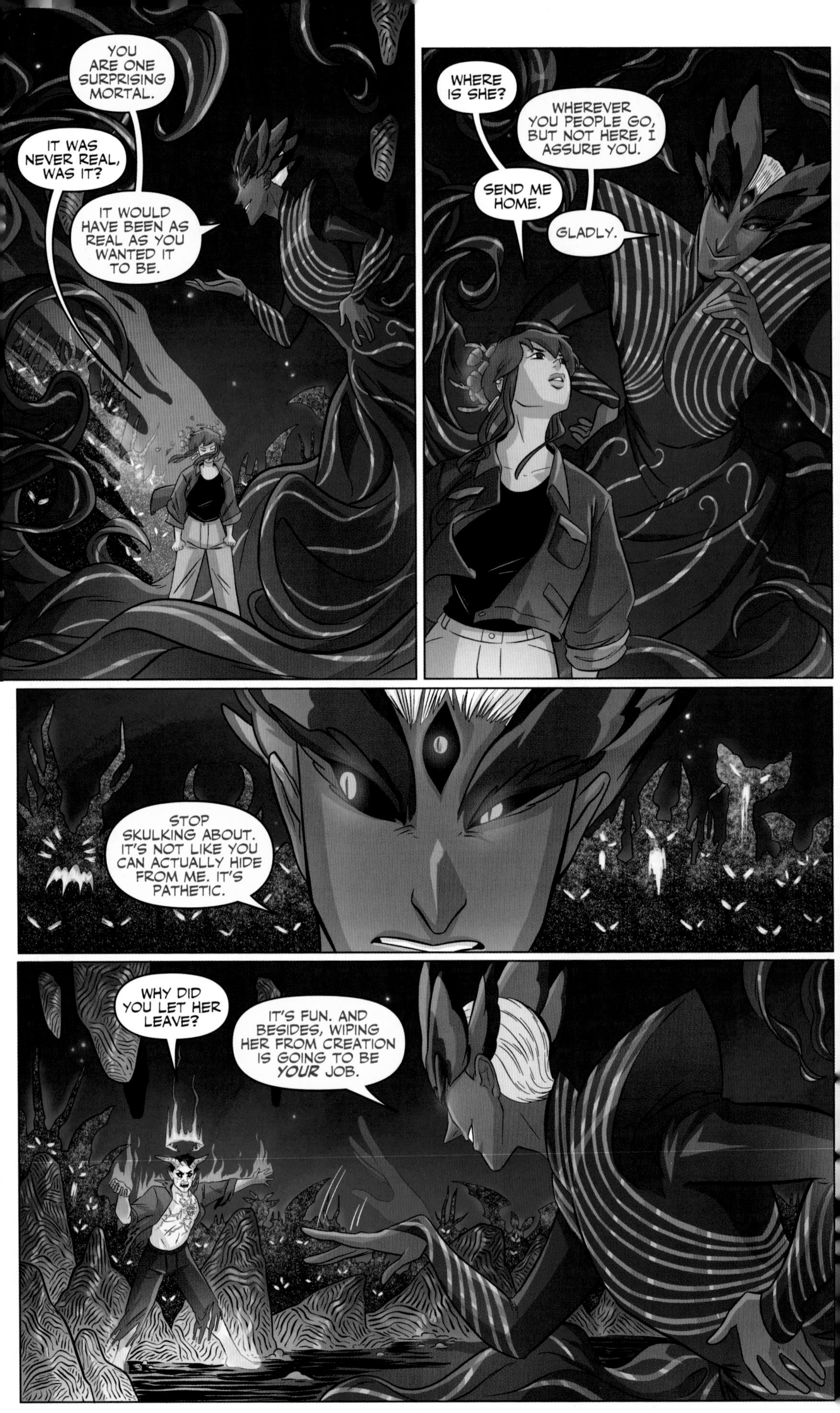
YOU ARE ONE SURPRISING MORTAL.
IT WAS NEVER REAL, WAS IT?
IT WOULD HAVE BEEN AS REAL AS YOU WANTED IT TO BE.
WHERE IS SHE?
WHEREVER YOU PEOPLE GO, BUT NOT HERE, I ASSURE YOU.
SEND ME HOME.
GLADLY.
STOP SKULKING ABOUT. IT'S NOT LIKE YOU CAN ACTUALLY HIDE FROM ME. IT'S PATHETIC.
WHY DID YOU LET HER LEAVE?
IT'S FUN. AND BESIDES, WIPING HER FROM CREATION IS GOING TO BE *YOUR* JOB.

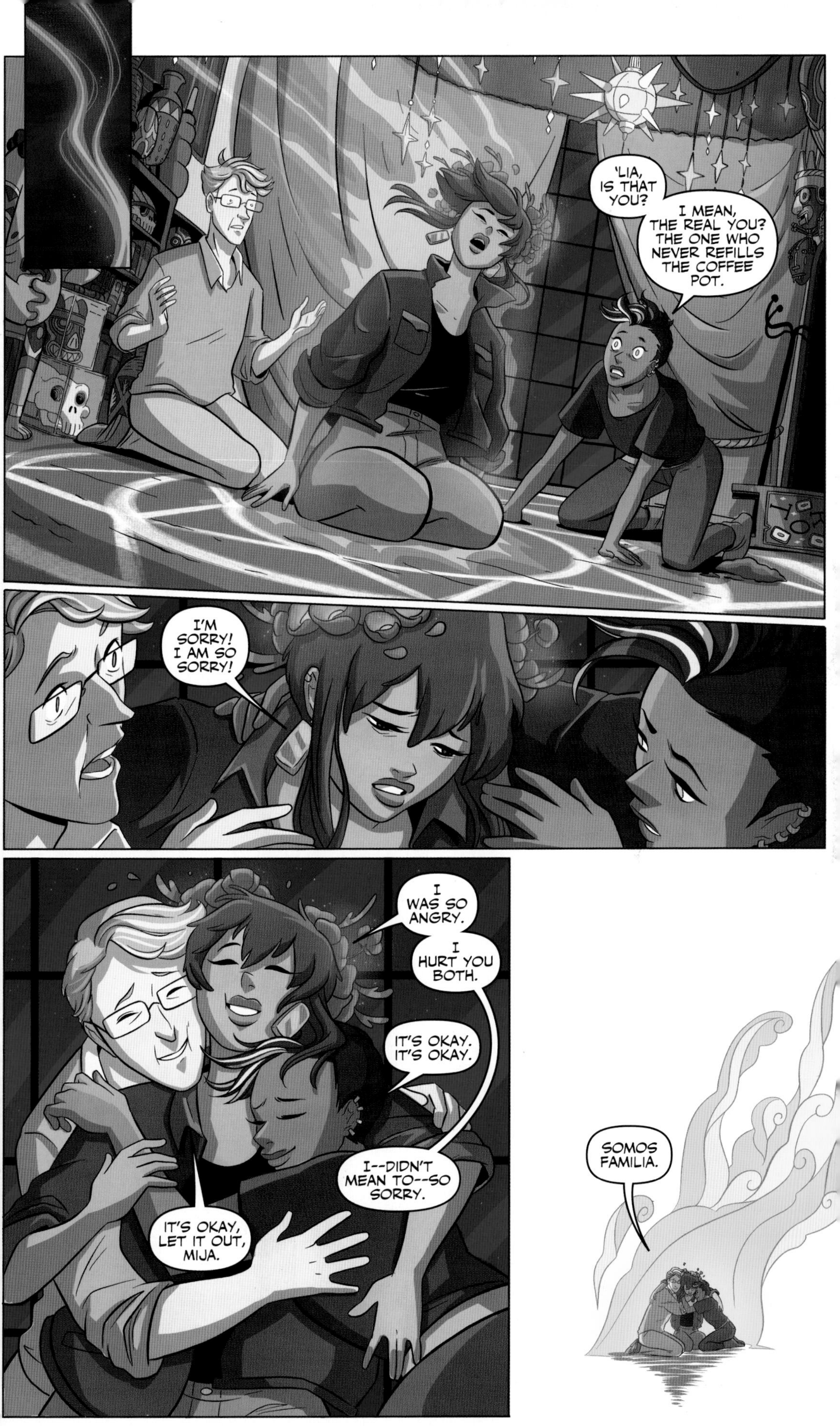
'LIA, IS THAT YOU?
I MEAN, THE REAL YOU? THE ONE WHO NEVER REFILLS THE COFFEE POT.
I'M SORRY! I AM SO SORRY!
I WAS SO ANGRY.
I HURT YOU BOTH.
IT'S OKAY. IT'S OKAY.
I--DIDN'T MEAN TO--SO SORRY.
IT'S OKAY, LET IT OUT, MIJA.
SOMOS FAMILIA.

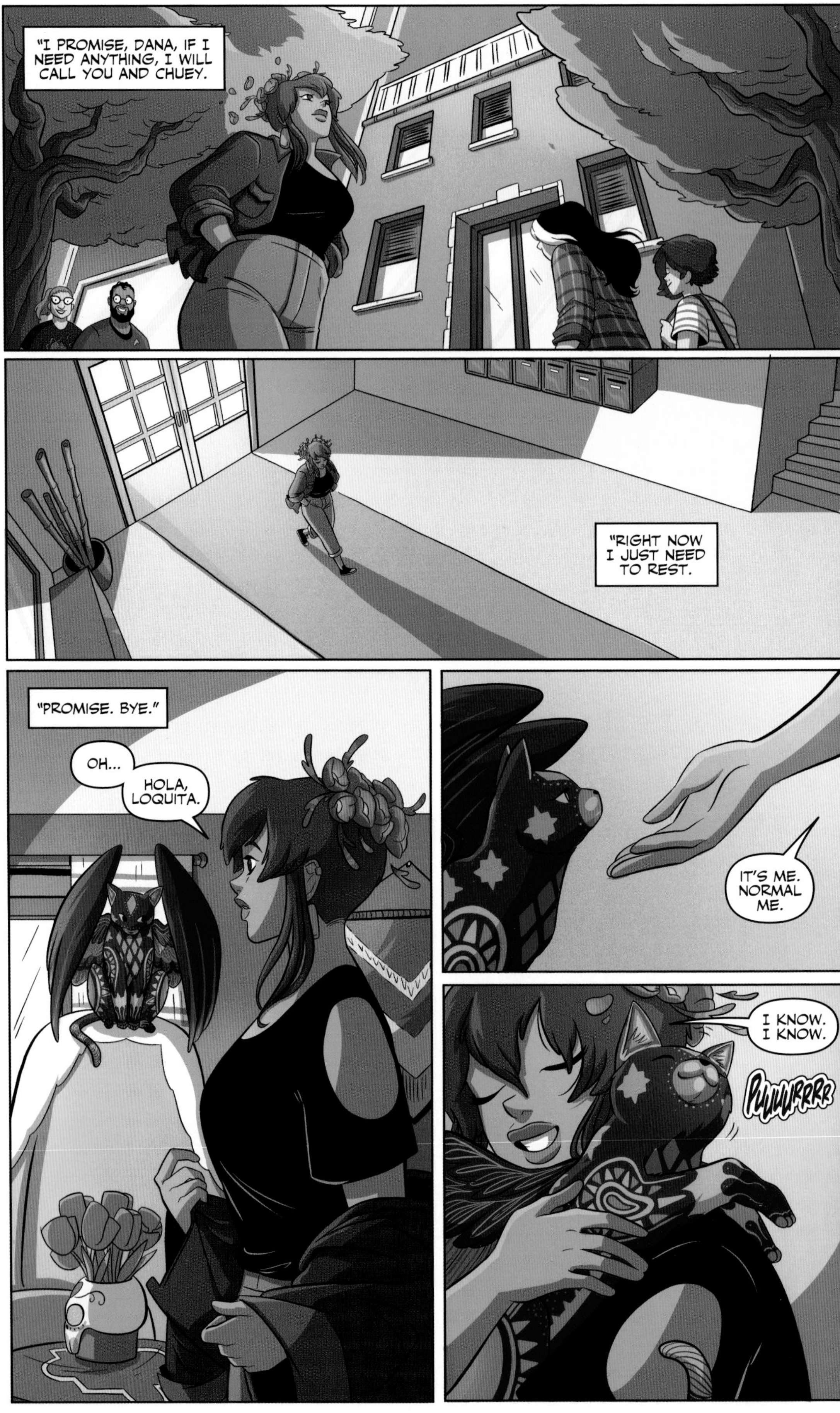
"I PROMISE, DANA, IF I NEED ANYTHING, I WILL CALL YOU AND CHUEY.
"RIGHT NOW I JUST NEED TO REST.
"PROMISE. BYE."
OH...
HOLA, LOQUITA.
IT'S ME. NORMAL ME.
I KNOW. I KNOW.
PUUUURRRR

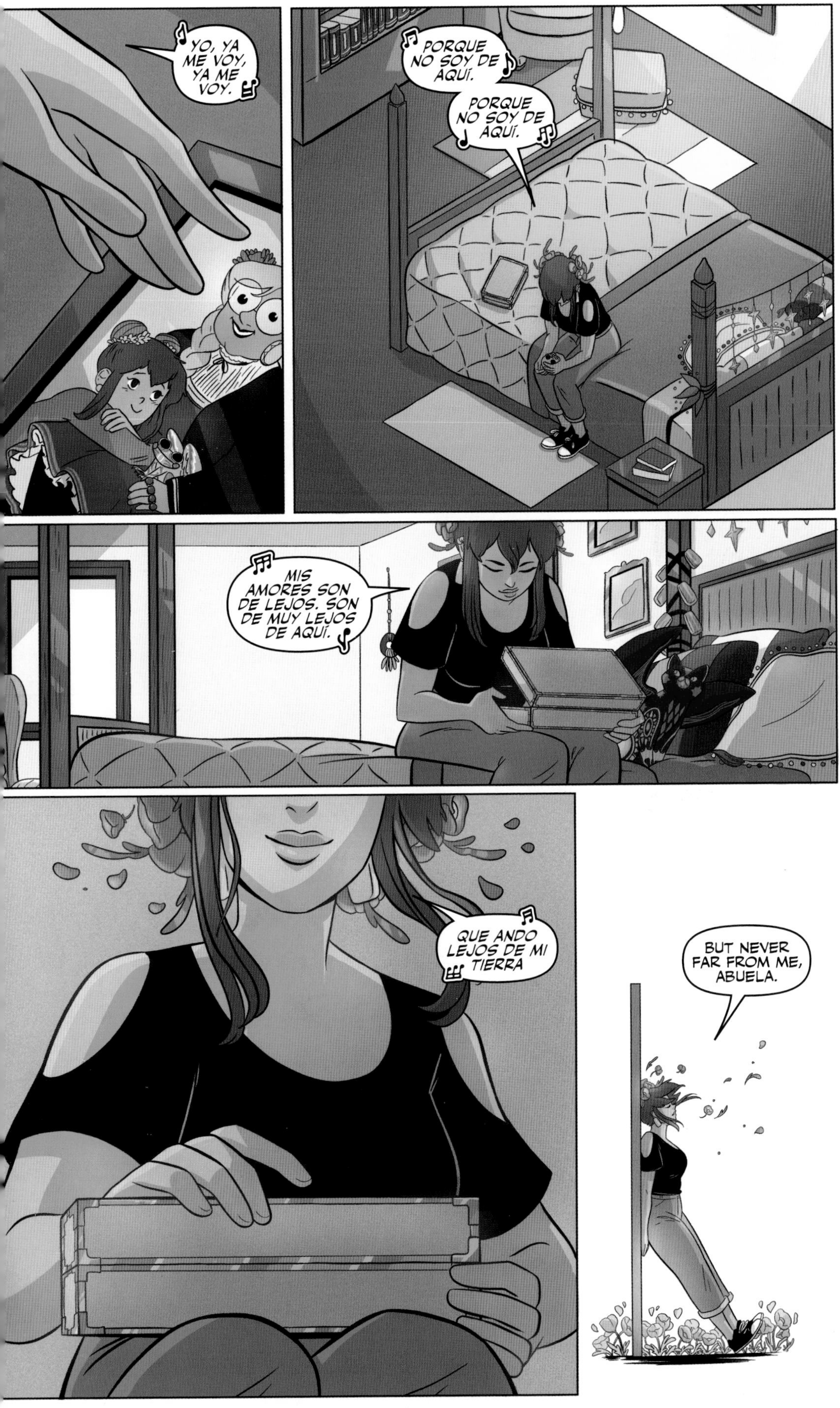
YO, YA ME VOY, YA ME VOY.
PORQUE NO SOY DE AQUÍ.
PORQUE NO SOY DE AQUÍ.
MIS AMORES SON DE LEJOS. SON DE MUY LEJOS DE AQUÍ.
QUE ANDO LEJOS DE MI TIERRA
BUT NEVER FAR FROM ME, ABUELA.

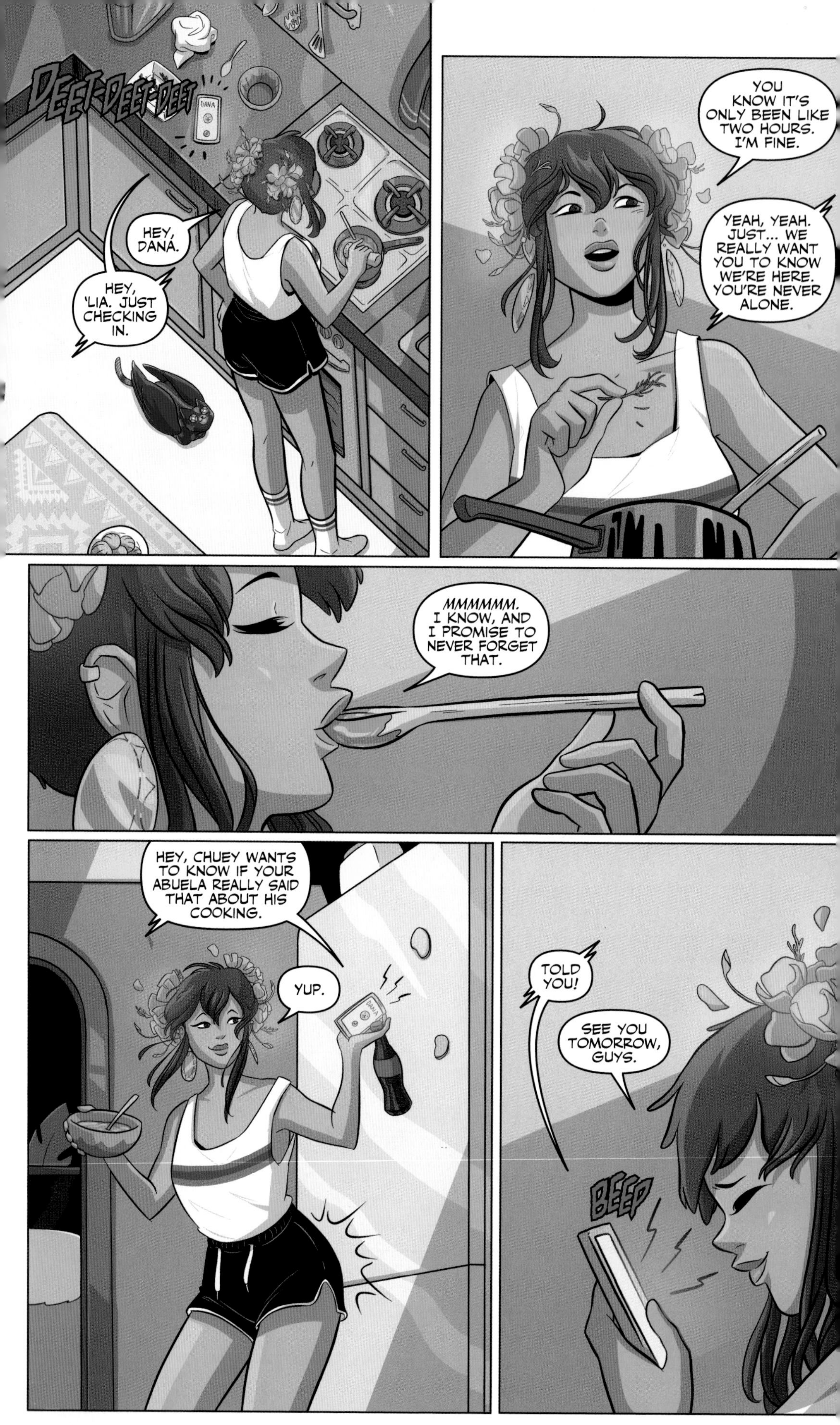
DEET-DEET-DEET
DANA
HEY, DANA.
HEY, 'LIA. JUST CHECKING IN.
YOU KNOW IT'S ONLY BEEN LIKE TWO HOURS. I'M FINE.
YEAH, YEAH. JUST... WE REALLY WANT YOU TO KNOW WE'RE HERE. YOU'RE NEVER ALONE.
MMMMMM. I KNOW, AND I PROMISE TO NEVER FORGET THAT.
HEY, CHUEY WANTS TO KNOW IF YOUR ABUELA REALLY SAID THAT ABOUT HIS COOKING.
YUP.
DANA
TOLD YOU!
SEE YOU TOMORROW, GUYS.
BEEP

OH NO! DON'T DO IT, LA SERPIENTE. DON'T LAUNCH FROM THE TOP ROPE.

OH MY GOD, SHE DID IT!

ONE.

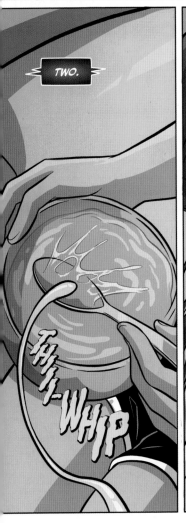

TWO.

THII-WHIP

THREE.

SHE DID IT! LA SERPIENTE IS THE NEW CHAMPION!

127

END

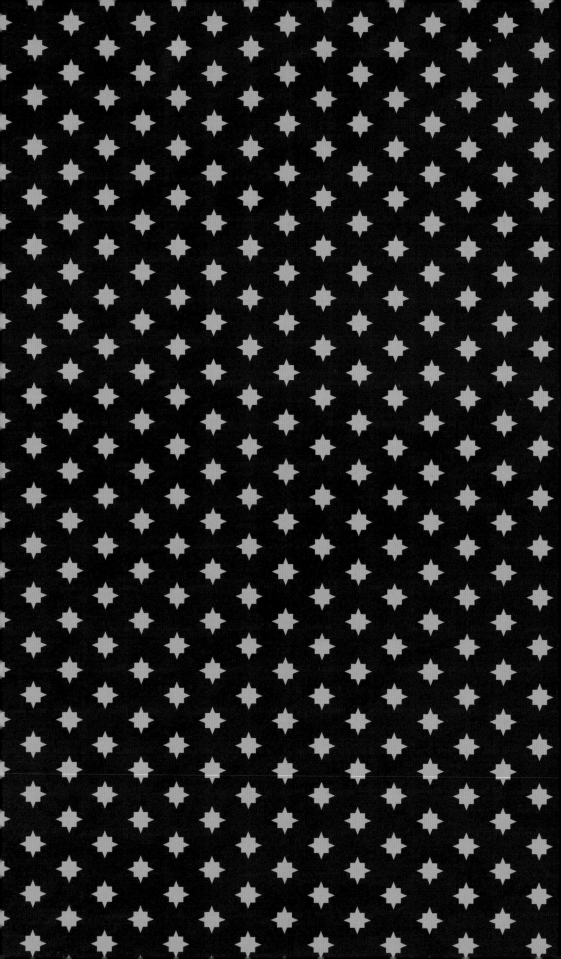

Issue 1A

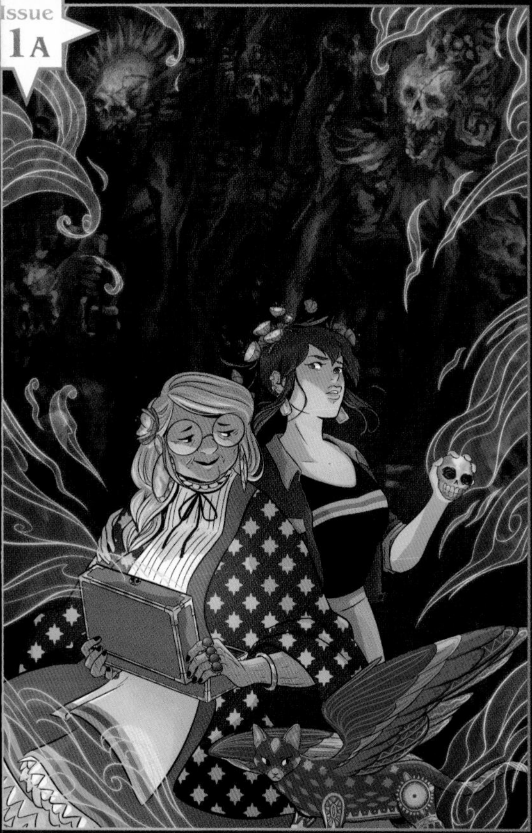

Issue 1B

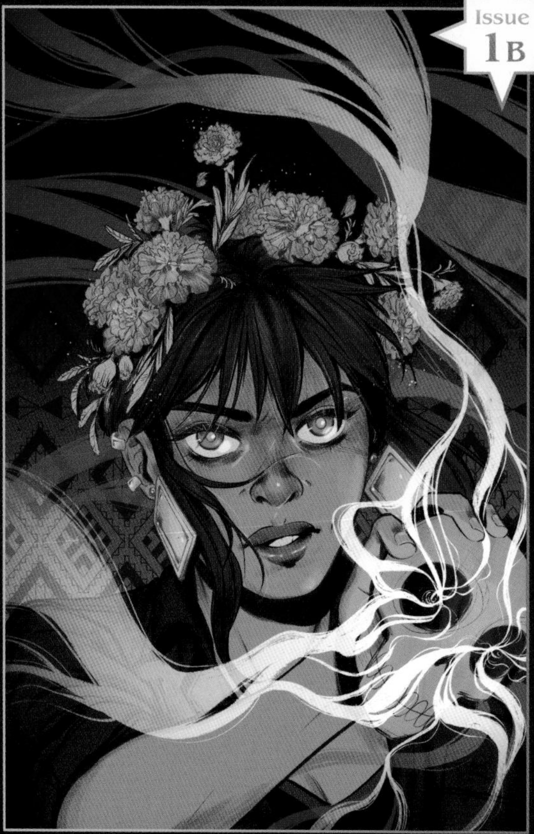

by Naomi Franquiz

Issue 2A

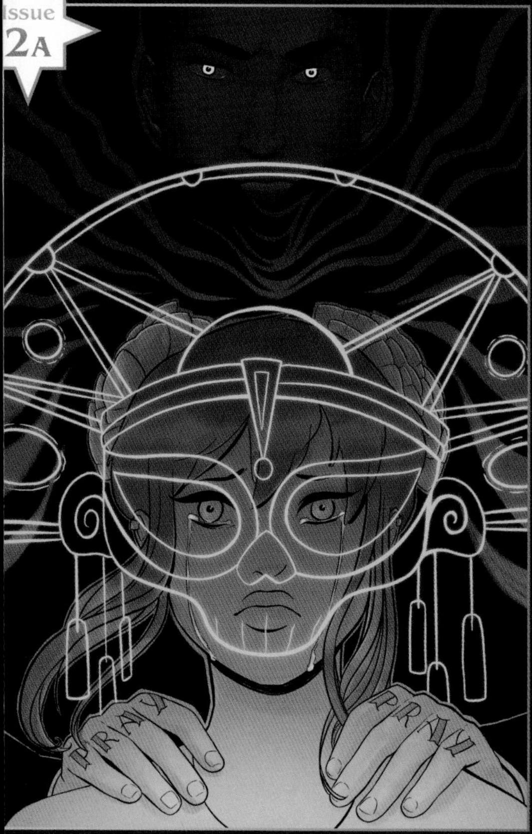
PRAY
PRAY

Issue 3A

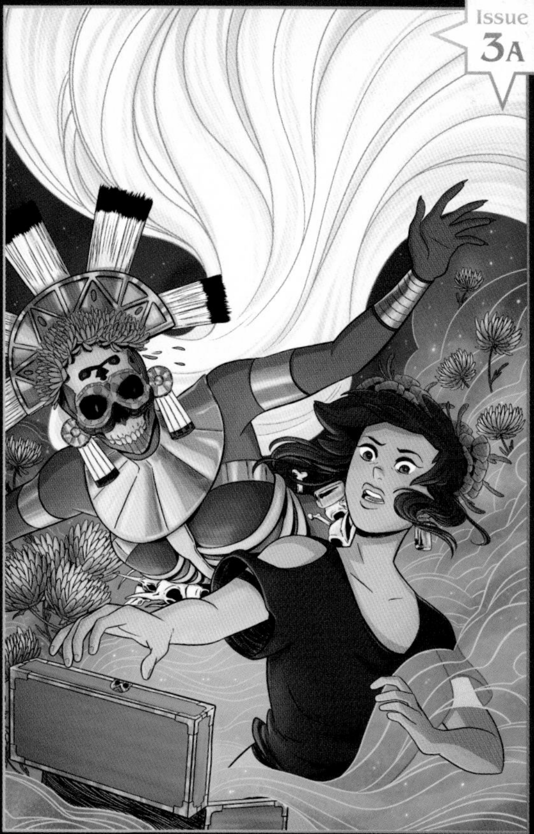

by Sara Soler

by Sara Soler

Issue 4A

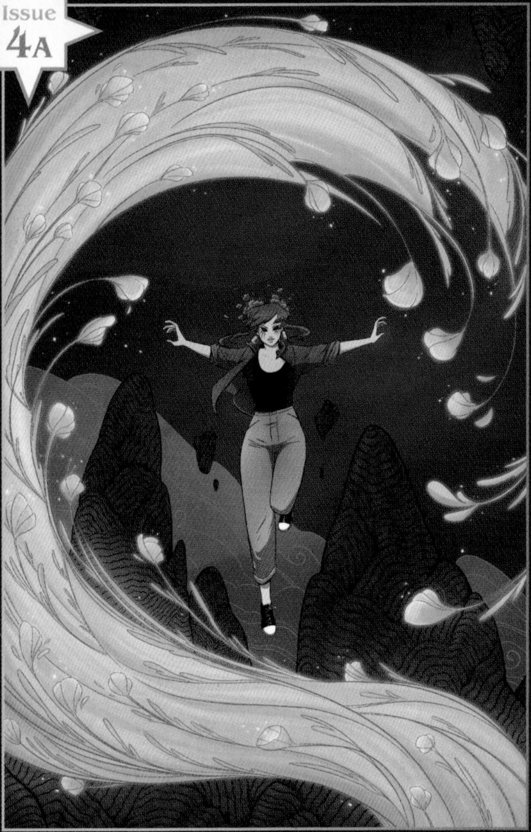

Issue 5A

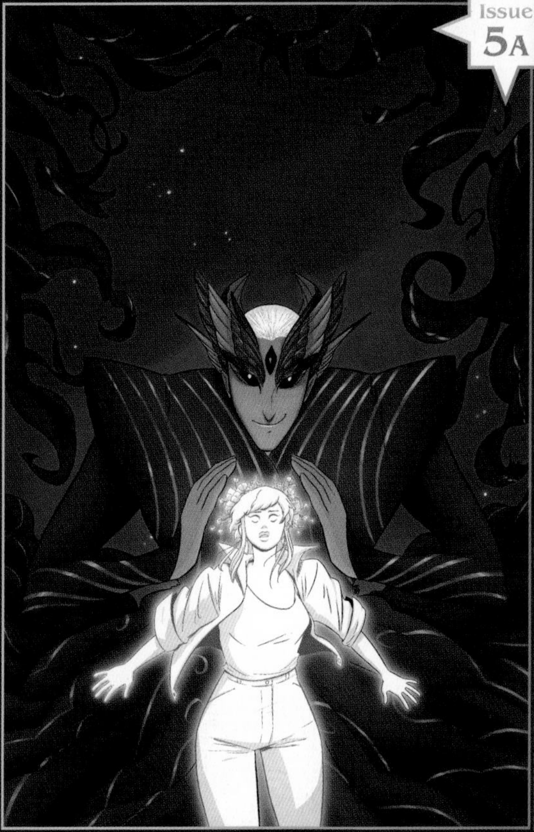

by David Aja

Variant

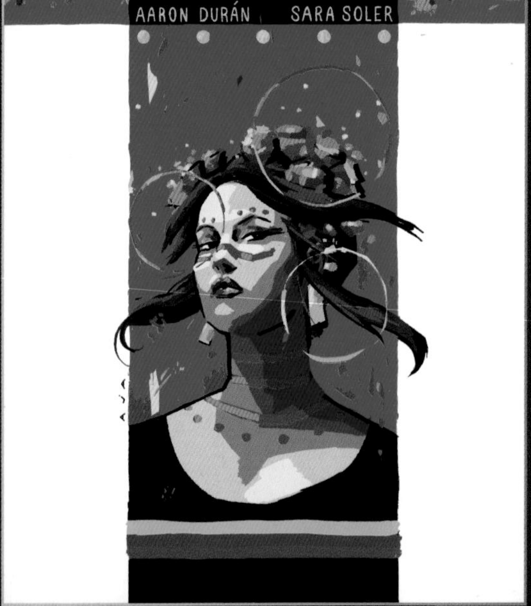
SEASON OF THE
BRUJA
AARON DURÁN
SARA SOLER

Poster

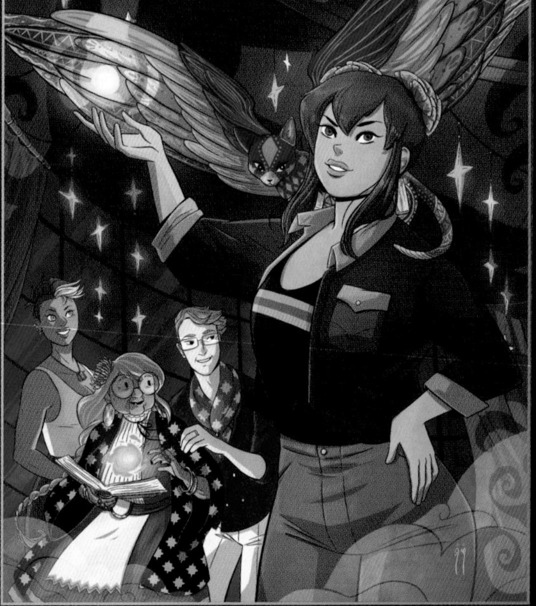

LY I KNOW HAS A VERSION OF THIS DISH, and with very few them are the same. Sure, each one uses a pasta: you have your fideo families, your alphabet ell families. Mine? We are star people, and I wouldn't have it any other way. It's quick and easy, foul mood or aren't feeling good, this trusted bowl of sopa will always make things better. And hat recipe on to you. SO HERE WE GO!

n Estrellas y Pollo (o con Setas)

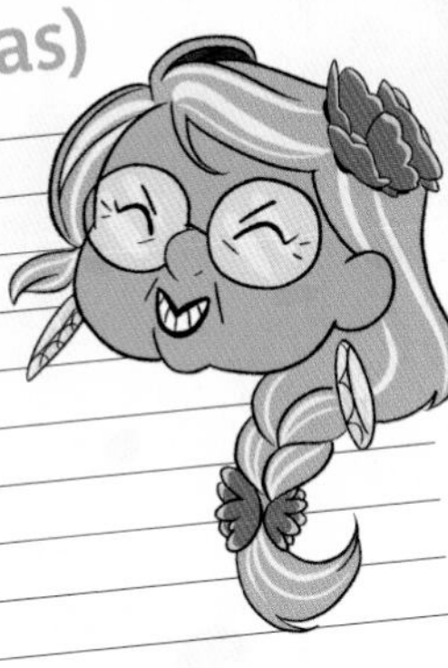

pasta stars
full package)
cken drumsticks*
ato sauce
ced scallions
espoons cumin

1 tablespoon salt
3 tablespoons vegetable oil
3 cups chicken stock*

Tools:
2 pots
1 mixing spoon

ons:

, put the chicken drumsticks in a pot with water, just enough to cover the chicken. Add 1 tablespoon of and cook until the chicken is ready. Once the chicken is cooked, remove it and set aside, but be sure to e the chicken stock.

the other pot, set the heat to high to get it nice and hot, carefully add the 3 tablespoons of oil. Once the comes to temperature, add all the pasta. Quickly but gently, stir the pasta until each piece is coated in oil nd you have slight browning on the pasta. Be careful not to burn them—we're just giving them different extures. It only takes one or two minutes. From there, lower the heat to medium-low (or low simmer).

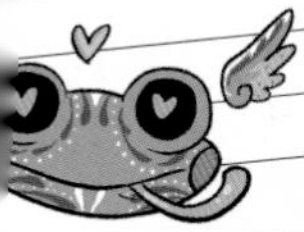

- Add the cumin and stir; again, just enough to coat the pasta. Next, you are going to add 8 ounces of tomato sauce and stir. It should look more like a chunky paste rather than soup.

Instructions cont'd:

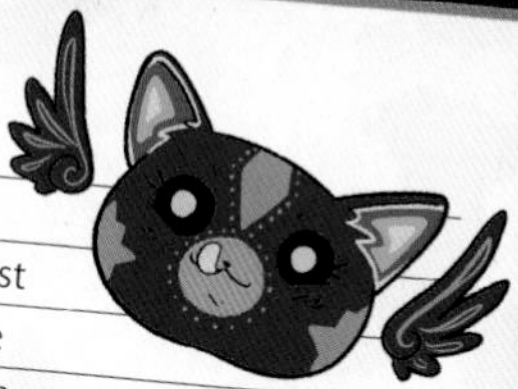

- Now add the chicken stock you saved (You did save it, didn't you?!). You need just enough to cover the pasta mixture by about an inch and a half. If you want more chicken flavor you can add some chicken bouillon, but don't use too much. The flavors are meant to be subtle.
- Keep it on a low simmer and stir. Once the pasta just begins to soften, add the chopped scallions and the chicken drumsticks. (My abuela liked the drumsticks whole, but I like shredding the chicken before adding. Totally up to you.) Keep an eye on the sopa, stirring every few minutes to stop it from sticking too much.
- Cook to your desired pasta texture, usually no more than 10–15 minutes. Those little stars absorb liquid fast.
- Serve with friends and bask in the goodness that is Isadora's Sopa con Estrellas y Pollo.

*If you want to make this dish vegetarian, it's relatively easy. Replace the chicken stock with vegetable stock. In lieu of chicken you can use portobello mushrooms.

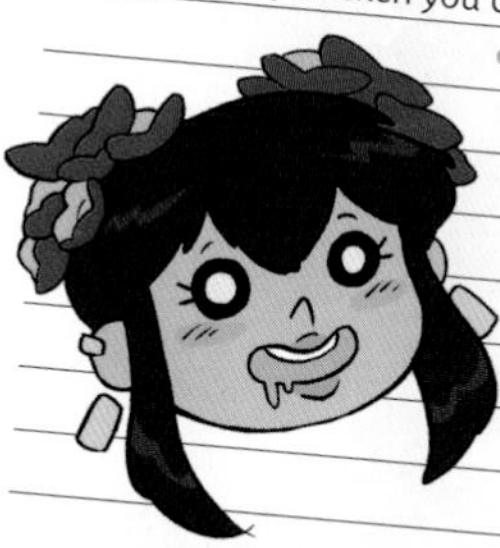

- Slice 2 large portobello mushrooms into thick slices and sauté them in oil and salt until tender.
- Then add the mushroom slices when you would normally add the chicken. If you are able to find mushroom sauce, add to taste for that extra umami kick.

¡disfrutar!

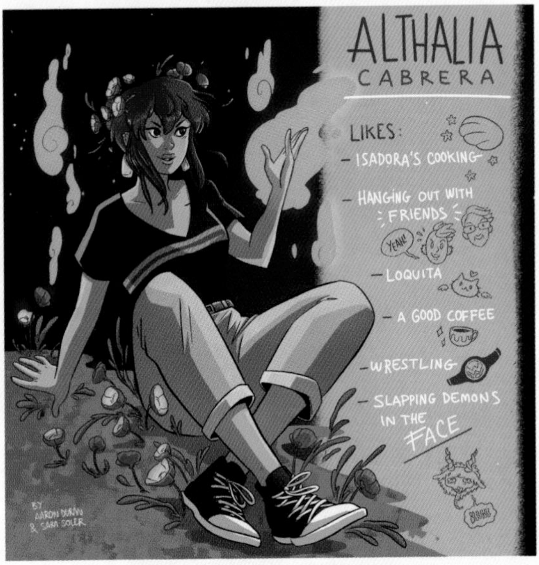
ALTHALIA
CABRERA
LIKES:
- ISADORA'S COOKING
- HANGING OUT WITH FRIENDS
YEAH!
- LOQUITA
- A GOOD COFFEE
- WRESTLING
- SLAPPING DEMONS IN THE FACE
BY AARON DURÁN & SARA SOLER

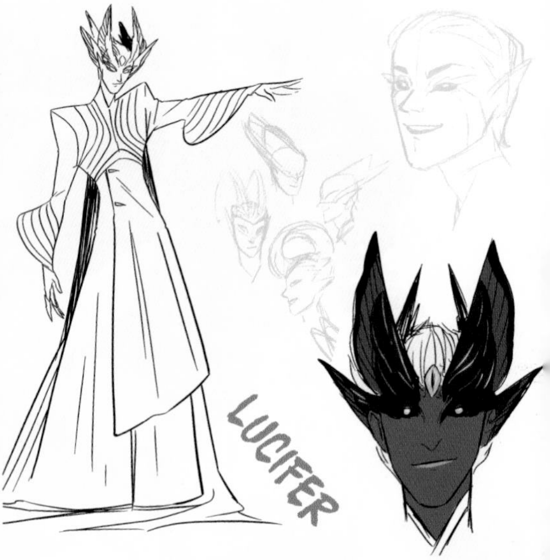
LUCIFER

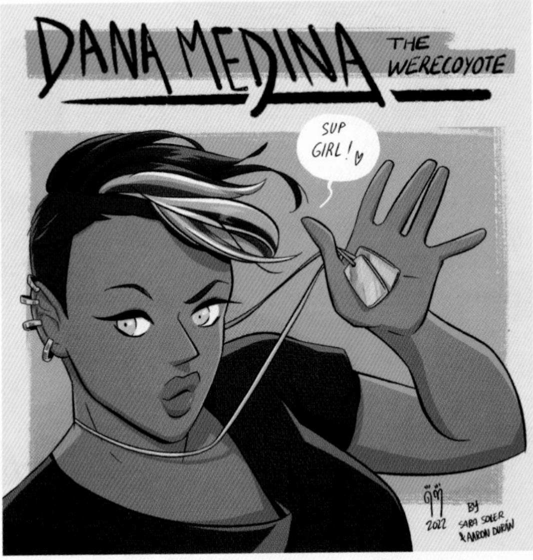
DANA MEDINA
THE WERECOYOTE
SUP GIRL!
2022 BY SARA SOLER & AARON DURÁN

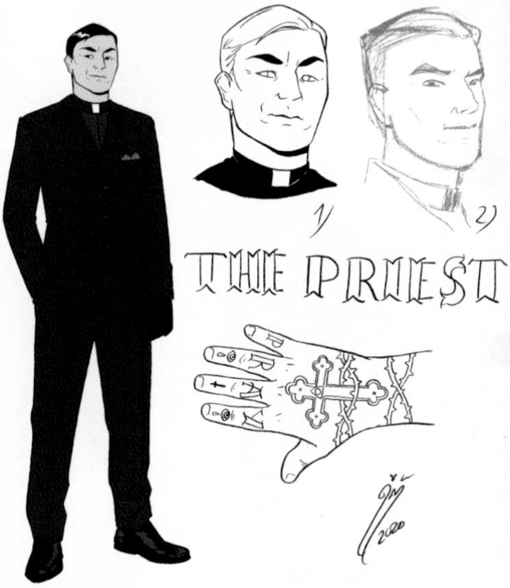
1)
2)
THE PRIEST
2020

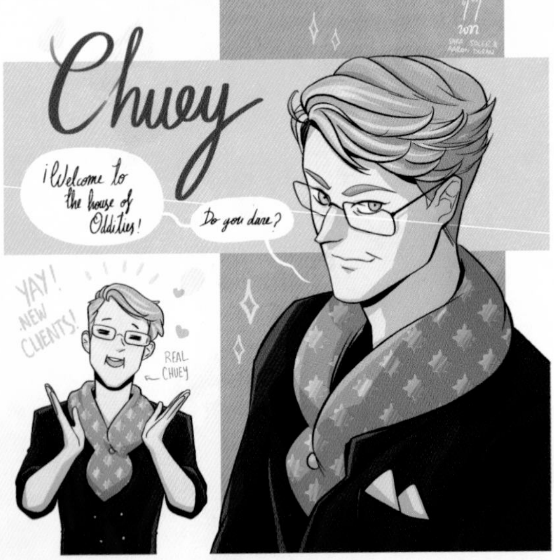
Chuey
¡Welcome to the house of Oddities!
Do you dare?
YAY! NEW CLIENTS!
REAL CHUEY
2022

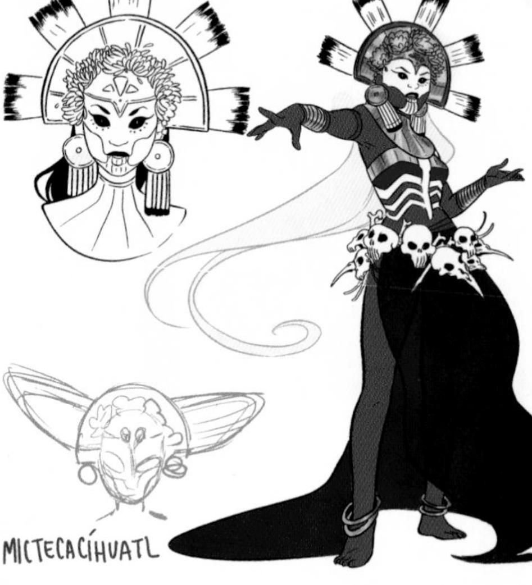
MICTECACÍHUATL

BEHIND THE BRUJA

Designs by Sara Soler

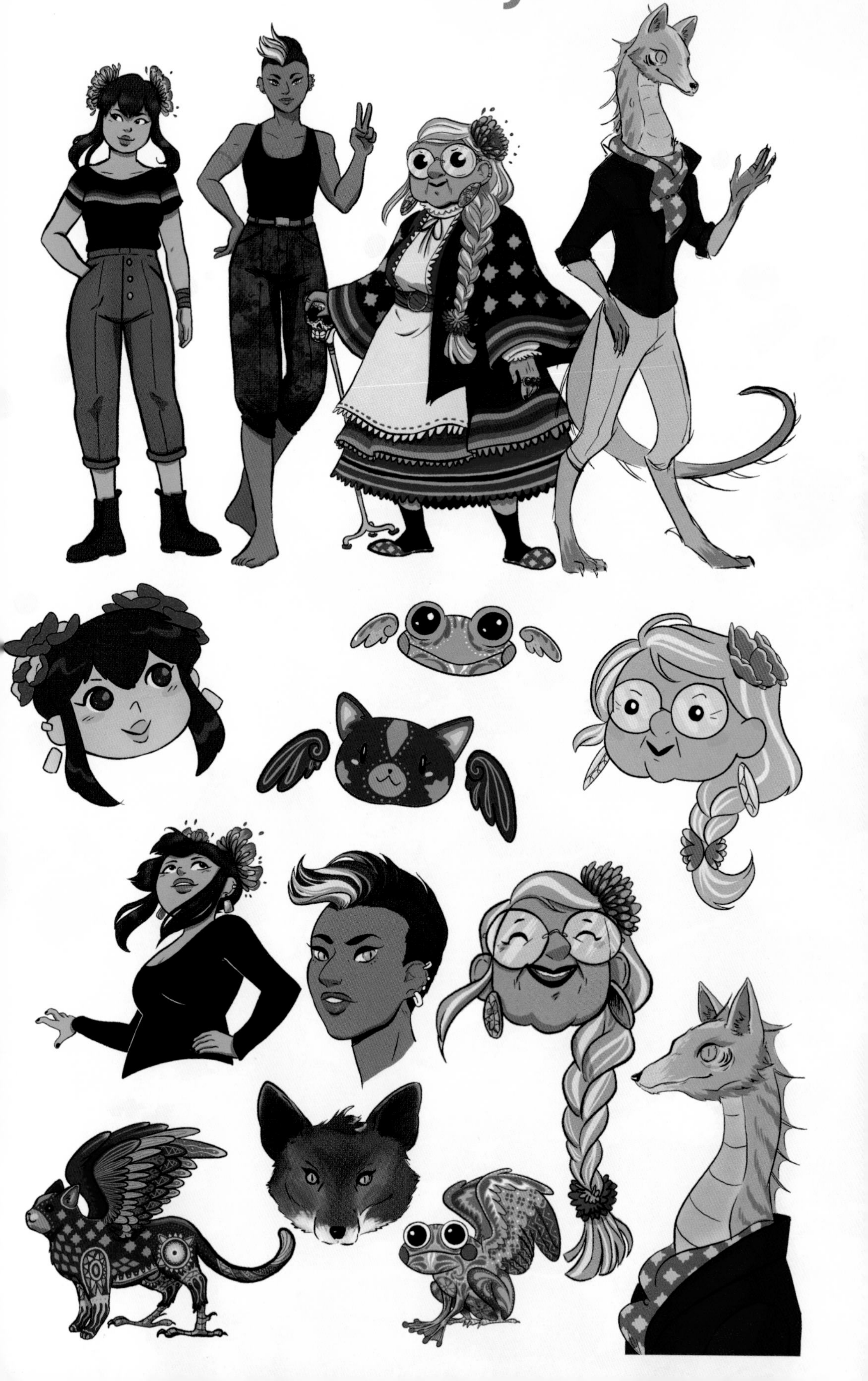

The journey from pitching *Season of the Bruja* to this afterword is about three years; but if I am being honest with myself, my journey with Althalia started a long time ago. I'm talking *grade school* long time ago.

I was in the fifth grade, and it was lunchtime at my school. Every other kid, including my friends, started eating their PB&J or tuna sandwiches. Me? Well, I was unwrapping leftover tamales from Christmas weekend. It didn't look like anything my friends were eating, and they were quick to point out how weird my lunch looked. This was my first true realization that, while I was born in America like my parents before me, I was not like the kids I spent time around, a feeling I'd experience on a semi-regular basis.

Trust me, it's odd when your friends on the playground call you mijo because they just assume it's your nickname.

If my life experiences were merely limited to how white American culture saw me, it's possible *Season of the Bruja* would never have happened. Except they weren't. And honestly, it often hurt more when I'd visit family in Southern California or run into some random Latinx person at a store or a restaurant. It always started the same way: the person would say something charming or endearing to me in Spanish. Without fail, I would just nod with a sheepish grin, followed by my mom telling them I didn't speak Spanish. Which was bad enough, but those interactions were always followed with a form of pity, and that is what cut deep, as though I wasn't good enough for what they knew. It's a common feeling among us mixed-race folks regardless of our backgrounds. We didn't feel like enough for either group to fully embrace us. So the emotional walls go up and the cultural dissociation kicks in. It was easier to just say I tanned easily, which is impressive in a small town that spends about six months under fifty degrees, and no one goes outside without being covered up head to toe. But through all of that I kept wondering when I wouldn't feel the need to protect myself from either group. Would I ever be comfortable just being who and what I am, a kid of mixed backgrounds?

This uneasiness between worlds led me to *Season of the Bruja* and to Althalia, who has followed the path I kicked off all those years ago in the school lunchroom. Because here is the truth of it all: I still don't know if I feel comfortable living within these two worlds. On one hand, I couldn't be prouder of this book. I've already seen the impact it's had on kids who see a little bit of themselves in these pages, and, honestly, I tear up every time I think of them. But for me there is still that fear. There have been times—more often than I care to admit—when I've asked myself, "Am I the right person to tell this story? Am I the authentic voice for *Season of the Bruja*?" Well, I am, but that still doesn't stop the fear that someone will think otherwise and remind me that I'm an unwelcome stranger within my own culture.

Then I think of the kids and the new readers who discover this book. They see Sara Soler's amazing art, and within that art they see a bit of themselves. They watch Althalia struggling to understand her place between two worlds, just as they might be navigating two or more worlds themselves. They see, I truly hope, someone who knows exactly what they are going through, and because of that they feel just a little less alone. And while I may never get past my own feelings of disconnection, I hope this book helps those readers get past theirs.

I'll keep writing and trying. I'd love for you to continue this journey with me.

AARON DURÁN

For me, *Season of the Bruja* began as a work-for-hire project. Yes, a very cool one with magic, adventure, and a very badass protagonist, but just one more project. I had previously worked as a cartoonist in the US, and I have always enjoyed the stories I have worked on, but in general I had done rather "mercenary" jobs in which you don't get emotionally involved at all. However, *Season of the Bruja* turned out to be a whole new world for me, both in terms of artistic and personal development.

I am Spanish, and, in fact, I know that Aaron's first concern when the editor put me on the table as a potential illustrator was if I would feel bad about drawing a story in which the Spaniards were, well...the bad guys! (Hahaha)

I fully understand his concern. I'm not proud at all, but what you usually learn in Spain when you are a child is that Columbus was a great discoverer of the New World. They teach you that the colonizers were heroes, and the day when "America was discovered" is celebrated. I have been saying for years now that this "discovery" should not be celebrated, and many times it is cause for discussion. Fortunately, there are more and more people who feel the same as I do.

At the age of fifteen, I was fortunate to have a history teacher who for the first time told us about what colonialism meant regarding Latin America. He told us about our shared history from a different point of view, different from all those sweetened stories that we had been told since childhood. For the first time I heard and understood the meaning of the word "decolonial." He taught us how rich the culture of Latin America was and how the lives of those people had been affected by white men who believed they had the right to take what was not theirs. So at that time, and having understood that, I thought that I was a totally deconstructed person. Nothing could be further from reality.

Season of Bruja has taught me so many things, things that you can only learn when you get involved and see with your own eyes the life experiences of other people. Reading this script and drawing the adventures of Althalia and her abuela Isadora have made it possible for me to be part of a wonderful story, but they have also allowed me to keep learning and deconstructing myself as a human being. As a queer woman, taking into account all the realities and points of view and being able to see and understand all the inequalities and oppressions that exist in our society is very important to me, and being part of this graphic novel has given me the opportunity to thoroughly self-reflect, something for which I am enormously grateful. Aaron's experience and kindness throughout the process have accompanied me all the time, and this is something I will never forget.

Season of the Bruja has been through many ups and downs. During 2020, I think the whole team thought that perhaps the project could end at any time, as the situation was so uncertain. Luckily, it didn't happen, and I think it's because we've all fought so hard for *Season of the Bruja* to come to life. We knew how important the story that Aaron was telling could be. Not only for the action and adventure but for all the truth that underlined his words. That has also made me try very hard to make my art worthy of such an important story. That has allowed me to fully involve myself in the character creation and, even without intending to, a little in the script as well. That Aaron has decided to share with me such a personal story fills me with joy and has made me feel that we have both been active parts of the project. It is not just "one more." I hope I can keep learning and enjoying my work as much as I did with *Season of the Bruja*.

SARA SOLER

AARON DURÁN

has lived in Portland, Oregon, for more than twenty years after a childhood spent in the desolate high desert of Northern California. He's worn many hats over the years, from film production to radio host, but writing has always been his love. In addition to his young adult novels, Aaron has written stories for Dark Horse Comics, Image Comics, and Activision. When he's not at his keyboard, he's in the kitchen experimenting with traditional Mexican ingredients to rediscover lost dishes.

SARA SOLER

began her professional career as an artist in 2017 and has worked for various publishers, including Dark Horse Comics, Planeta, and Penguin Random House. Her best-selling graphic memoir *Us*—about her relationship with her transgender girlfriend, Diana—was released by the Spanish publisher Astiberri in 2020 to widespread acclaim both at home and abroad. Sara lives in Barcelona and fuels her work with dark coffee and help from her dedicated and demanding assistant, Cimmeria the cat.